A DIVEMASTER RICKY ADVENTURE

JETSAM

TRACY GROGAN

WHAT PEOPLE ARE SAYING ABOUT RICKY

". . . a charismatic, nonchalant protagonist."

– Kirkus Reviews

"The world of scuba diving has a new heroine"

– Simon Pridmore — author of The Diver Who Fell from the Sky

"Ricky Yamamoto crashes through life with great joy and abandon. Smart but reckless, she always seemed like her own worst enemy . . ."

– Reedsy Reviewer Terri Stepek

"Ricky is an edgy and fearless protagonist, which makes for some sharp interactions and snappy dialogue. . ."

– Self-Publishing Review

". . . a likeable character thanks to her self-deprecating sense of humor and zest for life."

– BlueInk Review

". . . Ricky herself is a fun protagonist—a practical, down-to-earth girl who wants nothing more than to dive and explore and have frequent bathroom breaks thanks to her famously small bladder."

– IndieReader

WHAT PEOPLE ARE SAYING ABOUT THE DIVEMASTER RICKY SERIES BOOKS 1 AND 2

"As was the case in the first book, excellent plot crafting and a fiery lead character elevate this series far above action-heavy pulp fiction, resulting in a gripping high-stakes thriller."

Self-Publishing Review

"Having read the first Divemaster Ricky story, I was eager for this follow-up. I enjoyed Ricky's dry wit, and Grogan's descriptions of her dives made me feel as if I was the one diving, even though I've only ever snorkeled. The hijinks she got up to in the first book made me curious as to what she would get herself into this time. *DERELICT* didn't disappoint."

Amazon reviewer S. Honeycutt

"Ricky is an anchor in this suspenseful yet heartwarming story about connections and greed. The secrets and hidden agendas of every character introduced to readers will keep them engaged and guessing the whole way."

Literary Titan

"... *Derelict* is an accomplished work of mystery fiction that achieves everything it sets out to do and will entertain fans of thriller mysteries and leave them hungry for more."

Readers' Favorite

"With an appealing protagonist, interesting setting, and plenty of fascinating diver lore, Tracy Grogan's DERELICT (*A Divemaster Ricky Mystery*) has all the makings of a solid thriller."

IndieReader

"*Derelict*, by Tracy Grogan, immerses readers in a world full of culture and introduces readers to breathtaking landscapes and exotic locations deep in the northern parts of Africa. The author crafts a strong and quick-thinking female character that never gives up hope; and was one that I loved following. Ricky is an anchor in this suspenseful yet heartwarming story about connections and greed. The secrets and hidden agendas of every character introduced to readers will keep them engaged and guessing the whole way."

Goodreads contributor

"Grogan has released a much-anticipated sequel. Though this is part of a series, *Derelict: A Divemaster Ricky Mystery*, Book 2, is also a stand-alone story, even with returning characters such as Pascal. Grogan uses superb location descriptions, puts the reader alongside Ricky, and travels not only the world with her, but also shares her under-the-sea exploits. I would easily give, *Derelict*...5 out of 5 stars. This book delivers. The author's style is realistic with plenty of action and not at all boring. I found this book to be a real page-turner. I had to know what happened next."

Mary Maciejewski, a Goodreads contributo

Cover by Damonza

Paperback ISBN: *979-8-9850140-4-4*

Ebook ISBN: *979-8-9850140-3-7*

The superior man, when resting in safety, does not forget that danger may come. When in a state of security, he does not forget the possibility of ruin. When all is orderly, he does not forget that disorder may come. Thus, his person is not endangered, and his States and all their clans are preserved.

—Confucius

Only trust thyself, and another shall not betray thee.

—William Penn

.

1

NOT FAR ENOUGH

Hot damn, I've got a new job.

There were a lot of things I was going to miss about Dahab—the food from Falafel King, the house on the hill, the serenity of the Blue Hole. Friends.

But my last employer was still dealing with the aftermath of a fire and was nowhere near reopening. All the staff was either employed at other dive ops in town or had shipped out for new adventures. The guy who'd convinced me to come to Egypt in the first place had moved back to France, trying to repair relationships and legal complications.

And Sasha was dead.

It had been a triple-gut-punch holiday season. First Sasha went missing, next the shop burned down, and then I'd started off the new year finding his body. We'd brought him back from his watery grave, said our good-byes, and given his ashes to his parents, but his presence still hung over the town. The only way to move on was to leave his ghost behind.

Our boat's captain had already moved on to a new opportunity and had reached out to offer me a job. Captain Rich needed an expert diver, which was really all I had to know before saying yes. He had given me three weeks to pull myself together and get out there. I had said I'd be there in two.

I took the first week easy. Did some climbing. Visited some friends. Took one more dive to watch a team of archeologists and divers hurriedly empty a wreck before it slid into the deep.

And then I spent the next few days cleaning my Dahab digs, a house loaned to me by a friend of my mom. Once it was respectable, I left a note apologizing for the pillaging of the wine cellar, the destruction of the motorcycle, and the scratches on the bicycle, then locked the door for the first time in months.

On my way to the airport, I stopped by the local police department, where I had recently become somewhat familiar with their jail cells. This time I had only one task—drop off the house keys for a certain senior detective.

I was done with Dahab.

Sharm El Sheikh International Airport, a bit after midnight, was sleepy. I'd arrived with plenty of time to spare, for no other reason than wanting to begin the next phase of my life as soon as possible.

Other than a large duffel bag containing my dive gear, all I brought with me was a knapsack with a few clothes and toiletries, three paperbacks for the flights, one last box of falafel, a brand-new passport, and a one-way ticket to Thailand. I was first in line at the counter, half an hour before they even opened, and was seated at the gate two hours before boarding. That was a mistake. I never got past page 5 of the first novel. I spent the next two hours dwelling on the craziness of the past two months and all the things I wanted to leave behind.

Once airborne, though, I felt the tension begin to slip away. With each hour, I thought more about the future and less about the last few months.

I didn't ask for a lot. I just wanted to put as much distance between myself and the past as possible. Half a world would have been good, but I settled for forty-five hundred miles. Sharm El Sheikh, Egypt, to Istanbul, Turkey, to Bangkok, Thailand. Three flights. Thirty hours. Leaving behind a monumental pile of misery and trading it for a few months in paradise.

This was why I became a divemaster.

By the time I finished with an overzealous customs inspection at Phuket International Airport, explaining several times that my gear, which included multiples of pretty much everything, such as four dive computers, was typical for a divemaster and not for resale, I was in no mood for pleasantries.

"Howzit, beautiful?" Leaning out of one of the ubiquitous Thai three-wheeled transports, and with incredibly poor timing, was Captain Rich in all his glory. The only thing louder than his greeting was his shirt. On his six-and-a-half-foot body, it was more appropriate for a rugby player than a yacht captain. The thing had enough material to be a sail for a small boat. Not that I would ever say that to his face.

"None of that flattery stuff, OK? First, I know I look like shit. Second, we agreed no friends-with-benefits action on this voyage. We have separate cabins, right?" Captain Rich's childish pout just made me want to smack him. "Third, my follow-up discussion with my parents while I sat on a sticky airport floor during my layover was the worst phone call of my life. The topic, before you ask, is off-limits. So, let's just head to the boat and get started. All right?"

His wince seemed less theatrical than the pout. I might have actually scared him.

"Right-o," he said after a long pause. "Flattery is a no go. Separates on board, and I'll be getting my jollies elsewhere. Radio silence with regard to the parents."

With that, he heaved my big gear bag and carry-on into the open-air back of the tuk-tuk. "Easy in—this is a Frankenstein build . . . I've made a couple of modest modifications."

At least one was immediately obvious. The middle passenger seat had been replaced by a boxy contraption that I assumed was a cooler for Captain Rich's beer stash. I climbed into one of the two lone passenger seats in the second row as he squeezed into the single driver's seat in front.

The moment he turned the key, I nearly jumped out of my shoes. I'd been expecting the puny, typical two-stroke whose weak sound gave the tuk-tuk its name, but what we got was a roar. And a deep, bone-shaking vibration to match. To emphasize the point, Captain

Rich gunned the engine a half dozen times before turning back with his trademark grin.

"Modest modifications?" I was already white-knuckling the roll bar with one hand and a handle on the center contraption with the other.

"Six hundred cc engine. Local guy smashed up his bike pretty good, but the engine was still primo. Can you imagine that? People should have better respect for fine motor machines."

Having just trashed a $15,000 custom motorcycle during one of my last days in Dahab, an incident he was intimately familiar with, I bowed my head and inspected my feet—I might have blushed.

He adjusted the rearview mirror so he could better see me.

"Sorry. Too soon, yeah?"

It seems like longer, but it was only a little more than a month ago.

"No, yeah, you know everything is interlinked. You still mad about the bat?"

"Nah, sorry to bring it up. We're good."

Captain Rich had stayed at my house in Dahab following a police raid that had torn it apart. Not my fault. Not really. Loaner house from a guy who turned out to be a hacker and, unbeknown to me, happened to store a lot of things I'd end up getting blamed for. That was just one more reason for abandoning the Sinai Peninsula and heading around the world.

Anyway, Captain Rich had moved in after the raid and some ugly business involving guns. He took on the role of casual bodyguard and roommate without benefits. I was still dealing with a lot of fallout from the whole artifacts mess and was a bit on edge. His presence helped me maintain a degree of balance. As an additional safety measure, and knowing I have an aversion to actual weapons, he'd left a cricket bat by the door for protection when he wasn't around.

Mistake. In a moment of justifiable rage, after a particularly distressing phone call, I had thought of a better use. By the time I was done, Captain Rich's treasured cricket bat was little more than a carpet of splinters in the driveway.

But we'd both left the Sinai behind. He'd helped me get a new job. I was still enforcing the without-benefits rule, and the motorcycle mayhem would soon just be an embarrassing memory. So, I felt guilty about making him feel guilty about raising the subject. But it worked—he seemed sufficiently chastened. His mood, though, lasted only a minute. He was nothing if not irrepressible. Pausing for just a beat, he wiped his palms on his board shorts, goosed the engine one more time, gave a quick warning—"Tighten your seat belt and welcome to Phuket!"—and then zipped into a ridiculously small gap in the line of traffic.

Having been in Thailand before, I hadn't expected there to be a seat belt and hadn't even looked for one. But as we peeled off down the road to the sound of screeching tires and honking horns, I did. And when I found it, I cinched it up tight, then resumed my white-knuckling of the handholds. And my thoughts about the mess that was waiting for me back in the States.

2

TRIAL AND ERROR

"I KNEW YOU would come. I made a bet with Pascal—
he thought you would bail and head off to some
remote island."

Pascal. He would have been a great addition to the
trip. We'd worked with him back in Egypt, and he was
an exceptional diver and an even better companion. But
he had matters that required his presence back in France.
To put a finer point on it, he had matters that barred him
from leaving France.

Captain Rich whipped through traffic while talking
a mile a minute and barely glancing at the road ahead.
"This will be just what you need. Mellow bosses, no cus-
tomers, mainly solo dives. And great street food while
we're in port."

We'd worked together for the better part of a year in
Egypt, and he knew exactly what buttons to push—both
good and bad. These were good ones. So, when Captain Rich had pinged me about a three-month cruise on
a luxury yacht in Thailand as a dive guide and science

diver, it was an offer that was too good to turn down. I was sold even before he mentioned the salary he'd negotiated for me.

Fortunately, the drive from the airport was only a few miles. We survived. I'm not sure that it was a casualty-free trip, though, based on the honking and yelling that we left in our wake.

I had expected we'd be in one of the ritzy harbors or boatyards, but Captain Rich had passed them by and gone up an inlet for about a mile before pulling up to a locked chain-link fence. We were deep into a heavy canopy of tall tropical trees where sunlight didn't meet the ground. It was a far cry from the Sinai Peninsula, where you could travel for miles without seeing a tree.

He swiped a card at the fancy reader, and the gate opened. As soon as we passed through, it closed again. I couldn't see the boat yet, but the familiar smell of creosote, tar, and diesel fuel told me we were close.

Around a few wide turns, the road opened up to a large gravel parking lot fronting a boat ramp and a dock. There was a camping trailer, topped with a nice coat of moss, off to the side of the lot. And a pile of metal parts and bits that looked destined for the junkyard, or perhaps the start of a new junkyard.

Tied off to the dock and listing slightly was a yacht well over a hundred feet in length. A long time ago, she had probably been considered top of the line.

"She's a beauty, isn't she? The *Valkyrian*—custommade in Sweden. One hundred and twenty feet long. Twelve-foot draft. Built in 1966. Based on logbooks, it last sailed on the open seas six years ago. The property was abandoned just last winter." Captain Rich slowly led me down the dock, never taking his eyes off the decrepit hulk.

Luxury yacht, my ass.

I was already planning my exit. I was sure my cellphone battery was dead, but once I got back to the main road, I'd probably be able to hitch a ride back to the airport.

"Wait till you see your quarters—I spent the last two days on them. You're going to be in the lap of luxury for the trip. Leave your gear bag here. It's safe."

I sincerely doubted the first statement and was leery about the second, so I grabbed my gear bag before following the captain as he headed down the dock. He blathered on about some other mostly trivial boat details, but I was distracted.

How can I back out of my contract? It could be that Pascal had the right idea—a remote island. Maybe a new name.

"Actually"—Captain Rich paused and held up an index finger to make a point—"the *Valkyrian* has served us well. I'm guessing the previous owners either ended up in prison or on the run. It was a good boat before it was neglected. Looked like they left in a hurry. There were two caretakers living here in the trailer when I arrived. They were more than happy to scram once they were sure I was legit."

He slapped the hull just short of the bowsprit, which extended over the dock. The thud that greeted the slap instantly suggested the lovely *Valkyrian* was waterlogged. Captain Rich didn't react, though I'm sure he recognized the issue.

"Seems like they did a good job—no evidence of looting. Lots of shell casings, so it seems like it took a while for people to get the message. Lots of good stuff left behind. Some serviceable scuba gear, a compressor. A couple of cases of SPAM, if you're interested."

I tried to hide my interest, but it had been a number of months since I'd had a good SPAM musubi. As soon as I thought it, my brain went straight to Sumo, who makes a killer musubi, which then led me to think about our last call. I quickly lost my appetite.

It was not too long before I'd left Dahab. I had actually been sharing a bonding experience with Mom. Something we were decidedly lacking for the past decade. But things had turned monumentally ugly after I had given in to her request that I give Sumo a call. He had answered on the first ring before I could chicken out and hang up.

I'm pretty sure the memory of that conversation will stay with me for a long time to come.

And as usual, he had just launched into the conversation as if we'd been talking for several minutes, regardless of whether he knew the topic or not. In this case, though, he knew exactly what the call was about. But he was uncharacteristically evasive.

"Your mother said you would be calling, but she was, to be honest, just kicking the can down the road. I can see how Ingi thinks this discussion begins with me, but by all rights, it starts to her and then reverts to us."

I had no idea where this was going. "She told me nothing, and you've already lost me. What is going on?

All she said was that you and I needed to talk. What's up, and why was Mom the messenger?"

"Fair enough. OK, I'll start at the beginning. I'm not your biological father."

OK, that was more direct.

"You're yanking my chain."

"I wish I were."

Fuck me.

I decided I needed some time to process.

"I'll call you back."

I didn't.

Captain Rich had been keeping up a running commentary as I had spaced out.

". . . and the sleeping quarters were good, though we had to drag the mattresses out and burn them. Rats and worse. Sealed it up and fumigated it for three days. We got the stove and reefer running in a day. No running water, but it rains a lot. I'll switch to wearing my swim shorts during shower time from now on. No worries."

"Bathroom?"

"Portaloo right over there near the fence line. Just got it cleaned two days ago."

I could see holes in the hull above the waterline that made me suspect he was candy-coating it a bit. He kept on talking, but my head was no longer in the game.

"The compressor was virtually new. We replaced a few hoses, and the thing worked great. We used the steel scuba tanks they had on board hooked to nozzles to blow dirt out of the cracks in the rooms we needed."

His look suggested he'd developed quite a bond with the old, battered vessel. I had other ideas.

"Our employers bought the harbor and everything in it, lock, stock, and barrel. They got the land and the *Valkyrian*. They liked the privacy and being away from the yacht party scene. It's taken a turn for the worse since I was last here. Lousy with Silicon Valley millionaires. Trust-fund babies. Wall Street escapees. For me, avoiding that scene is a big bonus. This sort of suits my lifestyle. I can blast tunes at night while working on the repairs and upgrades, and no one complains about my super tuk-tuk. You're going to love it."

"That's what Pascal said about Dahab."

"Trial and error, Ricky, trial and error. This time it's going to be all smooth sailing. On land, we're totally secure—a lot more secure than the harbor, where anyone can walk on up and take things off."

I looked around, trying to find something anyone would even want to steal.

"There's a big resale market near the main harbor for tools that disappear from boats under repair. I don't need any of that. I haven't had to shoot anyone yet. Anybody who peeks through the fence sees the derelict *Valkyrian* and leaves."

I started to laugh, but then I remembered this was Captain Rich talking.

"You have a gun? Here?"

"I always have at least one."

"Probably best that you haven't shot anyone. That could bring unwanted attention. How about warning shots?"

"Well, yeah, maybe, once or twice. But if a gun is fired in the jungle and there's no policeman around to hear it, is it really a crime?"

He had a point about the location. Less convincing was his argument about warning shots. And it wasn't just his deal. If the authorities came, I'd probably get swept up in any dispute, and the last thing I wanted was to spend more time in a foreign jail cell.

Other than some short stints in an Egyptian lockup, intended to loosen my tongue but merely solidifying my resolve, my recent history of housing had favored free, out of the way, private, and comfortable. This checked the first two boxes. A bit weak on the privacy angle, but by my count, it would just be five people on a big boat. I'd have to check on the comfort level before marking that as a yes. My main requirements were a nice mattress and a shower where I didn't have to bend over to wash my hair. OK, I also needed a top-notch dive platform. Five. Given those five things, I'd get past the war-zone vibe soon enough. Wait. Six. Seaworthy. I'm not heading out to sea on a candidate for the next wreck dive site.

Those six things. If they were OK, I'd stay. If not— and I was leaning that way—I'd start brainstorming on my options. First and foremost, it had to be far from Hawaii. I made a mental note to check for jobs in Mozambique.

3

YOU HAD ME AT SIX HEADS

As I IMAGINED my options for a quick exit, Captain Rich gently pushed me farther along the dock. He was sort of babbling, talking to himself. But then he paused.

"A beauty, yeah, but this wreck isn't what we're taking on the cruise. We've just been using it for storing equipment and gear, temporary quarters—that sort of thing—while we work on the yacht."

He pointed farther down the dock and grinned a wicked grin. I could just see the bow of another boat.

Jerk. He totally played me.

Hidden from view by the huge mass of the *Valkyrian* and revealed as we picked up speed walking down the dock was a gleaming, sleek tribute to modern technology. Sort of. Totally, when compared with its next-door neighbor.

"Our home for the next four months!"

I felt my tense muscles instantly relax and punched Captain Rich for messing with my head. It was like hitting a punching bag. He didn't skip a beat or even acknowledge the blow.

"Italian. Custom-built in 2007, immediately back in the shop for upgrades, treated with kid gloves, used more as a day-tripping party boat than an ocean explorer. Kept in a boathouse since delivery in 2008. Eighty feet long. Seven-foot headroom. Draft of under two meters. Twin eight-hundred-horsepower Caterpillars. Listed cruising speed of twenty-six knots. Six heads—four en suite. Aft deck customized for diving . . . soon. High up on my retrofit list. Hydraulic swim platform for easing in the heavy gear and taking out the soil samples. New tender."

"You had me at six heads."

"I was won over by the headroom. No more skull knocking for me. Six feet, eight inches in the engine room. Welcome to paradise."

"You are so going to regret messing with me like that. So, what's the deal with this harbor?" I was ready to get off the dock and onto the boat. "The abandoned boat is creepy. Kind of an *Apocalypse Now* vibe. I was thinking that we just need mist rising off the water."

Captain Rich, I realized as I said it, would have looked and probably felt quite at home in Kurtz's squad. And not considered it at all creepy.

"What did they name her?" I hadn't taken the time to look and hadn't thought to ask after the *Valkyrian* trick.

The response was accompanied by a look that seemed to be an odd mishmash of grin and frown. A *frin*! A new word for Rickypedia.

"*Powerballer*."

"You're fucking kidding me."

"Apparently, that was also Margo's response."

"So what's their deal?"

"You already know the basics. New-money million-aires. Like they said during your phone interview, they're big-time environmentalists. Concerned about pollution ruining the sea. They've thrown some big money at elections in Australia and the UK. State politics in the US . . . North Carolina and Florida. Major sources of pollution."

"And we're going to monitor the waters off Burma?"

"Burma, Myanmar, whatever it's called now. But yeah."

"You've got a working refrigerator?"

"Yes, several, and I happen to have one or two cool beers with your name on them. But I got the keg cooler installed a few weeks ago, so if you'd prefer draft . . ."

It wasn't even sunset yet, though the thick canopy made it hard to tell exactly what time it was, and my watch had lost its charge somewhere over one of the -*stan* countries. But my body was so sufficiently confused about time zones that I figured a beer would help with the reset.

"A bottle would be great. Glasses break too easily."

"I aim to please. One Phuket lager, coming up. Adult beverages up in the pilot house? We're entering the mozzie hours, so it's best to stay inside. Quick tour, though, first?"

The ramp to the boat was solid and gleaming. No moss.

The hull was perfect.

Gunwale. Bulkheads. Decking. All in great condition.

As we passed into the salon, which was still a work

in progress, he tapped the built-in remote, and the stereo kicked in. He wasn't kidding about blasting tunes. I shouldn't have been surprised. There were times back in Egypt when we were returning from dives and could feel the vibrations coming from the boat when we were still fifteen feet down.

The first tune was "Highway to Hell." Captain Rich performed a few drum crashes on the furniture just to help the band along as we navigated past tools and scraps of wood on our way through the salon.

The boat was as pristine and ritzy on the inside as it was on the outside, once you looked past the tools, dust, and demolition. I had some idea of the changes the new owners were making, but it seemed excessive in such a new boat. I guess new money didn't care.

"Drop your gear bag here. We'll get it put away on the way back. Your cabin—excuse me, *stateroom*—is down this way."

The stairs down to the lower deck were wide and at a slope normally found in homes, not boats. Behind us, as we reached the bottom of the stairs, was a section with a taped-off, double-thick sheet of plastic.

"The lab. Last thing on the to-do list. Lonnie will be responsible for the final setup. All the staterooms are this way." He waved his hand in the opposite direction of the lab, which suited me fine. Camping out anywhere near a lab seemed like a recipe for failure.

On the way forward to my stateroom, we passed the first of several. It was over the top. Fancy wood with burl accents. Big-screen TV and full audio system. Most surfaces covered in plastic.

"Master stateroom. Master is ready to go. Just protecting it from last-minute sawdust. Yours is down a bit farther."

Having left my sandals behind as soon as we boarded, I was enjoying the full experience of the plush carpeting in this section of the boat. I wiggled my toes as Captain Rich blathered on.

4

THE BANNER OF BOAT SAFETY

Across from the master, I saw a second stateroom, this one with the doorway covered with plastic sheeting. Through the hazy material, I could see a pile of CD cases, a few video cassettes, and a messy bed. I guessed it was Captain Rich's.

"VIP. I'm not working on housekeeping much these days, twelve to fourteen hours a day getting things ready. Besides, it will be the last item on my list. You know, 'him that makes shoes goes barefoot himself.'"

"I don't get the VIP?"

"I thought you didn't want to share with me. I'll be in the VIP. There's room for two." He ducked, but I anticipated the move and succeeded in smacking the back of his head with sufficient force to register my unwillingness to go down that path.

He pulled the plastic back. "I guess we can take these down now. I've gotten this deck up to spec." I poked my head in and was impressed by the luxurious quality. But it was the closet that made me stop in my tracks.

"Are you kidding me? Do you think we'll need those?"

Captain Rich didn't have to stop and look. He knew exactly what I was asking about.

"Those will go up in the salon, and a few other strategic places, when I'm done with the retrofit and get the gun safes in place. Hidden panels in the walls. I'll show you how to reach them once we're done with construction."

"Lonnie knows you're doing this?"

"Knows? I've been sourcing these weapons at Lonnie's instruction. He's been transferring money to me this whole time. Five- and ten-thousand lots just dropped into my bank. I'm responsible for buying anything related to scuba or boat safety and operation. This falls under the banner of boat safety."

"Does this seem like overkill?"

"New money, new paranoia. They're primarily for close-quarters defense. Pirates. Opportunistic thieves. The waters around here are not the safest in the world. I agree, it seems over the top, but defense always looks that way right up until the moment you need it, and then you wonder if there was something else you should have added. Lonnie gave me the green light to get innovative if I found some less traditional defense tools in the marketplace."

I'd only had a glance and didn't know much about arsenals, but it seemed like ours was worthy of a small country. "You look like you're ready for war."

"Pirates. They can get nasty, and it's best to go large with them immediately. You'll see them turn tail right away if you come big and fast at them. You know what Pascal used to say: 'Trust not to God but upon good security.'"

"Sounds like him."

"You want to get trained up on any of this? We can always use an extra hand to announce our presence with authority."

"Announce our presence with authority? Another Pascal saying?"

"No, *Bull Durham*. Great scene. You want in?"

"You got a taser in there?"

"Hell, yeah, we have some tasers. I've seen your reenactment of your takedown of the bad guy in Palau, so I know you know how to use them. But how about I train you up on a shotgun?"

"Woot, a boom stick." I reached for the chunky device.

"Uh, yeah, we don't call it that, and please put it down. But good call. It doesn't require much accuracy but scares the shit out of people. Tasers are for close action. We don't want to get to that point."

"Close action is where I shine." I couldn't brag much on my fighting skills, but I had some success with stunning folks.

"So you've said. I don't want it to get to that stage. Better you learn some long-range shooting."

Crud.

"Let's stow your personal belongings and get those beers." He grabbed my carry-on bag. "Your gear bag can go on the sport deck. Let's leave it in the salon for the time being. The full tour can wait. And this is your bunk room."

He tossed my carry-on into the room, where it

bounced once on the mattress and then landed on the floor.

"I hope there's nothing fragile in there." His concern was a bit late.

"Not anymore."

I was traveling light and had left one sentimental keepsake—a ceramic tree—in storage back in Egypt. Lucky for me and for Captain Rich. I would have gone all Rikidozan on him, using the tricks I'd been picking up watching old videos of the Japanese wrestling idol for whom I was named.

That was back when I had thought I was half Japanese. Before the phone call that had obliterated the world as I knew it and I, in response, destroyed a cricket bat and some of the prettier parts of an expensive motorcycle. And back when I had thought the nice old lady who used to take me to the museum and bought me the tree I called Kuku at the museum shop was my grandma. I hadn't even thought of that part of my parents' deception. I'll bet she never knew.

My stateroom finished ticking off the comfort box. The mattress was brand new and just the right firmness. The shower head was more than high enough. Marble counters, the same wood cabinetry as in the master stateroom. A small TV, but that didn't matter.

"There's two more staterooms and heads in the aft for the crew. Separate access from the main level. We're running fairly light. I'm skipper, first engineer, backup diver, and chief bottle washer. Tao, who you'll meet in a second, does the rest. Second engineer, deckhand, and steward. Local guy. Lonnie and Margo got recommendations from some friends of theirs who have lived here for years. Good guy. Shy. You won't see much of him except during work hours."

"You haven't mentioned a chef. Is that part of my job description?"

"Hell no, there'd be a mutiny the first day. No, Lonnie and Margo are science officers and chefs. Captains during most night watches."

"I can do barbeque. Sort of. If need be."

"No need. This is a vegan voyage. No animal protein on the boat."

That stopped me in my tracks.

"You never mentioned that."

"Have I shown you the dive deck yet?" Captain Rich picked up his pace.

"Pathetic attempt at diversion. Are they good chefs?"

"They say you won't miss meat after you've had a few of their meals. I'm up for it. I could stand to eat a bit healthier."

"You should have mentioned it." He moved on at his new pace, but I stood stock still.

"You wouldn't have come."

"Maybe. Probably."

"Until they get here . . . there's an outdoor braai, and I've got about twenty pounds of meat in the fridge."

That got me moving again. "Barbecue? Bring it on!"

"Oh, it's already being broughten."

I sniffed around but found no sign of any barbecue in my near future.

Reversing our path, we headed up to the salon to grab a couple of beers. They were cold and plentiful, as advertised. The bar, as well, was fully stocked.

The galley was closed off but featured a large glass wall so that you could observe everything going on inside. The kitchen cabinets were, for the most part, closed, but two were open, and I could see they were stacked with first-rate cookware. The counters featured a variety of blenders, grinders, spinners, and a lot of other devices I'd only seen in catalogs.

"The galley is over the top! It almost makes me wish I cooked. Kind of a waste to only use it for vegan."

"Yeah, the oven can even be controlled from a phone. Like I could have it finish off a dish while I'm at the airport, picking up someone. If I cooked. It's a top-notch galley. Check it out."

The smell of Thai spices hit me as soon as he started to open the door. A young guy, likely a local Thai, was busily working pots and pans on the stovetop.

"Tao, this is Ricky. Ricky, this is Tao. Tao's our jack-of-all-trades. He'll be working with you on the soil collection. How much longer, Tao?"

"Just started. Thirty minutes, could be a bit more. I waited until I heard you come back. Meat goes on the gr—the braai—in a few minutes. Hi, Ricky. Nice to meet you."

"Hello, Tao. Looking forward to working with you." I'd already seen a pudding sitting on the counter, next to a plate of sliced pineapples.

I extended my hand, but Tao slowly bowed. I bowed back, sort of—keeping my eye on him to see if he reacted—hoping that was the correct response. I'm sure Captain Rich found my confusion amusing.

"Captain Rich explained you enjoy sweet Thai desserts. I do, too. The pineapples are not ready yet. I will put them on the grill later."

Yes, I was looking forward to working with Tao.

"It's a wait, but once you taste the food, you'll be in heaven." Captain Rich slapped Tao on the back. "It's not a vegan galley yet."

5

I MISSED WELL

WE LEFT TAO to do his magic and moved on up to the next level.

The pilot house was as spiffy as the rest of the boat. Even more high tech. It was as set up as any boat I'd seen, short of an ocean liner. All the familiar controls, navigation screens, and comms, plus a lot more. The captain's chair looked brand new and supersized for the new skipper. An iPad lay on a built-in desk beside one of the twenty-four-inch computer screens.

"Amazing how much I can handle with this little pad. I've got access to every screen and most of the comms. I can control the steering and power with a touch screen. And I have my entire catalog of tunes loaded on here as well." Captain Rich was in love.

A quick scan of the pilot house and I spied at least eight high-quality speakers.

"I spruced up the sound system a bit on the boat. You have a dedicated system on the sport deck, so you can control your own tunes. There's already an iPod plugged in. I made a mirror image of my own, so you've got a vast"—he did the little quotation mark thingy with his fingers—"library." He wasn't kidding. His iPod was famous for its broad range of music. He could almost always pull up a tune to meet a customer's request.

Cool.

"I have access to all the security cameras. I even have cameras beneath the surface, just to keep an eye on you."

"Creepy."

"And prudent." Captain Rich had enough tales about security breaches to make anyone a bit paranoid.

It looked to me like the boat was almost complete, though Captain Rich said it would be five weeks until we did our first test runs. We were waiting on some special equipment and making some last-minute changes, and there were some unspecified delays with the arrival of the owners, Lonnie and Margo.

"What more can you tell me about our new bosses that I didn't learn on the Zoom call?"

"Oh yeah. Lonnie. He's the mousey kind. You probably saw that. Short and skinny. Thinning hair. Dresses like a librarian on the day off."

"I have no idea what that means."

"Short-sleeve, plaid shirts. Khakis. I've never seen him wear shorts or T-shirts. I don't think he gets much dirt under his fingernails." He rolled his eyes. "Hard to imagine him working the soil at a golf course. I'm guessing he had others do the manual work."

He pulled up Lonnie's Facebook page and scrolled through the photos until he found the one he wanted. There was Lonnie, as advertised, in a plaid, short-sleeved shirt that looked like something from my grandparents' era. Captain Rich had forgotten to mention the oversize glasses. Lonnie didn't seem to have spent much time on Facebook, though he'd picked up frequency three years ago.

A few more swipes and Captain Rich handed back the iPad. "Margo." There were about two dozen photos—no selfies. It seemed like she wanted only one shot from each event they'd participated in, hosted by a who's who of countries at the forefront of investing in efforts to protect the ocean—Canada, Chile, Fiji, Indonesia, Jamaica, Namibia, Kenya, Mexico, Palau, Norway, and Portugal. When she did let someone take her photo, it was always well posed.

I wouldn't use the term *bombshell*, but Margo was certainly a few steps up from Lonnie. Along in her years a bit and definitely a life spent in the sun. She had her wrinkles, but she wore them well. Well-toned muscles, from what I could see. Her attire was definitely not day-off librarian. Designer shorts and a matching sailor blouse. Nice enough hair. Probably dyed and permed, but well done. We'd see what she'd look like after a couple of months at sea.

"So, d'ya wanna see it?"

"It depends on what 'it' is."

"You'll see."

He led me back out to the dock, where a large, boxy appliance lay covered up by a thick tarp.

The sled was the last thing on my preliminary tour, with Captain Rich performing a dramatic reveal worthy of a game-show host or a second-rate magician, whipping off its custom-made cover.

"Huh. I imagined something . . . I don't know, more high tech."

"You don't like it?"

"It just looks a bit, I don't know, homemade."

"Tao and I built it from scratch. Lonnie's design."

"It's beautiful."

The next morning, after another great Tao breakfast, Captain Rich announced that we were taking a day off for fun and games. We had fifteen minutes to get dressed—shorts, no long sleeves, sensible shoes—and then we were heading out.

Tao was already in the super tuk-tuk by the time I hit the dock. Captain Rich was last, but on time, lugging a big duffel bag that he tied down in back.

I'd already pressed him for the day's agenda, but he said that was on a need-to-know basis and that I'd need to know once we got there. But he promised it would be fun.

There was no dive gear in the back, so I figured it wasn't diving, which I'd been holding out hope for. He'd mentioned ATVs a couple of times over the past few days, and I was game for that. Tao had said they did some zip-lining but that it was somewhat boring. I could speculate all I wanted. I wasn't going to find out anytime soon.

But pretty soon, the potential options narrowed dramatically. We were following signs to the Kathu Waterfall, but there were also billboards for the local water park. Nothing else was indicated, so I figured it was one of those two. Since we weren't told to bring swimsuits, I figured it had to be the waterfall. I was cool with a hike and a plunge, even without a swimsuit.

But then Captain Rich threw us a curveball. Or maybe just me. Right after passing the water park, he swung the super tuk-tuk into an unmarked parking lot at the rear of a long, nondescript building. Once he'd turned off the engine, which was *uber* loud, I quickly figured out where we were.

"Are you planning on doing some shooting today?"

Captain Rich grinned but didn't say a word.

The parking lot was almost empty, though it sounded like a lot of guns were being fired somewhere. There were still no signs, except the one on the only visible door, which read—in many languages—Employees Only. Before we even got to the door, it opened from the inside. Captain Rich exchanged greetings and bro hugs with the guy who let us in.

The space we entered was surrounded by tall concrete walls on all four sides, was about the size of a football field, and was completely empty of shooters. The sound of firing, which hadn't slacked off at all, was coming from the one side that appeared to be part of a building. A sign on that door clued me in to the fact that I was looking at the entrance to the indoor range.

"We've got this place exclusively for the three of us for two hours. Let's get cranking."

"You know that guns aren't really my sort of thing . . ."

"Yeah, if you had a gun in Palau, you might have

been able to stop things before they got out of hand. Same in Dahab."

"I seem to have come out of both of those situations just fine. Unlike the guys who were trying to kill me."

"Dumb luck. Those guys, except for the one, were stooges. Couldn't get out of their own way to save their lives. Literally. And you did need a little help from your friends and, if I recall correctly, left behind a lot of destroyed property. For the record, don't even think that your Rikidozan moves will be of any value. They may be an amusing parlor trick, but if you end up in close quarters fighting with a Thai pirate, I can guarantee you that they will have a knife and be able to filet you before you land your first kick."

He handed me a manual. "Read this. We'll start assembling the gun in half an hour."

"It's ninety-two pages."

"They're short. Skip the first twelve pages and the last forty. Besides, there are a lot of pictures."

As I worked through the manual, I would glance over at Tao. By the time I was on page 15, he had already selected his two guns. By page 20, he'd broken down, cleaned, and reassembled a rifle. By page 25, he'd already worked through at least two clips.

Captain Rich had also, I noticed, been tracking Tao's progress. He called for a pause and a "cold" range after the second clip. "That means, Ricky, that you unload your weapon, open the action, step away from the firing line, and lay down your firearm on the shooting bench so Tao can safely retrieve his targets."

Given that I was only on page 30 and hadn't even

picked out my weapon, I was pretty sure I was in compliance. Tao had already done all of that and was standing at the ready to go get his targets. It seemed like a lot of work when just pointing the gun at the ground would achieve the same degree of safety.

"I know what you're thinking—that you could just point the gun at the ground or put on the safety or lay it on the table, without all the other stuff"—Captain Rich was in schoolmarm mode—"but you would be dead wrong. Actually, somebody else would be dead and you would be wrong. These rules only exist because of accidents. It's just like diving. You start skipping steps and people die."

I was duly chastened, but since I was still on page 30, I felt it was safe to continue reading. I did nod in his direction to acknowledge that I understood. I sort of understood, though I had no idea what it meant to open my action, but I would read that section twice when I got to it.

I hadn't noticed, but Captain Rich had brought a cooler. He reached in and tossed me a Krating Daeng—the Thai version of Red Bull.

"One. Too much caffeine and your aim goes to shit." He grabbed one for himself as well. Tao declined.

The drink helped. I was certainly more focused. Once I'd plowed through the manual, which took close to forty-five minutes, the class started off—slowly, very slowly. It kind of felt like I was on the learning end of a beginner's open-water training. I was increasingly hyped about firing the gun, and he was going on about safe handling, storage, posture. Stuff that was important, no doubt, but kept me from the immediate gratification I suddenly wanted. We were an hour into the session before I even tried dry-firing the M4.

I finally got to live fire and put a hundred rounds through it before Captain Rich told me to stop. Actually, I fired one shot and almost gave up. Captain Rich had explained recoil and even punched me in the shoulder—my "off" shoulder, he said, so that I wouldn't start out with a bruised shooting shoulder—to prepare me. The mule kick from the M4 was much worse. I almost dropped the weapon. We made a few adjustments to my stance and positioning and the way I froze my hips, and I tried again. It was easier the second time, and I got off ten rounds before I had to stop.

Captain Rich handed me a different rifle. An AR-15.

"What was the first one?"

"M4. Military issue. This AR-15 is set up for greatly reduced recoil."

We switched. My first shot was tentative, and my already bruised shoulder still caused me to wince, but there was definitely way less impact. I fired off ten shots in rapid succession and found the gun was easier to handle and the pain almost nonexistent.

We switched the weapon to automatic, and I raced through an entire clip. I also managed to hit the back wall with a couple of shots.

"For now, we stick to single shots, OK?" Captain Rich wasn't hiding behind a wall, so I figured I wasn't too wild.

"Why didn't we start with this one?"

"Because if we get into action, I want you to know

which gun to grab. We have two of these: one for you and one for Margo. We'll be back here for her training, and you can get in some more shooting as well."

"I still have two clips."

"Go for it. Aim for twenty feet ahead of the target."

"Pardon me?"

"Intentionally miss. When we start firing, I don't want you to hit people—I want you to scare them. But if you shoot above them or to the side, they don't really get it. Hit the water in front of them. They'll see the water splashes and realize how close you're shooting. It scares the hell out of them."

And so, I missed. I missed well and got rave reviews.

"Remember, we're trying to scare them, not make them mad."

Trying for shooting in front of the target seemed counterintuitive. I hit the target twice, but I think they might have been ricochets. That's the story I stuck with back at the boat.

We still had half an hour to go by the time I'd finished my hundred, but Captain Rich said it was finally his turn, and the duffel bag wasn't empty. But first things first. I cleared and locked the M4 with his supervision and left it on the bench. He said we could wait to clean it back on the boat when we weren't on the clock.

He pulled out a gun case and introduced me to his baby. Two big pieces, assembled and ready within seconds.

"The Denel NTW-20. Seventy pounds of pant-staining deterrence. Effective up to a mile away in the right hands. Not me. I'm a piker. But I don't need to hit someone with this. As a matter of fact, I hope I don't. This is just a great way of ending the fight before it begins. A few warning shots from a mile away and most bad guys will bug out faster than they came in. I'm using armor-piercing ammo. Nothing like ripping metal apart to encourage a hasty retreat."

"May I—"

"No. Hands off. I'm going to squeeze off a dozen rounds, and then you get your final test firing on a new gun." He pulled out some small sandbags like you might use for playing cornhole and a number of boxes—I counted four—out of the bag and arranged them to the left of the gun. "Box magazines. Each one holds three cartridges. It usually only takes one to send my opponent running. Or dead on the ground, depending on my attitude at the time. I was amazed I could get my hands on one of these. Incredibly expensive, but Lonnie was more than happy to pay."

I was happy to have the time off. My shoulder was beginning to throb, and my forearms were tired. I watched as Captain Rich tore apart a stack of car tires that had been set up at the far end of the range. I had thought about removing my ear defenders when I had stopped shooting but was glad to have kept them on.

The beanbags, it turned out, weren't for play— they helped stabilize the long barrel of the gun. I made a mental note to ask if we could use them for cornhole later.

He finally emptied the duffel bag and handed me one more weapon.

"SIG MCX semiautomatic rifle. We've got four of

these. Two long barrels and two short barrels. It might be your first go-to weapon if we run into trouble. Short barrel is less accurate but more convenient if moving about the boat to deal with imminent boarding. You can use the long barrel and stay in a fixed position. You might switch to the AR-15 if I change the battle plan to hitting the enemy. Then you might switch back to this baby if they get within fifty feet. At that distance, you might do some damage. At twenty feet, aim shouldn't be a problem."

I ripped through another hundred rounds with the machine gun, taking all of five minutes to run through all the ammo. The first fifty, Captain Rich had me aim twenty-five feet in front of the target. Then we moved the targets closer and went for kill shots.

I was exhausted, but to my surprise, really pumped. There was a perverse satisfaction in seeing my target up close with multiple hits.

"Do I get to try the grenade launcher?"

"No. Never."

Crap!

"But I'll gladly supervise you back at the boat while you clean the M4 and the SIG."

Crud!

"Before you have a beer."

Crud and a half!

Then he handed me a wet twenty-four-ounce plastic bottle filled with rich brown liquid.

"Thai iced coffee. Tao makes it extra strong and extra sweet. Have at it!"

Ooh, baby, come to Momma.

6

ONCE WE'RE UNDERWAY, THIS IS NEVER COMING OUT

I WOKE UP the next day with a stiff neck, arms, and back. My legs were a bit rubbery but OK. My right shoulder felt like I'd gone fifteen rounds with Muhammad Ali. I had a beauty of a bruise. My left shoulder, which had just taken a single punch from Captain Rich, also sported a large bruise but felt functional.

It took me a half hour to ease my way out of my cabin. I followed the sound of hard rock up to the pilot house, where Captain Rich and Tao were cleaning guns and discussing where to deploy them among the many secret hiding places that had been built into the boat.

My three guns lay on what looked like a black yoga mat. I noticed that Tao and Captain Rich had one each. Two more were rolled up and sitting in one of the captain's chairs. There were also manuals for the AR-15 and the MCX. I guessed that Captain Rich had decided my study of the M4 manual the day before had been sufficient.

"I cleaned the M4 for you. You won't be using it, so I took responsibility for its preparation. You can do the other two. Should take about forty-five minutes. Tao promised a great breakfast for you as soon as you're done."

I started working through the manuals. The AR-15 was not nearly as complex as I had thought it would be. Five pieces easily separated.

"Pretty simple, eh?" Captain Rich had been watching my every move. "Not so fast. Pay attention to the bolt assembly." He handed me an iPad loaded with a YouTube video. I watched it twice. Three times for one section.

It was fascinating to work through the process— almost erotic. When I was all done and approved by Captain Rich, I did the reassembly. There was something fulfilling about the clicking sound and feel as each piece was fitted back in.

"Pretty cool, huh?" Captain Rich and Tao were both staring at me. I figured it was because of the size of my grin.

"Yeah. A lot like servicing a regulator first stage but without all the O-rings."

"By George, I think you've got it! Now the MCX. And go a bit lighter on the cleaning fluid. That's why you're sitting on a tarp instead of the leather seats."

I looked down and realized my yoga pad and pants had significant dribble stains.

Crud.

The MCX was very similar to the AR-15, although a bit more complex and a bit dirtier. I managed the cleaning faster, though I failed that inspection. Too cocky. Too hurried. Captain Rich had me repeat the entire process. By the time I was done, the aroma of a Thai breakfast had been lingering for a few minutes.

The next weeks passed by quickly. Tao and I helped where we could—Tao more than me. All three of us returned to the range. Tao put me to shame with his rifle skills. Each time, I came away bruised—physically, not emotionally—but less than before. A slight adjustment in my stance made a big difference.

We also practiced shooting from a prone position. My aim improved dramatically, and Tao pointed out that it reduced my exposure to incoming lead. I made no bones about the fact that I preferred standing. In the prone position, my shoulder was taking a beating.

Captain Rich made some inquiries about a couple of special accessories to reduce recoil. Apparently, they were not as common on the black market as the high-powered weapons were. As far as I was concerned, we could hold off on the next training session until after they arrived. I might have mentioned it a time or two.

The next off day, we actually went to the water park instead of the range. On one of the rides, I swear Captain Rich screamed like a little girl.

We also talked about pirates. A lot. During meals, while observing the 11:00 and the 14:00 Thai dance demonstration, and while waiting for rides at the water park—after we'd assured Captain Rich that the next ride would be fine. We were, after all, near but not in one of the major piracy areas in the world, the Strait of Malacca. But the pirates, he claimed, were shifting their strategy to focus more on large ships carrying oil and diesel. Tao was also of the opinion that they were not a threat but agreed that deterrence was the proper response if we saw some. Captain Rich's opinion was that you plan for, and expect, the worst. And give them a bloody nose the minute they look at you twice. One pair of parents, apparently English-speaking, became increasingly agitated as we talked about which munitions we'd deploy against pirates and finally moved with their child to the rear of the line.

We quickly determined that the English translations of the Thai-language signs were abbreviated and incomplete versions, so Tao began translating the Thai words for us. After a particularly hilarious translation that almost left me with cola shooting out of my nose, Tao admitted he had made most of it up. He then switched to reading the English-language version, using his impression of a Southern accent. It wasn't too far off the mark but even more hilarious than his phony translations.

We practiced our weapon retrieval and positioning. My spot was on the deck just beside the pilot house, my gear just inside next to the outer door. Tao had reinforced the gunwale with steel plating. I was to lie flat and fire through a small opening just a few inches above the deck. Captain Rich had left small sandbags for me to stabilize the barrel while shooting.

"This is kind of freaking me out," I said. Captain Rich was stocking one of his hidden compartments. "It's like we're spending a lot more time preparing for war than getting ready to go diving."

"It's just a timing thing. You've already nailed down

all the gear and tools. We can't practice the diving or the sled until we get the boat out into the water. We still have a few things to do, and while we're at it, I just want to make sure we're ready for the highly unlikely scenario of pirates."

"You seem very concerned, and are spending a lot of Lonnie's money, for something highly unlikely." I was standing over him as he sat on the floor and halfway squeezed into the space under the pilot house desk. I chose my timing for a moment when he might feel vulnerable. That would at least put us on equal footing.

"This is just prudent. Lonnie has half a million dollars' worth of lab equipment that he'd hate to see stolen or smashed. And it would take up to a year to replace some of it."

He took the AR-15 I was holding and checked it to make sure it was ready for storage. I hadn't even put in a magazine, but he still checked the safety and the chamber. Satisfied that I'd handed him a safe weapon, he tucked it into the cradle he'd built for it.

"Relax. Once we're underway, this is never coming out."

7

JUST SHOWING OFF

FINALLY, AFTER WEEKS of increasingly granular work, we hit our first major milestone—the preshakedown shakedown.

Even though we would do the official in-harbor inspection once Lonnie and Margo arrived and then do a one- to two-week shakedown cruise, we wanted to make sure we had identified and resolved as many bugs as possible before they set foot on the boat.

It was hot and humid, with rain about half the days, but overall, the weather had been pleasant. On the day we began our preshakedown, there wasn't a cloud in the sky, and a moderate breeze, which we never got in the harbor, was a pleasing change of pace.

After we'd entered open water and were away from any traffic, Tao threw a couple of buoys into the water for handling practice. Captain Rich made a number of runs, progressively making his turns tighter as he wove the boat between the buoys. He used the thrusters to move sideways toward the buoys as well. On the last run, Tao hooked each buoy as we passed by. Like a pro.

Captain Rich had already run the navigation GPS receiver's system tests without detecting any internal errors in advance. Unfortunately, once we were out of the harbor and in open seas, he noticed an issue. As best he could tell, somebody had incorrectly input several parameters into the GPS that gave us erroneous data that became evident once we had gotten moving. Nothing serious, but we had to make some adjustments in open waters. It was more of a hassle than an emergency.

Once we had the navigation bugs worked out, we checked out the rest of the systems. That ranged from testing all the plumbing—water supply, waste disposal, running the dishwasher—to checking the electricity while the motor ran at full power. We ran maneuvers for turning and stopping. Tao further impressed me by cooking a meal—vegan, of course—while we were underway.

I'd set up my gear the day before, but we tested the onboard compressor on several tanks while running to a remote dive site. Actually, Captain Rich found the perfect spot—not a dive site, but an out-of-the-way location with a sandy slope. We were going to test a couple of gear configurations at a few depths.

Then it was showtime. I pivoted to turn on my gas before donning my gear. And then things ground to a halt.

"Hold it. Before we do anything underwater, we need to get Tao prepared to be a surface safety resource."

Captain Rich was nothing if not thorough. I gave myself a mental head slap for not thinking of that step.

I was too eager to get in the water. That sort of blinders-on thinking was what got people killed.

Rich had ten times the experience than I did with onboard safety and a hundred times more than I did in training up a crew member. Actually, I'd never done it. I'd done process reviews and briefings, but never a training.

I cooled my heels while Captain Rich worked through Tao's role, which would be relatively simple—unless things went south, in which case it could get very complex. His role was to keep an eye on the sled cable and listen in on the comms. After a few dry runs, it sounded like we were ready.

And then we weren't.

"Ricky, can you bring up your safety sausage?"

Duh! Of course! My surface-marking buoy!

Tao would be the one looking out for that. Mental head slap number two. This was not good. I had to get my head into the game and not just the fun part.

"Inflated?" I wasn't sure how real the demonstration was supposed to be.

"What state will it be in when he sees it under a real-life emergency situation?"

"Inflated." Captain Rich was good. Very good. A pain in the ass, but completely within his rights.

I unclipped the safety sausage from my buoyancy vest and unfurled it. Fully inflated, it would be six feet tall, enough to be seen when bobbing above the surface, even in rough waters. I hooked it up to a spare tank we kept on deck and inflated it to its full glory.

"Sometime this month, Ricky."

Sheesh.

Judging by their smiles, the guys were yanking my chain. I did my best game-show-hostess imitation as I displayed the six-foot-long orange plastic tube known as a safety sausage and how it might appear on the surface. I explained that it could merely be providing a warning to other boats that a diver was not far under the water and would be surfacing, so please stay away. Or it might mean that I was engaged in an extended series of decompression stops and that the boat would need to track me. Or it might mean that I was in trouble. It all came down to context, but for Tao, it meant to immediately execute a retrieval plan, which might very well involve him bringing the Zodiac inflatable boat to the vicinity of the safety sausage and waiting for me to surface.

We worked through various scenarios, each with the same resolution, and explained how the context of the moment might give Tao insight. And in each scenario, Captain Rich explained what he would do and why.

"And?"

"And, in the ab . . . absence of specific orders, I am responsible for getting the diver out of the water." Tao was a fast learner. And very good at following orders without debate.

"Well," said Captain Rich finally, "what are you waiting for? Shouldn't you be geared up?"

Now he's just showing off for Tao.

I geared up, indicated to Tao that I was ready, flipped off Captain Rich, and made my giant stride. The first dives, on a single tank, were only going to fifteen feet and only for a few minutes each. And I was going down a drop line, so I was never going to be separated from the boat.

I was diving with a full-face mask—actually, trying out three different masks—that incorporated a wireless communications system to the boat. This seemed like overkill, but Lonnie had insisted that I be in contact with the boat during dives to discuss where and how deep to take samples. I'd dove with them before, but they still felt odd.

I stayed shallow for the tests, fifteen feet, until I found one of the three that was the most comfortable. Once I'd settled on a mask, I reentered the water with the sled and descended to fifty feet, where we ran a couple of tests, then again near the bottom at seventy-five. The system worked fine. Sort of. I had balance issues and tended to dolphin a bit, rising and diving, but I was getting the hang of it.

We worked through the first run of tests faster than we had expected, and I was down for only thirty minutes. Tao had lunch—veggie stir-fry and noodles—ready as soon as I was dry. We ate and compared notes during the first half hour of the surface interval and chilled for the next hour before going over the plan for the second test.

Captain Rich moved the boat out into deeper waters—one hundred feet above the sandy floor—and I splashed back in and mounted the sled, this time with multiple tanks and a different gas mix. Afterward, we did some diver recovery drills with Tao. Normally, we'd do the deep dive first, but we didn't want to discover a problem on a deep dive when recovery might be tougher.

Again, everything went fine, including the full-face mask and communication system that I'd settled on after testing them all on the earlier dives. Both Captain Rich and I were new to this manufacturer and model, so we were concerned about the ability to communicate that deep. He'd kept the transponder immediately under the boat, and it worked fine—no need to lower it for deep dives.

8

I'M REALLY SICK AND TIRED OF PEOPLE DYING, YOU KNOW?

As I PREPARED to begin my ascent, Captain Rich called out, "Orca! We have a pod of orca on the surface!"

He couldn't contain his excitement, but I didn't completely share it. Although seeing an orca is a rare and amazing event, and being in the water with them even more so, I was immediately unsettled this time around.

I looked up. They were moving in the opposite direction of the boat, so they were about to pass over me. In the crystal-clear waters, I could make out the patterns on their bellies as they swam by. It looked like a small pod—I counted seven—moving slowly on the surface. Not hunting, just cruising.

"Captain Rich, hold off on raising the sled until they're gone. I'm just going to chill down here until then."

∽

"What was that about?" Captain Rich was in my face once I finally surfaced. He never danced around a topic. "Those were orca! They were breaching right by the boat."

"Yeah, I'm just not a fan of being in the water with them."

"Wait, you're afraid of orca? Ricky Freaking Yamamoto is scared of orca? You were always getting in the water with sharks in Palau. You were like the shark sanctuary goddess. There has got to be more to the story."

There is, for damn sure.

"I'm not scared. Just cautious." I was still wearing my gear and would have preferred to have this talk after showering and changing. Better yet, I'd rather not have the conversation.

"They've never killed or attacked a diver. Ever." Captain Rich had a number of triggers that could set him off. Two of them were people vilifying animals—especially marine animals like sharks and, I guess, orca—and people not confronting their demons.

"Yeah, well, a friend of mine was killed by an orca. Actually, two orca. Can we leave it at that?"

"Bullshit. No recorded attacks. Period."

"None in the wild. This was different."

"Christ. Was it the lady who got pulled down during the show?"

"You're not going to let this go, are you?" He was still standing between me and the gear rack. I still wore my neoprene suit. I tried to squirm by him, but he wasn't making way.

"OK. Short version is all you get. Bel was an environmental activist. Started with protest marches and graffiti in Honduras fighting for lobster divers' rights.

Longtime Greenpeace member. Save the whales. Save the sharks. Sort of a guardian angel. That's how we met. In Hawaii, right after I turned eighteen. We did our paramedic training together. I was still dealing with the whole Surf Slayer fallout and working through some complex issues. I could have wallowed in self-pity over the friends who'd been killed, or raged at the authorities and parents for not listening to me, but I channeled it into activism. But then I took my first assistant divemaster job, and we went different directions. She got even more radical and moved on to crew for two years on the *Sea Shepherd*."

"That's a pretty intense group. I've got a mate who's with them. They don't let many things get in their way."

I started to speak and realized I'd been holding my breath. I took a minute to catch it.

"Yeah, well, she got super-radicalized on the boat. But she didn't like all the posing and the media and decided she was going to split off and do her own thing with the orca. Protests at American facilities. Some vandalism. Then she went all in."

"It's an easy slope to slide down," Captain Rich said. He, of anyone I knew, would have had the best front-row view to that sort of thing. You couldn't do military and mercenary work for as long as he had without running into a few outliers.

"She and a couple of others set up shop in Alaska to prepare for a raid on a captive orca site in Russia. They were capturing them by the dozens and selling them to entertainment centers, mainly in China. Big bucks. They had twelve orca waiting for sale and transport. The guys she was with were underwater construction pros. Assembly. Welding. Inspections and surveys. The intense stuff."

"Deadly stuff. I've known a few. Heard stories."

I was still in my neoprene and, predictably, sweating like a pig, but I noticed that Captain Rich was developing a sheen of sweat on his forehead. I doubted it had to do with the temperature. Maybe he had more demons than he'd copped to.

"Yeah, well, they boated over to Kamchatka—you know, north of Japan, Russian territory. It was supposed to be a by-the-numbers action. They cut through two nets that were blocking the gap between the holding area and the ocean. Last thing was the metal gate, which they cut through. Took out a big chunk—big enough for a couple of orca to swim through at a time."

Captain Rich was definitely sweating. And uncharacteristically quiet.

"Bel's job was to chum the water with squid to encourage the orca to investigate and move out into open water, not that they needed any encouragement. Anyway, once the orca realized the gate was down, it turned into a fire drill. They came out more quickly than anticipated. The welders barely got out of the way. Three or four squeezing through at once. She was still in the water when they blew through. Her partners found her floating on the surface, already dead. As best as they could tell, she got crushed between two fleeing orca. No bite marks. Just smashed."

That all spilled out quickly. I couldn't even remember the last time I'd told that story. I'd repressed it for a long time.

"I've never heard anything about this. There's never been a report that I've seen. Sorry to question you like that." Captain Rich was seldom contrite, but it seemed like he'd gotten there with this exchange.

"There wasn't a report. The dudes who caught the orca didn't want any attention. The guys with Bel didn't want to spend time in a Russian prison. They took her body with them. Dumped her in Alaskan waters. Ended up in a fisherman's net. Medical examiner ruled it drowning from unknown causes. Satisfied?" That came out a bit more hostile than intended.

"Yeah. Sorry."

"I'm really sick and tired of people dying, you know?"

9

IS YOUR HEAD IN THE RIGHT PLACE?

I WAS CRANKY. Even though it was well past sunset, it was hot. Hot and muggy. Though hours had passed, I was still twitchy from the revived memory of Bel. And the AC in my cabin was on the fritz. I'd suggested to Captain Rich that I just move into one of the empty cabins, but he said he wasn't comfortable using them for anything other than shakedown testing. Having to change the sheets, clean the bathroom, yada yada. Whatever. So I left him and Tao to wrestle the unit out, repair it, replace it, and hopefully remove the stink of man sweat that had filled the room.

The AC issue was exactly why we were doing a preshakedown shakedown cruise. At some point, the owners would be joining us for the real shakedown, and we wanted to avoid any surprises. With three months of intense data gathering and scientific research ahead of us, the devil was in the details.

We were anchored in a fairly shallow bay around

thirty feet deep, tucked in among a grouping of around ten limestone pillars that rose about twenty feet out of the sea. The water was calm. The sandy bottom was almost pure white. It seemed like the perfect place for a relaxed night dive. I had to get the thoughts of Bel out of my head.

I poked my head back into the cabin to let the boys know I was going for a dip. I'm pretty sure that despite the vocal cursing each was unleashing, they heard enough to understand that I would be splashing in for a while. Just in case, I left a note about my plan and timing on the beer refrigerator, where I was sure they would be visiting when their task was completed, if not before.

We had several tanks already filled, tested, and racked, plus others waiting to be tested, part of our quality-assurance check of the compressor and our gas-blending station. I hooked my gear up to one we'd already tested, but I ran it through the analyzer again to ensure the right blend of oxygen and nitrogen. Then I hooked it up to my computer to check that it contained the right amount of gas. I did the same for the bail-out cylinder that I carried as an extra safety measure. I labeled each tank with its mix and related data, then filled in the blank dive log we'd bought for this trip.

The last steps involved a few modifications to my assembled gear, setting it up the same way I would for any night dive—adding two extra lights and a strobe tethered to the top of my tank. Even though neither of them was monitoring the comms, I stayed with the full-face mask. I figured more time spent on task, breathing through the unfamiliar gear, would make things easier in the long run. Besides, if Captain Rich needed to communicate with me, I'd be able to receive.

I went through my regular self-check routine to ensure that everything was where it should be and hooked up appropriately. Then I turned on my strobe light. If the boys popped up on deck looking for me, I wouldn't be hard to find.

Just as I slid into my harness, Captain Rich emerged from below.

"Up for some company? I was thinking I might come with you."

"Is the AC fixed?" I suspected his priorities had shifted.

"No, but Tao has it under control."

I didn't like this. I wanted to be alone. I didn't want a babysitter. I bit my tongue and waited. The only sound was the gentle slapping of small waves against the hull of the boat. It seemed like Captain Rich and I were in a staring contest. I gave in first.

"That's a two-person job. I'm just going for a little jaunt. I'll stay close to the boat, and I couldn't go deep at this site unless I had a shovel."

"All good, but is your head in the right place?"

"You didn't want to ask in front of Tao, did you? Thanks, at least, for that. I'm fine. I'm great. Setting up gear and going through my routine is helping clear my head. And you know, once I'm underwater, I'll be golden."

"Yeah, but . . ."

I saw no sense in continuing this line of discussion. "But nothing. Every single thing that's happened to me over the past year has been on the surface. Every. Single.

Thing. When I'm submerged, I'm in control. Now go back to the AC, or I'll make you switch cabins until mine is fixed."

"Fine, but let me do a buddy check."

I let Captain Rich double-check all of my gear. He even checked the dive log. There were no signs that I was off my game, even after an extended layoff. After giving my harness straps an extra tug, he patted me on my head. "Good to go."

And with that, I stood up, walked to the edge of the dive deck, and stepped off the stern of the *Powerballer* and into the waters of Thailand.

Despite being warm, the water temperature was still several degrees below that of the outside air—and far cooler than my muggy cabin. I couldn't call it bracing, but even the slight difference helped clear my head. I floated to the surface, slipped on the fins I'd worn around my wrist for my entry, and then—since the big lug was still standing there watching—signaled to Captain Rich that I was descending, gave him what was becoming my traditional middle finger, and slipped beneath the surface.

I slowly dropped down to just above the shallow, sandy bottom. An unwelcome but familiar sense of melancholy and dread grew as I descended. This wasn't how it used to be—how it was supposed to be. I paused and tried to relax, humming my longtime comfort tune—the *Barney* theme song—and focused on being in the moment. That was normally all I needed to settle into a calm breathing pattern and a relaxed body posture.

But not this time.

10

IT FELT A BIT LIKE A REBIRTH

OVER THE PAST year, I'd been feeling increasingly separated from my usual peaceful state. I hadn't enjoyed a dive in months—and I'd been on dozens. For some, my heart wasn't in it, and for others—the worst—they were just damn heartbreaking. I needed to reconnect with the calm and creative juices that had been coursing through my veins ever since I had discovered the joys of diving and climbing.

But forcing myself to calm down was completely counterproductive. The more I tried to relax, the more tense I became. The more I tried to be unfocused and one with the water, the more I became rigid. I was thinking it was time to end the dive.

As if on cue, an undulating, red creature swam by. *Swam* might be the wrong term—the aptly named Spanish dancer contorted, furling and unfurling, to propel itself through the water. In all my years of diving, I'd never seen one swimming. I'd read about it. I'd seen videos. I'd even seen them crawling along the seafloor or along reefs, but I'd never been blessed with seeing one swim.

A few bubbles escaped from my mouth as I grinned.

The Spanish dancer's choreography is slow. I'm talking somewhat comically slow and lacking in direction. I followed it for a couple of minutes—while it traveled no more than fifteen feet—until it settled on the reef and reverted to crawling.

I hadn't immediately noticed, but it was as if a switch had been turned off in my head. My whole body relaxed. My breathing returned to a natural rhythm. My head didn't buzz with ugly memories.

The moon was almost full and high in the sky. The sand reflected it back with an intensity equal to a cloudy day. Although I carried them, I didn't need my lights; in fact, they hindered my eyes' ability to adjust to the natural lighting. My strobe, even more so. With some degree of difficulty, I managed to reach behind my back and turn it off. The flashing was immediately replaced with a feeling of calm.

With my lights extinguished and little to no movement, I soon blended in with the fish life. A large barracuda gently cruised by, taking a moment to assess me before continuing on. An octopus slid along the seafloor and up into a patch of coral, hunting for crabs, most likely. I returned to the Spanish dancer and watched it working its way along the reef. I was probably never more than thirty or forty feet from the boat as I puttered around, just letting the marine life be and doing my best to remain nonthreatening.

As divers go deeper, they use more breathing gas for

each minute that passes. At the shallow depths beneath the boat, I had only used about one-third of a tank after an hour. Every once in a while, I heard a bang resonating from the hull of the boat, suggesting that Captain Rich and Tao were still struggling with the wonky AC unit.

Although I'd been trained to follow the dive professional's mantra of "Plan the dive and dive the plan," I sometimes found room for a bit of flexibility. I'd planned on an hour, but this was too good to stop. I abandoned any thought of surfacing on schedule.

I'd passed a small opening at the base of one of the pinnacles during my meandering and decided to circle back and give it the attention it deserved. Limestone can be riddled with open spaces—holes, tunnels, caverns, caves. Some go on for miles. Most much less or even almost nothing. But a fair number allow the enterprising and trained diver to navigate through twists and turns, tight passages, even tighter restrictions, and wide-open chambers, sharing the space with fish that spend most of their time in the shadows. These spaces, many of which have never been discovered, are among the world's last uninvestigated mysteries.

I had no idea how this one might turn out.

After only a few feet, the illumination from the moon had dwindled to zero. But the hole opened up wider, higher, and deeper, into a space that allowed easy navigation and, if necessary, an easy retreat—which only made me more curious about what I might find.

I'd been having nightmares about caves for the past six months. The year before, through no fault of my own—and in fact, totally unrelated to diving—I'd found myself being chased through a dry cave by a tough-guy wannabe who most likely would have ended up killing me if he'd caught me. He didn't. He tried, but he died. Still, half a year later, I continued to wake up in a sweat after some terrifying dream about caves, both above and underwater.

I've always been fairly good at confronting my fears, and I hoped this time would be no different. Nightmare or not, though, I was going to need at least a little light. I turned one of my lights to its red setting, lighting up the cave with a soft glow. Not only was it less intrusive to my own eyesight but also to that of the fish. They seemed unimpressed by my presence or the new, weird lighting.

The crack turned out to be somewhat complex. It reached deep under the pinnacle, sometimes turning narrow and tall, but wide enough for me to wiggle through, and at other times widening into a very shallow restriction that almost made me turn back. A little bit of twisting got me past and into a larger chamber. Beyond the chamber, through a gap that looked to be about fifteen feet long, I could see the white sand and the bright moonlight—meaning that I'd reached an exit of the tunnel. But that last restriction turned out to be a puzzle.

I looked at a gap not so high as to allow me to squeeze on through with a tank strapped to my back. And if I shifted my tank to my side, instead of my back, it was high enough but not wide enough. And either way, there wasn't enough room for me to propel myself by finning. I didn't have enough room to move my legs and fins.

It looked like the restriction was rock above but sand

below. That meant there was some leeway in squeezing through—by working back and forth, I could shift the sand to make for more space. Of course, that also meant silting up the water and reducing visibility. Squeezing through a restriction when you could see the options ahead was one thing—squeezing through with zero visibility was quite another.

I could turn back. I had plenty of breathing gas and maneuverability to just turn around and retrace my path in. No shame in making that move. But what would be the fun in that? I did a mental coin flip, and it came up heads. I would continue forward.

I took a minute to make sure my breathing was regular and relaxed. Backing out slightly into the large chamber, I removed my tank and bailout bottle from my buoyancy vest. Then I took off my fins, slipping their straps over my wrists. I was a bit discombobulated, but I'd successfully done this before and had confidence in the decision to move on. Aligning my tank and bottle straight ahead of me, I gently pushed with my feet and began to ease into the restriction.

Divers tend to reside entirely in one of two camps when it comes to handling tight restrictions. There are those who expect they will freak out and don't try it, and there are those who maintain their calm as they work through spaces that would cause a claustrophobe to panic even above the surface of the water. There is, for the most part, no middle ground. Fortunately, I was in the second camp, though I respected the risk and always assessed it thoroughly before proceeding.

I mapped out the space in my mind, anticipating

challenges and how to move past them. Almost like a gymnast or a slalom skier playing the moves ahead in their mind, I spent a few minutes inspecting the space and devising my approach.

It went smoothly . . . until it didn't.

About ten feet in, probably halfway through the restriction, my vest snagged on a small irregularity in the rock surface above me. I wiggled left and then to the right, trying to slide off it. No luck. I couldn't see where I was hung up, but I knew generally where and what the potential snags on my vest were.

My body was relaxed, my breathing calm. I was mentally in a good place.

I wiggled back a few inches and felt it release, slid sideways a few inches to get around the problem, and then wiggled forward. My legs were now in the most restricted spot, and I was unable to get any significant push, so I used my left hand to push the tank and the bottle and the right to find and use a handhold for pulling. It was a lot like climbing, searching for that sliver of rock for a secure fingerhold. But there was nothing on my right. I switched hands, planting my right hand on the tank and feeling about with the left. I almost immediately found a substantial handhold, pulled gently, and was soon writhing and pulling through the gap, making slow but steady progress until the tank, the bottle, and I were clear into the final chamber.

It felt a bit like a rebirth.

It only took me a minute or two to recombobulate and return my tank and fins to their normal positions. Back in a part of the swim-through, illuminated by the moonlight reflecting off the pure-white sand, I turned off my light, paused for a few minutes to enjoy the serenity, and then finned out into the open water.

After easing around for another half hour, checking out the little night critters, basking in the rich light of the moon, and holding fast to the joy I'd rediscovered, I slowly ascended to the dive deck of the *Powerball*, where I found Captain Rich and Tao apparently sharing fart jokes.

They had a large cooler filled with ice and what looked to be a case of beer. Captain Rich slid it my way with a push of his foot. I popped one open and downed half before I even took off my gear.

They yakked away until I pulled off my wetsuit. I noticed that Tao went silent. Captain Rich filled the void with a long story that had something to do with . . . actually, I can't even recall what it was about. I was checking out Tao, who was working hard not to check me out.

It took most of the evening, and a little help from me, but the boys finished off every can in the cooler.

To each their own. I was starting to get back in touch with my inner Zen goddess. This trip was turning out to be exactly what I needed.

11

SOUNDS WICKED

LIFE CAN BE tough. But it doesn't have to be. I was in Thailand, pulling down a larger salary than I'd ever had before, and had just finished a fairly uneventful—except for the AC—preshakedown cruise on a $3 million yacht. We'd perform a final inspection prior to the extended voyage, though the boat had been subjected to so much fine-tuning that we didn't expect much.

The temperature gauge back on the aft deck had remained pegged at ninety for the days leading up to our departure. One drawback of the private harbor our bosses had bought, tucked into the jungle as it was, was the lack of a cooling breeze except on the windiest of days. It was a relief to get out on the water. And into the water. My gills had been drying out.

Tao's brother, Shway, and sister, TK, showed up at the gate shortly after 08:00, bearing a variety of paper and plastic bags. Soon the galley was filled with the familiar smells of garlic, ginger, lemongrass, and cumin. And a few others I couldn't identify but made me drool.

There was also a large jug filled with Tao's "super-iced coffee," made extra sweet just for me. If it was too sweet for Captain Rich, I'd gladly drink the whole thing. As a matter of fact, I planned on drinking most of it while he slept in.

When Captain Rich finally emerged from his state-room, Tao pointed him to the salon. "Hangover food. Best stuff."

He was right. Two bowls of spicy noodle soup went down quickly and didn't come back up. He followed that up with a bowl of chicken drunken noodles and—"secret cure," Tao had said—a bottle of Singha beer.

After a shower and a short nap, Captain Rich was back to his normal self. The White Stripes' "Seven Nation Army" blasted from his room as he set about cleaning the guns. I noticed that the armory had expanded and that he'd been able to source some of the "less tradi-tional" weapons Lonnie had hoped for. I doubted that we'd ever have to put them into play, but if we did, I hoped that Lonnie knew how to use them.

Lonnie and Margo were unknowns for me. Captain Rich had met them years before, when they dove with him on a liveaboard in the Philippines.

"Back then, it was budget, but now it's bazillions."

"How so? Stock options? Inheritance?" You ran into all types on dive boats, from people who scrape together money every year or two to make a big splash trip to those who have money to burn on boat charters, private guides, and all the pampering you could imagine.

"American lottery. Powerball."

"Oh, I thought the name meant . . . never mind. Wow. Lottery. That can be big bucks."

"You have no idea . . . actually, neither did I. They have the news article framed up in their stateroom. Just over a hundred million. They don't talk about it. But Lonnie dropped three million and change on this boat. The private harbor was another half million, and they had to put at least another half million into the boat. He's never said no to any expense I've raised with them. You should see the lab equipment they've got in there. I have no idea what any of it does, but I did some searches, and there's several hundred thousand dollars' worth of gear in there."

Turns out that Lonnie had been a groundskeeper for a major golf course in Rangoon, Myanmar. Apparently, he'd bent Captain Rich's ear about seeing the impact firsthand: sediment choking out plant life in the estuary, pesticides killing large populations of fish, fertilizer causing algae blooms that smothered the reef. It took him almost an hour to paint that picture.

Margo ran a nursery that supplied the golf course and a number of local resorts. "As she put it," Captain Rich said with a grimace, "over time, their romance 'bloomed.' They both do that—silly horticulture jokes. Got married before they got rich, so it appears to be true love. They didn't get religious about the environment until they suddenly had the bucks to be independent. Then they went hog wild."

"When do they get here?"

"A week or two. Give or take. They're at some conference in Australia with ocean conservation mucky-mucks. Sylvia Earle is there."

"She rocks. One of my few heroes."

"Yeah, they seemed more interested in meeting the *Sea Shepherd* folks. Lonnie said they got a tour of one of the boats. I'm surprised they haven't asked me to get a water cannon fitted on the foredeck."

"Are they looking to rumble?"

"Nah, they're pretty meek. They just like to think they're badass. They loved the articles about you in Palau. Not the ones where you were blamed for killing the two Yakuza gangsters with the truck axle and chain. The later ones where you're the hero and you killed three hoods. Never mind that one of them fell into a crocodile enclosure while you were still tied up and the other two piled into the rocks chasing you—those final few articles left our new bosses thinking you're the next Katniss Everdeen. Lonnie and Margo like to think that the five of us—you, me, Tao, and them—are a 'small but mighty squad.' But I could scare Lonnie by just yelling, 'Boo!' Kind of high-strung."

"Sorry, who?"

"Lonnie. Margo. The people who are paying you to be on top of things."

"No, Catnip somebody?"

"Katniss. Katniss Everdeen. *Hunger Games*? Survivalist? Bow and arrow? Savior of the freaking rebellion?"

"I got nothing. I don't read the news very much. Sounds wicked."

A new tune started, and he paused to turn up the volume for the Red Hot Chili Peppers, which I knew was going to delay us for a few minutes. He joined the band on his own version of drums, which consisted of armrests, the wheel, and any part of the console that didn't have a screen or a gauge. By the end of the tune, he'd worked up a sweat. And a thirst.

"Beer?" He nodded at my empty hands.

"Nah, but knock yourself out."

Without even leaving the captain's chair, he popped open a small, discreet refrigerator and pulled out a bottle of Singha.

"Where was I?" He took a long pull on the bottle. "*Boo.*"

⤜

The next week passed quickly as we knocked off, added, and then knocked off a variety of increasingly minor tweaks and cleanup on the boat. We had barely finished when we got word of the upcoming arrival.

It was getting on toward dusk when Lonnie and Margo, the boat's owners and my employers for the next few months, arrived. The music had been turned off hours before in anticipation of their arrival.

My hopes for Lonnie's firearm expertise and battle readiness diminished almost immediately upon his arrival. Not that looks can tell you much about a person, but Lonnie's lack of battle readiness was immediately obvious as he stumbled when stepping off the dock onto the boat. Margo caught his arm with such speed and grace that I suspected she'd had a lot of practice. Lonnie shot a look at the dock as if to find blame, but there was none to be found.

After the formal introductions—sort of unnecessary, since we'd interviewed on Zoom—Captain Rich and

Tao trotted back to the limo that had brought Lonnie and Margo to the harbor and hauled their luggage—matching bags, eight in all, plus a golf bag—to their stateroom. Lonnie followed, but Margo went back, tipped the driver, and sent him on his way.

Golf?

Captain Rich had spent the afternoon checking navigational issues such as tide times, heights, and streams, and the weather forecast. He and Tao spent some time in the engine room as well, checking fluid levels and belts. They ran the engine for more than an hour, checking the exhaust and running through various RPMs.

Finally, Captain Rich headed to the pilot house. I was following and had to stop on the ladder as he paused and took in the smell and feel of the place. New room, new chairs, new gauges.

"I'm actually getting a bit tingly."

I don't think I'd ever heard him express an emotion like that. New captain's chairs can do that to a man.

While we had been working through a checklist to document the seaworthiness of the boat and the dive operations, a list that closely paralleled the exact items we'd already checked before and during the preshakedown cruise, Margo and Lonnie were inspecting the habitation portion—testing electricity, water, AC, toilets, and everything else they needed for comfort and pleasure. Margo was checking the temperature in the wine cooler when Lonnie turned on the stereo, and she nearly jumped out of her thousand-dollar leather boat shoes. Dropping the volume level before they arrived had somehow failed to make it onto our checklist. Despite that misstep, Margo pronounced the boat and its crew A1 and ready to roll.

Lonnie, on the other hand, was not yet done. He followed Tao and Captain Rich down the stairs to the staterooms, pausing to run his hand along the polished wood of the salon. He paused again to sniff his palm in a creepy way. Well . . . actually, I'm not sure there's a noncreepy way to sniff one's palm.

Lonnie was a piece of work. He was skinny, with an oval head that was wider than it was tall. His hair was a pale ginger. His mustache was too thin and patchy to be called a porn-star 'stache, but it was not a good look. He was short. At least three inches shorter than Margo and a good six inches below my five feet nine or ten. He was, however, dressed perfectly for an afternoon yacht outing. If we were in Newport, Rhode Island.

Margo, on the other hand, clearly still had her strength and muscles from her years working in the nursery. And she was a bit of a hottie as well. Not that I notice that sort of thing.

My admiration of Margo's skill set was interrupted by an eruption from Lonnie, who had, unfortunately, found the remains of Captain Rich's chicken drunken noodles as he worked his way through the boat to inspect the armory. Tao leaped into action and apologized, claiming that the food was his, not the captain's. An interrogation ensued until Lonnie was satisfied that no kitchen tools, plates, cutlery, or cloth napkins had been employed in the eating of the soup. Tao bagged up the leftovers and took them out to the parking lot, promising to throw them away in a public dumpster on his way out.

Captain Rich immediately set about distracting Lonnie, popping open the hidden compartments and pulling out the full range of the arsenal. Lonnie began cooing in pleasure. His creepiness rating raced upward.

"Only one shotgun? I specified four."

"My supplier was almost exclusively military weapons, and shotguns are rarely available. They get top dollar, and he only had this one, and it was in his private collection."

"I specified shotguns. We might need them for close combat . . . with pirates. You got the knives, right?"

"Yeppers. Just short of a dozen. You can have your pick."

I gave Lonnie another looking over and found it hard to imagine him in close-quarters combat. I guess a shotgun at twenty feet. No way with knives. But this was his wet dream, so I kept my mouth shut and tried not to smile.

"I do have flash-bangs. And grenades."

"Grenade launcher?"

"Would I let you down? I bought five, one for each of us."

"Shame about the shotguns." Lonnie, literally surrounded with an arsenal that would make a drug lord proud, seemed inconsolable. "Any chance we can get some more before we head out?"

"I'll check. Same price limit?"

"Double it."

Criminy!

"You have time at the range with any of these?" Captain Rich wasn't about to let him handle anything without some qualifications.

"Range and field. ROTC marksman qualification. Combat-situation simulations. Then army reserve for six years."

Weekend warrior. But better than nothing. More than I have.

"We'll get out on the range, the two of us, before we leave."

Trust, then verify.

Captain Rich wasn't cutting anyone any slack. Although I was surprised to hear that he'd gotten a grenade launcher for me. I guessed we wouldn't be training on that at the range.

"Did you get the night-vision goggles?"

"Two sets, just like you asked, but I got reamed on the price. I warned you. US military grade. Waterproof and built to take a beating. You get what you pay for."

"No worries. Better to have them than not."

"Good, I'm glad to hear that. I sort of extended the request."

"How so?" Lonnie had never complained about prices, according to Captain Rich, but perhaps this time he'd gone too far.

"I also got two night-vision binoculars. Easier to fit with a variety of face types. Makes switching from scanning to focusing a lot easier."

"How much?"

"Three times as much as the goggles. About fifteen grand US each, once the middleman got his share."

"Next time, ask. But good call on your part."

After that, Lonnie seemed satisfied. Except for the shotguns. He was finally able to pull himself away from the arsenal after identifying several pieces he wanted stored in the secret compartment in the master suite. Then he headed for his pet project.

A sizeable chunk of the lower deck had been converted into a lab. I heard him squeal with joy as he and Captain Rich entered. I dropped down for a quick look-see. Peering in the door, I saw him gently running his hands over dials and switches, muttering various acronyms. I figured he'd be busy for a while.

While Lonnie drooled over his new lab, I headed out to the parking lot to rescue the exiled food bag before the rats got to it. The trailer had a small kitchenette where I sat and ate until the containers were empty. I popped a couple of mints that I'd grabbed for the meet-and-greet with the bosses and hoped I wouldn't burp near Lonnie.

12

YOU DON'T REALLY NEED TO UNDERSTAND THE SCIENCE

SHWAY HAD BROUGHT more fresh fruit to augment the papayas, mangoes, and limes that Tao had collected on the property. I was down with that. The three fifty-pound bags of rice, though, had me a bit concerned.

Shway hadn't been involved directly in any of the maintenance work, but he'd be staying in the trailer while we were gone, providing site security. The tools were locked up in a fairly solid storage shack, and the small dive boat had been pulled onto shore and chained to concrete blocks in a section of the harbor hidden from view, so really, the only exposed item was Captain Rich's tuk-tuk, but Lonnie and Margo were clear that a caretaker was a justified expense. Shway promised to guard the super tuk-tuk with his life.

A private harbor pilot also popped in during the afternoon for a last-minute consult with Captain Rich and Lonnie. He reviewed the charts that Lonnie and

Captain Rich had plotted for the first two days. Beyond that, we were going to be planning as each day came.

Amid all the activity and visits, Margo dropped by my cabin, followed by Tao, with one of her many suitcases. If she knocked, I missed it.

"You can store your personal clothes, other than swimsuits and casual deck wear, in the *Valkyrian*. I'm told it won't sink, and several of the cabins were brought back up to livability standards." She lazily waved her hand in the direction of the abandoned hulk that shared our private marina.

Does she even know my name? She hasn't used it yet.

"Thanks, Margo. Yeah, Captain Rich showed me the cabins that were ready for storage. I actually travel quite light. I don't have anything other than swimsuits and a couple of changes of boat wear."

If she heard me, she didn't react or respond. "When you are working, though, I have clothing for you. We want to present a certain image." In the suitcase were a number of outfits that you might find in a Lands' End or Abercrombie & Fitch catalog. Not my style, but not revolting. There was even a very nice bathrobe. The *Powerballer* monogram was a bit much, but it's not like any of my friends were going to see me.

She plowed onward.

"I took the liberty. I hope you don't mind. Don't consider these a uniform, just a set of clothing coordinated for the look of the boat. Also, here are new toiletries, including organic, sea-friendly toothpaste;

lotions; shampoos; and feminine hygiene products. We want this voyage to have minimal impact on the ocean."

"Great. Stellar. Thank you!"

"Stellar"? I'm using Sumo's terms? I'd prefer to get him out of my head.

I realized, though, that Margo seemed like she might be the type to post social media photos during or after our journey. I decided I'd make a conscious effort to be elsewhere when her camera came out.

"You might want to wear the bathrobe," she added, "when wearing your swimsuit."

Yeah, no, that's not likely.

Our last evening was spent going over the details of the plan for acquiring and archiving samples. Margo had handed that responsibility to Lonnie, then retired to their cabin almost immediately. Tao delivered her dinner and a bottle of chilled white wine and, later, returned for her plate.

We were seated around a table up in the pilot house. It was big, heavy, and fancy. Looked like it came from a single tree trunk. It could probably seat a dozen people.

Included in that discussion was a review of the custom-built storage racks for the samples I'd be collecting. We'd never gotten that detailed about the collection process, so I was glad to go over it before hitting the high seas.

According to Lonnie, our mission was simple: "Determine the extent and source of pollution pouring out of Myanmar into the Andaman Sea."

Lonnie's rants had gotten very intense and detailed anytime we strayed into that topic. It made sense. They'd dropped five million bucks into this project, their biggest investment of time and money so far, according to Margo. This was the first time it was being discussed as a focused topic. Lonnie began by saying that he was looking for our input. His following words made me wonder how true that really was.

"You don't really need to understand the science," added Lonnie, with what almost looked like a contemptuous sneer. "All we need from you is to collect the samples."

Well, thank you, Mr. Snotty McSnotpants!

"We want as many core samples from the sea bottom as we can get and then water samples from the water column as you surface. The gear is simple to handle, and Tao will assist you at the surface. We've plotted the drop points. There are almost one hundred and seventy that we plan to sample in a six-week span."

"I thought we discussed something on the order of eighty when we spoke." I'd seen scope creep and had expected it might happen here, but doubling the workload was going to be a problem.

"We have to keep the plan fluid, based on what we find. If we're getting consistent readings, we'll decrease the number of sites tested. That's a very real probability in the early weeks, as we're a good distance from the delta. Consider this the maximum and eighty being the target. But we'll collect from as many sites as we need and not a single site less."

"We're clear." As he said it, Captain Rich tapped my foot with his. I was guessing he had this under control.

I'd have to keep an eye on our interactions. If he had

a major stick up his butt, I'd need to tread gently. Not my strong suit.

"That's four a day. That's a lot of up and down. We'll have to work up the tables on how one diver can do this. But at this point, I'm not seeing it."

"We don't think so."

Again, with something looking like a sneer. I tend to get a bit combative when someone hires you for your expertise and then decides to mansplain your business to you. Captain Rich had witnessed that before and delivered several kicks to my leg.

Message received.

I kicked back to acknowledge his communication.

"We're thinking you can hit multiple sites on one dive and do the whole day's work in two dives. You go to site 1 and take a core sample from the soft bottom. Then you stay deep and go to site 2. Take another core sample. Then you stay at site 2, ascend to middepth, and take a water sample. Move on back to site 1 at middepth and take a water sample there. Move up to shallow depth at site 1 for the final water sample for that site and finish off with a shallow-water sample from site 2. You'll just weave back and forth as you move up the water column."

"How big a spread are we talking about?"

He pulled out a chart.

"They are spread out in an array of concentric arcs. The closer we get to the mainland, the smaller the arc and the fewer the samples. We expect that we'll be choosing appropriate sampling sites approximately two miles apart along each arc."

At least he'd planned it out.

"Why didn't we have this discussion before I signed up?"

Captain Rich kicked me under the table.

"Hey." Lonnie held up his hands in surrender. "This is just a starting discussion. You're our lead diver. I'll tell you what's needed. You tell us what's possible. If we have to extend the trip, then we'll do so."

Nice sentiment, but the past five minutes had made me believe that it was Lonnie's way or the highway, and I wasn't looking forward to being fired in the middle of the Andaman Sea.

"Extend the trip? Something else we didn't discuss."

This time, Captain Rich planted his foot on mine and left it there.

"Do you have a job waiting for you when you return?"

"No, but I have feelers out, and people have expectations."

"You do recall that the contract does include provisions for extra days at double the pay, don't you?"

"Good point. No worries, I'm in, but just trying to calibrate expectations with our actual capacity. Two miles? We're still planning on using the sled, right?"

"Planning and confident. We've studied this every which way." Lonnie grinned. It appeared he was considering me his setup lady today. "We're looking at three options. Captain Rich in one of the Jet Skis towing you and extra tanks underwater in a sled. Two knots per hour. One pass at no more than sixty feet to get core samples and water samples. Sample drop-site 1. Travel two miles to drop-site 2 for its bottom sample. The next stop at thirty feet for water samples. First with drop-site 2 and then drop-site 1. The last at fifteen for water samples. Drop-site 1, then drop-site 2. That's three hours. Six samples. Only one descent and one ascent. We've already done the tables."

Sure you have. I'll be doing them again, thank you. Amateur.

"You can easily do that on the gas mixes we've evaluated—subject, of course, to your approval."

"Yeah, I'll be plotting these out with a software package I use. And then I'll confirm manually."

"Right. As I was saying, then you'll have a three-hour surface interval and another set of passes. That's four drop sites a day in two dives. Within our planned calendar."

"What's the second option?"

"Same plan but using the boat. And going faster. The Jet Ski isn't as smooth and might throw you around a bit at higher speeds. Maybe we do six drop sites a day, but we're planning on sticking with four."

Six? No fucking way.

Captain Rich was tight-lipped but seemed to be increasingly tense as the conversation developed.

"Option three?"

"Stay with the Jet Ski idea. Captain Rich does the second dive, and you do a third. You trade off with him in driving the Jet Ski. Fewer days but longer hours. Option four is the alternative sled driver but with the boat and me driving the *Powerballer*."

Oh, hell no!

"Yeah, too long. Though I'm sure I would have some fun towing Captain Rich. Yeah, no, that probably would be a bad idea. Can we check out the sled again?"

We left Lonnie to his charts and headed for the flybridge.

13

PURITANICAL PRISS

As soon as we were out of sight and sound, I gave Captain Rich a head slap. I think he was expecting it but didn't duck. Probably his way of serving penance.

"You could have mentioned the scope creep."

"First I heard about it. As soon as he started talking about it, I decided to speak with him privately. He doesn't take well to challenges, particularly in front of others. You really need to stop and think before reacting. Better yet, let me handle any discussions about agenda, job roles, or scope creeping."

He was right. There was nothing to be gained by making Lonnie look bad. But it felt good.

"Deal. But I'll give you about ten seconds, and if you don't step up, I'm jumping in."

"So anyway"—Captain Rich chose to move on without comment—"the sled. We'll run tests to see what's possible and what isn't. Then we have a discussion and revise the chart or the plan as necessary. Deal?"

"Deal. Can you modify the sled if we need to?"

"Sure. We're always up for a welding session."

"Then I'm good to go for testing."

"OK, that's the message I'm going to deliver to Lonnie. In private."

The sled was not unlike a sled I'd ridden as a teen in Colorado. And I'd often done that drunk, so this would likely be simpler. It had a much wider frame with an equally wide steering bar. The frame reached higher, with room for two breathing gas tanks in back and racks for the samples up front. There was a padded bench on which I would lie, with openings in the flooring on both sides, just off-center, for me to acquire my samples. It had a fin with foot pedals, giving me a second steering mechanism. And it had a control panel with gauges for depth, direction, bottom time, and even a roll and pitch sensor—with blinking alarm, Captain Rich mentioned, in case I got a case of the wobblies.

Some sled.

"Next topic. What's the deal with Lonnie and pirates?"

"Oh, you know how it is. New wealth. Focuses on money and how not to lose it. He's read about the Malacca and Singapore Straits and figures it's all the same no matter where you are in Southeast Asia."

"So, you're not worried about pirates where we're going?"

"Not at all, but it was fun collecting all that gear."

And with that, we left the topic behind.

'Nuff said. Maybe he's just compensating.

I suspected Lonnie hadn't had me in mind when he designed the sled—he had probably modeled it after his own dimensions. At five nine or ten—I'd stopped keeping track of it in high school when it became awkward being taller than most of the boys—I was still taller than most men, even in the United States. We had to adjust both the peddles and the steering bar almost to their limit to accommodate my tall frame. The handgrips and foot pedals, though, were just about right for my freakishly small hands and feet.

Lonnie had noticed and commented on my hands, probably not the only body part he had studied, and we even did a hand-size comparison. At five or six inches shorter than me, his hands were still noticeably larger than mine.

He had tried to interlace his fingers with mine, just for a moment. I would have thrown up in my throat if I'd had food in my stomach and decided that I would kick him in the shin if need be. He wouldn't survive one of my kicks in the head.

"I think you'll find that I'm a more-than-reasonable employer. We hire the best and pay the best for one reason—failure is not an option."

We were all back in the salon, having our end-of-the-day libations. Lonnie was five minutes into a speech that was, originally, a response to a question about our schedule.

"If we have to delay and wait for equipment to fix a problem we find on the shakedown, so be it. We are well ahead of storm season. I put significant buffers into the planning. Captain Rich, Tao, and I can handle that. And if we have down days, you and the captain can get in some dives. The local reefs are crowded, but I'm told you can head out early and beat the crowds." He waved his hand toward the end of the dock, where one more boat sat—a twenty-five-footer, rigged for diving. "And"—he waved like a game-show host—"for those of us with weak bladders, it has a small cabin down below with a head."

Dude!

So far, our employers were scoring OK. Lonnie could be creepy, Margo cold and controlling. But they paid well, didn't overwork us, gave us some perks, and seemed to be dedicated to saving the world's oceans.

The next day was the beginning of the big test.

Tao had wavered between nervous tension and cockiness as we approached departure hour. He and Captain Rich had been quite diligent in practicing castoff procedures before Lonnie and Margo arrived. There's nothing that starts a trip out on the wrong foot like blowing the castoff.

Before that could happen, though, we had to make sure we had a clear path to the bay. Tao took one of our Jet Skis out through our narrow channel to remove the chain that blocked access.

With a few comments and suggestions from the private pilot, Captain Rich eased us out to the main waterway, ready to head south through the otherworldly Phang Nga Bay, around the southern tip of Phuket, and into the Andaman Sea. Tao reconnected our security chain and eased the Jet Ski back to the boat. And onto the lift. He was remarkably self-sufficient, a real find on Lonnie's part.

Within minutes, we were cruising out into the marine traffic. I hung out on the foredeck, taking in the fairy-tale islands and craggy rock outcroppings that made this a favorite place for James Bond movies.

Once we were out of boat traffic and into open waters, a water taxi met up with us and took the pilot back to shore. He saluted Captain Rich as he boarded the taxi. Captain Rich responded with a rather sloppy salute. It had probably been years since he'd practiced that particular skill.

For our first day, Lonnie and Captain Rich had planned for a southernly route to Ko Racha Yai. It was expected to be a quick leg, giving us time to discuss any boat-related issues that cropped up and giving me time to do a checkout dive at a shallow, sloping site with Margo. Despite our agreed-upon schedule, Margo asked Captain Rich to cut his speed by half. A couple of times, she had him circle a new, dramatic island.

My dive with Margo was delayed but not canceled. Light was a bit dimmer than I would have liked, but it was good enough. I shortened the planned dive time by fifteen minutes, just in case. The conditions were perfect—warm water, great visibility, almost no current. No other divers to be seen.

I guided Margo through a series of exercises to test her skills, a bit faster than normal due to the shorter dive time. She wasn't perfect, but she wasn't scary bad. We'd get in some more easy dives during the week, and I'd have a handle on what she could manage before we set out in open, blue water. Surfacing among the peaks of Phang Nga Bay was almost a spiritual experience—we floated on the surface, jabbering about things she needed to work on while Tao patiently stood on the aft deck, waiting to help us out of the water and our gear.

That afternoon set the tone for the voyage. Schedule and route be damned, if Margo wanted to deviate, deviate we did. Lonnie fumed at times but never overruled her. He was more focused on the mission than she was. I could see how he had the right attitude to be in charge of maintaining a golf course.

For the next week, we worked our way through all the sea tests. It was, essentially, exactly what we'd done during our tests before Lonnie and Margo had arrived, but it gave them peace of mind, and we were getting paid well, so who's to argue?

We spent the better part of a day doing tests on the sled. We performed several of the collection arcs, fine-tuning the stops and turns and depth changes that Captain Rich, Tao, and I had already reviewed during the preshakedown shakedown.

Lonnie was micromanaging, intent on demonstrating the perfection of his design. He quibbled about decisions we'd made, based on actual experience, in how to control the sled, but he was up top, and I was down below, so I ignored his input. He'd never know. But we did tweak the sled a bit as we executed more and more demanding tests.

Lonnie took notes; Captain Rich and Tao made fixes. Margo and I talked, checked out the view, studied the water as I gave her guidance about currents, and looked through fish ID books that Captain Rich had thought to buy on one of his trips into town.

I was able to squeeze in enough time to train Tao. I didn't have official paperwork with me, but he fulfilled all the requirements to be a certified diver. He was a quick study. Hopefully, it wouldn't come down to needing him, but the extra depth of talent was helpful. He was, unfortunately, painfully shy whenever I was stripped down to my swimming suit. I noticed on the fourth day that my bathrobe was hung out, waiting for me on the dive deck, when I got out of the water.

Margo! Puritanical priss!

Lonnie and I had a few inconsequential chats. He was pretty focused on the science. I wasn't really able to contribute much except from the ethical side. I was totally in support of how they were choosing to spend their money and time, but I didn't really understand the ins and outs as he explained them.

"I've been meaning to ask you," he said during one lull in the conversation, "because, at first, I thought it was just a case of bad Zoom contrast—you know, flat lighting and all that—but once I met you, I just had to ask: Yamamoto. You don't really look—"

"Yeah, I get that a lot. All my life. I'm a bit of a mutt."

"I don't mean to pry."

"Yeah, that's a good policy."

And that was that. I would tell the world one person at a time, and the Lonnie/Margo team was nowhere near the front of the line. I had a lot of backtracking to do. My racial and family history had been a key marketing tool for one of my prior employers. I figured they should probably know before they got blowback for misleading advertising.

Captain Rich spent an inordinate amount of his time in the pilot house, which left me with hiding out in my stateroom, engaging Lonnie in a discussion of the environmental impacts of golf courses, or bugging Captain Rich. I did a mental coin toss, and my three-sided coin came up Rich, so I headed upstairs to investigate.

It was the end of the planned workday, so I guess he couldn't be blamed, but he wasn't exactly the stereotypical ship's captain as he kicked back in his new captain's chair, headphones on, and played air guitar. The bottle of beer beside him in the console cup holder looked to be empty.

Spying me, he slipped off his headphones. I could hear AC/DC blaring out from a dozen feet away.

"I could die in these chairs. Best I've ever had."

I slid into the matching chair on the right. I couldn't argue with him—pretty darn perfect. Except . . . I couldn't reach the cooler and had to get an assist. That was probably by design. He was quick, though, to hand me a tall, cold one.

Near the end of the shakedown cruise, as our schedule lightened up, Margo and I squeezed in a couple of recreational dives. One in particular stood out.

We were on a relatively deep dive, a remote shelving reef that featured an easy slope to fifty feet and then a straight drop-off down to over three hundred. We'd already seen some large schools of fish, trevallies, and fusiliers, along with a couple of good-size turtles.

I'd seen a tiger shark and tried to get Margo's attention by pointing and whispering through the comms system. I don't know why—it's not like the tiger shark could hear me—but she was staring at a family of clown fish zipping about in their host anemone. I decided afterward that it was probably best that she didn't see one just yet. Tiger sharks have a somewhat undeserved reputation as indifferent eaters, going after whatever looks appetizing. I wasn't sure how she'd react. I hoped we'd have another chance once she was more comfortable with her skills.

Later, Margo and I were finishing up on the wall, working on her buoyancy skills, when Captain Rich pinged us on the comms system. "Margo and Rick, look up now."

Crap.

The last thing I needed was to get tweaked about orca again, but as I looked up, I saw a large silhouette. A mature whale shark—even larger than a full-grown orca. It had to be forty feet long. Slowly, gracefully cruising along the surface. Probably feeding on microscopic plankton.

And between it and the boat, splashing and struggling to keep pace with the gentle giant, was Lonnie.

By the time Margo and I did a slow and safe ascent to the surface, complete with safety stop, the whale shark was gone. No thanks to Lonnie for all the kerfuffle as he tried to get close.

As we got back in the boat, I realized that Lonnie had

been so quick to get in the water with a mask, snorkel, and fins that he hadn't bothered to change. Today was a new twist on his standard style—seersucker shorts, pale-blue stripes, and a white linen shirt, all of which were soaking wet and hung pathetically on his skinny frame as he shivered in the high-eighties temperature.

Margo draped him with a towel. "Lonnie is very sensitive to even the slightest cold. We have to pick our destinations carefully."

"Well, thank goodness for global warming!"

My glib response earned a scowl from Margo, who hadn't yet warmed up to my sense of humor.

"Climate change."

"Yes, I sometimes fall back into old terminology. Sorry. Actually, his reaction is not all that uncommon. Lots of people get cold in eighty-degree water with wetsuits, and he's got no thermal protection at all. No surprise that he's cold."

Lonnie, I think, nodded in appreciation for my concern. Either that or it was just a cold-induced spasm.

As Lonnie shivered and Margo ignored him, Captain Rich motored toward our next stop, a sheltered cove in the Andaman Sea. He called out, uncharacteristically, for Tao and me to come join him in the pilot house, ASAP. Normally he'd say ASAFP, with an emphasis on the *F*, but I think he skipped it in deference to our bosses' presence.

"Really," he shouted when we didn't instantly appear, "now!"

14

KEEP THE JEWELS
OFF YOUR BODY

UNFORTUNATELY, LONNIE TOOK it upon himself to join us. And he was first in line with questions.

"What's the emergency?"

"No emergency. Just a situation. We just need to discuss how we'll handle it."

"OK, then." Lonnie was getting frustrated. "What's the situation?"

"Don't look back. We're being shadowed."

Lonnie looked back.

"I said don't look back!"

"But I didn't see anything."

"That's because you don't have binoculars. If I wanted you to look back, I'd have given you binoculars. Everyone just act normal. If we can see them, they can see us. I'd rather not tip our hand. And I can assure you that their captain has his binoculars focused on this pilot house right now."

"Please give me the binoculars." Lonnie put out his

hand expectantly. Captain Rich brushed it aside and leaned past him.

"You can't have them. Ricky is an experienced spotter."

I'm not sure what that meant or how I'd earned that ranking, but I wasn't about to argue.

He reached his arm around Lonnie and slipped me the massive pair of marine binoculars—the type you use when panning the horizon. Captain Rich pointed with his chin in the direction we'd come.

"Be discreet. Get down on the deck and move to the rear. Tell me what you see."

I took the binoculars, did my best to discreetly drop to the floor, and then slithered to the rear of the pilot house and out onto the adjoining sundeck. I braced them on the lowest bar of the railing and focused on the trailing boat.

"So?"

"Give me a minute. I'm trying to figure out what they're up to. Could just be a fishing boat. Although they look a bit too orderly for a fishing boat."

After a few minutes, I figured I knew enough. "Not good," I announced. "They're wearing uniforms and they're handing out weapons. They definitely look like they are following but seem to be taking their time to figure out if they want to engage."

"Pirates?" asked Lonnie, with a certain amount of fascination in his voice.

Margo had come up at some point while I was handling the binoculars. As soon as Lonnie piped up, she elbowed him in the ribs.

"Worse. Pirates we can handle. Marine police. Military. They're not as reasonable as the pirates."

"I heard about a trip where the pirates raided a boat one day out of port. They took the TVs, sound system, booze, and the coffee machine."

Thanks, Tao.

My ears perked up. "Would they take the keg?"

"Doubtful." Captain Rich was trying to regain control. "Not easily recognizable. They tend to come in fast, work fast, and get out of the area. The keg is in a built-in. Same with the weapons. I have my priorities."

Lonnie was hard to read. Nervous, but excited. It looked like he was ready to rumble.

"Did they take prisoners?"

"Nope. Not a soul. Not worth the hassle." Tao was not getting the message to zip it.

Captain Rich jumped in again. "Prisoners can be unpredictable and end up dead. No one wants that. They left all of us alone. Didn't take anything from the passengers. They know that if they keep the crime to the boat, which is insured, and don't harm any foreigners or take their money, the heat won't come down on them. Easy peasy. They never take the comms and navigation gear, either. Pretty unique and identifiable, plus it's a small resale market. And buyers for this level of stuff are more than willing to pay retail and not mess with secondhand gear. Not worth the time or risk for the pirates."

"The coffee machine?" Margo was horrified.

"Yep, they figured it was early Christmas shopping for the pirates."

I eased over to Tao. Either he'd get the message, or maybe I'd distract him enough that he'd shut up.

Lonnie looked back and forth from me to Captain Rich and back again. It looked like he was about to soil himself.

"I have cash."

"Hide it. These guys are usually bribe-proof and can run us in and seize our property if we offer them money."

"But the guidebook said—"

"Screw the guidebook, Lonnie . . . respectfully. Here's what you need to understand: These guys are military. This is the Royal Thai Navy, not some traffic cop. They don't take bribes, and they don't break rank. One, do not argue. It's 'Yes, sir,' and 'I understand, sir.' Second, anticipate their needs. We have a folder in the salon with photocopies of all our passports. Ricky, can you get it? Three, Lonnie, explain our mission—simply. We are doing government-approved research on pollution emanating from Myanmar and spoiling Thai waters."

"Actually, we are subsidized by several privately held entities."

"OK, fine, you can tell them that. And after they leave, you can tell us why that never came up before. Deniability is much easier when you're working for the government."

"What if they find the guns?" We were losing Lonnie to a major freak-out.

"If they find the guns, you can blame me. I'll tell them you knew nothing about it, and after they arrest me, you can fire me. I'd deserve it for failing to properly hide them. But that's not going to happen because I designed and built the gun storage units, and no one is going to find them. So please, honestly, chill. Besides, we don't even know if they're going to board us."

It was almost an hour before the frigate decided to engage, but once they made that decision, it was a matter of minutes before they caught up.

"Hey, guys." My voice cracked a bit, not exactly the level of professionalism I'd hoped to display. "They just took a tarp off a large, mounted gun on the foredeck. And their wake is churning more. They're speeding up."

"That lovely lady has a top-end speed twenty percent greater than ours." Captain Rich pointed to the iPad beside him, where a search engine displayed a page that explained exactly what we were up against. "We can outmaneuver her, but in the open ocean, she can close a one-mile gap in less than ten minutes. Besides, if we run, they don't have to catch up. If they're outfitted like a typical Thai navy frigate, they've got antiship harpoon missiles. They can hit us from more than fifty miles away. Prepare to smile."

He accepted the inevitable, helping matters by cutting the engines and sending us off on various duties. We were at full stop and had our dinghy lift down before they even got close.

He, Tao, and I all lined the aft deck, ready to receive their lines. Margo and Lonnie, at Captain Rich's instruction, stood nearby and out of the shadows. Lonnie had the passport photocopies.

Eight of them came in their dingy. They waved off the dingy lift and tossed their aft and stern lines for us to secure. Two kneeled off the forward portion of the dinghy with assault weapons at the ready. Lonnie whistled and whispered—loudly—to Margo, "HK33s, very sweet." The next sound out of his mouth was a muffled yelp as Margo sidestepped and planted her heel on his bare foot. She left it there, despite his whimpering.

The first two men off the dingy pushed all of us back. Politely but firmly. With a minimum of contact. We didn't resist. As we moved back, Margo finally remove her heel from Lonnie's foot. He let out a loud sigh of relief, so she kicked him in the shin.

The third man aboard appeared to be a lieutenant, based on the number of stripes on his rank insignia. He paused, taking his time to assess each of us. Three more jumped aboard. After they were all stationed, spread out on the aft deck, the lieutenant signaled Tao to step forward. A rapid-fire but muffled conversation took place, with Tao pointing at one or another of us in response to the lieutenant's questions. The last two sailors stayed in the dinghy and kept their assault rifles trained on our group.

Finally, once he was satisfied with Tao's answers, the lieutenant spoke to Captain Rich.

"You are the captain?"

"Yes. I was hired by the owner of the boat"—he swept his hand in Lonnie's direction—"to captain it during a three-month period, including time here in Thailand. We have the proper paperwork."

"I get the sense that the owner is useless." The lieutenant gave a thin smile. His English was impeccable. My experience as I've moved around the world is that ambitious military and police tend to work on their language skills. It greases the skids for promotion if they are able to manage foreigners. And English tends to be at the top of the list.

"He tells me where he wants to go, and my job is to get him there safely. Without him, we would still be in port. He is quite smart."

Lonnie, still wincing from Margo's kick, tried to stand as tall and authoritatively as he could. It didn't do much to dispel the impression that he was a secondary character in this charade.

"We are looking for drugs. You can save yourself time and misery if you tell us now what you have."

Lonnie jumped in. "Nothing. Medications for anxiety and seasickness, and small amounts of painkillers in the medicine kit, but that's it. I have the prescriptions."

"Perhaps I was unclear. We are looking for smugglers. Large quantities of marijuana, heroin, methamphetamines. We are not looking for personal usage, but if we find it, we will act."

Captain Rich tried to wrest control of the responses from Lonnie. "We are a scientific venture aimed at helping the people of Thailand and better understanding the global impact of pollution. I invite you to search the ship."

And search they did. They tossed the place. Politely. But they made no effort to put things back together once they were done. The galley was a mess. The staterooms as well.

They never found the guns.

After two hours, they packed it in, gave us additional warnings about smuggling, suggested we cut our trip short lest we run into pirates, and motored back to their frigate, where I noticed for the first time that there were two sailors manning the large deck gun.

"Your English is excellent, by the way. US university?"

I should have let them go without engaging a potentially sensitive topic.

"Nah, American grade school and prep school. Dad was diplomatic corp."

"I understand. Based on your experience with Americans, do you have any advice for our owners about dealing with the pirates? Americans tend to be a bit edgy, as you probably know."

The lieutenant gave a knowing smile and turned to Lonnie and Margo. "Stay back, keep your mouths shut, and let the captain do his job. And even though they likely won't steal them"—he dropped his voice a bit, looked directly at Margo, and pointed to her rings, necklace, and earrings—"you might want to keep the jewels off your body and keep your body covered."

I nodded sagely, then gave Margo my best Zen divemaster look of confidence.

And I made a mental note to start wearing the *Powerballer* bathrobe.

15

IN FOR A DIME

"We can handle our stateroom," announced Lonnie, "but Tao and Ricky, get the salon, lounge, and galley in order. Galley first. Tonight, we had planned a feast, and we're not going to let those guys ruin the mood."

I shot Captain Rich a look, gave him ten seconds to respond, and was about to protest, but Rich beat me to it.

"Pardon me, Lonnie," he interrupted. "That's not part of Ricky's job description. Tao can handle it."

"Ricky will do what I say," bristled Lonnie, "as long as I pay her salary."

Another sharp look from me got the desired reaction.

"Lonnie, let's take this upstairs." Captain Rich gently pointed the way, and the two disappeared up into the pilot house, Lonnie limping slightly. They returned no more than two minutes later.

"Change of plans," mumbled Lonnie, his arms crossed. "Tao, if you please, you may start with the galley. Then the lounge and salon. I'm going to lie down. I have a feast to prepare."

That earned Captain Rich a brief smile and wink.

When he returned from his brief nap, Lonnie appeared to have regained his mojo. Margo followed shortly after, no longer bedecked in her expensive jewelry. She did, wisely, keep a simple wedding band on her hand and silver studs in her earlobes.

"Tonight," Lonnie announced, "we celebrate seitan!"

"Satan?" I wasn't opposed. I just wanted to make sure I didn't make some sort of social faux pas.

"Say-tan. It's plant-based meat. Tastes almost the same. I know vegans who won't eat it because it tastes too much like meat."

"OK, I'm game." Given the lack of alternatives and that the chef was the person who was paying my salary, enthusiasm seemed like the best strategy.

I'll admit that the food smelled excellent. I'd seen the last grocery delivery, and it had been heavy on excellent spices and herbs. It seemed like Lonnie used them well. I could smell the ginger all the way back on the aft deck. It even covered the lemongrass smell of the cleaning liquid I had used to cut through the meat smell in the galley. I picked up on some intense pepper, right before a sneezing fit.

Margo had taken second seat in the kitchen but then had been busily chopping and washing as Lonnie manned the stove. She was setting out serving dishes as quickly as Lonnie was finishing up.

I recognized pad Thai—a favorite of mine—as well as pineapple rice, which Captain Rich had turned me on to during our weeks outfitting the boat. The mango salad seemed completely normal—"We replaced fish sauce with soy, but you won't be able to tell the difference." The eggplant stir-fry with peanuts smelled awesome. I was thinking that vegan might not be as bad as I had imagined.

Meal prep had taken Lonnie and Margo a long time, and it seemed, judging by the stack of pots, pans, and bowls that they'd generated, as if they had pretty much depleted the boat's supply. Tao had noticed the same and was looking rather forlornly at the kitchen, having spent the better part of an hour putting it all back together after the search. He was in for a long post-dinner night.

They had also made satay, which was my favorite street food in Phuket, but I realized the square chunks weren't meat but tofu. I considered tofu to be just a step above packing material in terms of taste. I filled my plate high as I worked through the assembly line that Margo had laid out. I'd even taken one of the tofu satays, but really only because I'd touched it before realizing my error and figured it might be career limiting to put it back while Margo was watching. The final dish, the ginger-laden masterpiece, was a large pot—guaranteeing leftovers for at least one day—of chicken curry. Only it wasn't chicken. It was the seitan they'd mentioned before.

In for a dime, in for a dollar.

"Here, let me help." Margo popped over, seeing that my plate now required two hands. "I can tell you have a healthy appetite."

She scooped up a large ladleful of the dish and then poured it into a bowl, which she handed to me with a smile. I smiled back, immediately wishing we had a dog I could pass scraps to.

It took me a long time to work through the meal. Some of it was outstanding. The satay was OK and even better when covered with a lot of peanut sauce and a local hot sauce.

But the seitan. I'd cleaned my plate, and Tao had removed it to the galley to join the immense pile of dishes awaiting cleaning, so the big bowl of curry sat directly in front of me. There was no getting around it. I was going to have to eat it. At least 80 percent. Seventy-five? But I'd definitely have to lower the level in the bowl by a lot.

I've got to tell you, my first interpretation of the name as *Satan* seemed spot on to me. I developed a strategy of holding my breath while I chewed and then taking in a gulp of cold beer. "Spicy. Good, tasty, but spicy. I'm going to need another glass of beer. Be right back." I stopped at the head on my way to the beer and spit out a particularly obstinate piece of Satan. My jaw was already getting tired from all the chewing, but this piece was over the top.

I finally managed to get through at least half of the bowl before insisting that I couldn't possibly eat another bite. But I made sure to add, "It's surprisingly good. I can't rave about it enough!"

"Great!" cried Lonnie. "For some, it's an acquired taste, and I know a lot of vegans who don't like it, but I think my preparation is really quite popular. I'll make sure to make it again during the cruise."

Just shoot me now.

Tragically, we did have it again—for lunch. Even more tragically, Captain Rich pointed out that I really shouldn't drink beer at a midday meal. It was a nondiving day, so I had another gulp and flipped him off. Duly fortified, I worked my way through another bowl and tried to convince myself that it tasted better the second day.

That night, over a more regular meal of stir-fry and rice, Lonnie announced that he and Margo were satisfied with the shakedown and were "certifying" the boat ready for our mission.

Although Captain Rich had already told me that he was going to suggest that same conclusion to them in hopes of ending a few days early, he jumped up and thanked Lonnie and Margo for a great display of leadership. He'd already plotted a direct route home and announced that we would leave a little early the next day, the "anchor up around six and cruise all day" so that we could make it back before dusk. He then asked me to join him in the pilot house for a quick consult.

"We'll get back by five-thirty, have the boat put to bed by seven-thirty. I heard Lonnie and Margo arguing. Margo scheduled a stay at a resort down along the southwest coast for a few days as soon as we tie up at the dock. She's already called and arranged for a limo. Apparently, Lonnie had other plans in Bangkok, and a plane was waiting for them."

"So . . .?"

"So, we may be in for some rough seas with those two. We need to grab our mental health days when we can. I've already been online. There's a place in southeast Phuket. It's a bit of a drive, but we can be there by eight or eight-thirty. I already made a reservation for three people. We'll take Tao—did you see the color he turned when he tried the Satan? We need to cleanse. This place has the best beef in Thailand, bar none."

"I'm in. Are you driving?"

"Yeah, but we should stay overnight. Maybe a day or two. I've got a buddy that lives within walking distance from the place. Big house. You can have a bedroom. Tao, too. I'll grab a couch."

"I'm in. I need to detoxify from that meal."

16

GETTING BUZZED

Being away from the boat and the owners gave me time to recalibrate. Here I was in beautiful Thailand. I had no expenses, a luxury stateroom, and minimal duties. I had a bodyguard and guardian angel in the form of Captain Rich, and Tao was anxious to take on any task. I was earning big bucks. I'd survive the food as long as I avoided Satan, and I could put up with some nouveau riche owners.

And the beef, in all types and forms, was as good as advertised.

We got back to the boat a day ahead of our required return and made sure that we'd fixed everything that had been upended during the search. We found a few items in need of repair, but Tao and Captain Rich made quick work of them.

Captain Rich had been overjoyed to discover that the searchers had found a previously unknown storage unit in the pilot house that contained a full setup for welding and two drones. No rhyme or reason for why they were up there, but he was pleased with the discovery. He immediately took one drone and control up to the foredeck for some trial runs.

My attempt at a chill session in the foredeck hammock was immediately cut short. I was getting buzzed. I might have been able to tolerate the high-pitched insect sound, even the irritating Doppler effect as it moved around and above the boat, but Captain Rich's practice low-level passes were getting too close for comfort.

Besides, Tao had begun working on his welding skills on the dock within twenty feet of where I lay.

Boys with their toys. Ugh.

Later that afternoon, Tao proudly presented me a chunk of metal that he'd cut and welded. I thanked him. I was pretty sure it was a . . . actually, I had no idea what it was. He said it was an angel.

"Does Tao have a crush on me?" I asked. Captain Rich and I were up in the pilot house.

"Why? Would that be a problem?"

"It just seems like sometimes he reacts to me by getting very distant and shy."

"Between you and me, I don't think he's had much experience with women. And probably none with women a head taller than him. You can be intimidating."

"It's usually when I'm wearing my swimsuit."

"Yeah, I can see how that might be intimidating. You have a bathrobe, you know."

Sigh.

Captain Rich had finished the charts for the first leg of the trip, and I was happy to see that it terminated at an island known for its remote and deserted beaches. I had no reason to complain. Yet.

When Lonnie and Margo's limo arrived the next day with a new supply of vegetables and flour for Satan in cloth, reusable bags—emblazoned with the *Powerballer* logo—we were ready to head out. Margo had a deep tan, but Lonnie looked pale. They wordlessly boarded the yacht. She headed to the foredeck while he oversaw the unpacking and folding of the grocery bags. Then he headed out into the parking lot.

Lonnie, after a thorough inspection, certified the braai as meat-free. He commandeered Tao, who had nothing better to do at the time, and reviewed some meal plans, the first of which involved grilling.

As the sun set, Tao built up a massive braai fire. While the wood slowly turned to embers, he cut an array of vegetables and tofu, whipped up a couple of sauces, and set the table. After working some magic on the grill, he served up an amazing predeparture meal, for which Lonnie took credit.

I don't know what had gone on between those two, but while we ate, Margo stewed.

17

THE LOGBOOK

OUR FIRST REAL travel day began, as would become our norm, with anchors up at 06:00. Captain Rich was by nature a light sleeper and tended to wake up before sunrise, ready for action. Probably a good trait when you're a security consultant but a bit bothersome when you're the captain of a luxury yacht. When Margo emerged from the master stateroom, she looked the worse for wear.

I couldn't wait to see how she might look when she learned that Lonnie had signed off on the travel plan, including the departure time. Those two had some serious communication issues.

Captain Rich was taking a quick breakfast break. Tao had the wheel. "Margo!" he called out before remembering he had a mouth full of food.

She cringed but turned to talk to him. She looked very pale. We'd never discussed her history on the open sea, but we did have a store of seasickness medicine if need be.

"That was off the charts. Thank you. I just saw it

this morning when I took the helm up to warm up the engines! Thank you!"

He turned to Tao and me, who were confused by his effusiveness as well as wondering what the hell he was talking about.

"Margo gave me a leather-bound logbook." He held it up for us to see. It even had the *Powerballer* logo embossed on the cover. "To track the journey. Its pages have space for things like date, destination, current weather and forecast, water conditions, length of trip, crew, passengers, and ports visited. Also fuel and water consumed, damage incurred, reprimands issued to the crew"—now it was Tao's turn to wince—"and expenses related to the boat and travel."

He grimaced and patted—more like thumped—the logbook and laid it on the bench beside him. "There are even sleeved pages for me to store the printouts for each day's planned route and actual route. Sweet!"

I bet dollars to doughnuts that an accident would befall it before the third day of the trip.

We didn't really have a full travel plan. We needed to get up to the northern reaches of the Andaman Sea by the end of March, beating wicked currents and winds that we'd be dealing with in April and May.

Lonnie leaned in as Captain Rich worked to finish off his breakfast. "What's our ETA for the first testing site?"

Captain Rich estimated that we had sixty to ninety cruising hours to get there, depending on winds and currents. Breaking that down to ten hours a day, we were looking at a week to a week and a half before we reached our first testing site. Given Lonnie and Margo's tendency to change plans and deviate from course and timing, I was thinking two weeks. Either of those projections still got us up to Myanmar right around the start of April. No later than the third. At least that's what Captain Rich had estimated just before we had shipped out.

"Well, we're two hours into a trip that will take at least a week," he said, "so I'm not working off a lot of data, but so far, so good. ETA remains seven to ten days, barring changes in course or delays along the way."

Lonnie glared at Captain Rich, likely thinking that the crew shouldn't speak to the boss like that. I'm not sure how he had missed that trait, either during their Philippines trip or during interviews, but he certainly hadn't hired a yes-man.

"Daily updates, please."

"Absolutely, at the end of each sailing day."

Lonnie extracted himself before there were any further challenges to his authority.

Margo most definitely wanted a low-stress trip. She recovered a bit as the day progressed, even spending time up in the pilot house. As we'd pass islands, she'd ask Captain Rich to move in closer for a better view. He was busy with charts and preferred to stay in deeper waters where there was less chance of uncharted obstructions, but he also didn't want to piss off the boss. At least no more than necessary.

In our first few days, we stopped a handful of times as Margo went for swims or explored the beaches and coves as we came upon them. Lonnie tended to stay to himself, reviewing charts, weather reports, and academic papers about the Andaman Sea. Captain Rich tended to add on a little cruising time at the end of the day to compensate for her delays.

Lonnie was in a huff. "There's almost no analysis of tides and currents! How is it that you have almost no documentation?" He raised the issue for at least the third time since we'd left Phuket, and he'd been at it before we had left as well.

"You've searched as well," Captain Rich replied.

Lonnie started to comment, but the captain continued, a little bit louder and a little bit more emphatic. "The analysis you're talking about doesn't exist. That area is a mix of four countries. Countries that don't particularly get along. Coordinated research is nonexistent." He'd done his homework. And he had anticipated Lonnie's complaints.

"Well, then." Lonnie's huffiness continued. "We'll be the first. If Margo ever lets us get there."

"Truth be told, we're pushing about as fast as is safe. And Margo's not delaying us. I built in wiggle room. Ten hours at the wheel is a long haul. I'm not good with cruising at night. You've already said it—there's not a lot of documentation on this area. You wouldn't want me to put a rock through the hull, now, would you? This pace is good. I'll get you there within the two weeks we agreed to. Despite slowdowns—whether it's currents, winds, or Margo—we've been making good time."

It was hard to blame Margo. Not only were the beaches pristine and jaw-droppingly gorgeous, but the terrain frequently featured more dramatic limestone cliffs whose pale walls were perfectly framed by the blue-green waters of the Andaman Sea. I certainly took advantage of most stops to grab my fins, mask, and snorkel for a little spin around the block. It seemed, though, that there was a definite he-versus-she vibe developing as Margo insisted on more and more unplanned stops. But I wasn't going to let that harsh my mellow. I'd never before in my entire career as a divemaster been able to relax and appreciate the natural beauty of our seas. I decided I could get used to it.

Good call, Captain Rich.

18

MARGIN FOR ERROR

DAY FIVE WAS tense.

It started out with a predawn rant by Captain Rich. "Between Lonnie's constant revisiting of decisions already made, Margo's stops, and that damn logbook, which adds an hour to my day, I'm back up to twelve- and fourteen-hour days. Last night, he asked to meet first thing this morning. Of course, my first thing and his first thing are quite different. I've been waiting for him for hours."

Tao had taken the wheel as soon as Lonnie had popped up into the pilot house so that Captain Rich and Lonnie could argue. I eased over to listen in. They were poking at a map as Lonnie tried marking a route using a permanent marker.

Captain Rich was livid. "If we go through the archi- pelago, we'll be in Myanmar. That seems too much of a risk." More vein-popping. He was going to stroke out on this trip if he didn't watch out.

"It's actually safe. We all have visas, and they've

been letting in cruisers and divers from Phuket for years now. I've got paperwork up the wazoo with specific permission for sports diving and golfing."

"Golfing?"

"Yeah, they have a course down here. And a casino. I didn't work on the course but know the guy who did. We've got a tee time set up for next week. I'll miss it, but the appointment gives us even more credibility. Pretty smart, huh?"

Possibly, maybe, just this once.

"Besides"—Lonnie was puffed up about his local expertise—"they rarely patrol down this far. There's nothing for them to protect. It's a shorter route, so we'll make up time. Plus, I believe you said there were some bad weather patterns forming out there. This gives us more protection. From where I lay my head, in the master stateroom of *my* boat, it seems like the smart thing to do."

"And from where I sit, in the captain's chair, my passengers are safer going around a country in turmoil. I don't want unnecessary attention. This is more than enough boat to handle the bad weather. We'll get wet, but that's about it."

It seemed like Captain Rich's days of accommodating Lonnie might be a thing of the past. I tucked myself into the couch and watched the fireworks.

"Look, we got searched for two hours by the Royal Thai Navy, and they never found the lab. And if we get boarded and searched again, all the equipment is still sealed and in pristine condition, never used, so they can't claim we've been doing testing in their waters. I've talked with a dozen cruisers who have been through here, and we are not the concern of the navy. They don't even have a coast guard unit. They're underfunded and under-manned. If they do go after someone, it's a drilling ship or a large-net fisher that they followed from up north."

It went on, back and forth over the same issues, for an hour before Captain Rich relented. Lonnie put together, in case he was wrong, a packet of copies of passports and visas and the survey plan for testing open waters in the Andaman Sea for pollution.

Tao was sent off to set up all four sets of gear so that the part of our cover that we were divers seemed legit. He hosed down the boys' wetsuits and gear so that it appeared they'd been diving. I'd clipped their computers to the sled at the beginning of the trip so that they even had some recorded data.

Captain Rich took the wheel, but he wasn't done.

"Oh, since you're at it, beef up the passport and visa copies with about two million Myanmar kyat and a hundred thousand Thai bhat. In Myanmar, bribes are wise business. Put about the same in the safe in your stateroom in case they really shake us down, and put the rest in the safe in the lab. No one is to know about that."

"Except, you mean, her." Lonnie jabbed his thumb over his shoulder to point at me. "If any of that money goes missing . . ."

I covered my ears, then my eyes.

"I heard nothing. I see nothing. I know nothing."

Dick.

Score another one for Lonnie. By my count, that made two.

We took the right route. The islands of the Mergui

Archipelago were phenomenal. My bet would be that most of the reefs had never been dived. They'd certainly never been charted as dive sites.

Everything slowed down—literally. Despite the decreased wind and current, Captain Rich kept our speed down as he navigated through the eight hundred islands that made up the Mergui, some so small that we'd be within a hundred feet before we could see them. He started his days a bit later so that he had good light and ended them earlier. With the more direct route, we weren't eating into our margin for error.

Margo, in turn, asked for even more stops. Her interest in land animals and birds increased, which meant longer stays on the islands. Lonnie was increasingly irritated but never seemed prepared to limit Margo's impulses. Besides, we were still going to reach our destination within the two-week schedule that he and Captain Rich had agreed upon.

Captain Rich's timetable had built in a healthy number of extra days in case of the almost inevitable delays that hit a cruise—bad weather, broken equipment, navigational issues, pirates. But it also meant that we had less and less wiggle room.

"Pirates!" Captain Rich had roared over the PA system, and then all hell had broken loose.

As soon as Tao reached the wheelhouse, Captain Rich had him take the wheel and flew down the stairs on the way to his stateroom. Lonnie, who'd been napping on a couch in the pilot house, followed.

"We fight!" screamed Lonnie, striking a pose worthy of Gen. George Patton. All he needed was the swagger stick.

"No, we scare the fight right out of them!" Captain Rich barked in response before he stopped at the bottom of the stairs, where he grabbed Lonnie's golf bag and dumped his clubs unceremoniously on the floor, then continued down to his cabin.

The boat jumped forward. Tao must have jammed the throttle to full power. Judging by the way the boat whipped about, he must have begun to slalom through the islands in full evasive maneuvering. Lonnie tripped and fell but scrabbled his way up and pursued Captain Rich below. Margo, who had been sunbathing on the foredeck, was busily putting her swimsuit back on.

I'd stood frozen at the top of the stairs. Back at the shooting range, it had all been fun and games—I hadn't really considered what I'd do in a real firefight. For lack of a better plan, and with a good idea why the focus was on Captain Rich's cabin, I followed Lonnie.

What I came upon was a scene from a comedy. Captain Rich had tossed the golf bag to Lonnie, who stood in the doorway, loading rifles into the bag as fast as he could.

"Go, go!" Captain Rich pushed Lonnie in the direction of the stairs. He handed me some sort of gun with a barrel that could handle a potato, a cylindrical magazine like an old-fashioned six-shooter, and three bags loaded with what looked to be large bullets. He snatched the golf bag back from Lonnie and took the stairs two at a time, heading for the aft deck.

"C'mon, damn it!"

I realized that was for me, still standing there holding the weird gun and the bags. I quickly followed.

When we got to the aft deck, I could see the issue. A scruffy, overpowered, and overloaded speedboat was struggling to overtake us. Tao was smart, choosing maneuvering over maximum speed: every time they took a turn, the boat threatened to capsize or take on water.

Captain Rich dumped the bag on the aft deck and handed out guns.

"I've already got one," I said as he thrust an assault rifle in my direction, emphasizing the point by holding up the one he'd given me below.

"Yeah, no. That one's mine." We exchanged guns, and he grabbed the ammo bags I was holding.

Margo appeared and grabbed a compact assault rifle. It looked good on her, matching her gray bikini to a T. I looked around for a bathrobe to toss her way, but none was available.

"Everyone get set for a sharp turn." Captain Rich grabbed the PA mike from the wall and barked, "Tao, as close to the island as you safely can, sharp turn to port, then slow to half speed."

Tao almost immediately launched us to port, throwing Lonnie and me about as we struggled to maintain a good base. The boat slowed. Behind us, though, the maneuver had worked like a charm. Three of the pirates were thrown into the water as the boat almost capsized, trying to match our sharp turn. The driver swung starboard and killed the engine.

That's when Captain Rich went primal.

"Tao, go straight until I tell you to turn. Ricky, get to your firing position."

The Denel that he'd used to pulverize car tires back at the shooting range was lying on the couch. He grabbed it before I had a chance, then two of the magazines containing its massive shells and a sandbag, and headed to the sundeck. Taking up a position on the deck, he tossed the sandbag forward, nestled the rifle into it, and began sighting the pirates.

"This will scare the hell out of them."

The pirates were still struggling to retrieve their fallen when he squeezed off his first shot, blowing the top off a small rock pinnacle just offshore and a mere twenty feet from the boat.

Nothing. The pirates were still dead in the water but were handing out guns.

The next shell tore up the water just to the side of the boat, spraying several of the pirates with a wave of water.

And they still continued to prepare for a fight. And I stood there frozen.

"These guys must be desperate. My next shot, if I took it, would be a kill shot. But let's try something else first. Ricky, since you're still here—the grenade launcher and a bag of shells." He'd plopped the odd gun and the shells down near the captain's chairs when he'd gone for the Denel, so I grabbed them and laid them beside Captain Rich—all while he kept the Denel aimed at the pirates, just in case. Their motors began to belch smoke as they prepared to reengage.

Captain Rich quickly loaded six of the giant shells,

rose into a kneeling position, and fired off three quick shots with what I'd compared to a potato gun. Each of them exploded right in front of the dead-in-the-water speedboat and sprayed the pirates with huge waves. He then shifted his aim away from the boat. The next shot landed on a rock about ten feet from the pirates and erupted in flames. Flames shot up from the pirate boat as well.

"Pyrotechnics," Captain Rich said with a grin. "Just one of the tricks of this baby. The first three were low explosive. The last two, if things turn to shit, would have taken them out . . . high explosive. Tao!" He was yelling, even though they were almost side by side. "Same speed, cut to starboard but a wider turn, so we keep them in view."

We reversed our turn, although at half speed, and circled in a path that would put us behind the pirates' boat, though their attention was firmly on putting out the fire with blankets and buckets of water. Their three soggy comrades had finally made it back to the rear of the boat.

Captain Rich fired off one more round, aiming behind the speedboat. Judging by the splash and the noise it made, I figured that was one of the high-explosive rounds. It was all the inspiration they needed to haul their friends aboard and beat a hasty retreat.

Captain Rich handed me his special weapon and sprinted up the stairs to the flybridge, where he pulled one last trick. I could tell by the buzz that he'd deployed one of the drones. He flew down the steps from the flybridge, bumped Tao away from the wheel, and brought the boat back up to three-quarters speed. Having turned the tables, he began to chase the pirates.

Alternating between paying attention to the boat and to the drone, he harassed the pirates from behind as they impotently swung wildly and fired pistols at the tiny, buzzing machine. After a few miles, Captain Rich backed off and swung the boat back in its original direction.

"That," he called out to Lonnie, "is how you handle a pirate. You don't fight. You scare the fight right out of them. They never even fired a single shot at us. If you see a fight coming, walk right up to the biggest guy and punch him in the face."

Lonnie, for once, was speechless.

After catching our breath and letting our pulse drop to reasonable levels, we stashed the extra guns and the golf bag in the salon, then all headed back up to the pilot house.

Captain Rich was focused and barely clocked our arrival. His hands were shaking from the adrenaline—I noticed mine were as well—and he spun about, looking for new threats or a return of the last one, though none of us expected them to be crazy enough to come back.

I tapped his shoulder and handed him back his magic gun. "I figured you might want to keep this one close by for a while."

"Thanks. But next time, be in your firing position. You were standing there like a sitting duck."

He was right. I had just stood there. It was surreal being in the middle of an almost gun battle. Captain Rich cradled the potato gun.

"This did the job, but if we attract official attention,

we'll want this baby tucked away. It's a Milkor—a multigrenade launcher. Made in South Africa." He looked lovingly at the beast. "I trained on these babies. There's a fourth bag with smoke bombs. I could have landed them right in the boat and freaked the hell out of those rats. Kicking myself; I forgot that bag." He reached under the dashboard and opened one of his secret compartments, sliding the Milkor and its ammunition onto the lowest shelf and then resealing the hidden door. "Does anyone have a cigarette?"

When we all professed to be without cancer sticks, he mockingly mimicked anger. "Fine lot I've thrown myself in with. Until now, I could always find someone with a smoke after a good firefight."

"Keep going?" I asked, pointing back the way we'd come during the chase.

"Yeah, I'm guessing no one is going to bother us after that. But we play it safe. Tonight, everyone has a six-hour watch. Two people on watch at all times, walking the deck and wearing night-vision goggles or holding on to the night-vision binoculars."

I quickly volunteered for the first watch, walking the deck. I was so wired that it would be therapeutic.

"Your call. But you need to be on your game the whole time. A third, either Tao or me, will be watching the radar. We should do check-ins every fifteen minutes. It's good, but it's not perfect if someone tries to slip in. During the day, I want someone besides me on watch as well. Hey, Tao! Fucking great driving. Fucking great."

Tao returned the compliment with a perfect, crisp salute.

19

RETURN TO PARADISE

IT TOOK A few hours to settle down, and it would be a while before we relaxed, though we maintained the nighttime vigil for the rest of the trip. Nothing popped up, but Captain Rich maintained the fifteen-minute check-in ritual throughout.

I'd floated the idea of turning around.

"What about we return to paradise?"

It was like talking to a wall.

"Y'know, Ricky . . ." Captain Rich stopped talking and stared out over the darkened water, his feet up on the dashboard and the iPad, with the radar display on, in his lap. It was my sixth check-in of the evening watch. I was wondering if that was a vote of no confidence pointed at me.

His attention focused for a moment on something on the horizon, but then he relaxed. In one hand, he held the grenade launcher, which he'd taken to carrying each time we stopped for the night, and in the other, a beer—also a recent habit. He had a pair of night-vision binoculars strapped around his neck. Tao had been wearing a pair of goggles, but they sat on the desk as he rested his eyes. Captain Rich had promised to limit himself to a single beer until our watch ended and that he'd put away the launcher before he had a second beer, after we'd been replaced by Tao and Margo at 02:00.

He started again where he'd left off.

"Y'know, Ricky, I've lost mates as well." That was about as specific as he ever got about his side jobs as a security consultant. "Us non-state-aligned resources are expendable. They'll leave us behind, unlike their own troops. And they don't tabulate our losses in any report that reaches any senior staff. So, I think I get how you feel about your friend."

"Sasha? Bel?"

"Yeah, Bel. Sasha's death gutted me, too, but I'm talking about Bel. I'm talking about going into a nonviolent action and running into the unexpected. We didn't plan on war, but that's what we almost stepped into. There's little room for indecision in conflict. And none in the heat of battle. That just adds to the damage. You hear me?"

"Yeah, but excuse me for caring."

"Nothing wrong there. And no issue with not wanting to be in the water with the orca. But up top was a different matter. Indecision has its time and place, just as long as it doesn't get in the way when we need you most."

Captain Rich was using his downtime to clean the guns. For the third time. I guess the exposure to saltwater spray was enough to concern him. Or he just felt more in control while working with his toys.

I helped by breaking down the AR-15. I got a nod of approval before he rearranged the parts on the mat.

"I was ready to shoot, you know." I looked to see if he'd heard me.

He continued cleaning the barrel of the AR-15, squinting as he inspected his work. "I don't know about that. Not how I saw it. You were a statue. I've seen it enough times. That's less than worthless. It means I not only have to worry about stopping the bad guys, but I have to worry about you."

"Don't. I can take care of myself."

"Next time, prove me wrong—if there is a next time."

We continued our route northward, but we agreed to limit our stops to areas where there were other boats. Strength in numbers, though I assumed none of the others had armories like ours. The insistence on no more private beaches seemed to dampen Margo's beach lust, so we picked up our pace quite a bit.

If the navy had heard about our little incident, they either couldn't find us or didn't care to. After five uneventful days in the Mergui, we headed west through the wonderfully named Mermaid Passage and out into open water. As the GPS showed us leaving their territorial waters, Tao lowered and removed the Myanmar courtesy flag that had been flying above our Thai flag.

Despite the pirates, I made a mental note that I wanted to return to Myanmar sometime in the not-too-distant future.

20

FACE-PLANT

WE'D GONE WITH option two for the sled operation. The boat was towing me. It ended up being an easy call. Our underwater comms system wouldn't work unless the boat stayed in close proximity, so the Jet Ski would have been dangerously close—at least when in choppy water—to the boat as they both motored along.

My first ride on the sled was a crack-up, in more ways than one. There were several steps required to get us up and running. First, we had to try a run with no additional weight. This required precise positioning on my part—anything other than being fully centered meant the sled would veer. Correcting by shifting my weight usually resulted in oversteering.

We spent more than an hour working on the balance. It reminded me of the summer when Mom had enrolled me in circus camp. Camp Winnarainbow. I sort of learned high wire and did a lot of trapeze. I loved the aerial work. Letting go of the bar and flying was the best.

But the sled was a different beast altogether. Very minor shifts were magnified several times over by the broad plane of metal. Bit by bit, we worked on the speed of the boat and the art of staying level and then of turning.

Then the learning curve started a steep climb upward again with air cylinders mounted on both sides. That actually made the sled less responsive, which made me cocky—less chance of overcorrecting.

Despite the added stability, the response to my own shifts was exaggerated on deeper dives. On our first seafloor pass, I performed an unintended nosedive into the sandy floor and got thrown off. Fortunately, we'd planned for that, and I had my own scuba gear strapped on as a backup to the tanks mounted on the sled. The sled, on the other hand, required some pounding and welding to bring it back to its proper shape.

It took a few days to fine-tune the sled and our towing procedure. Once we laid out additional line to four times water depth, I was able to control the sled without wrestling. Even when a run was completely loaded down with tanks, two core samples, and a half dozen polyethylene bottles, I had come close to mastering the maneuvering. I'd even gotten Captain Rich to up the speed to three knots.

With the monster winch we had, once I'd notified the boat that I'd taken the final sample at fifteen feet, I could be back at the boat in ten minutes.

There were days when Captain Rich and I got quite chatty during the dive, but more often than not, we were radio silent except for sampling stops and turns.

We agreed that he did not need to share his music, unless asked, and I would turn off my mic anytime I hummed. For some reason, he wasn't a fan of the *Barney* theme song.

I quickly realized that I'd soon be battling boredom as I glided over the moonscape to the Irrawaddy Delta outflow. There was little or no coral to be seen, almost no plant life, and as a result, almost no fish. Just long runs over brown-gray muck.

That night, I approached Captain Rich with a list.

"What's this?"

"My playlist. The beginning of my playlist."

He took it from my hand and slipped on his readers. "R.E.M. Cowboy Junkies. Alejandro Escovedo? Cool. Yeah, Dan Fogelberg, I've got him covered."

"Can you just pipe in music during my sled runs? I'll give you a longer list, but can you make those happen for tomorrow?"

"Sure, I've got them all. A little light on Alejandro, but I'll have enough for the day's runs. You will listen for me if I interrupt, right? The whole idea of the comms package is to manage the dive."

"Yeah, you can hit 'Pause' and talk all you want. All you need."

"OK. Shall I tee up some Eagles and Green Day?"

"You know it. Feel free to add some that I might have forgotten."

"Insane Clown Posse? Nickelback?"

"Please, no. OK, maybe some Nickelback, but no Insane Clowns. Check that—no Nickelback."

We were clocking our runs in at just under two and a

half hours, so the workload was manageable even when working seven days a week for multiple weeks in a row. We got a day off after week three, and Lonnie promised another one after week five.

The playlists made the tedium much more manageable. Captain Rich slowly slipped in more new music that was almost always a welcome addition.

Lonnie was excited about the results he was getting, but I really didn't want a science class, and Margo kept reminding him that others might not find it as exciting as he did. His pouting didn't diminish our resistance.

21

SIMPATICO

ON ONE OF our days off, though, I did broach one aspect of the mission that I hoped wouldn't devolve into a science lesson.

"Why Myanmar?"

"Why Myanmar what?" Lonnie preferred precision in his discussions.

"Right. Sorry. Why did you choose the waters near Myanmar for your study? It doesn't seem to get a lot of press from the environmental community."

"And that's one of the reasons." I could tell that Lonnie was about to go on a roll. I'd opened Pandora's box. "There is almost no academic or scientific study taking place in Myanmar. The Brits did a study last year, but it's got big gaps. It's been a closed-up nation for decades, even when the populist vote is bringing in the liberal regime." He paused and checked his watch. "What day is it? I think they got sworn in last week. Not that it matters. They have so many issues to deal with that environmentalism is going to take a back seat."

Reason number two, according to Lonnie, was that the rivers of Myanmar produce around 20 percent of all the Himalayan sediment being poured into our oceans each year. Twenty percent, and that's a dated and conservative estimate, he said. There are studies that suggest it is likely the third-largest contributor of sediment load in the world.

"That alone"—he was in major rant mode by this point—"is altering the landscape and killing off coral. Altering the climate. That's interesting, and we need to understand the long-term implications, but that's not our focus.

"But reason three," he said, finally getting to the real answer, "is why we are here."

He then ran off a list of chemicals that was totally lost on me. But the basic story made sense. "That sediment contains chemical waste from agriculture, manufacturing, and yes, even golf courses. It lasts for years, emitting poison bit by bit. Last, the three major rivers come from three distinctly different geological zones. We are able, by looking at things like the mineral content of the water and sediment, to determine which river is delivering what levels of pollution. Once we document that and publish our results, other organizations, including the government, can figure out where the polluters are and apply pressure to mitigate their output."

"That was incredibly succinct!" Margo patted Lonnie on the shoulder. "Lonnie has a master's in chemical analysis from the University of Aberdeen. He can talk your ear off about spectro thingamajigs and chromo photography all day long."

"Thanks. I practiced it a few times in hope we'd have this discussion. And it's spectrometry and chromatography. I was going to go into environmental science. Nonprofits. But Aberdeen has a great golf course, and I kind of got sidetracked after working summer jobs there. I actually fell a wee bit short of completing my master's."

"When we met back in the States, he was on a mission to decrease the use of fertilizers on golf courses. Bad for the rivers and oceans. I ran a nursery that focused on organics and drip irrigation. We were simpatico."

"I could have been a golf course superintendent, but you know, politics. I was viewed as a loose cannon."

"I think people found his enthusiasm threatening." Margo seemed to be encouraging another rant on his part. Frankly, *threatening* and *Lonnie* were two terms I didn't expect to hear in the same sentence.

And he's off to the races.

"All things considered," he said, "it was a worthwhile sacrifice. I reduced the amounts of nitrogen, phosphate, and potash at our course by more than thirty percent in ten years."

I'd seen the impact of golf courses on a couple of my trips. Portions of the Great Barrier Reef, according to people smarter than me—like Lonnie—were slowly being suffocated due in large part to the substantial amounts of nitrogen and phosphorous dumped onto golf courses.

"Yeah, I've seen it. Nutrient-rich waters promote algae growth, which smothers the coral and—"

"Exactly." Apparently, this was Lonnie's time to shine, and I was expected to nod and applaud. I signaled that he should continue. "What goes in the ground doesn't stay in the ground. It enters the groundwater and works its way out to the sea. We did a study—"

"Settle in," Margo chimed in as she grabbed an extra pillow and adjusted her position on the couch. "This will take a while."

✍

As we got closer to the mainland, my runs began to change. I was seeing firsthand what Lonnie was talking about. The seafloor was shallower, thirty feet or less, which meant one less pass and one less water sample. Visibility was dropping because the sediment-rich water was denser closer to the source, so we slowed down the passes to give me time to react to obstacles.

The slower speeds meant the sled maneuvered more like a recreational vehicle than a sports car. I worked a lot harder, and the runs took longer, even though the distance covered was less. And that meant I had less time between runs.

I asked Captain Rich to switch to edgier tunes to keep me on my toes.

"Jane's Addiction? Hendrix? AC/DC?"

"Hell, yeah."

"Grunge?"

"Pearl Jam, yeah. Early stuff. *Ten* or the *Vs.* album. Soundgarden. You got it. I'll stop you if you go too far or not far enough. Oh, anything from the Tragically Hip."

Tao, though, made my surface intervals easier as time went by. He was there to pull in the sled while Captain Rich backed up toward me. He'd developed a routine of hopping into the sled and hoisting up my samples, sparing me the originally planned task of handing them up. He made sure that my lunch came out no more than fifteen minutes after I had finished a run so that I had time to digest and chill. And warm towels, fresh from the sundeck.

But he also was a sponge for information. He was anxious to continue his training and get in the water, although actually doing the sampling was not in the cards for a new diver. But he would take advantage of the downtime to pepper me with questions about dive theory and how to deal with things like the poor visibility in turbid water.

"Yeah," I told him, "turbid water is the shits. Not what I had in mind when I became a divemaster. There are divers who work in those conditions for a living. Welders, for example, who work in cold, dark, restricted spaces, sometimes for hours without a break. Not for me. Give me warm, gin-clear water and colorful reefs."

"Do they make good money?"

"Oh, hell yeah. A lot more than divemasters."

"I could be a welder."

"Yeah, Tao, you could. We can hook you up with a couple of schools that produce great underwater welders."

Tao's grin made the exhaustion from the day's work seem to melt away.

In addition to the physical toll, I was more fried at the end of the day from the tension of being towed with minimal awareness of what possible obstructions lay ahead. Captain Rich, and sometimes Lonnie or Margo, with him watching over their shoulders, would check the sonar and let me know if I was going to do a face-plant into a wreck or big rock, but that didn't do anything to diminish the focus it took to keep moving along in low-viz conditions. Slower runs meant less time for Tao to turn things around. He stopped asking questions, which made me feel guilty, so I tried to volunteer when I was up to it. Those offers were always greeted with a big Tao smile.

Come to think of it, if I did smack into a wreck that wasn't on the charts, it might be a toss-up between whether Captain Rich's first move would be to see if I was all right or mark the GPS and declare we'd found a new historic site. Maybe sixty-forty for hitting the GPS first.

22

NEW CRICKET BAT

THE SHALLOWER WE got as we moved closer to the mainland, the more excited Lonnie became. Despite Margo's pleas, he often dominated dinner talk with his observations. He was picking up pollutants that pointed to heavy dumping of both liquid and solid industrial waste. The mineral fingerprints for the three rivers were so distinct that he was able to identify source waters on the fly. It seemed like no river was immune to the waste issue. More than fifty million people in Myanmar, he pointed out with regularity, were getting their drinking water from highly contaminated sources.

One day, per Lonnie's instructions, instead of my taking a quick rinse in the dive-deck shower, Tao began vigilantly hosing me and my equipment down after every dive. Before I even got off the sled.

"Lonnie says that Margo was complaining about all the mud on the deck." Tao shrugged his shoulders. As far I could tell, he had always hosed down the dive deck after I'd showered and left. "She likes things clean."

I'd already taken to changing into my not-a-uni-form—or at least the bathrobe—before heading inside. And after another Margo edict, we'd taken to using extra towels on the deck to ensure my feet were dry. Something didn't compute, but Margo and I didn't spend much time bonding, so I decided to hold off on asking until an appropriate opportunity appeared.

Tao had also taken to working in running shorts and nothing else, hosing himself off after handling my gear, the samples, and the sled. He was doing a lot of hosing. I tried not to notice, at least not stare, but damn, he had a fine body. I asked him one day about his tattoos. *"Sak yant,"* was his reply. He very shyly explained that the tattoos were part of his daily meditation and were also intended to ward off negative energy.

I didn't ask him about his scars. I was more con-cerned about the changes to our usual routine.

Captain Rich and I were sharing sundowner beers at the end of the day.

"Have you noticed that Lonnie changed my post-dive protocol?"

"You mean the sexy shower show on the sled?" He gave me a sly wink. "I was going to ask you about that."

"Thanks. Yeah, that."

"Did he say why?"

My conversation with Lonnie had taken place just outside of the lab. I'd gone there to get his side of the story since there did seem to be two sides. The door was closed when I got there. He'd taken to closing and locking the door as soon as Tao delivered the latest samples. Sometimes he'd stay in there for hours, and I had never bothered him before, but this was weirding me out.

He took a few minutes before responding to my knocks, and then, when he came to the door, he slipped out and into the hallway for the discussion. He was uncharacteristically vague. After an uncomfortable period of silence as I waited for more, I got the hint and left. As I stomped up the stairs, he remained standing in the hallway before hurrying back into the lab and relocking the door.

"Pollutants. Nothing specific. Said they were minor. He said that was one of the reasons for the full-face mask, and he'd let me know if I should be worried. But he wants to keep it off the boat. The weird thing is that Margo said it was because of the messy mud on the deck. Has he said anything to you?"

"Nope." Captain Rich just shrugged. "Does it have you worried?"

"I'm spending hours down there in water he doesn't want to touch his precious deck, so yeah, I'm concerned. It feels like he's keeping things from us. He and Margo seem to be having quite a few private conversations."

"Husband and wife. You have no idea how common that is. Perhaps a little tension in paradise."

"Do you think I should have another talk with him? See if he can be more specific?"

"You aren't going to take my new cricket bat, are you?"

I hadn't planned on it, but now it seemed like a good idea. A very good idea.

"No."

"I hid it."

Damn it!

"Ye of little faith. I'm just going to talk."

"Yeah." He sort of flinched. "But you and talks about full disclosure have a way of escalating. Seems like I remember you being behind bars back in Dahab after one of your conversations with the police. And that recent dustup phone call with your father."

"His name is Sumo. I had a difference of opinion with Sumo."

"I'm just saying, Ricky." It was somewhat comical to see this six-foot-six, two-hundred-fifty-pound mercenary pressing himself against the wall out of an unfounded fear that I was going to attack him. "You have been known to get a bit revved up."

"I happen to think that my reaction to Sumo was quite reserved and proportionate."

"You destroyed my cricket bat and battered a twenty-thousand-dollar motorcycle."

"That bat was quite old . . ."

"Don't you dare go there. That was my lucky bat."

He was still pressed against the wall, but I could see the veins beginning to pop out on his forehead.

"OK, my bad. I'm sorry. It was quite a shock, and I just grabbed the first available smashing tool. But you have to admit, I had every reason to be pissed."

"Yup."

"And it's not as if he was the first person to betray me."

"True enough. But . . ."

"But what?"

"You seem to be taking more pleasure in the violence. Those three guys in Palau. And your business partner. And then there was the cop."

"It's therapeutic. And in every case, my actions were proportional and justified. The three guys in Palau, which I wish you'd stop bringing up, had kidnapped me and got killed during my escape. Not by me. My business partner, as you call him, was just a minor investor and a major scumbag who was about to send me over a cliff. I'll cop to my attack on Officer Uchel, which was an unfortunate mistake, and he forgave me. You can barely see the scar on his forehead, and the ribs healed within a month. The desk duty probably was a good break for him. And I was never arrested for any of that."

"The two guys in Dahab?"

"I was jailed, but I wasn't ever arrested or charged. That's just how they do things in Egypt."

"Maybe. I'm just saying, I should tag along when you go to talk to Lonnie."

23

A PROVERB FOR WHAT HAPPENED NEXT

IN THE END, we decided that nothing more could come from a discussion with Lonnie. At least one that didn't involve the cricket bat. I took longer showers after the hosing, just in case.

We were tracking perfectly against our schedule. My one day off gave me time to sleep in and recharge my batteries. I hung out on the foredeck, enjoying the top-side view and hydrating heavily. Tao, though even more shy since our conversation about his tattoos, would regularly refresh the ice in my water. But he had stopped making eye contact.

He'd closed up as soon as I started asking about his upbringing. I still had a lot to learn about Thai culture.

The vegan menu, once Captain Rich and I copped to the fact that we couldn't eat another bite of Satan, was actually pretty good, though we'd run out of most of the fresh vegetables, and we were unable to find any villages that could help us replenish. We did have lots of apples to go along with pastas, beans, rice, potatoes, squash, beets, cabbage, and rubbery carrots. Both Lonnie and Margo turned out to be very good cooks, though Lonnie could be a bit anal about precise measurements. I was invited to stop helping in the galley.

Several times we stopped at islands Margo thought had the potential for edible vegetables. I was leery of eating unfamiliar foraged food—in Hawaii, we'd eat wild mangoes and guava, sometimes sea grapes, but we knew from our parents that these wouldn't kill you. I learned the hard way that raw breadfruit was on the don't list, even though cooked breadfruit was a do.

Out of her many suitcases, Margo had pulled a reference book on edible plants of the Andaman Islands. She made soups from acacia, boiled bamboo, ficus sprouts, and a variety of nuts and seeds, as well as a stew-like dish from banana flowers, a slow-to-acquire taste.

"It took several years to convert me from a carnivore to a vegan," offered Lonnie during one of our dinners, "but her yard supplied us with almost everything we needed. All organic. She eventually sold me on plant-based proteins. And it was a treat to just wander around the yard, plucking fresh lettuce for a snack."

For perhaps the first time in my life, I craved green salads.

We were halfway into week five and had over 120 sites sampled. We'd been incredibly lucky. The weather had held out, and other than a few squalls while I was under—which affected Captain Rich more than me—I hadn't even known about half of them until I had surfaced. For the few storms I did notice while submerged, it was merely a matter of slight shaking coming down the towline. We'd had calm weather. We'd seen a few boats, but always at a distance, and none of them seemed to take an interest in our activities.

Lonnie was emphatic, despite the one incident, that all firearms be stored in the secret compartments in the pilot house and Captain Rich's stateroom. Our speedy response to the first pirate approach had convinced him we didn't need weapons out and ready. Having ended our all-night watch parties, Captain Rich was OK with stashing the grenade launcher in the pilot house secret compartment once again. He was, though, spending more time up on the flybridge with binoculars. I think the rest of us would have preferred the grenade gun be at the ready, but it wasn't open to discussion.

Pascal would have had a proverb for what happened next.

On the last day of week five, just before heading out for sites 139 and 140, Lonnie interrupted our prep.

"We're changing things up a bit."

I never liked the sound of that.

"I'm getting great data. Yesterday's samples are giving me exactly the type of detail we need. I'm seeing very well-defined bands of effluent. As we get closer, though, the waters from the rivers will be less defined and more blended, leaving the sediment mixed and useless for our purposes. This is the sweet spot. We're going to start executing a tighter grid. More samples on each pass and much shorter distances between passes. We're only four miles from Myanmar waters, so we want to be careful."

We spent the next thirty minutes going through his plan. Both Captain Rich and I made minor changes to the grid pattern, but it made sense. I'd be taking samples three times as frequently as before, which would put a strain on Captain Rich's maneuvering, but he was up to the job.

Tao listened in but had nothing to contribute. The new schedule meant he'd be working even harder. We all would—especially Captain Rich. As long as he kept to the GPS coordinates, Lonnie pointed out, we'd be fine.

I was halfway between sites 151 and 152 when I felt the sled slow down. We were working in shallower waters, less than thirty feet, so my first thought was that we'd encountered a major obstruction. Captain Rich cut the engines.

"Captain Rich, what's up?"

Silence.

Crud.

The comms had been working just a few minutes earlier. My first thought was a loss of power and electrical systems. But we were within spitting distance of a foreign country with unique troubles, which led me to an alternate theory that was validated almost instantly. I heard a different set of engines and could see the silhouette of a large boat moving in beside the *Powerballer.*

Crap!

Without the pulling action of the luxury yacht, the sled drifted deeper and settled on the seafloor. As I lay there, considering my next move, Captain Rich finally came back on the comms.

"Ricky. Myanmar military. Leave the sled, and come

on up following the towline. No hurry—do your safety stop. Blow lots of bubbles so they see you coming. And surface slowly in a nonthreatening manner. Stay on the dive deck once you're on board. Do you copy?"

I tried to process his instructions. I didn't want to mess this up. "Should I come up away from the boat to avoid surprising them? Should I send up my safety sausage before popping up?"

"Both good ideas. Take it slow. Gotta go."

Since I'd taken to always doing the sled dives with a full tank strapped to my back, it was a simple task to pull on the fins I'd strapped near the foot pedals, release from the sled, and begin my ascent. I'd never been below thirty feet on the run and had only been down for just under an hour. Science said I could perform a normal ascent. I took my time. And blew lots of bubbles. It would be hard not to notice.

I was hoping they'd pull away by the time I surfaced. Within two minutes, though, I was fifteen feet below the surface doing a mandatory, three-minute safety stop in the shadow of the two boats. I was about the same distance behind the dive deck.

Normally, the safety sausage is used in open water. This use, right behind the boat, was a new one for me. I unrolled the orange plastic tube and used my backup regulator to fill it with air. It slowly rose until it popped up to the surface. I tugged on the line, pulling it tight so that the tube stayed upright while I continued my three-minute countdown, which slowly ticked away on my dive computer.

Once the readout indicated that I was cleared to surface, I slowly worked my way up the line, keeping the dive platform in sight. As I got to five feet of depth, about five feet behind the boat, I began to rise straight up. I kept my eyes on the dive ladder but saw a sudden movement as Tao appeared at the edge, then tripped and did a face-plant in the water.

Except it wasn't a trip.

Fuck!

His eyes were open, and a few air bubbles escaped from his mouth. Blood washed out of his back. More blood seeped out of his mouth. There was little doubt that he was dead.

And then, above him, two more men appeared. With weapons. Pointed into the water at me.

For not the first time in my life, I held on to my regulator as I vomited.

A third man appeared above me, hands plunging into the water at Tao's feet, and dragged Tao onto the dive deck by his ankles as the other two remained with their rifles, threatening me with the same outcome. I surfaced a few feet away from the boat and raised both hands, releasing the safety sausage as I did. I didn't understand what they were saying, but they clearly were motioning me forward with their rifles. I slowly finned myself over to the boat, the water around me still pink with Tao's blood, and grabbed the ladder.

I had an issue. I normally didn't climb with my fins on, and I didn't want to reach down to release them and get shot. I decided an awkward climb was the better of two evils. Swinging my left leg in a semicircle, clearing the ladder, I slid my fin over the first rung. But my extra-long Endorfins wouldn't let me get my foot onto the rung, so there was no way to climb. The soldiers were getting more adamant about my exit, and I was getting more rattled. I spat the regulator out of my mouth and tried to communicate my issue. They just got louder and more emphatic with their rifle barrels.

I finally turned and managed to raise my foot above water level so that they could see the issue. One of them knelt, wrestled the fin off my foot, and tossed it onto the dive deck. Then I presented the other, and he did the same, except this time he missed, and my fin flopped into the water and began to drop. As valuable as my prototype fins were, I was not about to make any sudden move to retrieve it. In the grand scheme of things, that was a minor issue. I climbed the ladder and surrendered to the soldiers.

I had no idea what was wrong, but I wasn't about to mess around.

I heard a splash and turned in time to see Tao's body, stripped bare, begin to float away.

There were three bullet holes in his back.

As he drifted away from the boat, I heard an officer bark out what must have been new orders. Suddenly, a gunner on the large machine gun on the aft deck began firing bursts at poor Tao. By the time he stopped, what was left had sunk below the surface.

24

DON'T TALK BACK

I WAS LED up to the foredeck by the pair of armed soldiers. Everyone else was gathered there, seated, hands behind their backs. There were five more armed soldiers and one officer with his sidearm drawn. Scattered among them, I could see Margo vainly struggling with the zip ties that held her, right up to the point where one of the soldiers toed her in the ribs.

My arms were pulled behind me and zip-tied. I was then shoved down into a kneeling position and then into a seated position like the others.

This was real.

Way too freaking real.

Margo was wheezing and tucked into the fetal position. Lonnie was surprisingly stoic, staring straight ahead. Or scared shitless and unable to react to anything. Captain Rich was scanning the deck and probably what he could see of the other boat. It was smaller than the Thai frigate that had searched us before and looked a little more run down, but the gun on the foredeck looked sufficiently menacing. As did the man standing at the ready to use it. Given that half the people on our foredeck were his fellow soldiers, I didn't know how that would have worked out, but I was not going to try to find out.

I could hear noise below deck. I was guessing they were looking for additional people. But it seemed like more than that, like they were tossing the boat. That seemed a bit over the top.

But so had killing Tao.

Finally, the soldiers who'd been down below came up and spoke quickly with the officer. They then joined the rest in watching over us.

"International waters!" Lonnie had come out of his silent funk and had been muttering that same line for a few minutes.

No one seemed to be paying attention to him until the officer tilted his head in Lonnie's direction and barked out an order. Two men shouldered their weapons and yanked Lonnie up and back toward the aft. Or toward the salon. From my position seated on the foredeck, no matter how much I twisted around, I couldn't see beyond a few feet behind me. I thought, though, that I heard Lonnie squeak.

We weren't allowed to speak to the soldiers or even to each other. It was fairly miserable, sitting in the sun without water for what seemed to be several hours. I was still zipped up in my wetsuit, which had long since turned into a sealed sauna. And I needed to pee. Making matters worse, it had been hours since breakfast, probably past the lunch hour as well, and I was hungry. Hot, hungry, and soon to be humiliated if I had to pee in my suit.

Margo had mouthed off twice. Once she got another kick and the second time a slap. Captain Rich wasn't reacting, but I could tell he was calculating. He did hiss at Margo—"Don't talk back." I'm sure he'd memorized every slight against each one of us and would retaliate when the right time arrived. If the right time arrived.

Finally, just as I was figuring out if I was going to pass out or scream, Lonnie was led back. Dragged back might be more accurate. His legs were barely keeping up with him, and the guards didn't make a pretense of letting him down slowly. They just dropped him on the deck.

Following not too far behind was the officer. He was accompanied by another officer, one who seemed to be subordinate. The senior officer glared at each of us and then spoke a few words that I couldn't understand and assumed to be Burmese. The subordinate then said in almost impeccable English, "You are now prisoners of the Myanmar Navy."

The senior officer then spoke again, this time for longer. The translation was even more disturbing than the first. "You have illegally entered Myanmar territorial waters for purposes of conducting a clandestine investigation. You will hereby be transported to appropriate facilities within mainland Myanmar and subject to detention and criminal prosecution."

The senior officer tapped the subordinate on the shoulder, whispered in his ear, and then spoke again. The subordinate waited, nodded, and then said, "The owner of the boat claims that your research was not conducted in secret. He was unaware that you had entered Myanmar waters and said that the captain must have mistakenly taken the wrong route. This information will be submitted to prosecutors for evaluation."

Captain Rich barely flinched at that last portion, but I could see him glancing at Lonnie. I could not believe that Captain Rich had made a navigation error. Lonnie had, I suspected, thrown him under the bus. Whatever the Myanmar officer had done to Lonnie during his interrogation would pale in comparison with what I assumed Captain Rich wanted to do at this moment.

We were pulled up, one at a time, and led to the aft deck, where we were transferred to the naval vessel via a narrow plank. Despite my hands still being zip-tied behind my back, I feigned slipping and fell into the water. I immediately peed while vigorously treading water. The relief, both for my bladder and my internal thermostat— despite the hell we were going through—was worth the rough treatment I got as I was snagged with a mooring hook and then dragged onto the foreign boat.

After an equally rough and overly intrusive body search, I ended up being tossed into a windowless cell in the belly of the boat with Margo while Lonnie and Captain Rich set up housekeeping in one opposite from us. Lonnie cowered like a trapped mouse as Captain Rich glared at him. I truly worried for his safety.

A door separated our cell area in the bow from the rest of the hull area, and a narrow passage separated each cell from the other. We heard activity off and on for the better part of an hour before four of our captors—two with guns, one with a cutting tool, and one with a pile of clothes—pushed the door open. The soldier, whom I forever after nicknamed Walmart, pushed a mash-up of women's clothes through the bars into our cell before the one with the cutting tool—Edward Scissorhands—mimed that we were to stand with our hands toward the bars so that he could cut our restraints. When Margo and I both stood, he barked some indecipherable order at us. Guessing at what had triggered him, I sat back down and let Margo go first. Once she was reseated, I followed suit. They repeated the exercise with the boys. The sight of Captain Rich with his hands free only served to make Lonnie more nervous.

Although it appeared that they had found the appropriate clothing for Captain Rich and the much smaller Lonnie, they had only brought clothing from Margo's room for us. She was polite enough to give me first pick, so I got a matching pair of shorts and a sleeveless shirt. She got a cocktail dress. But at least she had the clothes she had been captured in, as sweaty as they might have become. All I had on after my body search was the one-piece swimsuit I wore under my wetsuit. I made the boys turn around as I removed it and slipped into the shorts and shirt.

I was going commando, but that seemed like the least of my worries.

Not only did we have no windows, but no watches. They'd been taken away, along with Margo's inexpensive substitute jewelry and Lonnie's wedding ring, when we were searched. Beneath his mop of curly brown hair, I saw that somehow Captain Rich had gotten to keep his earring.

Captain Rich developed a basic set of mimes to communicate with our captors. A few of them, like "I need to pee," were open to misinterpretation, but the guards seemed to understand.

We got fed periodically. Mainly noodles with a little meat. Captain Rich made Lonnie give him his meat. We were taken to the bathroom when we complained enough. We slept when we could.

Captain Rich figured we were captured about 150 miles from the coast, "unless the GPS was wrong," insisting that all of his data had told him that we had been ten miles short of the Myanmar territorial waters when we had been captured and never less than two miles away during any of our passes.

Captain Rich stood over Lonnie, who slithered up the wall to at least present a less cowering posture. "Did you play with the GPS when you were on watch?"

"Why would I do that?"

"Yeah, exactly. Why would you do that?" Captain Rich had moved even closer, pressing Lonnie into the corner.

"Leave him alone! We're all in this together." Margo, who seemed to defer to Lonnie for more than was warranted, sounded like the voice of reason for once. I guess self-preservation was a greater motivator than nuptial loyalty, given that we all knew who represented our best chance of escape. Two guesses—and it wasn't Lonnie.

"They're nervous. On edge. That's not healthy for us or for them. The guy who shot Tao didn't even give him a chance. All he was doing was running to help Ricky. I don't want any of us to be the next accident. So please, everyone, just chill."

Captain Rich backed off a bit and seemed to calm down.

"Warn. Warn. He was racing to warn Ricky." Lonnie seemed to find a distinction. "If he hadn't had a crush on her, he would have stayed seated. She didn't need help. It was stupid. No reason for him getting himself killed."

"Bullshit!"

So much for everyone chilling. Lonnie was pushing all of Captain Rich's buttons—hold accountable, he always said, but never blame.

"His people came from Burma. He was first-generation Thai. He'd heard all the horror stories. His uncle had his forearm hacked off—almost died. Family members disappeared. He was scared to death of the Myanmar military. He only came along because of the money we promised him. It was just as likely that he was going to dive in the water—over Ricky, if necessary—and try to swim away. They had him that scared. I promised him a dozen times that we wouldn't get in any trouble. I gave him my oath."

It seems like the two had bonded more than I had realized during their time working on the boat.

"I didn't expect you to guide us into territorial waters."

Lonnie must have had a death wish. The veins in Captain Rich's neck were bulging out. He pointed at Lonnie. "When this is over, we're going to have a long talk."

You know that moment when the quarterback loses the support of his team? Yeah, like that.

Lonnie couldn't stop himself. "In the end, it didn't matter why he went running. The guy on the aft machine gun didn't wait to figure out what was going on. I don't see that changing. They're still high-strung. Could be some of them are on meth."

Captain Rich wasn't much for conjecture. Even when it was rather obvious.

"Meth?" I blundered into the conversation. "You think? The guy who wears his shades indoors was definitely tweaking." That would be the one I'd nicknamed Wile E. Coyote. Luckily, Edward Scissorhands seemed to be safely mellowed.

Margo was, if nothing else, observant. "Probably half of them were cranked up."

The jury was still out on that. We'd see how they were once the adrenaline had left their systems. But yeah, meth was a wild card in this whole play. The fewer who did it and the less they did, the better for us.

"Ricky." Captain Rich seemed to have collected himself. He sounded thoughtful. "Sorry, but how many exit wounds?"

"Exit?"

"Yeah. Any wounds in his chest?"

"None. Why?"

I hoped there was some real value in this because picturing Tao dead was making my stomach do a dance.

"How many in his back?"

"Three."

"Large and jagged?"

"No. Small and clean."

"Tao was executed. Full stop."

Lonnie rose from the floor, holding his arms out in exasperation. "Oh, for Christ's sake. Can the melodramatics."

"Lonnie, you're out of your element." Captain Rich held it together, but his neck and ears were flushed red. "Almost every man and boy on that boat was armed with a rifle or submachine gun. The guy on the bow deck gun was operating a .50 caliber. Three close-up shots from any of the rifles or machine guns would have gone through and through. The .50 would have torn him apart—correction, did tear him apart, as they let his body drift away. I saw only two guns, possibly a third, that could have left three shots, all closely grouped, inside of Tao. A pistol. The first was an enlisted man, whose compact machine pistol was in a ready position the whole time. But he began working his way toward the bow as soon as he got on the boat and was nowhere near the aft deck. Then there was the officer, who had one that never left his holster, and he came up to the pilot house as soon as he boarded the boat. The third one was the most intense in the way he carried himself. Not wearing a naval uniform, but some sort of official clothing, with a Sig Sauer in his hand—and when he came across, he headed straight for the aft deck with two other men. To where Tao was. Not to the wheelhouse, where he'd expect to find the captain and maybe the owner. The aft deck. Like he was looking for someone. Tao was executed."

"Are you out of your mind?" Lonnie actually laughed.

"It's a working theory. We surely don't know for certain, and I don't know, even if we did, what good it would do. Understanding their intentions might help. You have to know each piece on the board, what it's capable of, and why it's moved to a particular square. This guy was no pawn, and his beeline for the aft was no coincidence."

Captain Rich had slowly walked over and put his arm around Lonnie's shoulder. He slid down the wall, bringing the resistant Lonnie with him, until both their butts hit the floor. He pressed against and whispered to Lonnie. It went on for a couple of minutes, and when he moved away, Lonnie remained pressed into the corner.

"Lonnie says I'm in charge now," he announced before settling down on the one cot in the cell.

"I did not."

Margo and I shared the single, narrow cot in our cell and kept our eyes on the boys.

25

UP SHIT CREEK

WE HAD NO sense of time or day. We took turns guessing, and we were across the board. It had been at least eighteen hours, or twenty-four. Thirty? Thirty-six?

More talk about Tao. Turned out he was a former Buddhist monk. But he'd left that way of life and joined the military, which could explain a number of things. His focus on serving. His early-morning training, the scars. His history as a monk would account for the meditation tattoos and his shy nature. According to Lonnie, it could be that he had died a celibate.

"*Sak yant,*" offered Lonnie, who had been working very hard to avoid any conversation and certainly any that involved offering opinions. "It was a *Sak yant* tattoo. I started to get one, but they use really pointy metal spikes that they jab into your skin. I bailed out on mine fairly early."

Margo made a priceless face. "You never told me that. That spot on your back? I thought that was just a dark freckle." Clearly, mocking Lonnie was not off-limits. At least to her.

Lonnie, though, got me thinking. I tried to avoid the thought that I'd somehow led Tao on. But all that happened was I kept replaying our interactions. He certainly had spent increasing amounts of time with me on the dive deck.

I decided it was time to hum the *Barney* theme song to relax, but I couldn't keep the rhythm going. It didn't stop me but made me work harder, which was actually helpful in keeping my mind off Tao.

Margo shot me a look this time. I suspect she was thinking about mocking me but thought better of it. I did, after all, have Captain Rich as my bodyguard. But then my mind pivoted in a different direction.

"Hey." I slid my leg between the bars and tapped Captain Rich's butt a bit more firmly than necessary. "Where was everybody as I was surfacing?"

He looked at me cockeyed. "I'm not sure. Hadn't thought about it. I was paying attention to where the boarding party was going. Everyone on our team was out of sight. I was the only one in the pilot house. I set the PA to full boat and told everybody to slowly move to the main deck with their hands visible. Lonnie had most likely been in the lab working on your first set of samples. Margo, who knows? Tao was, as far as I know, at his station on the dive deck. Then I immediately pinged you."

"Who said Tao was running? And if he was, where was he running from?"

"Lonnie or Margo. I can't recall. Things went wonky very quickly."

"I think he was already back there. Where he was supposed to be. Did you warn him I was deploying my sausage?"

"No. I don't think so. Jeez, you think he ran because—"

"No, I don't think he ran. He wasn't running. He was shot in the back turning to help me . . . because . . . he saw . . . my sausage."

Captain Rich fucked up and Tao died.

Maybe.

At some point, there had been a subtle change in the engines. They had been at a steady RPM for the first part of our captive voyage but were now shifting from high to low and medium speeds and back again. We also seemed to be maneuvering more. I was lost in a funk of going back and forth between blaming Captain Rich, myself, or just dumb circumstances.

"Delta," said Lonnie. "Sort of the midway between sea and land. It spreads for hundreds of square miles, but it means that we're heading inland. My guess would be Yangon. You probably know it as Rangoon. That's where much of the police force works. Almost half."

"Thank you, Professor Lonnie," grumbled Captain Rich, who was stretched out on the cot. He'd been awfully quiet, probably also considering the possibility that Tao had died because he had been trained to respond to the safety sausage. Because Captain Rich had trained him to react immediately if he saw it. Because he always did the job as he was told. "You seem to know an awful lot about the area for someone who can't even keep a navigation system running right."

"I'm getting a little tired of your accusations, Richard."

Uh-oh.

"And yes, I do." Lonnie was, uncharacteristically, showing some spine. "I worked at a golf course in Yangon for several years. I've spent a lot of time on the river and in the delta. I can speak the primary language, somewhat, and know the culture. And how to work with the authorities."

Captain Rich rotated into a seated position on the cot. At some point, Lonnie was going to push one too many buttons, and there would be a confrontation he stood no chance of winning. "Oh yeah, we saw how well that worked when they dragged you back to the *Powerballer.*"

Lonnie stiffened. "Dealing with the military and dealing with the police and government authorities are two very different things. Getting close to Rangoon means we're almost to our destination. And proper authorities I can talk to."

Lonnie seemed quite sure of himself. I wondered if he could actually have something to offer at this point.

"Oh, goody. Are you going to throw me under the bus again when we get there?"

"How about you stay quiet and let me manage this? You might be surprised what diplomacy can do compared with brute force. We'll be there in a couple of hours."

He'd shifted away from the corner and was sitting up a little straighter. From where I sat, I could see Captain Rich's face. Not only was his jaw clenched, but there were veins popping out in his neck and forehead where I never knew veins existed. He was clearly doing a slow burn, but it seemed like the threat of physical violence was not imminent.

Lonnie had a death wish. He just couldn't shut up. "You know, maybe the officer went to the aft deck because they'd seen that we were towing something. I'm sure they had their glasses on us the entire time they were closing in."

He had a point. I was sure that wouldn't stop Captain Rich from crushing his face if the opportunity presented.

The time dragged on, far more than his projected "couple of hours," and Lonnie's confidence in his estimate for our arrival appeared to wane. He shut his yap and sat in the corner. Captain Rich occasionally slapped his hands on the floor or stomped his feet near Lonnie's—just to keep him on edge.

At some point, not long after we got what we thought was our evening meal, all movement stopped, and the engines stopped as well. We noticed our guards nodding off. We quietly agreed it was nighttime and all tried to get some sleep, though the lights stayed on. Some handled it better than others. Margo and I settled in together on the cot.

Some hours later, the guard shift changed. The new set seemed perky and well rested. They brought a thermos of tea and served us what looked a little like breakfast. It included what seemed to be fresh bread. Then the engines fired up, and we resumed moving.

"Let's see now. First, a nighttime stop. Then fresh

bread. Now, I'm just a brute, but to me, that means someone was able to leave the boat, and there is a town nearby. Any new assessments of our travel, Professor Lonnie? I'm thinking we're up shit creek." Captain Rich was clearly not embracing diplomacy. Can't say that I blamed him, given Lonnie's blame game.

Whenever he looked at Lonnie, Captain Rich began clenching his fists. Lonnie just stewed.

26

WHEREVER HERE IS

THE HOURS PASSED with little or no change. The boat churned on. Lonnie remained in a pout. The only improvement was that Captain Rich's veins had stopped throbbing and his fists were no longer clenched. This uneasy peace was disrupted when the boat shuddered to a sudden stop, knocking one sleepy guard off his stool.

Captain Rich was up and looking around. "If we start flooding, what are the odds that they let us out? Hey, do you have the keys?"

I wouldn't call it panic, but I could imagine that boat captains spend a lot of time envisioning the worst-case scenario so that they can either avoid it or respond to it. Locked in a jail cell, he had neither option. One guard ran upstairs while the other one took a vigilant stance, gun in hand.

"Do . . . you . . . have . . . keys?" Captain Rich wasn't of a mind to sit back and wait. "Ricky, Margo, watch the decking for moisture. If you see so much as a trickle, start screaming bloody murder. Bang on the hull, stomp your feet. You, too, Lonnie."

He, in turn, resumed screaming at the guard about the keys. The guard might as well have been deaf.

A few minutes later, the first guard came back down with Edward Scissorhands, carrying zip ties this time, and the officer who had originally boarded us, with pistol drawn. They took Captain Rich away without explanation, hands zip-tied, but at least in front of him rather than behind.

It was several hours before he returned. No trickles had appeared in the hull, but he was soaking wet, a bit muddy, and in a foul mood. The guard, Walmart again—who, it seemed, was responsible for keeping us properly clothed—was carrying some dry clothes and tossed them into the cell just ahead of Captain Rich.

"Well," he said, staring at Lonnie, "that was fun. We're still towing the *Powerballer*, but she got stuck on a sandbar. It took a while for me to get her off, and then I convinced them to let me check for damage. I even grabbed my rig and a tank to check the hull from underneath . . . with a goddamn rope tied to my ankle so I couldn't escape. And no wetsuit. Idiot on the other end kept pulling the rope tight, so I had to fight to check the full hull. Some scrapes, but the hull is intact."

He stripped off his clothing, every stitch—which got a smile out of Margo—and tossed it on the cot. He took a minute to towel off with the cot's blanket, then pulled on the new shirt. The shorts went on last. Margo never looked away.

"Professor"—Captain Rich continued to be snarky—

"I changed my mind. You can have the cot. Seems that I've convinced our hosts that I need to be in the *Powerballer* for the rest of our navigation to keep us off further sandbars."

Lonnie appeared to consider responding, but Margo not so subtly stamped her foot, and he closed his mouth, doing that silly "locking my lips and throwing away the key" mime.

"And I have a few updates. One, we are way, way upriver from Rangoon. The river is narrower, shallower, and more crowded with small boats than you would see in or below a major seaport. Two, they're trashing the boat. Seems like our staterooms, the salon, and even the pilot house are preferred sleeping quarters for the sailors. They're not very big on housekeeping, and Margo, your satin sheets are gone. Last, all the liquor and beer are gone. I'm calling the UN first chance I get. That should be a violation of international law."

With that, he banged on the bars and was let out to resume his captain role, in a limited sense. Lonnie tossed the wet clothes and blanket off the cot and settled down in his corner, waiting for it to dry.

The next time we saw Captain Rich, several meals later, he showed up with new clothes for each of us and a bucketful of news. He distributed the ladies' clothing before he was led back into his cell. He tossed the rest of the clothes to Lonnie. We'd noticed the engine speed dropping off just before he arrived.

"We're here, wherever here is. The *Powerballer* is already docked. We'll be docking in just a few minutes. I've been watching our progress and haven't seen a city all day. We're in the middle of nowhere. No city. No buildings, for that matter. A dock that leads to a dirt road that leads into the jungle. A couple of small boats, painted to look military, but I don't think they are."

He took a deep breath. "There are a dozen armed soldiers on the dock. I use the term *soldier* loosely. All armed, but with a variety of weapons that don't appear to be recent or standard military issue. Not all are wearing uniforms, but most are wearing fatigues that are made to look official. There are others, unarmed, making no attempt at a uniform. They might be wage earners, or they might be prisoners. Hard to tell at this point. My guess is we stumbled into a guerilla operation. What I can't figure out is, what concerned them a hundred fifty miles from shore?"

The hours passed. We had been docked for quite a while without a sign of our captors or a hint that there was going to be a change in our status.

"So, Lonnie," Captain Rich deadpanned, "earlier, you mentioned that we are sponsored by some American corporations. Do you care to expand on that?"

"Not really. None of your business, and not relevant to the current situation."

"I must disagree with that stance." Captain Rich, for the umpteenth time, rose as high as he could above Lonnie. "I think everything having to do with this voyage is our business, and we get a say in what's relevant. So, I ask you again, would you care to provide more detail?"

"OK. First, they're not sponsors. Their names are not associated with us in any way. They subsidized us

JETSAM

because they have business interests in the region that they wish to protect."

Criminy.

"And I never said they were American or even corporations. They are business entities. And I'm pretty sure the moment they find out we've been taken, they will start shredding documents."

"Lovely. So I'm guessing we shouldn't be asking to speak to them on the ship-to-shore. Was there anybody back home that you did or should have contacted the moment we saw the hostile ship?"

Lonnie shrunk back as best as he could. "No. This was our deal. No one's going to come racing to help us."

"Lonnie always insisted that this study be part of our growing personal brand. No sharing the glory." The way it came out did not sound like Margo was praising this strategy.

169

27

AS CAGES GO, IT SEEMED
FAIRLY NORMAL

THE DOOR TO our section of the bow flew open, and six guards entered, the first four carrying weapons. Our private guard jumped to attention—an impressive act, given that he had been snoring just seconds before.

Without instruction or explanation, we were all recuffed and removed from our cells.

Even before we got to the top of the stairs, we noticed the difference. The topside air, despite the killer humidity and the stench of heavy jungle, was a blessing after being locked up in the ship's hold for what had to have been days. The midday sun warmed us as we stood on the deck of our captors' ship. I had been in its belly, which alternated dramatically between nighttime cold and daytime heat, so long that I'd ceased to notice the temperature. I didn't have much cause for pleasure, but the sun made me smile.

Behind us, the *Powerballer* was a bed of activity as a handful of ragtag soldiers and nonuniformed workers removed food, equipment, and our personal effects from the boat. Weapons, too. But it did not appear that they were stripping it. I didn't see any cushions, bedding, or other comfort items in the things being schlepped.

A hodgepodge of small and medium-size boats lined the shore. Upriver, at least four large barges that were in the beginning stages of being loaded were carrying massive logs.

A rickety ramp led from the deck to the dock. At least this one had cables on both sides. My legs weren't used to standing or walking, so my steps were unsure and erratic. But we all made it down without drama and were prodded to follow the ship's goods as they disappeared into the jungle on a narrow, rutted dirt road. The narrow road leading through a path cut into a bamboo forest thirty or forty feet high felt both stately and a bit imposing.

Our walk didn't take long. Within fifty feet of shore, we came upon a large building with metal siding. It was substantial, both in size and construction. It sat on a deep concrete pad. The metal plates were riveted together. Its double doors were open, and I could see workers inside wrestling fifty-gallon drums off a fork-lift and onto a stack of similar drums. One worker was hosing down the piles of drums, and the water was running from a pipe that extended out of the concrete pad. Beside it lay another concrete pad of similar dimensions, with the metal skeleton of a second building rising next to it. Sparks flew from several spots as welders, in heavy protective outfits and helmets, suffered in the hundred-degree heat.

A third pad, also a hotbed of activity, comprised multiple teams who seemed to be modifying midsize metal shipping containers. They were the same length and width, but shorter—less than five feet high.

I must have slowed down because one of our guards poked me in the ribs with his rifle.

Nothing to see here, folks; nothing to see here. My ass.

Within a hundred yards of the dock, we came to a sloping area broken up into a mishmash of clear-cut circles, each hosting half a dozen or more buildings. *Buildings* might not have been the right term. Some were essentially tents strung up over what looked like timber frames, flaps tossed back to provide some degree of ventilation. Others were little more than palm-frond shacks. Each clearing, though, appeared to have at least one Quonset hut in its center. We were guided through a string of these clearings, the buildings in each successive one appearing to be more upscale than those before it.

At least three forklifts, each carrying four drums on pallets, slowly passed us by. Our guards made sure we were well off the road before they passed.

We were paraded through several more of the clearings, heading upslope, until we reached a fenced area. In the center stood a welded metal cage, about the size of a shipping container. A nudge from one of the rifles pushed me in that direction. A minute later, a much firmer nudge encouraged me to enter. Margo and the men followed.

As cages go, it seemed fairly normal.

The sides were thick, vertical bars that stood about

six inches apart, held together with two thicker horizontal beams spaced at about three feet and six feet off the ground. It had a metal floor. Unlike the shipping containers we'd seen near the boat, this cage was at least eight feet high. The structure was topped with metal bars covered with palm leaves. The door was chained and secured with a large padlock.

On the plus side, it was larger than the two cells combined on the boat, and it provided fresh air and light. On the negative side, there were no cots, and there were creepy-crawly things on the floor. And the floor retained a lot of heat.

On the abysmally horrible side, we were in the middle of nowhere, in a cage, surrounded by a large number of men with assault weapons.

As we stood or sat in our cage, watching the goings-on of the camp and providing entertainment for those on the outside, I'd occasionally see members of the original crew. The one who had served as the translator on the boat, I'd heard him called Wai, was all over the place, trotting from one group to another and shouting orders. The others treated him with deference. I saw Edward Scissorhands at one point and called out to him. His reaction was similar to that of the two men he was with—they all stared at me quizzically.

It hadn't rained for the past two weeks, but of course, that day the skies opened up. The breeze was slight, but rain still blew in on two sides. And ran from the jungle across the naturally heated floor. Of course, the palm-leaf ceiling leaked.

Other than quick glances and the occasional stare,

no one seemed to pay much attention to us, so we all moved to the corner farthest from the rain and stood. For hours. Finally, an officer noticed our plight and, after some discussion with yet another officer, instructed a group of soldiers to throw some tarps over the top and down the sides. Part of the sides, about one-third. The rain continued coming in, though it hit a smaller area.

Based on the following interactions, we concluded that Wai was the commanding officer's aide. He almost immediately appeared and flagged down the officer who had ordered the tarps, then seemed to refine the solution. There was a brief exchange between Wai and the soldier, accompanied by lots of nodding. The soldier immediately pulled a sheet of corrugated aluminum from a nearby stack. The thing was taller than he by a couple of feet and wider by even more, so he resorted to dragging it over. He then leaned it up against the cage, making a functional barrier. He trotted back for a second. Then a third. At that point, he figured out what was obvious to all of us in the cage, or he heard our comments. Or Wai gave him further instruction. With the plastic sheeting on the inside and the metal panel laid over it, water still ran down the opening of the ribbed sheet.

He finally enlisted another soldier, who clambered up on the cage and pulled the tarp out so that it lay over the metal barrier. With his buddy on top and making adjustments each time, our savior dragged a total of eight sheets over, overlapping them by a couple of inches and forming a wall that kept the sheets of rain out. The only drawback was that the sound of the large raindrops against the metal sounded eerily like the sound of gun-fire. Or it was masking real gunfire. I couldn't tell.

The downpour stopped coming in through the sides, but the water flow at our feet continued. And the humidity within the cage shot up.

All things considered, it was one of the worst days of my life—except nobody had died. Yet.

28

I CAN GET THIS SMOOTHED OVER

I FIGURED CAPTAIN Rich, of anyone in the group, might have some ideas. "Have any thoughts on what's going to happen next?"

"No, I don't. And I don't think they do, either. I'd be surprised if this was a standard operation. There have been no reports of disappearing luxury yachts. The pirates always leave people alive and boats afloat. And I don't figure the current Myanmar government approves of what's going on here."

Another drawback of the tarps, other than the intense humidity, was that we couldn't see what was going on outside. Although, given what we'd seen before the tarps had blocked our view, most everyone had stopped working and run for cover.

We'd been without food and water ever since before we'd left the boat. We took to pushing our hands out through a gap where two sheets of aluminum didn't overlap and collecting water for drinking.

Captain Rich mentioned that in the jungle, he'd

often resorted to eating bugs. We certainly had enough of them crawling around with us on the floor of the tent. He pointed to a large cockroach. "Those fellas taste a little bit like vanilla. Lots of calories, too. The crunch is off-putting, but once you've got it mashed, it's not bad."

About half an hour later, with hunger pangs dominating my thinking, I made a grab for one. Captain Rich quickly leaned over from where he sat and grabbed my wrist before I could get it to my mouth.

"Kidding! Geez, Ricky, you can be so gullible. That's disgusting. Put that thing down!"

"Do you think they'll feed us soon?" I was thinking that disgusting might be the lesser of two evils.

"I don't think there's a method to their madness. Some of these guys have no training. Did you see how they hold their guns? A couple of them have their itchy fingers on the trigger. That's crazy. Like the guy who shot Tao. They're wild cards—no way of predicting their behavior."

Thank you, Captain Sunshine.

OK, Captain Rich's threat assessment presented an even worse aspect of our situation. I'm not sure if his reference to Tao was denial on his part, but I was pretty sure the guy who had shot Tao had just been following orders.

"Take it easy, then, Rich." Lonnie had a smile that seemed to communicate that he knew things we didn't. "There is no reason to rile them up. The guerillas around here are in it for the money, not for politics or religion. If we play along, they'll let us go. Maybe just a raft to go downriver, but enough to get home safely. Follow my lead."

"Yeah, no, but these aren't guerillas. No way they have a fucking navy patrol boat and can bring us halfway up the blessed Irrawaddy without even being stopped. This is, at best, an official group doing unsanctioned activities. The new government just got installed, and no matter how progressive they might be, they're inheriting a mess. If I'm an opportunistic member of their military, this is exactly the time that I'd go rogue and monetize the hell out of my job."

Lonnie blinked, but he pushed on. "Official, rogue official, or guerilla, they don't mean us harm. They could have dumped us with Tao back at the beginning and saved themselves a lot of trouble. No, we'll be on our way soon. If this is for ransom, I have people who will make it happen and make it happen fast."

Captain Rich, on the other hand, didn't blink. "Forgive me for doubting your assessment, but given that you are a liar and incompetent, why should we trust you now?"

They were on a collision course. I had no idea when it would happen or what the catalyst would be, but Captain Rich's patience had worn thin. The vein on his forehead was making more frequent visits.

"Best that you remember that I'm still your employer." Lonnie was not very good at reading people. Playing the employer card with Captain Rich was like waving a red cape in front of a bull. "Like I told you, I lived and worked here, at a Rangoon country club. Many of our members were military. Others were profiteers. Businessmen who skated the edge of the law when they thought they were being watched and definitely

JETSAM

went off-book when they knew they weren't. I got to know them all. I saw them betting. I saw them cheat. Sometimes quite brazenly, almost taunting their opponent to call the bet off. I'll wager I can get this smoothed over with the leader of this group in just a few hours."

"The problem is," said Captain Rich as he unfolded himself from where he sat, "you're betting with our lives. And I, for one, want to know exactly what makes you think you've got the winning hand."

And with that, Lonnie scurried over to the far side of the cage and started calling to the guards in what I assumed was Burmese.

29

YES, YES, THE BEST

THE RAINS HAD stopped, and several of the metal sheets—the ones facing the jungle and uphill—had been removed. The others, which were facing the direction from which the rain and wind came, remained.

Lonnie returned without a celebration cake and sporting a sour look on his face. He was accompanied by five soldiers, one officer, and four guards—two with pistols and two with carbines. We watched as he was prodded down the path to the cage.

Captain Rich leaned against me and whispered, "Betting dollars to doughnuts that huddle didn't go as well as expected."

Lonnie's assessment differed. "I've made significant progress. Met with the head man himself, a General Thandar. Good man. Seems quite reasonable. The discussions are a work in progress, and everyone"—he looked directly at Captain Rich—"is to be as forthright as possible but not speculate about things you don't absolutely know. This takes a level head and good negotiation skills—leave that to me."

Margo was taken next and returned in a pissy mood. She didn't want to talk about her session. She pulled Lonnie aside, and they spent a short time in whispered discussions. Then she went into a corner and gently beat her head against the bars.

During the remainder of the day, we each got our turn at being interrogated. After his, Captain Rich found a stick just outside the cage and was able to reach it. He began wandering around the cage, stopping every couple of feet to scrape the end of the stick against the floor.

"Making a shiv for your big escape?" I had high hopes for his next moves.

"Close, but better."

Once he had worked the end of the stick into a close approximation of a knife, Captain Rich quietly climbed up each wall, using the crossbars of the cage, and made small, half-moon-shaped cuts in several places a few inches below the ceiling level but above the remaining metal sheets.

"We've been blind to a major part of the goings-on. This gives me a three-hundred-and-sixty-degree view." He could only use them when the camp above us was quiet since his imposing bulk was hard to miss for anyone looking into the cage.

"Lonnie, your lab has been relocated. I doubt they know what they have, but they seem very excited. By the way, Thandar asked why we had an encrypted radio in the laboratory. I'm pretty sure my shock underscored my denial of such technology. Care to explain?"

"I don't have to explain my processes to you," Lonnie spat out. "It's a toy. OK? A silly toy. I wanted to feel like I had my own little domain."

"Your own espresso machine would have done that." I was getting into the spirit of Captain Rich's browbeating.

"He had one of those. Very nice. Ground multiple types of beans. We had to tear out several panels of teak to run a waterline where you couldn't see it. Took Tao and me more than a day. For a stupid espresso machine. But we never saw a radio. Sort of explains the locking of the door."

I was the last one called.

About half an hour after I returned, Lonnie was led away for a second session, but this time, according to Captain Rich, into one of the nicer buildings. When he was done, he, an officer, and Wai bypassed the cage, diverting to the trail toward the river and the *Powerballer*. Captain Rich, still observing, noted that it looked like all the workers on the *Powerballer* were dismissed for the day.

We'd gotten in the habit of debriefing after each session, although we waited this time until Lonnie was gone. Captain Rich and I, who were more than happy to talk about our interrogations, had basically the same experience. We were taken to a cell, probably the same one. Two chairs and a table. A bare-bulb light hanging from the ceiling. No offer of water. They started with a lot of basic questions, lots of requests for details about our route and activity. My work on the sled led into an extended line of inquiry that didn't seem to go anywhere. Most of the questions had to do with the lab and its results. I had nothing, but they weren't inclined to believe me. My most noteworthy moments were questions about the sample results—"'Um, duh, I don't know . . . I just collected them'—and your navigation skills." I nodded at Captain Rich. "I told them that I once saw you drop a diver directly on top of a two-inch-square dive computer, a hundred feet down, two days after a diver dropped it while climbing into the boat." Apparently, Captain Rich was asked a lot about course, navigation, and how we ended up in Myanmar waters.

"I swear, Ricky, we were still a couple of miles outside. The GPS showed a couple of miles of clearance."

Periodically, he climbed the walls to observe the activity outside our cage.

Lonnie, Wai, and the man who was apparently a senior officer returned about a half hour later. Lonnie, Captain Rich reported, looked like he'd been rolling in off-white powder and was sweating heavily. Wai was carrying four briefcase-size bricks sealed in blue plastic. They, too, had powder residue. We watched through the uphill side of the cage as Lonnie went with them to the fancier buildings and were still watching when he was finally returned.

Next up for a second round was Margo. I hoped she kept the snark to a minimum. It wouldn't play well, not with this crowd. Her visit was shorter than Lonnie's. She, too, was then taken somewhere other than the cage. It looked like she and Lonnie were sent to the same building. I didn't know how to interpret that, but I feared the worst.

Then they came for Captain Rich.

"They're playing us against one another. I'll bet Lonnie's been selling me down the river."

"Downriver might be a good way to go." I tried to keep things light.

"Not if you're wearing lead boots."

As with both Lonnie and Margo, it was the same five soldiers. It might have been my imagination, but it seemed like they gave Captain Rich more space and kept their weapons in ready positions. The officer pushed him as he slowly walked out the cage door. Bad move. Captain Rich came to a full stop and turned his way. It was a short standoff—I think he got his point across. He also got jammed in the kidney by a rifle butt. I would want more than a few guards with me if I'd pissed him off. He, too, was taken to the same building that Lonnie and Margo had gone to.

I was alone. Well, Lonnie was there, but it was as if I was alone.

And then they came for me. Unlike my first time, I was led into an office. Interrogation was not top on my list of highly anticipated activities. So, color me surprised when the bigwig's opening gambit was to offer me tea and a seat on a cushioned chair.

"With sugar, please. Three spoonsful."

The translator from the boat, who was also, it would seem, Thandar's assistant, Wai, served it and carefully measured out the sugar. The cup was high-quality china, though I noticed the saucer was mismatched. I didn't mention it.

Our conversation began and continued for several minutes in that awkward manner you might expect from a captor trying to make small talk with his captive in a remote jungle enclave.

"Welcome. My name is General Thandar. You are Miss Ricky?"

"Uh-huh."

"You have a very nice boat."

"It's not mine. I'm just their dive guide."

"Are you a professional diver?"

"Yes, for almost ten years. I'm an instructor and dive guide."

"I have done some diving. I am open-water certified." He seemed impressed by his entry-level certification. "Myanmar has some of the best diving in the world."

"Yes, very nice, from what we have seen."

"Among the best?"

"Yes, yes, the best." I worried that was laying it on a bit too thick. Thandar, though, was probably used to people providing over-the-top praise.

"Very pleasing. Do you like your job?"

"I do. I get to travel and see the world."

"I have never traveled. When you live in paradise, you don't need to go elsewhere. I joined the military when I was fourteen. Lied about my age. I wanted to be part of the best military in Southeast Asia. How do you like Myanmar?"

"Beautiful, what I've seen of it."

"Yes, it is beautiful. We invest much money and people to make sure it stays that way. Are you being treated well?"

"I haven't been beaten. Yet."

Mistake.

It was a bad move on my part, but Wai smiled. I wasn't sure how to interpret that.

"Yet? You think we are savages who beat our prisoners?"

Crap. I think we just moved beyond the awkward small talk.

"No. I'm sorry. Bad joke."

"Yes, it is not wise to joke in your situation. We have limited resources out here. We don't have a hotel for our prisoners. Would you like your conditions to improve?"

Thandar rose, signaling for me to stay. He and Wai left the room, but I could hear them on the other side of the door, having a muffled conversation. I resisted my compulsion to start sorting through the papers on his desk. Given that they all appeared to be in Burmese, I figured there would be no value in doing so, and I also figured there was a camera pointed at me from somewhere in the room.

Thandar returned, without Wai.

"Your passport says your name is Riccarda Yamamoto. An Italian first name and a Japanese last name, but you don't look like either."

"Yeah, I get that a lot. I stopped trying to explain it when I found out that the guy who claimed to be my father wasn't."

"Yet you keep the last name. You perpetuate the deception."

"This was just a few months ago. I'm not sure yet how I should react. This is kind of personal."

"Are you a spy?"

"No, no, just a very confused young lady." It stung

a bit to say it, but I figured playing the young lady card might help with this guy. He'd certainly been checking me out as I had entered the room.

Wai returned to the room and leaned in to whisper to Thandar, who raised his eyebrows but said nothing. Wai stepped back and stood at attention just to my right.

"What is your true heritage, if not Japanese?"

"Nobody knows. I'm not sure who I am anymore."

"Go on."

Suddenly, it seemed like my captor was about to become my latest therapist.

"Nothing. Just a bad joke. A really bad joke."

Like one of those cruel jokes that life throws at you at the worst possible time. I thought nothing could be worse than the shitstorms of the previous two years, but 2016 was putting them to shame.

Thandar stared at me. Wai was prodding me. I guess I'd zoned out a bit. I had a feeling that afternoon was going to keep popping up in my head for a long while.

"Sorry, I'm still processing. Sort of zoned out. This is all quite stressful and unexpected. What was your question?"

The interrogation continued. Why were we in Myanmar waters? What was the nature of our research? What route had we taken? Had we been in contact with any other boats? What did Lonnie's research show? Why did I get hosed down before boarding the *Powerballer?* Was Tao a spy? And then back to questions about my heritage and name.

Most of my answers pled ignorance. I didn't know. Lonnie had never shared. It was all above my head. I just did the sampling. And I swore that my name really was Yamamoto.

Although I wasn't about to tell him this, I was strongly considering changing it.

30

WHERE THE HELL ARE WE?

THAT SORT OF *mental detonation that my dad's nonpater-nity announcement had provoked was not something I was prepared to discuss or handle without a plan. That was one of the positive things that had come out of working with my therapist.* Therapists *would be more accurate—over the years, I'd bailed on a few before one stuck. Until she didn't. But some things they had told me had made sense. I needed to avoid reacting with-out thinking about it first. And as each of them had tried to make clear to me, I needed to get in touch with my emotions.*

Boy, did I ever get in touch with them as soon as I had hung up.

It had been a too-cold Egypt night. I'd had to dig out a pair of climbing leggings and my only pair of socks. I'd been jittery even before making the call and should have thought twice. But if I had considered the pos-sibility that a serious conversation with my dad would aggravate me, I never would have made the call. Not that night, for sure.

If I'd known Sumo was going to drop a shit bomb on me, I definitely wouldn't have called that night. Not any night. Not in this lifetime.

But I had. And he had. And now I had a lot of feelings to work through.

Trey, my landlord—and I use that term loosely since he didn't charge rent and let me slowly drain his wine collection—had left behind a garage filled with beautiful rides, including a fifteen- or twenty-thousand-dollar motorcycle. In addition to a variety of his possessions I'd managed to break, the motorcycle was totally trashed during a mad dash to escape some goons who had thought I knew something they wanted to know. Actually, it survived the mad dash in very good condition—most of the damage occurred when the goons drove over it with their truck. Trey had gone radio silent ever since the authorities had raided the house and found some very illegal, high-tech equipment used for hacking, so I had no guidance on what to do with the carcass. But the motorcycle seemed—at least to me—to be clearly ready for the junk pile.

It seemed like the perfect target for an emotional outlet.

The tailpipe was already folded like origami. I merely added a few more dents. I did my finest work on the gas tank. And the gauges.

After adding my enhancements to the trashed bike and managing to destroy most of the bat, I returned to Trey's abandoned futuristic home, grabbed a pad of paper, and made notes. Questions, predicted responses, my retorts. Otherwise, I'd just resort to screaming and swearing. Then I'd start stammering. Again. Just like after the day Mom had chased Dad—not Dad—naked through a group of my friends, swinging a Ping-Pong paddle.

I still had the notes and still hadn't made the call.

෴

My brain checked in and out as the questions came. Thandar was picking at scabs, probably unintentionally, that I preferred to keep. Ultimately, he dismissed me with a frustrated wave of his hand.

Wai led me directly back to the cage, where I found that the others had been returned. We shared our experiences and assessment of Thandar and the other interrogators. Margo thought Wai was kind of creepy. He seemed to spend a lot of time in the shadows, watching us. Everyone agreed that Thandar was rather random in his inquisition. Captain Rich wanted to know when the thumbscrews would come out.

Rather than thumbscrews, we were treated rather fairly for captives. By that, I mean none of us bore open wounds or broken bones from the interrogations. We all reported, in varying degrees, being allowed to wash up, being provided better food than in our cage, and being accorded a degree of respect that we didn't see when we were confined. After discovering my sweet tooth, Thandar had Wai get me a second helping of coconut cake. It might have sweetened my disposition, but only slightly, and it did nothing to loosen my tongue. I had already told him everything I knew.

Wai came by frequently, checking on our needs. Sometimes he made small talk. His English was even better than Thandar's.

"Duke University. Political science with a public policy minor. I hope to go into politics. Gen. Thandar has several American university graduates. Texas A&M. UCLA. Michigan—go blue!"

Clearly, Thandar had his own unique methods and an interesting circle around him. Wai also had a darker side. "You know it was me who shot your man on the boat?" he asked me.

I didn't allow him the pleasure of answering. I looked away and hummed. Ignoring him had the right effect but an unpleasant outcome. He turned my head so that I faced him, then spit in my face before leaving.

At least that settled that question. No one seemed to feel a need to discuss it after he left.

Dinner that night was some form of stew. Vegetarian. I'm not sure if that was at Margo's request or if meat was just a rarity here in the jungle.

Day two was, essentially, a repeat of day one. The questions dug deeper into details. Thandar's agenda, though, remained unclear. Wai hovered around even more.

It seemed like we could be coming to a point where the issues might be resolved. Lonnie was very confident that we'd established our case well. The boat had been searched, even torn apart in some places, yet it didn't seem like they had found the weapons. Lonnie had been taken down to review the lab with them, and his preliminary reports were given to Thandar. That might be a sticking point.

Day three took a turn for the worse.

I was brought down to the boat to discuss my role in collection. The sled had been brought back to the boat after we'd been captured, so I demonstrated, on dry land, how I did my sampling. Then I was returned to Thandar.

"Why were you taking radioactive samples?"

"I think you have incorrect information. We were testing for chemical contamination. Dangerous for sea life or people who eat fish or plants contaminated with the chemicals."

"And radiation." He seemed quite clear on that. "We have studied the laboratory equipment. We have read the logs. And we've reviewed the medical kit. Your team was monitoring radiation. It makes no sense to lie."

And just like that, I realized I didn't really know what Captain Rich knew. In fact, I didn't really know Captain Rich all that well. Was he really that clueless?

Crap! Is there anyone left that I can trust?

31

NO SHIT

WHEN I RETURNED, it was Margo and Lonnie's turn. Together. They passed me on their way to Thandar. I didn't have a chance to confront them about any radio-activity, but I wouldn't have put it past them to have put me at risk without warning.

Captain Rich and I had spent the past three hours being interrogated, although in a relatively polite way— not what I expected from a totalitarian regime known for slavery and murder. And certainly not from one that suspected us of spying.

Or at least, that's what he told me about his side of things.

They felt that I was feigning ignorance, but as too often was the case, I was truly ignorant. Other than poor navigation, I had no idea what we had done to warrant this attention.

But what if Captain Rich was somehow directly involved? I'd only known him for less than a year. And what I knew was the stories he repeated, time and time again, about his captaining and mercenary exploits.

Fuck!

"OK, there's more going on here than just a lumber camp, right?" I was trying to figure out the purpose of the camp in the middle of nowhere. I'd seen streams of men going back and forth, muddy or covered with dust, their tools packed into two-wheel wagons towed by water buffalo. "We've seen bundles and those cubes wrapped in plastic. Where are they going? Small boats? The barges?"

We'd been so busy talking about how to get out of there that we hadn't really discussed why, of all places, that was where they'd brought us.

"Two things I can see. They're mining some sort of minerals or precious stones, and obviously, they're harvesting teak. The teak is going down the river. The mine output is going into some storage sheds. But yeah, it's got to be leaving here somehow. They also seem to be collecting goods from locals. I see civilians going into buildings and coming out with bags or cardboard boxes. I doubt either is legit." Captain Rich had leaned in to whisper. "Plus, I think Lonnie is passing information to the general."

"Thandar? What could Lonnie possibly have that would be of interest to him? And what information? They have everything we had on the boat."

Captain Rich kept whispering. "Did you and Thandar talk about shotguns?"

"No, why?"

"He asked me where the shotguns were. He laughed

when I said there was only one. Like he was expecting us to have more."

"But we didn't. Lonnie knew that. Margo knew that. I knew it." And then I realized what Captain Rich was thinking. "Unless Thandar was expecting them from Lonnie before you delivered the bad news about only one shotgun. Lonnie was certainly bent out of shape about them."

I was liking Lonnie less and less by the minute. But Thandar had never asked *me* about them.

Is Captain Rich making this up?

"Uh." Captain Rich had that toddler-caught-with-his-hand-in-the-cookie-jar look. "My brain went in an entirely different direction. I was thinking that my gun connection might have turned us in to Thandar back when I gave him the original list. It sort of makes sense—he makes a profit off the gun sales to me, then gets a bonus from Thandar for finking on us, maybe gets the weapons back to resell. But it doesn't really hold. How would he have known to tell Thandar rather than any of the other possible officers in the navy? Your idea might be right. It's simpler."

"For sure, but we can't rule out your gun guy."

Was Captain Rich the problem here? Navigation? Backstabbing supplier? Special weapons on Lonnie's dime?

Crud.

"Did Thandar ask you anything about radioactive samples?" I had thought it was just a random, crazy question, but . . .

"Yeah, he did. Told him to sod off, that we were

doing scientific testing for pollution. Not radiation. There's more: earlier today, Lonnie took a crap in the bucket and then checked it out."

Ugh.

There were so many reasons I didn't like the direction that this conversation was going.

"Like, picked it up and looked at it?" I instantly regretted even conjuring up that image.

"No, but he looked in the bucket for a minute and poked it with a stick . . . and then I think he signaled the guard. Did you notice that they took the bucket away and gave us a new one?"

"Yeah, but that's just good hygiene. Maybe he saw something wrong with his, you know, his sh . . . stool." This conversation was going in entirely the wrong direction. Well beyond my comfort zone.

"Kak. We call it kak."

"Yeah, like that's a big improvement. As if it's more polite than *shit* or *stool*."

Captain Rich shrugged. "I say *kak* in mixed company. Anyway, what did they do with the last bucket?"

"Waited until it was almost overflowing." That memory was one I was hoping to scrub from my brain. Small chance of that now.

"And then?"

"They dumped it outside of our cage. Like five feet away."

"Bingo. They took this one away. You think they are suddenly all about hygiene? In the direction of the main buildings? I knew a guy who swore he passed intel by swallowing micro SD cards—you know, those ones in cameras—and then shit them out a few days later. I think that's what Lonnie did. Maybe he's passing on the lab results, and we really *were* testing for radioactivity."

"You're shitting me."

"This isn't a joking matter." Captain Rich gave me the stern teacher look that he gave to flippant dive students.

"You have to admit, though, that it was a good joke."

Activity around the camp had been nonstop and occurring in multiple locations. A mix of soldiers and, judging by their gaunt condition and tattered clothes, prisoners formed ant lines carrying or pushing various containers—buckets, boxes, sacks, wheelbarrows, carts, even a couple of boar suspended on a shoulder yoke between two men—into and out of the camp.

Few, if any, looked our way. Lonnie and Captain Rich, on the other hand, seemed to be doing nothing but watching them.

32

NOTHING I WOULD
WORRY ABOUT

"What the hell is the deal with you and Lonnie?"

It was dark. Our only guard was asleep. Lonnie had been taken away more than an hour ago for a late-night conversation with Thandar. And Captain Rich was sitting on Margo's chest. She probably would have complained that she couldn't breathe, but I'm pretty sure she was too compressed to even do that.

"You're going to kill her." I was getting quite nervous. I'd seen the results of chest compression on two kids we'd treated back when I was an EMT in Hawaii. The sand cave they were digging had collapsed on them. There couldn't have been more than a one-minute difference in the amount of time they were under before we pulled them out. The first survived with no residual effects. The other was dead at the scene. I was betting Margo was closer to the latter.

She was close to losing consciousness. I tried pushing him to let her up. But he was like a rock. A big, heavy, stubborn rock.

Finally, Captain Rich shifted so that his knees were on the ground and his shins were pressing heavily on her upper arms, but at least she could suck in air. At first, there was no reaction, and I was going to freak, but suddenly, she started to suck air. Rapidly. Maniacally. All the while she glared at Captain Rich. He didn't seem to care.

"I'll give you a minute to catch your breath. In case you forgot the question, it was, 'What the hell is the deal with you and Lonnie?'"

Eventually, her breathing returned to normal, but she continued to stare him down. And he continued to ask the question, again and again. I noticed he was beginning to shift his weight back toward her chest. She noticed as well.

"He's trying to talk our way out of here. We have more money than the general could dream of. Lonnie is convinced he can find the right price."

∽

"Get . . . off . . . my . . . chest!"

For somebody who had been ambushed minutes after returning from the general's office, or whatever he called it, Lonnie had shown surprising fortitude during Captain Rich's primitive interrogation. Our guard had called over two others. It appeared they were making cash bets on the tussle. Straight up, I'd have to take Captain Rich on that bet.

Margo watched but made no move to stop Captain Rich—not that she had a chance of doing so.

Lonnie had been taken to the point of unconsciousness twice, yet he continued to insist there would be no conversation until he was released. It didn't look like the third time would be any different. Captain Rich finally wiggled off. He was almost as wrung out as Lonnie. He twisted himself into a lotus position and began taking some healing breaths. Lonnie just lay on his side and panted.

"OK, I'm off. Talk."

"Jesus, you're an . . . asshole." His wheezing made it difficult to talk and harder for us to understand, so he took another minute to catch his breath. "I'm working with General Thandar to come up with a plan for our release. OK? But I've got a backup. At least one of the guards is paying close attention. And Wai seems to be very focused on being our friend. If we can't get a full release, I'm willing to bet that we can get an assist in escaping. At least I'm trying."

"Escape? Why would we need to do that? This was a simple and stupid navigation error. Isn't this why we have diplomats?" This was getting more complicated. I had been hoping for simple.

"They're not buying the story. They've been going over the *Powerballer* with a fine-tooth comb. They found the weapons. Or at least most of them. They might have missed a stash or two. They think we're spies. And they say we were a mile inside their border." Lonnie was sticking with the calibration-error theory.

"That's not right. I caught a minor error before the shakedown cruise, and I recalibrated it when we were at the dock. It was spot on."

Lonnie smiled, but he looked in any direction but at Captain Rich. "Well, then something happened when you were operating it. Or your reset didn't work. You must have broken the system."

"No way." Captain Rich pushed himself out of his seated position. "I've dealt with GPS in jungles and the open sea. When I do it right, it stays right. I don't set it up wrong, and I don't mess with equipment. I say you were the one." His finger jabs were coming close to Lonnie's face. "You had plenty of opportunities during your night watch. You just had to have more data, didn't you?"

"This is going nowhere." Lonnie was getting his cockiness back. "There's another complication. It might be our saving grace, or it might be a giant problem. In case you haven't noticed yet, Thandar is rogue. This operation, or at least parts of it, no way are they on the books. He's got mercenaries mixed in with uniformed non-comms and prisoners. He's got two different storage facilities. One out of four of the canisters I've seen is unmarked. No way any embassy gets involved or even hears about this. Thandar is judge, jury, and executioner. And he's certainly not going to let anybody else hear about this operation."

Shit.

That got everyone's attention.

"OK. Coming clean. Trust me, we didn't expect this. But we did leave out some details. Part of our research was looking for traces of uranium mining, processing—that kind of shit."

Lonnie was slowly recovering. His voice was shaky, but he seemed to want to talk. Captain Rich backed off a bit to give him room. I couldn't see well enough in the dark, but I imagined the forehead vein was throbbing at maximum levels.

"The Andaman Sea had been surveyed before, but we couldn't identify the source of the uranium, which was likely either the mine or the processing plant. We'd be happy to find either. We were tasked with finding signs of where the pollution had entered the water. Period. That was the sanctioned mission. Christ, I think you broke some ribs."

Margo finally joined in. "Water samples, core samples. We were getting a clear picture of the source by looking at what other elements were coming down at the same time. That's Lonnie's area of expertise."

Now it was me that began to crowd our two clients. "So, if the samples were radioactive, that means I was diving in radioactive water? I thought Thandar was just baiting me."

"Small, trace quantities. Nothing I would worry about." Lonnie's lack of concern for the health and safety of his crew, and arrogant dismissal of my concerns, was becoming increasingly aggravating.

"Of course not. You were in the boat. Would I set off a Geiger counter right now?"

"You're being overly dramatic, Ricky. Our projections were that your exposure would probably be below safety thresholds. We wouldn't have done this if you were going to get radiation poisoning."

Margo had an arrogant sneer. I was heading for a fight before I even thought to stand up. Captain Rich had grabbed hold of my hair, so I was unable to reach her.

"Yeah, because you've been so transparent up to this point. So, you don't really know. Did you calculate my exposure after you tested the samples? Did you implement processes to reduce the risk of handling it?" I felt a little silly challenging her with my head tilted back, but Captain Rich wasn't letting go.

"There was too much to do. We were closing in on identifying the source. That was our leverage with Thandar. We had Tao hose you off better. Besides, at that point, it fell into the bucket of 'it is what it is.' I mean, I would have thought you would consider this your patriotic duty. This uranium could be destined for a terrorist bomb."

"If I'd been asked . . ." I stopped myself, distracted by a very patriotic vision of smashing her in the face. Captain Rich had now grabbed the waistband of my shorts and pulled me back.

"Wait." Things began to click. "You said you were tasked. So, this is government sanctioned. You're spooks. CIA." I was sort of shooting in the dark, and it sounded like a TV show, but I saw Margo twitch.

All Captain Rich said was, "Spot on."

I'd bet he'd already figured it out. I wondered when he had been planning on letting me in on the secret.

"That's absurd. We're rich. We don't work for anyone." I have to admit that the way it came out of Margo's mouth, it sounded quite sincere and ridiculously obvious.

"Yeah, great cover story. Don't you think the news article in your stateroom was a bit much? Clumsy CIA cover." There had been red flags, and I had missed them.

I'd had some experiences with government agencies, and I hadn't yet found one that I trusted.

Everyone went quiet.

"That's really not fair. You think you're so good at spotting the CIA?" Margo actually snorted as she laughed. "We're not like the FBI. We know your history with them, but you shouldn't judge us based on their behavior. I've read the psych profile, and it's amateurish but not far off the mark. Even more amateurish was their fieldwork. But they did catch him."

"After I found him!"

"Or he found you. A few minutes later and you might have been victim number four."

"Number eleven if you count the other states. And that was the first time I had to deal with them. I caught the next guy and delivered him hog-tied to the feds."

"I stand corrected." She did the laughing snort again.

I wasn't sure what she had to laugh about—Margo had given up any hope of pretense and certainly, given that we were caged in a jungle compound, had not yet displayed great fieldwork. Captain Rich let go of my hair and waistband. That was way too easy.

"You had researched my history before you hired me, yes? You lied about our task. You exposed me to radiation. You put us in the hands of a rogue general. Without giving us a chance to say a patriotic yes or a forget-you-not."

At some point, I'd made enough contact that Margo was on her butt on the ground. This could have been the moment where Captain Rich acted like the adult in the room and stopped me, but a glance confirmed that he was quite content with watching the drama play out. He did, however, tap me on the leg.

"You know, your proclivity for violence is really ramping up. If you don't clean it up, you might find yourself having trouble getting another job as a divemaster. Even with my glowing recommendation."

"That?" I glared at him. "That's what you worry about at a time like this?" There was a fair chance that I was about to launch myself at him in a feral rage.

Lonnie, on the other hand, had backed away to the farthest and darkest corner of the cage. It was also, by coincidence, the closest spot to the dumping ground for our toilet bucket, so no one seemed inspired to go get him.

Margo pushed herself up into a seated position, took a deep breath, and pulled out the ace up her sleeve. Delivered with that irritating laughing snort.

"Your mother thought you would be great for the mission."

33

GET A DOG

"My mom?"

Pascal didn't have to be with us to have a presence and an influence over my thinking. Ever the philosopher, he once told me—long before these last two revelations—"If you want a trusting relationship, get a dog." If I managed to get out of this, I might very well go that route.

We'd been competitors back in the waters of Palau but had formed a strong friendship on land. Despite legal troubles back home in France, which until recently had him keeping a low profile in backwater countries, he was always willing to step up when I needed it. He had been privy to my trust issues. Cynicism was a trait we shared, though I had him beat by a country mile. True, his brother had thrown him under the bus and framed him in a drug deal to avoid jail time, but I had a far greater history of betrayal—twenty-nine years of it, now that the fact that one of them wasn't my parent had come out. I ranked that fracture of our relationship a little bit ahead of the time they had asked a serial killer called the Surf Slayer to give me a ride home. But this latest revelation, sending me on a suicide mission that could end with my skin peeling off and tumors crowding my belly, might have leaped to the number-one slot.

It would have been good to have him here, except I'd already pulled him into two bad situations that led to him fleeing the country, first Palau and then Egypt. And I guess it was my fault he'd ended up getting shot with a speargun. No need to have him irradiated as well.

Thanks, Mom.

"What about my mom?"

"Life is full of amazing coincidences. When Captain Rich suggested you be part of the team"—she glanced in his direction, and I noticed him wince, though mainly he seemed to have drifted off into a quiet haze—"I pinged Ingvold and took a sounding on her thoughts. She was quite enthusiastic and felt it would be a good change of pace for you. She was concerned that your divemaster duties were putting you at risk."

"As opposed to rogue generals and radiation poisoning?"

"Neither of those was supposed to happen. And in any case, you have perfect deniability. You had no clue what we were up to. You could pass a polygraph or even torture. Plausible deniability. You were just window-dressing. With badass fighting skills if needed. We had you covered."

Captain Rich added, "Except that you intended for us to get captured."

"This was always intended to be covert, with a very small number of people clued in."

"OK, covertly get captured. That's just another twist of the truth." Captain Rich looked like he was in the sitting-on-the-chest mood again. He loomed over Margo. "Either someone messed with the navigation and placed us inside territorial waters, or—and I can't believe I didn't see this earlier—our capture was prearranged. You wanted us to get here. You wanted to get face to face with Thandar."

"That's a fantasy." Margo pushed herself up into a standing position, but she was still a foot shorter and had to crane her neck to look Captain Rich in the eyes. "You're just making that up. We had one mission: Find the source and give our diplomats the ammunition they needed to tighten the screws on the current government to stop mining and reselling uranium to bad actors. You saw that. You saw what we were gathering."

"Bull. Lonnie passed—and I mean that in multiple ways—something to the general. He had to have swallowed it two or three days ago, before we were captured. I saw him inspecting his shit." Captain Rich had even more experience with government agencies and liars than I did. He was picking up the pieces faster.

Margo shifted her attention from Captain Rich to Lonnie. I shifted mine to Margo.

"Wait. This needs to slow down. How the hell do you know my mother?"

"We traveled in some of the same circles."

"Like James Bond circles?" I did not like the direction this was going.

"Organic gardening. I was even a guest on her cable TV show. What was it called? *Grow Organically?*"

"*GroGantic*. 'Grow gigantic produce the natural way, with your host, Ingvold Lindelöf.' Yeah, I have the whole intro memorized. You know, that wasn't her real last name. It was Elg—that means 'moose' in Swedish. She thought a name that translated to 'laurel leaves' would be more appropriate. Besides, I think she was still legally a Yamamoto at that point." At the mention of Sumo's name, my eyes glazed over as I spaced out, rehashing my own history with that name. Perhaps, when this was all done, I'd change mine to something more appropriate, like *Uh-oh*. Maybe *Whoops*?

My thoughts were interrupted. Suddenly, Lonnie was the center of attention.

"Let go of my arm!"

Margo had Lonnie's left arm twisted behind his back at an angle that would have made a yoga instructor proud. He was facedown, dangerously close to our bathroom bucket, and her knee was in the small of his back.

"Tell me, now!"

"He's wrong. I was just checking my stool for blood."

"Try again."

"Those thugs hit me hard from behind as they were moving us along the deck. You saw it. I've been checking my piss and shit every time to make sure I don't have an internal injury. Between you and Rich, I think there's a good chance that I now do have at least one."

Captain Rich moved forward, looking to add to Lonnie's pain.

Lonnie stared directly at him. "Look, now is not the time for violence. When we need you to go into mercenary mode, we'll let you know."

"I never said anything about mercenary." He looked at me, but I just shrugged. It hadn't come from me.

Margo sighed. There are moments when you have to decide whether it's best to continue a lie, come up with a new lie, or offer the truth. "We knew who and what you were when we hired you. It's not like your second profession is a state secret."

"I'm a boat captain. That's my only profession."

"Bullshit." Lonnie was suddenly full of bluster, but it was a poor choice of words, given that he was only minutes removed from having his head shoved into a bucket of possibly radioactive human waste. I paused for a microsecond to think of the movie that could result from that scenario. Lonnie pushed forward. "Private security. Security consulting. Incident relief. I've seen the write-ups. You're good. That's why we hired you. Our ace in the hole. A back-pocket winner. The unforeseen change of tide."

Captain Rich moved to pin him down again.

"OK, OK, wait. Getting carried away. Back off, Mongo."

Lonnie had that deer-in-the-headlights look that he'd gotten when Captain Rich had first been released from his bindings. The comment had exactly the opposite of the intended effect.

"Wait a minute . . . was Tao a mercenary?" Captain Rich now had Lonnie pinned with one knee just under his rib cage. He released it a bit to let Lonnie catch his breath and reply. "How did I miss this?"

"Tao was a man of many talents. We hired him for all of them. Of course he had military skills. Mandatory service in Thailand."

We'd taken so many things for granted. He had known his way around a rifle and had been as toned as a cheetah. But that would describe most Thai men. And Thai fighting monks. He had handled the boat like a pro, but that hadn't immediately registered as military-trained mercenary skills. The cooking skills hadn't fit with that picture, either, but in retrospect, his interest in learning scuba certainly had. The fact was, I hadn't spent much time getting to know him. Although some of that was on him. He had been reserved unless he had been trying to learn.

"Did you tell him he might need to use his mercenary skills? That you'd be taking him into risky waters?"

"Nobody had to tell him anything. He was a Buddhist monk warrior. Muay Thai. They don't wait for orders. They act when they see the need."

Captain Rich wasn't letting this go. "Why did Tao run?"

"Stupid. He was smitten with Ricky and ran to protect her."

Captain Rich wasn't buying the bullshit. "Or he was running to protect something else. Like his own ass. Or your lab."

"You're fantasizing. It was a simple crush and a reckless attempt to be a knight in shining armor."

Lonnie never saw the punch coming.

34

WHERE THE HELL ARE WE?

WAI CAME TO us in the night. Inside the cage.

He roused Lonnie first. Despite what might have been a concussion, he stirred quickly. Captain Rich was a notoriously light sleeper, and he had been aware of Wai's entry before he even got to Lonnie. He tapped me with his toe. Margo was the last to wake.

Our guard was gone. The cage door was ajar. And Wai was whispering to Lonnie.

Lonnie reluctantly pulled Captain Rich in. I shifted over quickly. Any discussion was going to involve, at the very least, the two of us.

"Wai is our way out of here. Thandar has no need for us, and that usually doesn't turn out well. Wai thinks that tomorrow might be a bad day for us unless we leave now."

"And Wai is suddenly our friend because . . . ?"

Captain Rich nodded at me as I asked. I'm sure he had the same question. I was just faster.

"Thandar is crazy. He's expanded his dealings to

include meth and opium he buys from the locals. He's using his own product. A lot. I want to go back to the States. I can make it happen." Wai's English seemed even better under pressure.

"Product?" That was the first I'd heard of this.

"Opium." He looked at his feet to avoid looking any of us in the eyes. "Heroin. He has a refinery. Crystal meth, he just distributes. We should go now."

I wasn't buying it. Seemed like an invitation to walk out right into a firing squad. But staying bore its own risks. This could go several ways, and none was attractive. This was one of those mental coin-toss moments. Heads go, tails stay. I imagined the coin spinning in the air and landing. I closed my eyes before it hit the ground, though given that it was all in my head, that didn't change matters. It was heads.

Crap!

"Guard change is in three hours. I knocked out and tied up Moe—your current guard."

"Moe?" I would have giggled if I hadn't feared for my life at that very moment.

"Was a Burmese name long before *The Three Stooges*. Not everything was invented in America."

"Can we stay on point?" Captain Rich tensed. His breathing was a dead giveaway that we were in unfamiliar territory. "Wai, what's your plan? And what's in it for you?"

"We'll have a three-hour head start if we leave now. I have to leave, even if you stay. Thandar will suspect me when they find the guard. He doesn't need proof to execute someone. Suspicion is more than enough."

Wai seemed sincere, but it could be I was reading more into his slight North Carolina accent than it deserved. There was something about Duke men that made me nervous.

Lonnie broke the silence. "It's never going to get any better than this. Even if we end up being captured by the actual Myanmar Army, our chances of survival and a diplomatic solution are better than with Thandar. Margo and I say we go. Now." He glanced at her to make sure he had her support, and she nodded. "With Wai's help, and your"—he looked at Captain Rich— "skills, we can get back to Thailand in three days."

"I'd like to point out that you hired me to be the captain. If you had wanted to hire a security specialist, you would have paid the security specialist fee, which is three times that of a captain."

"Agreed. We'll pay you three times. Now help us."

"Problem is"—Captain Rich moved closer to Lonnie, the veins bulging in places I didn't even know existed—"you've left security specialist territory way behind. That was what I got paid to help you avoid situations like this. *Avoid*. Now you're into extraction-services territory. That's a much bigger nut to crack. Ten times my captain's wage. One hundred forty thousand dollars a month."

"You're crazy."

"No, far from it. And believe it or not, along with Wai, I'm your best hope." He pointed at me. "She's your next-best hope, and you're now paying her five times her rate. Retroactive. For both of us. Back to the day we set sail."

"This is blackmail. You're bleeding me."

"It's not even your bloody money. Your Uncle Sam won't even notice the pinch. So should we stay or should we go?"

"Deal." Lonnie looked broken. "Let's get out of here."

"Excellent." Captain Rich gave him that hard look. "By the way, the last guy who crossed me, he didn't make it back."

"You abandoned him?"

"Nah, I killed him myself."

We slipped out of the cage and headed west. Lonnie let Captain Rich go ahead of him.

∽

"Isn't there about a thousand miles of Myanmar territory to the west?" Captain Rich knew his geography, and he had a scarily accurate internal compass. He was only trusting Wai so far. But if he was going to turn on us, it seemed that would have been within a few minutes of leaving the compound.

"Yes, but the Irrawaddy River is to the west, and it's the most logical way to quickly get out of the country."

"Isn't it also the most patrolled and visible way out?"

"Yes. That's why we're not going to take it."

"Then we're going west because . . . ?"

Captain Rich pulled up to a stop. I was following closely and bumped into him, starting a chain reaction, with Margo hitting me. Lonnie was lagging so far behind he avoided the whole mess. "I'm not going anywhere until we sort this out."

"Because . . ." Wai sighed as if dealing with an insolent child. "Thandar will expect that. We'll turn back when we get to the next ridge. It's hard rock. They'll lose our tracks. Then we head east."

"Still a long way." Captain Rich wasn't buying it.

"There's a vehicle waiting for us."

How the heck?

"But all the mountain passes have security stops." I guessed Captain Rich was taking some aspects of this run to freedom at face value.

"We'll bypass them."

"How?"

Wai looked at Margo, who was grinning from ear to ear. All she said was, "I know a guy who sells balloons."

Oh, great. And cotton candy?

"OK, odd, but one last question." Each answer was leaving me more confused.

"Shoot."

"Where the hell are we?"

35

TRUST, BUT VERIFY

WAI HAD PUT a lot of thought into this. He had printed maps and GPS directions. He had water and energy bars for all. He had an answer for every question and a plan for every concern.

Captain Rich, though, had the emergency-extraction wisdom. He led us in a variety of directions, sometimes looping back, to make sure we couldn't be followed. We chose where we stepped carefully, often detouring to hard rock instead of loose trail. We avoided breaking twigs. I suspect that Captain Rich would have been happier if we'd collected the mosquitoes as we slapped them and put them in our pockets, lest they be a beacon pointing in our direction.

Margo and Lonnie kept to themselves and deferred to the captain and Wai. We were two hours in before we took our first break. Ninety minutes later, we took another. In all that time, we heard no alarms, no shouting, no crashing of trees as if a mad pursuit was taking place. It was half an hour past the changing of the guards, and we seemed to be in the clear for the time being.

After about ten miles of hiking—check that, it was more like twenty the way we kept changing directions, but ten as the crow flies—we came to a hardtop, four-wheel-drive SUV. A fancy one, though—a Suburban. Banged up, covered with mud, filled with bags of fertilizer, floor to ceiling. Spare tires and jerry cans on top.

"Voilà!" Wai was pleased with himself. I'll admit, I was pretty impressed.

"So, we dump the fertilizer here?"

"No. It stays. Camouflage for you." He opened the second-row door. The third-row seats were removed, and the second row folded down—plenty of room. The fertilizer, in thirty-two-pound bags, was packed along the side and the rear gate. It actually left a significant space. Maybe not for four adults, but significant.

"You expect us to fit in there?" Captain Rich was leading this line of questioning. I had no doubt that Margo, Lonnie, and I could fit in there with no problem.

"Dude, it's a Chevy Suburban. Used to be the property of the diplomatic corps. Biggest cargo space around. Even with those bags, you've got almost eighty square feet of space. I measured. It's almost forty inches wide. Wider than two coach seats on some planes. And you got eighty inches of length. Still beats coach. I gave you four extra bags, one for each butt. You're welcome."

"No, yeah, thank you. It's not that we're not pleased. We're just stunned at your resourcefulness. And you know—trust, but verify."

"I get it. Not a Range Rover. Get in. Be happy. Stay

quiet when I tell you. Anybody need a potty break?" He held up a box of tissues. Margo grabbed it and headed into the trees. I followed.

By the time we returned, Captain Rich was situated all the way in the back. Legs spread. It seemed like he had dibs on the space, but he soon explained the logic.

"We'd be crushed side by side. Instead, we do it like we're on the Olympic bobsled team. I'm biggest, so I'm in back. Ricky, you're next, with those long legs of yours."

"And small feet, an advantage for the people ahead of me."

"Yeah, as I was saying, you're next, scooted back up against me. I've pulled a bag up along the floor for your cushion. No hanky-panky, I promise. Then you pull up a bag for Margo's cushion. Finally, Lonnie, you're in the driver's position up front. Please refrain from simulating steering and making *vroom* sounds."

I have to admit, it made sense and gave us room to stretch out our legs and wiggle our arms. Wai finished repacking the back, sealing us in with several dozen heat-producing, smelly bags of rich, organic fertilizer. If the pile moved, Lonnie would bear the brunt. I was OK with that.

"Sorry, no seat belts. Hold on." Wai's muffled announcement was immediately followed by sharp acceleration and bucking as we headed down the rutted dirt road. Sure enough, the top bag slid backward and smacked Lonnie in the face.

Wai stopped and adjusted the pile. Lonnie's glasses took the brunt of the blow, and we were sure to get a few hours of grumbling as a result.

"Well," I offered as I wiggled around, looking for comfort, "isn't this special."

"By the way," whispered Captain Rich, "a vehicle loaded with fertilizer and jerry cans of gas . . . in South Africa, we call that the door-knocker special. Just saying. Remember Oklahoma City."

According to Wai, we started out near the Bago River, about 150 miles upriver from where it merged with the Irrawaddy, around a hundred miles from the Thai border. He kept up a running travelogue as we rumbled along the unmaintained back roads, although we could see nothing of what he was describing. He could have told us we were passing the Taj Mahal and we would have believed him. Time passed slowly.

"I was thinking."

"Me, too," Captain Rich quickly replied. "You go first."

"I was wondering if it was better to just let the whole left side of my body stay numb or if I should twist around and make the other side numb." I'd progressively lost feeling from my hip down to my feet over what seemed like the past hour.

"Twist. You don't want to stay numb for too long. Keep alternating every ten minutes. We can coordinate. When I pull up my left knee, you can do the same."

He was full of all sorts of good ideas. I tapped Margo's shoulder, but she had already bought into the idea. "Got it. Left knees, then right."

"Want to hear what I've been thinking?"

"Shoot."

"I think we're still heading west."

Crud.

Captain Rich began banging on the hard metal ceiling of the Suburban. "Hey, Wai! Hey."

Wai slowed the big beast down.

"We need a lavatory break back here. Pronto. It's Ricky, and she's not good at holding it."

True enough, though the numbness sort of masked my need to pee. But I was happy to take a break if it helped Captain Rich.

Wai agreed to pull off at the first minor clearing he could find. At the slow rate we were moving and the ruts he was bouncing through, he probably could have stopped in the middle of the dirt road. It's not like another vehicle would come bearing down on us. After moving some fertilizer bags and unfolding ourselves from our economy seating, Margo joined me as I headed off into the jungle, carrying the tissue box that we'd sort of taken ownership of. The others squeezed out to stretch their legs.

Captain Rich seemed to be in conference with Lonnie and Wai.

When we returned, Captain Rich had Lonnie in a bear hug, and it clearly wasn't one born of newfound camaraderie. Lonnie's feet dangled a good six inches off the ground.

"Tell her. Now."

"We're heading west right now. We have a plan. But we have to go west-northwest a few more miles to connect with the guy who can get us out."

"And . . ."

"And it involves taking a lighter-than-air balloon up into the mountains and over the ridge to Thailand."

"And . . ."

"And we know this will work because this was all planned out months ago to enable us to meet with Thandar and arrange a deal to resell some of his product. There's a guy waiting for us. No one is chasing us because Thandar wants us to make it back safely so that we can complete the transactions. He let us escape, and he's signed off on the plan. But we have to cross the border without officials knowing. So, we're taking the balloon." Lonnie paused, and Captain Rich squeezed him hard. "And, OK, yes, we are CIA," he gasped. "The *Powerballer* was our first payment. Untraceable by the time he's done with it."

"And the grand finale . . . ?" Captain Rich squeezed a bit harder but released enough for Lonnie to wheeze.

"We're working a side deal. Outside of our CIA remit."

Fuck me.

Lonnie looked defeated. Captain Rich dropped him to the ground and sat on him. Again. He shifted to give Lonnie a chance to breathe.

"The truth, the full story, and I let you breathe. A single lie and I'm back on you."

"We've known for years that Myanmar was mining and selling uranium. Mainly to China. The new regime has already made it clear they're going to stop both the mining and the sale of uranium. We were here to negotiate a deal to buy the uranium for the US. But it wasn't for processing or use. It was so that we could turn around and supply it to aligned nations. Enhance relations. Maintain control. And—big bonus—we keep it out of the hands of bad actors. But as you might imagine, our new administration didn't want this to be public. There are already messy political battles being waged regarding foreign access to uranium, and this would just be throwing gasoline on the fire. That's where you guys came in. And the seizure. Good cover story."

"And we weren't told any of this because . . ."

"Because the key to you providing the best cover story was if you believed it."

Captain Rich shifted his weight back onto Lonnie, held it there for a minute, and then backed off.

"And we didn't think you would go along with the plan if you knew all the details. The pirates, by the way, were not part of the plan."

Lonnie winced in anticipation of another Captain Rich attack, but the captain seemed content to let the story come out. "And the side deal?"

"Problem was that they had always been stealth, so there were no records of the mines, which created the opportunity for profiteering. Thandar has been skimming for years, without consideration for who they were or why they wanted it. Iran? Probably. Terrorists? Maybe. We were going to be taking it off the street. If we don't, Thandar and others like him will sell to the highest bidder, and that's usually someone we don't trust."

"So, to net this out: you are unheralded heroes." I know I was being snarky, but this bullshit had gone on long enough. "This is all about patriotism. Right? And we should be happy to have been asked to serve our respective countries in fighting terrorism?"

I had lost my patience. Captain Rich, having already heard this while we were off having a pee, was much calmer.

Margo had been quiet but was suddenly all self-righteous. "You have no idea. We've been undercover for four years. We devoted four years of our lives to building up this lottery story, four years without seeing family, away from our pets, making up lies as we went along."

"I am so sorry. I had no idea." I was taking my snark to levels never before seen—except, maybe, by my mom and Sumo. "It must have been torture, yeah—living in a mansion, driving nice cars, ordering the hired help around, drinking expensive wines, making sure you're seen at all the best restaurants, international trips on private jets to meet with fancy environmentalists . . ."

"The private masseuse was actually the best perk."

"Fuck you. Oh, I'm sorry, did I say that out loud?"

∽

The rest of the ride to meet up with the balloon guy was quiet. Between Captain Rich occasionally kicking Lonnie in a none-too-subtle reminder that he had plans to crush him and my threat to punch Margo in the throat, there wasn't much room for chatting.

Captain Rich and I had discussed it. We had no idea what we were walking into, but we also had little or no chance of getting home if the balloon story was more trickery. It was agreed that I'd shadow Margo and he'd shadow Lonnie. If anything seemed off, we'd take each of them down, for whatever that was worth. Wai was a wild card but actually seemed more trustworthy than either of the spooks.

We'd arranged a signal since we were still wedged into the fertilizer cocoon. Wai was to bang three times on the ceiling when we got there.

After a quick stop, which I hoped was the end of the road, we headed off again. Somehow, we were on roads that were even more rutted than before. We heard animated, one-sided conversation from the front but couldn't make out much of it. Wai was on the phone or radio. That left me uneasy. Captain Rich just shrugged when I twisted to look at him and raised my eyebrows. We were most definitely in "It is what it is" territory. All we could do was stay alert and be ready to react. Our only weapon, it appeared, would be bags of fertilizer, so I didn't give that strategy much of a chance, but it was what it was.

After somewhere around an hour, we stopped.

Some of the bags shifted, threatening Lonnie once again, as Wai pulled out a couple of the top bags by the side door. Light poured in and, with it, some badly needed fresh air. Multiple pairs of hands set to removing the bags and creating enough space for us to crawl out: Lonnie, then Margo, then me. Captain Rich had Wai clear out a few more bags before he squeezed out. Whatever our next steps might be, and at whatever risk, one thing was a definite plus: the place smelled like paradise.

"You smell like shit." We had a new player. I guessed it was the balloon salesman.

"Nice to see you, too, Fritz. It's been a while." Lonnie was grumpy but put on a good face.

"I didn't know if this day would even come. I was beginning to have my doubts. Five years."

There had to be more backstory to this. Hopefully we wouldn't have to sit on Fritz to get it.

"Fritz, meet the rest of the team. Of course, you know Wai." Margo was better with social skills than Lonnie. I'm sure she felt a bit uncomfortable with me standing behind her and holding one elbow. It didn't show.

Fritz didn't reply. He was eyeing Captain Rich.

As Lonnie had said, this plan had been long in the making. Perhaps it was best to let them roll it out without pushback, as unlike me as that might be.

"The tall, good-looking one standing behind Lonnie is Rich."

"Captain Rich," the tall, good-looking one corrected. He had both of Lonnie's arms pinned to his sides, so he chose to forego the traditional handshake.

"Captain Rich. That will be a bit of a problem. You see, I'm Captain Fritz from this point on, and those two names are close enough to cause confusion."

"Can we call you General Fritz?" At this rate, I figured we'd all have ranks before we made it home.

"Naw, too much responsibility. You can just call me Fritz. Nice to meet you, Captain, but I'm still in charge."

Captain Rich just nodded. It seemed to be a point he'd only push when he needed to.

Margo put on the charm. "The other one here, who I'd describe as tall and even better-looking, is Ricky. You've been briefed on both of them. I'd say they are relatively consistent in behavior and skill, as the briefing indicated, though they are both more prone to violent behavior to resolve disputes than we'd been led to believe."

Fritz replied with a smile. "I consider that a positive trait—depending, though, on who is involved in the dispute."

Margo removed her scarf and showed Fritz the bruising on her neck.

"Oh my, duly noted. Hi, Ricky. Nice to meet you." He held up his hands to suggest he came in peace. "I mean you no harm."

36

NO OFFENSE INTENDED, RICKY

FRITZ HAD A barn. And four water buffalo. "*Buba-lus bubalis*," explained Fritz. "I got them originally just because I loved their scientific name. They are my draft animals. They pull the trailer for the balloons and basket. And they help me in the field."

"You work the land?" I was not beyond being surprised by our motley crew. "Aren't you CIA? Like them?"

He shot Margo and then Lonnie a look.

Lonnie raised his hands by his sides with the palms up in that universal "Duh, I don't know" signal.

Margo sighed. "We made the call. It was better that they knew. No worries. They are in no position to expose the operation."

"Classic. Well, I guess we've moved past plan A." It was equally a statement and a question. "OK, yeah, I am with the agency. Do you have a problem with that?"

"Nope, just wanted to make sure we're clear on roles. We've had some transparency issues in the past few weeks."

"OK, yeah, so I'm a spook and you're not. But most of my time is spent developing and keeping my cover story. So, I farm, sell off my harvest, and a couple of days a week, I head down to Bagan and take people for balloon rides. I was inserted five years ago for just this kind of situation." He glared at Lonnie.

Margo jumped in. "It had to come out. They would have revolted and thrown a spanner in the works if we hadn't told them. They had different ideas about breaking out and leaving the country. And they weren't buying the cover story." It appeared she'd taken over the lead for Lonnie at this point.

"So, it's plan B." Fritz smiled. He seemed relieved.

"Yes, but let's keep plan C in our back pockets, just in case." Margo was definitely in control.

"OK. Stop," I said. "No side agreements, no euphemisms, no secret plans. What the hell is plan C?"

"Plan C . . ." Margo sighed. "Is always punch the biggest guy in the nose and run like hell."

"Roger that. That's usually my plan B. My plan A is to punch the biggest guy in the nose and stand my ground." Captain Rich seemed to be relaxing. He released Lonnie, who quickly moved away and stood behind Fritz.

I looked around at the bucolic scene. Besides the water buffalo, there were pigs, goats, and ducks. And past the fence, fields of soybean and, cut into terraces on the hillside, rice paddies. I didn't see any balloon operation.

"Is that pot in the greenhouse?" I recognized both the aroma and the leaves.

"Yeah, it seems like the best cover you can have in

Myanmar is being part of the black market. If you openly break the law, they seem to figure you're not doing anything underhanded on the side. Do you want a sample?"

"No, I get tested in my line of work. But thanks." That sounded lame as soon as it came out of my mouth— and it seemed like everyone was staring at me rather incredulously. It looked like even the water buffalo were eyeing me differently.

"So, are we going flying or not?" If I was going to look like a goody two-shoes, I might as well play the part. I had scanned the open area and couldn't figure out where this magical balloon was coming from.

"Yeah, we won't take off until after dark. Weather's looking good. I'd say it's a fifty-fifty chance that we have a smooth takeoff around twenty hundred hours. But we can start getting things ready. I need a volunteer to help me with the roof. Captain Rich, you're elected."

"That's not how volunteering works, but I'm all in."

"Great. There are four long ladders in the barn. Pull out two, and lean them up against the two corners on this side of the barn. Leave the other two inside. OK, ladies, let's get to work in the barn." Fritz then led us in the exact opposite direction.

The water buffalo perked up as we approached.

"Ricky? Margo? How are you with animals? I'd like to introduce you to Fred, Ethel, Lucy, and Ricky. No offense intended, Ricky. His name predates my hearing of your participation in this mission."

He opened the gate and led us into the pasture with the water buffalo, which were standing belly-deep in a large pond, grazing away on water plants and greens.

Water spilled out of their mouths each time they pulled their heads up.

"The boys are the ones with the five-foot-long horns. The other two are the girls. Ricky is the one with the longest horns."

Fritz turned and started walking toward the barn. The water buffalo followed, so Margo and I, after dodging Ricky's horns, took up the rear. Lonnie, avoiding the horns, slipped and fell in something that I was pretty sure wasn't mud. I caught a satisfied smile on Margo's face before she turned away.

The five of them, Fritz and the buffaloes, and the three of us stopped at the side of the barn. I recognized two sets of wooden racks mounted on the side of the barn as yokes, although far larger and more primitive than what I'd seen at county fairs in Hawaii. Then again, Fred, Ethel, Lucy, and beautiful Ricky were far larger and more primitive-appearing than any cows I'd seen yoked back in the day.

"OK, we're going to get these four yoked up. Margo, remind me, your family farm was . . ."

"Manhattan, and it was a window box. I'm not touching those animals."

"Ricky?"

"Never tried. Never wanted to. But tell me what to do, and I'll give it a try."

Lonnie stood by with his hands in his pockets. Fritz glanced his way, then turned back to Margo and me. "Perfect. You just need to assist. The beasts will do the rest."

It went surprisingly smoothly, the buffalo doing

most of the work, almost eager to get hooked up to the yoke. Margo kept her distance but provided some colorful commentary about the male buffalo. By the time we were done, Captain Rich had gotten the ladders up and ready to go. He'd found a pickax and dug holes for the feet of each ladder. I was sure he had a story about how he'd learned that trick. By this point, I still didn't know if I could trust him, but I knew I couldn't trust Lonnie or Margo, and the jury was still out on Fritz. So, for lack of a better alternative and for better or worse, I figured I'd hitch my yoke to Captain Rich.

"OK, now I need the two of you"—he nodded at Margo and me—"to get the balloon basket ready." It appeared he'd written off Lonnie as worthless. "It's buried in that haystack." He swept his hand toward a stack of hay that must have been fifteen feet tall and twenty feet wide. "I didn't want any prying eyes wondering why I had a fancy basket up here. One that doesn't look like the one I use in Bagan." He pointed to a trailer loaded with an oversize metal crate and a worn and battered wicker basket adorned with advertisements—in English—for massage parlors and bars.

I wandered over near the haystack and pulled a pitchfork from the wall.

"That's right. The basket is pretty much dead center in the stack. It rises from the ground to about three feet and is six feet wide. I built a frame around it, so once you get to it, it will be easy to pull out with the aid of the lads and lasses here."

The Ricardos and Mertzes, with each couple now

yoked, had returned to grazing on the floor of the barn and expressed no interest in their mention.

"Just poke into the stack with the pitchfork, and you'll find the basket. Then just start pulling the hay away and tossing it to the side."

Margo was gingerly testing a pitchfork for balance and heft, avoiding doing work as much as possible. I launched in, found the basket with my fourth probe, and began pulling. The hay fell away easily, and I got a good rhythm of pulling, scooping, and tossing to the side. Once we could see the basket, Margo tentatively joined in. By the time we'd cleared the basket, my clothes were soaked with sweat. Actually, they were Margo's clothes since that's what I'd been handed way back in the cell of the naval ship.

God, how long ago was that?

The water buffalo had patiently waited while we worked, occasionally moving as a team to get some of the hay we were pulling down, but once we had the basket cleared, it was their time to work.

Captain Rich had already set up the last two ladders inside the barn and was up in the hayloft on the other side of the building. Lonnie was nowhere to be seen. Apparently, the twenty-five-foot height had him anxious. I didn't see how he was going to handle the flight. Not my circus, not my monkey.

"Just hook up the two ropes from the basket to the beam that runs between Fred and Ethel. Then just give them a pat on the rump to get them moving. There's a weighted bag hanging from the rafters. Have them stop when the center of the basket is right underneath."

Easier said than done. The hooking-up part went fine, but the pat on the butt did nothing.

"Again, with enthusiasm!" Fritz was enjoying this.

So, I slapped harder. Ethel turned her head around and gave me the stink eye. But no forward movement.

"Try food. Go out to the pond and grab a handful of grass."

After two slips and almost a submersion, I was able to get a big, dripping handful of aromatic water grass. Standing in front of Fred and Ethel, I offered it up. That got movement, both of them pulling on the basket, stretching their necks to get the grass. I backed up, keeping about three feet of distance between their mouths and the grass. More stink eye from Ethel. Finally, we had the basket positioned just right. I handed the grass to Ethel, which earned me some stink eye from Fred.

Tough, Fred. You should have expressed your needs more clearly.

"Hey," called Fritz, "you had better get Fred some grass, too. You don't want to get on his bad side."

I trotted out to the pond and, with a bit more grace this time, got another handful.

The next task was pulling out the fuel tanks, which had been stacked on a sled behind the basket. This time, it was up to Ricky and Lucy. Fred and Ethel watched while a similar drama played out, but eventually, we were ready with a pile of large, unmarked metal cylinders.

"Just leave them there. Captain Rich and I will get them installed and hook up the hoses."

"Isn't there more?" I'd been in hot-air balloons before, and there's a humongous burner that sits in the center of the basket for heating the air in the balloon. I leaned against the basket to see if the burner was in there, and the whole thing slid at least two feet.

"What the . . ."

"Yeah, be careful. Can you pull it back to where it was?"

I gave it a pull, and it slid back. "We could have pulled this out without the buffalo."

"Yeah, but I would have missed out on the comic relief. Besides, you needed Lucy and Ricky for the sled with the hydrogen tanks. It weighs somewhere over eight hundred pounds. I figured you would get experience with the smaller load before I brought in the big guns."

"Hydrogen, like the *Hindenburg*?"

"Yeah, but safer technology."

"Bulletproof?"

"Pretty much so. It would take a lot of bullets to open up a big enough hole. It likely won't ignite. At that point, with a steady stream of bullets, I think you would be better off worrying that some of the bullets would hit you. But I've got that covered. I think."

"That's reassuring. Thanks, Mr. Happy Face."

37

ARE YOU LEGAL?

FRITZ TWITCHED, AND his attitude changed in a flash. He looked toward the road and muttered a few obscenities. Through the trees, I could see a cloud of dust heading our way.

"Captain Rich, kick over the two ladders to the hayloft. Stay up there, as well hidden as you can possibly be. Margo, Lonnie, and Ricky, get in the haystack under the plywood."

He was already outside and laying down the ladders before I could even ask a question.

"Wai! Are you legal?"

"Yeah, here with Thandar's permission. Not AWOL. Why? Who's coming?"

"Most of the folks who come to visit are chill and don't drive that fast. Could be *federales*. I'd say it's a fifty-fifty chance they're here just to shake me down. What's the status of the Suburban?"

"Registered in my name."

"That might stick out like a sore thumb. None of my

cars are registered. OK, let's shut the barn and head to your car. What's your cover story?"

Wai was ready. He pointed at the bags in the rear of the Suburban. "This is a gift that you're going to take down to friends whose land was scrubbed by the typhoon. I brought it here from the Bago basin, where my uncle has a farm. You paid well for it. Bago soil is the best in Myanmar. Your friends will be very, very lucky and appreciative to receive this."

By the time the plan had jelled, we'd squeezed into the haystack, and Fritz began pushing the basket back in front of where it had been. "Get into the basket. I'm pulling down some hay, so duck your heads." And with a few frantic jabs of the pitchfork, we were shrouded in darkness. We could hear, but we couldn't see.

Squatting in the basket, loose bits of hay shifting around, I was afraid I might sneeze. I squeezed my nose tight and hoped. We couldn't hear much from outside of the barn. Slamming of car doors. A lot of talking. More slamming of car doors.

Fritz finally opened the barn doors again and dug us out.

"No problem. Just a little shakedown. A friend of a friend of one of the members of our local police department saw Wai's fancy ride coming up the road. The police seldom pass up a chance to make a little extra cash. In this case, fertilizer. They took half the bags and half a pound of my best weed. No loss. In a few hours, we say goodbye to this place and everything on it. Besides, Bago fertilizer can't beat what I pull out of the pond each week."

Great. After days of no showers, that's where I ended up taking a bath.

"Let's chill for a bit. I'd hate to have a return visit."

"Speaking of chilling, I could use a ladder up here."

Oops. Captain Rich.

"So sorry about that, dude. But while you're up there, you can help me with some recon?"

Fritz jogged down to his house and returned with a pair of binoculars. He and I then replaced a ladder, and he carried the binocs up to Captain Rich. Just below the crossbeams, he slid open a panel in the side of the barn.

"OK, just stand here on the ladder and keep an eye on the road for dust, a vehicle, or even people on foot. Half hour at the most. Thanks, dude. Back soon."

"OK, let's get moving. They might be watching and wonder why Wai is still here. Or they may not care. I'd say it's fifty-fifty, so we'd better be ready to launch as soon as it's dark. Sunset is at eighteen thirty-five, so I suggest we lift off at nineteen hundred hours."

That gave us three hours.

We got the basket back and centered; attached lines, tanks, and ballast; loaded in supplies; and discussed some of the practicalities of launch and flying. I'd been in hot-air balloons, but hydrogen was a different beast.

We seemed to have halted. Everything that needed to be connected to the basket had been, and everything other than us that should be inside the basket was. And there we sat, in the middle of the barn.

"OK," said Fritz, "now it's time to huff and puff. Time's a wasting!"

Margo and I led the four buffalo out of the barn.

They were much more compliant this time. Once we were ten feet past the door, Fritz yelled for us to stop.

He'd clamored up a ladder to the roof with two long coils of rope and was busy tying them off to eyebolts under the peak of the roof. After a few test tugs, he tossed the coils down toward us, scaring Lonnie, who hadn't been paying attention. Neither Margo nor I had felt inclined to warn him.

"Hook one rope to Fred and Ethel and the other to Ricky and Lucy. Make the ropes the same lengths."

We did, and they were.

"Now lead them toward the pond."

It took no encouragement to get the big beasts to move, though they both stopped in their tracks as the rope to the roof tightened.

"Now slap them!"

I gave a slap that could be heard a hundred feet away, and Margo tried to do the same. It worked. The beasts leaned into their pull and began to tilt the entire roof off its supports. Bit by bit, they tore at the soil with their hooves and slowly dragged the roof to a vertical position. The vertical walls of the now open-air barn now stood something like fifty feet on one side.

"And . . . stop!"

We repeated the process on the other side, moving even more quickly that time. When we were done, with two and a half hours remaining before liftoff, the barn was a roofless, forty-five-by-sixty, open-air space.

Fritz had one more surprise up his sleeves.

We lifted the second inside ladder and positioned it opposite the one that Captain Rich was on, still watching for bogeys. At Fritz's request, Margo and I scampered up to the loft. Fritz, who'd climbed down on each outer ladder as the beasts of burden had raised the roof, followed us up. Then Captain Rich joined as well. Starting at one side, we located and began to roll out the balloon—"envelope" is what Fritz called it—passing it to Fritz as he shimmied out, spreading it over the loft floor and centering the essential parts as he did.

Things sped up at this point. Fritz did most of the work, flying about under the open sky, connecting lines to D-ring hoses and interior lines where they needed to be.

And then he turned on the gas.

Everyone but Fritz was sent back down. I sat on the ground near the basket, watching in awe as the envelope filled. It spread across the entire width and most of the length of the barn. Heading outside, I saw nothing. The raised roof hid the expanding nylon sack and would, Fritz said, until the final thirty minutes, which would be just after sunset.

I still didn't understand how we were going to launch. Fritz had a nonchalant attitude that inspired both confidence and concern.

"Have you ever done a flight like this before?" I asked.

"Nope."

"But you do have experience with this balloon, right?"

"Nope."

"Other people? Have other people done something like this?"

"Define *like*."

"Nighttime over mountains and through a mountain pass?"

"Not anyone who has lived to talk about it."

"People have tried and died?"

"None that I know of, but I'm getting tired of your questions. Suit up. And don't forget to put on your parachute."

"Parachute?"

38

AS EASY AS FALLING OFF A CLIFF

It was becoming clear that Fritz was not on the same page as the others. "Didn't Margo or Lonnie discuss any of this? Christ almighty."

He looked their way. Lonnie was staring at Margo, and Margo was staring at her shoes.

Fritz seemed a bit intense. Wired. If I had to guess, he was in a chemically enhanced state. This seemed to be a common thing in Myanmar. Not that there's anything wrong with that. And who am I to judge?

"Are you ready for this? Do you think this will work?" I really wanted to get some positive vibes from him on this. What with the fact that I was putting my life into his hands and trusting a technology I'd never used and had no idea how to operate if things went sideways.

"I've been ready for five years. This is what I've trained for."

"You don't actually mean exactly like this." I still felt leery.

"No, I do mean exactly like this. This is why I was

embedded. Carrying up to five passengers, launching from this very spot, aiming for the Thai border. Night flight skimming the treetops. OK, I haven't practiced skimming treetops at night, but I've been doing some serious contour flights . . . hopping over buildings, skimming lakes, buzzing temples . . . that sort of thing. That is all I've trained for. And not really aiming for the Thai border. This thing can't be aimed. It goes where the wind takes it. But the prevailing winds from here almost always go due east to the Thailand border." He pointed skyward, and I hoped he was pointing in the direction of Thailand—though my impression was he was pointing south.

"I have calculations for any weight up to one thousand three hundred and twenty pounds of 'cargo.' That's six two-hundred-and-twenty-pound Navy SEALs. Or four three-hundred-pound diplomats." He eyed Captain Rich, likely doing a mental calculation. Fritz was as tall as Captain Rich but probably a hundred pounds lighter. It looked like he could slip through a crack in the door, whereas Captain Rich would just knock it down.

"I check the weather and wind six times a day. Every. Single. Day. I generate projections of weather patterns, upcoming storms. I'm telling you, this—what we are doing today—is what I've trained for, and there is no one on this earth, or in the sky, who is better prepared to save your behinds. So please, enough with the questions, and let's get on our flight suits and parachutes."

I looked around for support. Margo seemed to be comfortably and silently waiting beside a packed chute and bundle of clothing. I shot her a nasty look. Captain Rich was bouncing on his toes. I gave him a "what's up" look, but he was totally focused on Fritz. Wai's eyes were darting around. Parachutes? One more omission of a data point I would have appreciated knowing about. Margo's conscience didn't seem to be bothering her.

I raised my hand. Fritz sighed.

"It seems like we should have known about this."

"That is because you were not here, and there was no way to train you in advance under plan A. I don't know why, once we shifted to plan B, they didn't give you all the details. So"—this time it was he who shot Margo a nasty look—"that is why you need to listen to what I say and do what I tell you to do. It's a precaution. Just in case. BASE-jumping chute. Should save your ass if you pop the chute above two hundred feet. I'd advise three hundred above the treetops just to play it safe. Now, does anyone here have experience with parachutes?"

Lonnie and Margo raised their hands, but Fritz waved them off dismissively. "Yeah, yeah, I know. You trained at the farm. But have you ever done a BASE jump?"

They both lowered their hands.

I thrust my hand up like an overanxious sixth grader and shouted, "Me," and then pulled it down a bit when I noticed everyone staring at me. I realized my enthusiasm might have been a bit over the top.

Fritz raised an eyebrow, and I immediately took it down a notch. "Yes," I said, more under control. "I've done a bunch of BASE jumps. Some legally. I recognize the rig."

Captain Rich jumped up, waving his hands in the air and shouting, "Me, me!" in a shrill voice I had to assume was mocking me. I stamped on his foot, but he didn't seem to notice.

"Yep, I trained with my unit in the Forty-Fourth Parachute Brigade. We were airborne ops. Air-landed assault troops and heliborne. Primarily heliborne, but we practiced both for high-altitude covert insertion and low-altitude, quick response using BASE rigs. Night jumps, high-wind jumps. We jumped in a rain cloud once. The air force guys called us dirt darts. Do you have one in extra-large?"

He managed to make my over-the-top response seem sedate.

"Roger that. Not technically a BASE jump when it starts in a helicopter. Then again, it's not a BASE jump from a balloon, either. I'll give you a pass on that. I think you'll need the diplomat-size rig."

"Thanks. We also did vehicle and heavy-artillery drops, but I'm guessing that's not part of this operation. You'd be surprised how often that came in handy when I was privatized."

I glanced over to see if Captain Rich was foaming at the mouth. He continued to bounce on his toes and had been talking a mile a minute. If I didn't know how adamantly he opposed drugs, I would have thought he'd been sharing some of Fritz's stash.

"OK, cool. Wai, how about you?"

Wai stood near the back with eyes the size of dinner plates. He seemed to have lost some of his cool. He made some slight stammering sounds that I took to mean that not only had he never done a jump but that he wasn't in favor of giving it a try.

Fritz smiled. "Don't worry. It's as easy as falling off a cliff."

His humor didn't resonate well with the team.

"Ok, then." Fritz shrugged. "Let's get everyone set up." He slid open the door to a toolshed and then a second door inside of it. "Captain Rich, we've ascertained that you get the *mucho grande* large. Grab the flight suit, and chute up there at the far end. The chute will definitely fit and is designed for substantial weight. I think the flight suit will fit. It's the largest I have, so it better."

Captain Rich trotted over to the big-and-tall section, kicked off his shoes, and unrolled the flight suit. It made a crinkling sound. We all watched as he worked his way in and zipped it up.

"Pretty spiffy," huffed Captain Rich after the struggle with the zipper. "What's this material?"

"Something that's been developed for the military and siphoned off by the agencies. Waterproof, windproof, bugproof, but most importantly, it doesn't show up on night-vision technologies. Neither the balloon nor our bodies will be emitting an identifiable heat signature. Totally stealth."

The rest of us did the appropriate head nodding and grunts of approval. It did seem like he had a handle on this.

"Now," continued Fritz, pointing at Captain Rich, "step into your harness and start cinching it up."

"It's been a few years, and this may be slightly different from what we used in the Special Forces." Captain Rich seemed a bit less cocky, perhaps after watching my interaction with Fritz. His cheeks and ears began to turn red. "Can you give me a hand?"

"Legs, arms, chest!"

Captain Rich continued to stare at the rig lying on the ground. Fritz finally gave in. We all circled around while Fritz walked him through each step of the process, explaining why a mistake with any one of the secure points could be fatal.

"OK, pick up the rig, and hold it at about hip height on your left side. Left side, not right. Now put your feet through each of the leg holes, starting with the left leg. OK, one leg per hole. I've widened them as far as they can go, but you're not going to get your right leg in there with the left leg in the same hole, no matter what. OK, now pull up the shoulder straps, and slide your arms in, left arm first. Excellent. Now put on the chest strap, but keep it loose. Now squat and tighten the leg straps. There's not a lot of extra strap, but for those who are watching"—he waved his hand at the members of our assembled group, who were studiously observing the operation, including Wai, whose eyes had gotten larger, if that was possible—"roll up and tuck in any excess strap into the crotch. And you'll have to undo and redo all of this each time you take a bathroom break, so keep that in mind as you hydrate and eat."

I raised my hand. "Can we just—"

"I know what you're going to ask. It's the first question from most of the Navy SEALs. Sure, you can piss or crap in the suit if you wish, but the reason it blocks your heat signature is because it's sealed and nonporous. Anything you put in that suit will stay in there, warmed by your own body heat, until you remove and clean the suit. I've been there when people who've tried that route have taken off their suits. It empties the room quickly."

"OK, thanks. It's easier on scuba dives."

"She knows of what she speaks," added Captain Rich. "Trust me on that. Every. Single. Dive."

That wasn't exactly true, but close enough that I didn't challenge it.

It was the beginning of dusk and becoming harder to see when the outdoor lights clicked on. "Light sensitive." Fritz nodded. "Every night. Then they're on a three-hour timer to turn off. If anyone is paying attention, it will all look normal."

Except for the giant balloon in his backyard.

Fritz asked each of us our physical particulars and then pulled out the suit and chute he thought best fit our size and weight. I wasn't comfortable with the way this was playing out. I had no reason to doubt Fritz, but I also had my own protocols to follow.

"If you don't mind, I'd like to repack my chute."

"Because?"

"Because I always pack my own chute. No disrespect intended, but I need to be accountable for my own gear."

"No offense taken. There's a concrete pad right over there. Have at it. Take your time, but don't make us wait. Wheels up at nineteen hundred hours with whoever is ready."

The pad was a mess, and there was no way I'd safely pack a suit on it, so I got a broom and cleared away an area long and wide enough for me to spread everything out.

Fritz handled Margo and Lonnie their parachutes and flight suits. After I'd swept the entire pad, Fritz strolled over with a battery-powered blower. Grinning, he offered, "You might want to do one more pass with this."

Jerk. But a playful jerk. I can handle that.

After blowing the pad, which helped quite a bit since I've never been good with a broom, I unpacked the chute, fold by fold, to see how Fritz had done it. He was good. His creases were sharp, his folds precise, his symmetry and seams perfect.

Once I had it all laid out, I reversed the process. Fritz stood near the basket, but I could tell he was watching.

"You can come closer if you want to observe."

"Frankly, I would. You're my responsibility, no matter how experienced you are." He came and stood beside me. Everyone else was done, after some grunting and wheezing, and joined him. I'm pretty sure they were just waiting for me to make a mistake. I took far longer than I expected with Fritz standing over me, but I ended up with a packed chute that met both of our approvals.

"Not exactly how I do it, but the end product looks good. Not bad for an amateur."

Well, freak you very much.

"Can we get on with the show now?"

I nodded. *OK, point taken.*

The rest of us, including the very reluctant Wai, got our suits on and our chutes cinched up—Fritz had promised the rest of the team that the chutes had been inspected in the past week and that he had packed each one himself. In his current hyper state, this was less reassuring than I imagined he had intended it to be.

"OK, now here are your packs." Fritz pulled something like half a dozen black nylon packs out of a wheelbarrow he'd brought out while we were struggling with our suits. My suit was actually pretty easy to pull on. He'd given me a large so that my wrists and ankles weren't exposed. Like a good tailor, I guess he'd noticed my rather long limbs.

"In your packs are the basics you will need for what I expect to be a thirty-six-hour journey. Fifty to fifty-five if the winds don't do us a favor. I packed mainly protein and hydrating fluids. Also rehydration powder in case we go to ground and find a water source. This is not a Michelin three-star restaurant. You will not enjoy the food or drink, but it will keep you alive while taking up a minimal amount of space. You have freeze-dried coffee beans for when you need to be alert. Be conservative with them—they pack a punch. I have extra water as well, should you run out. It will be doled out on a rationing basis. You've got bug spray and wipes. Use them."

He quickly looked at Margo and then me but just as quickly turned away. "Ladies, you have an item called a ShePee. It's a shaped funnel that is used for relieving yourself. Please let me know if you need instructions, but frankly, I hope to avoid that."

I gave Margo a nod. "Used 'em before. Easy peasy."

Fritz had overheard and seemed quite relieved.

I noticed that there was one extra pack in the wheelbarrow.

Oh no. Tao.

Fritz had packed for six passengers, but now we were only five.

Crud.

"You will also find a beacon to be used if you become separated from the balloon and/or the group. Use it judiciously or not at all. We can't control who might pick up the signal. I've monitored this frequency and never heard any chatter on it, but that doesn't mean the army isn't also monitoring it. Each pack also contains a bare minimum first-aid kit and a signaling mirror."

"Weapons?" It was Captain Rich, still in a highly excitable state.

"No. No guns. No knives. We've found that both are counterproductive to the safe operation of balloons. If we have to exit the balloon before reaching civilization, you will not need to worry about defending yourself against foreign troops. Ten miles to the east"—this time, I could swear he pointed north—"is jungle. Even if we're sighted, no troops are going to try to track you down and engage you in the jungle. Do, however, watch where you put your hands, as we have not supplied antivenom in your kits."

"Is that going to be a risk?" Margo, such a worrier.

"No, you're much more likely to die during your landing than by encounters with some living thing on the ground." His smile suggested he was joking.

"How often do people die during landings?"

"Only once. Each."

39

LIKE A GYMNAST DOING
A DISMOUNT

It was 19:00 hours and had already been dark for an hour. We'd been in position for the past half hour. We had a little over twelve hours until sunrise. Fritz had gone over every inch of the basket and the balloon three times. We were all getting twitchy.

Wai held the carabiner at the end of what Fritz called the crown line. It was, as best as I could tell, the only thing keeping us on the ground. Fritz made some last-minute adjustments to the ballast, shifting weight so that it was in Lonnie's corner, opposite from Captain Rich's corner. I guess a few of us glanced in his direction.

"OK, I get it. I've gained a few pounds. Sometimes a little extra mass comes in handy. But I own it. Damn street food."

Fritz smiled but resisted any commentary. He pointed at Wai. "OK, walk toward us, taking in the slack. Always maintain tension on the line. This is very important. If you give it slack, the balloon will begin to rise, and it will be difficult for you to get in the basket. If it rises so that part of it is outside of the protective shield of the barn, it might drift and get torn on a rafter. But start giving it slack. Slowly." He watched Wai creep forward with precision I'm sure was drummed into him in the military. "That's good. Wait for me to say, 'Now,' but when I do, put one hand on the side of the basket where I'm pointing right now—you see it?"

Wai nodded. Nervously.

"Keeping tension on the line, you put one hand on the basket. You got that? We'll call the hand on the basket your first hand."

Wai nodded again. He licked his lips and gripped the line even more tightly than he had been. "First hand. Basket. Yes."

"OK, then, with the second hand, give me the line and carabiner and then grab on to the basket. You will have both hands on the basket. The balloon will stay grounded. Then you're going to climb into the middle section with me just like we practiced. OK?"

Wai glanced about, looking as if he might run, but nodded yes and pressed up against the basket.

"Now!"

The carabiner was handed off, and Wai grabbed the basket.

"No!"

We all swiveled to look at Lonnie. He was holding a pistol and pointing it at Wai.

"Wai stays. I don't trust him. Everything has seemed too easy up to this point. We know he was part of Thandar's honor guard. Right-hand man. What if this is all a setup?"

"To exactly the fuck what end?" Captain Rich fumed.

"I don't know. But we don't need him anymore. He can disappear into the hills and get back to his past life."

"Or get captured and shot." I figured I should get my two cents in. Wai seemed like a truly virtuous person. He had a nice aura.

"Or tell them exactly where we're going. And how." Margo had entered the fray.

Lonnie waved the gun at her, and she froze. "Good point. I should just kill him." And he turned back toward Wai, who was no longer where Lonnie had expected him to be, having released the basket and begun running for the barn door.

The next few moments were a blur. Fritz swung down toward Lonnie's gun hand with some sort of tool, but Lonnie swung his arms away, and Fritz hit air. Lonnie was up instantly, and this time, the gun was pointed at Fritz. Captain Rich, who was in the partition behind me, started to make a move, but he was too far away and had too many walls to get there in time. Margo was a statue.

Something in my brain fired, or misfired, and suddenly, I was pulling a Rikidozan move.

I vaulted using the partition divider, swung my entire body toward Lonnie, wrapped my legs around his gun arm, and did a full twist. I landed on my feet, but my momentum still carried me forward toward the edge of the basket and the long drop beyond it. Luckily, Lonnie was in the way, dragged down by the arm that remained pinned between my legs. I banged into him with a grunt, smacking my hip into his face and, fortuitously, my ankle into his groin, before I dropped to the bottom of the basket in stunned disbelief of what had just happened. But somehow, I wasn't done yet. The gun lay at my feet. I grabbed it, rose, handed it to an equally stunned Fritz, and sprung back into my section of the basket like a gymnast doing a dismount.

The whole thing couldn't have taken more than thirty seconds. Probably more like fifteen.

Lonnie cradled his arm. Fritz had the gun pointed at him. Captain Rich just stared at me. Margo remained glued to her spot, unblinking. It looked like she had something to say, but she didn't.

Whoa. Did I just do that?

Lost in all of this was Wai, who had taken advantage of the distraction to do the only thing he could: he was running out of the barn as fast as possible. The balloon had begun rising. We had no control over the next step. It was decided by physics—Wai was not coming along.

Lonnie's stupor cleared quickly. "Shoot him! He can turn us in!"

"If so, that's on you. What were you thinking, and where did you get the gun?" Fritz was shaking, I think with anger as opposed to fear. His face was a bright shade of red. He backed away within his partition, putting himself a good five feet away from Lonnie. He held the gun in an up position, near his face, finger off the trigger.

"I'm more resourceful than you think. I found it in the Suburban's toolbox."

"Wonderful." Fritz popped bullets out of the magazine and shoved them into his pocket. He checked the chamber, slammed the empty magazine back into the magazine well, clipped a carabiner on the trigger guard, and shoved the gun into his flight suit's waistband.

"Less resourcefulness from now on. This is my flight. You take my instructions as orders, and we'll get out of here safe and be drinking cold Singhas the day after tomorrow in a nice Thai restaurant. If you don't, I can't be held responsible for the outcome. Sorry," he said, staring right at me, "but the bar for trust on this little voyage just got a lot higher, and you dug yourself a hole."

As we drifted up and away from Fritz's barn, Wai came back out from where he had been hiding. Although his English skills were excellent, this time he used sign language to communicate his feelings. In the lights of the barn, it was hard to miss his signal—his upraised middle fingers spoke volumes. I just hoped that he wasn't going to go running to the authorities.

If I were him, I would.

40

ONE OF HIS SIGNATURE MOVES

IT WAS DARK, with no noise like you would have from a hot-air balloon. There had been a noticeable breeze when we were on the ground, but up in the balloon, pushed by that same wind, the atmosphere seemed calm.

Except for Lonnie.

"You stupid bastard! You should have let me shoot him. You've signed our death certificates! They'll track us down and put us in the ground."

"Oh, shut up, you whiny little worm! I'm busy saving your ass right now, so I'd appreciate a little silence. And if Wai had come along per the plan, he wouldn't have had any chance to notify the authorities."

That had the effect of shutting Lonnie up for at least a short while. He returned to pouting and gently cradling his arm.

"Credit where credit is due." I'm pretty sure that was Captain Rich's subdued way of saying that I was kind of badass and that I'd definitely saved the day and probably Fritz's life. And there was probably an apology tucked in there as well for criticizing my threat response to the pirates. We were both sitting on pull-down seats that Fritz had thoughtfully designed into each partition of his reinforced, camouflage-painted, super-secret balloon basket.

"The dividend of watching endless hours of my namesake on Japanese wrestling shows. That was one of his signature moves."

"You've been practicing?"

"Not that one. I never thought I could pull it off. That came directly from my lizard brain."

"You should listen to your lizard brain more often."

So much for that being an apology.

Fritz was focused. He alternated his attention among the altimeter; another instrument for tracking our ascent rate; a GPS tracker on an iPad; and, flipping his night-vision goggles on, the slope rising in front of us. As time passed, he spent less time on the instruments and more on the terrain ahead.

After about half an hour, as he seemed to relax, I ventured to break the silence. "How far above the ground are we?"

"It's a bit of a guess, but about three hundred feet. My altimeter is pretty useless with the rapidly changing landscape below. The incline of the mountains is fairly shallow right now, and there are no man-made threats in this area, like cell towers or power lines, so we can stay low. The thrilling part will be the last twenty miles, when the hills rise faster and we play the game of staying high enough to avoid collision but low enough that we don't pop up into visual range. But at night we have more slack."

"Will they be able to track us by radar?"

"Nah! We're too small and slow to show up on any of their instruments. It's nighttime and we don't use flame, so there's no heat signature. We're all wearing suits that block our heat signature, dropping it by more than ten degrees. They could aim their gear right at us and never pick us up. Besides, they have no reason to be looking for us, and even if they did, they wouldn't be able to predict our route, even if Wai were to warn them." He glanced over at Lonnie, who had been rubbing his wrist and pouting since we had lifted off. "Wind currents are unpredictable up here. I don't even know over what turns and arcs our path will take us. Within an hour—and long before Wai could notify anyone—we'll be, as they say, in the wind."

The fluttering of hands that accompanied that line was probably intended to lighten the moment, but no one responded.

"Besides"—Fritz was on a rant—"Wai isn't informing anyone. He's an escapee, too. He had plenty of opportunities to sneak away during the day, and he didn't. He was ready to join us in the balloon, and once he was in here, he'd have been as vulnerable as the rest of us. Chill. I've got this."

I cleared my throat. Not my normal thing, but it seemed like a good way to get everyone's attention. "I didn't mention it before because I thought he was just playing the big man, but Wai said it was him who shot Tao."

Captain Rich glanced at me and raised his eyebrows but said nothing. After several minutes, he replied, "He looked familiar when I first saw him at the camp. Could have been. Or he could have just been trying to throw you off, make you vulnerable. Water under the bridge now. Maybe, though, Lonnie did us a favor."

In the darkness, even as my eyes adjusted, I could barely see the others in the basket. But I could see well enough to catch Lonnie. He was muttering and staring darts in Fritz's direction. I also noticed that Fritz kept to the far side of his compartment, putting as much distance between him and Lonnie as possible. He had also moved the gun to a cargo pocket on his thigh. Unless Lonnie had some other trick up his sleeve, he wasn't much of a threat. Despite that, Captain Rich just stared at Lonnie and flexed his hand open and closed. The air was cool and perfumed with the smell of the jungle, but it was heavy with tension. I got twitchy.

I hadn't taken the time to check out my flight suit when we were on the ground, but Fritz's transfer of the gun made me think. I rooted through my knapsack and relocated a couple of items to the pockets.

And that's how we spent the first night: Lonnie pouting; Fritz piloting; Captain Rich staring; me nervously alternating among sleeping, standing, and rechecking my pack and pockets. Margo has been silent for most of the ride. She hadn't spoken to Lonnie since the gun incident.

Fritz was a pro. He kept us above the tree canopy but did a great job of matching our ascent to the hills and mountains as we climbed away from the camp and toward the safety of Thailand.

And so it went. We drifted along in the dark, with Fritz fidgeting to add or subtract gas, at that point not even bothering to check his instruments or look up at his controls, depending on the slope. Once we almost brushed a treetop, and he scrambled to get us some altitude. I worried he might be falling asleep, so I dragged myself up into a standing position and kept watch. And provided a frequent burst of chatter. After an hour or so, everything had settled into a steady rhythm.

Then Captain Rich stood up and stretched. He climbed over the partition that separated him from the operator's area, spoke briefly to Fritz, then slung his leg over the partition into Lonnie's section.

"Incoming."

"What the hell are you doing? You're standing on my leg."

"Feel free to move it. I've had enough sleep, and I figure you might want your gun back, which I intend to keep from happening, so I'm going to buddy up with you till we sort this all out."

I scooted over to be as close to them as I could. The possibility was that they would use this time to conspire. The likelihood that this was much more than a series of accidents now seemed all too real. I listened, mostly, for Captain Rich's deep voice.

In the quiet of the night, I think I heard him fart.

41

WE WAIT

BEFORE I WAS aware of it, Fritz sensed that sunrise was coming. That, or he had set an alarm on his watch. Whatever—he rousted us all and started barking out instructions for the morning's maneuver. Wind speeds had died dramatically during the night, and the morning air seemed quite still. I could barely make it out in the waning darkness, but the landscape seemed to be moving beneath us in slow motion.

Fritz fiddled around in his pack and pulled out a can of something—I couldn't tell what—and stretched his arm out over the side of the basket. A thin, white line arced out from the can and fell to the earth. He watched it until it hit the tree line and dispersed.

Several of us stared at him.

"Shaving cream." He held up the can and grinned. "Light enough to get carried by the wind. I can tell how fast and in what direction the ground breezes are going. We're good." He tossed the can back into his bag and cleared his throat to get the attention of the whole group.

"It's starting to get light. The helicopters, if there will be any, will start up soon. I don't expect any, but if they behave anything like I think they will, they'll perform an expanding zigzag, starting with our last known position. If Wai spilled the beans, that means the house. If not, and they're looking for us to head to the border in a straight line from the camp by truck or car, then they'll probably start down by the main intersection and focus on roads heading west. If so, they'll never be near us. We're already fifty miles from the nearest road and won't get any closer."

That all made sense but did little to diminish the sense of foreboding that had stayed with me through the night.

"Regardless, we're going to anchor up about two miles ahead for the day. Figure about twenty to thirty minutes at our current speed. The terrain here gets quite steep—that'll give us a good backdrop, but I want to be as close to the canopy as possible. So, the first thing we need to do is secure ourselves to a strong tree. There will be some up there that will do the trick."

"Captain Rich grew up on a ranch." I was quick to volunteer his services. The closest I'd ever come to roping was attending a rodeo with my mother. She'd dressed me as a baby seal as part of a protest against the treatment of rodeo animals.

"Even better," said Fritz, "so you know how to lasso. You have the rope. It's essentially forming the floor for your compartment."

Captain Rich and I both looked down and realized

that he'd been sleeping on a coil of thick, stiff rope, wound into a near-perfect circle.

"Thanks, Ricky. Thanks a lot." He did not look pleased as he assessed the rope. "It was an ostrich ranch. You know, big birds, and I never tossed a lasso around any of them. Admittedly, I did learn a trick or two with the rope. I can give it a try. If . . . big if . . . I'm the only option." He also shot a look at Lonnie, who had risen from his corner. "You can sit down. We don't need your help."

"This should be fairly easy." Fritz's confidence wasn't exactly shared by the rest of us. We nervously shifted our eyes among the approaching trees, Captain Rich, and Fritz. "We're above the trees, and you just need to hang the rope down and snag one far enough down the trunk that it will hold us. Then we can hook onto others for more security. Just make a really big loop."

"Yeah, I'll give that bad boy a whirl."

I gave him a helping hand as he climbed back into his compartment, adding a wink and a smile. "You've got this, cowboy."

Captain Rich almost smiled as he took the rope and played out some line. It formed a stiff loop more than three feet across. He let out a little bit more and leaned toward the side of the basket. I quietly pointed out that he was standing in the middle of the looped rope and would be pulled overboard if he didn't watch out.

"I knew that," he said as he moved his feet to the side. But he and I both knew that he hadn't.

Fritz had a second rope in his hands, so I figured

we did have an option number two, but he didn't offer Captain Rich any relief.

"Just one other thing." Fritz sounded as if he had forgotten something. "Once you've set the loop, don't hold on to the rope. Just let it play out—it's already secured to the basket. If you try to hold it, you'll lose a hand."

With a speed of under five miles an hour and Fritz's deft handling of the balloon, we were soon passing toward the exposed top of a trunk of a substantial but dead tree. Its pale-white trunk stood out in contrast to the rest of the trees. Fritz nodded. Captain Rich lowered the loop, snatched the tree, and tugged to set the line. Just like a pro. He let the remaining length of rope run out until the balloon tugged to a violent stop, accompanied by the loud cracking of the tree as branches broke, but the trunk held under the stress. The balloon bobbed back and forth a bit before settling.

We were about a hundred feet above the tree canopy. Using a set of pulleys attached to the D-rings on the balloon, we pulled back most of the line and anchored ourselves just fifty feet above the treetops.

Fritz said, "Let's tuck in a little bit more. We have plenty of clearance to the side." He and Captain Rich, with the aid of the pulleys, muscled the balloon down another twenty feet. Fritz then tied off the rope and worked his way around the basket, dropping lines from each of our partitioned sections.

"These don't tie off to trees. These are just in case we need to make a quick exit. If we do, don't forget to take your knapsacks. That's your only food and water if we have to take to ground."

"Do those reach the ground?" Margo pointed at the ropes, beating me to the question by a second or two.

"I don't know. But they're closer than the basket. Besides, once you're in the tree canopy, you can grab branches and climb down. It's not perfect, but it's better than the alternative."

"What now?" Margo was setting the pace for asking the nervous questions. She'd lost quite a bit of her swagger since handing over the lead to Fritz.

"We've got about eleven hours before we start our next ascent. With good wind, we should hit the border around four hundred hours. Plenty of time to get over the top and drop into Thailand. The copters, if there are any, won't be flying at night, so it will be safe to pop up over the ridge for a few minutes."

"And while we wait?"

"We wait out the day. Full stop. There's nothing out there that can help us now. We've got plenty of food and water to last us for another forty-eight hours, so even if we don't make the border tomorrow morning, we're good to go on subsistence rations until the next day."

Captain Rich had already begun checking out his food stores, and his body language suggested he was far from pleased. "The bars are past their sell-by date. And how old is this dried meat?"

"Those are just advisements. The bars can last for decades. They get a bit chewy, but they're still nutritious and probably won't kill you. Same with the meat. It's smoked as a preservative. I vacuum-packed them myself. They'll be good for a decade. Make sure you drink plenty of water with them. Otherwise, they'll stop you up like rush hour in New York."

"Speaking of which, what are we doing for toilet facilities?" I could be counted on to be the first and most frequent to cover that topic.

"You want to piss, follow the same protocol as last night. Men, through the hole in the side that you use for a step, as long as you're not facing the wind. Ladies, use the ShePee. For everything else, use the bucket."

I had already become quite proficient with the ShePee back in my Colorado days and had guided Margo through its use the night before. I'd used the bucket once at night and was OK with using it again, even though I'd no longer have the privacy of lights-out nighttime. Margo insisted she could wait until tomorrow.

"Wait," said Margo, "there's meat in my bag?" She tore into one of the vacuum-sealed bags. "Omigod, it smells wonderful. Hell, yeah."

"Wait—you're a vegan, yes?" Captain Rich asked.

"That was part of our cover story. You have to make them deep to be believable." It was one revelation after another. The depth of their deception was getting clearer.

Captain Rich got up and leaned across the partition to get right in her face. "You mean we had to eat that vegan crap for six weeks because it was a cover? My fee just skyrocketed. And my motivation to save your asses just went down."

Fritz said, "OK, everyone, best if you hunker down while we're stationary. Keep our profile static. Get some shut-eye if you can. I know most of you, Captain Rich excepted, didn't get much sleep last night. Most of all, I need my sleep and don't need you knocking around and waking me up. So sweet dreams, and I'll see you around eighteen hundred hours. And give me a shout if you hear copters, OK?"

Oh, you didn't even need to ask.

"Captain Rich, back off from Margo. Believable background stories are concocted by our handlers, and the vegan part has proven to be quite compelling."

42

AND THEN THERE'S . . .

IT WAS, FOR me, a restless day. The basket partitions were not designed for sleeping, it was ungodly hot, the bugs—despite a liberal application of bug spray—were insistent, and at least three of my fellow passengers snored. I couldn't turn off my ears, and every new sound brought me back to a hyperalert state. I never heard any helicopters, but I imagined about a hundred other threats. Like, can those tree snakes climb up the rope?

Finally, after the sun had dropped behind the ridge and even though it was still hours until dusk, I got up to look around.

If it weren't for the current circumstances, which sucked on so many levels, it would have been a beautiful sight. The hillsides were thick with jungle, with no sight of human contamination—no buildings, towers, or roads to be seen—and the sky just over the treetops was filled with birds feasting on the same insect life that had been trying to feed on me. The delta was trippy—small tributaries looped in; small side channels spun out. It was like a massive, shimmering fractal.

Fritz, either because of my movement or his inner alarm clock, or perhaps even his magical watch—he'd called it "the ballistic"—emerged from his partition. The basket, I noticed, rocked a bit as each of us repositioned. Within a few minutes, everyone was in some state of waking. Margo looked a little worse for wear. I suspected she usually spent some significant time in front of the mirror under normal circumstances. It could be, though, that was only spy Margo, and real Margo, or whatever her real name was, never touched makeup.

"So, as I listened for helicopters, I was wondering if there were any other sounds we should be listening for. Any other threats?" I worried that I'd get an answer I didn't like, but given that I'd spent much of the night wondering exactly that, I figured it was time to put it to bed.

"Nothing, really, that you would hear in time to act. I guess there's a chance that one of the rebel armies might see us. But would they consider us a threat? I don't know, maybe a fifty-fifty chance. But even if they did, would they have the firepower to do anything about it? Some of them are barely equipped with modern guns. And it's really unlikely that any of them would be this far south. Well, except for the SSAS."

"SSAS?"

"Shan State Army–South. They sometimes show up this far south."

"How many rebel armies are there in this part of the

country?" I was getting a bit concerned that Fritz had been less than forthcoming.

"Well, of course, you have the SSAN—the Shan State Army–North. But they let the SSAS take care of this patch. And the TNLA, that's the Ta'ang National Liberation Army. You've probably also got the MNDAA. That would be the Myanmar National Democratic Alliance Army, and then there's the AA, the Arakan Army. This isn't even their district, but they will join anyone in the fight for independence. Massive group. Maybe thirty thousand strong. Well equipped, too. They've raided the Myanmar Army posts for years. Artillery. Automatic weapons."

"And you didn't think to mention this before?"

"No sense in doing so. This balloon is, by far, our best option. And there's absolutely nothing we can do about the armies. They are unlikely to see us, even less likely to engage, and then completely unlikely to be able to bring us down. Why worry about what you can't control?"

Captain Rich, sensing that I was about to violently express myself, reached across the partition and put a heavy hand on my shoulder.

"Do you think there might be some way we could look out for their activity? Maybe, just maybe, so that we could have some forewarning?"

"Realistically, no. By the time you hear artillery, it's either missed you or hit you. Same with their .50-caliber machine guns. And they can be over a mile away and still tear this thing apart with a few good blasts. No, if you see them, they've already got us dead to rights. On the plus side, it seems like none of them have incendiary rounds."

"And those would be bad news because . . . ?"

"Poof!" Fritz accompanied the sound with a mimed balloon explosion, which seemed rather unnecessary.

"Well, then, that's just dandy."

Captain Rich's hand pushed me farther down in my little section of the basket. "I hate to say it, Ricky, but he's right." He removed his hand from my shoulder. "They're not going to see us as we travel at night, and if they see us in the day tied up to this tree, we're sitting ducks. Nothing we can do. But Fritz, buddy"—he moved his hand to Fritz's shoulder, which noticeably sagged—"we're all adults here. How about we work a little bit on trust and transparency?"

"Point taken." Fritz squirmed his way out from under Captain Rich's beefy hand.

We all stayed fairly still and quiet as the afternoon passed and dusk approached. I, for one, had now added a whole new set of sounds that I was tracking—basically, anything like metal or that changed the natural soundtrack of the jungle.

As color disappeared and shadows began to blend into the night sky, we prepared for the second leg of travel. Fritz had Margo and me pull up the drop lines on our side of the basket. He pulled his up. Captain Rich's was hooked to the tree, and I was wondering how they were going to pull it off.

Margo and I followed Fritz's lead, bundling and tying off our ropes and dropping them into his section

TRACY GROGAN

of the basket. My bundle looked more like one big knot, but I was rushing not to be last.

The wind had died down a bit, which had Fritz doing some calculations in his head. We could tell he was absorbed in something meaningful because his lips were moving as he thought.

Captain Rich leaned in. "Care to share? Transparency and all of that?"

"I'd say our progress yesterday was about what I'd expected. We're a bit farther to the south, so the ridge is a bit higher out this way. And the wind seems like it will be less helpful tonight, so I'm thinking we are looking at hitting the ridge right around sunrise. The last couple of hundred or thousand feet, depending on where we cross, is above the tree line, so we'll be pretty much committed to making the run for the border at that point. But there wouldn't be enough time to scramble helicopters and reach us, so I'm feeling good about our chances."

Captain Rich didn't seem as confident. "And plan B?"

"We're past any plan B or C. This is it. We're going for it."

Captain Rich leaned in farther. "Are you open to any input?"

"Look. You're bigger than me. I get it. But I've been anticipating this plan for five years. I've run through every scenario in my head. Our ability to hide during the day diminishes as we go higher and the topography changes. Once we take off today, there's no stopping. So, give me all the input you want and try to intimidate me to your heart's content, but we're going. Balls-out."

Captain Rich shrugged. "OK. You're the expert. I'm all in. Balls-out. Let's do this." He shifted himself back into his partition.

Fritz leaned back into his. "So," he asked with a slightly demonic grin, "are you ready to rock 'n' roll?"

"I thought you said no knives." Captain Rich stared at the shining blade in Fritz's hand. It wasn't all that big, but it was most definitely a knife. And the edge looked sharp.

"No military knives. Nothing for fighting. This is for the ropes. Unless you want to climb down and work your lasso off the tree trunk."

"Nope, I'm good."

"We still have those three lines we dropped over the side in case we need to tie off again, but that's not in the plan." Fritz nodded to bundles on the floor of his partitioned section. "When we get to Thailand, we just drop and drag until the balloon deflates enough that the wind stops pushing it."

He had us return to our prior launch positions, moving our bags as well.

"We're going to lurch—no way around that. But if everyone is sitting, it should go smoothly. Captain Rich, can you get back into Lonnie's compartment, just in case he thinks about taking advantage of the distraction to go for the gun?"

"Absolutely. My extreme pleasure." We heard a loud, high-pitched grunt as he landed in the opposing compartment, but Lonnie was smart enough to limit his protests after that.

With threats minimized, Fritz made the cut. The

basket jerked heavily but then settled quickly, and we slowly rose.

It seemed like our rate of rise was less than the rise in the hillside. Twice we brushed against treetops, but soon we were getting some separation, and within a few minutes, we'd risen to a comfortable height of several hundred feet. I realized my shoulders were hunched, and I'd probably been that way since we had practiced the knife transfer. I settled into the basket and did some breathing and stretching exercises. It was going to be a long and tense night and, if Fritz was right, a particularly tense morning. Despite his assurances that the helicopters weren't coming, and if they were, they wouldn't see us, I listened intently again as we glided silently upward.

As we moved onward, Fritz had each of us practice standing, hooking our knapsacks to the front of our harness, standing on the foot holes in the basket, reaching for and finding our pilot chutes, and imitating the throwing motion for after we leaped from the basket.

"You're shitting me." Lonnie was fumbling with the carabiners on his harness, trying to hook up the knapsack. "We're supposed to do this in, like, five seconds?"

The four of us looked up. All of us had already secured our knapsacks, though I noticed Lonnie's hung by only one 'biner. Fritz reached over and deftly attached the other.

"You could just secure it now and leave it that way. But that will get uncomfortable after a short while. This is just a prudent precaution. It's not like you have anything else to do. I'm not expecting that we're going to jump. That's a last resort, and I don't foresee it coming to that. At worst, fifty-fifty."

If he says 'fifty,' one more time . . .

I couldn't sleep. Didn't really want to. I hate being unable to control events and felt completely helpless as we drifted in the dark. Worse yet, I shared Captain Rich's misgivings about Fritz's willingness to share. He had painted a good enough picture, but we kept finding flaws. I'd periodically check with Fritz, and I was sure he found it irritating, but the status checks at least made me feel a bit more centered.

We passed four in the morning and were still over jungle.

"Once we hit the tree line, the wind speed will pick up. I'll increase our rate of climb. Things will get noisier as we approach the ridge, from the wind rushing over the landscape and top, and then we'll pop up. We'll probably climb at least five hundred feet after we crest, and I'll start our descent. We should be down within ten minutes of cresting. I'll be looking for a field for our landing, but no assurances."

"Fifty-fifty?" I figured that was as good as I was going to get.

"Yeah, I'd say fifty-fifty odds we nail a crop landing."

The last time I'd checked with him, it was just past five in the morning. There were fewer stars in the night sky as dawn approached.

"Even in predawn light, no one can see us. It's only once the sun actually comes above the far horizon that we'll be visible. By then, we should be in Thailand." I noticed, though, that he was checking his fancy watch more often. "We've got less than a thousand feet to go. I can see the tree line up ahead. Pretty soon, things will start happening much more quickly."

43

IN THE EVENT OF AN EMERGENCY . . .

He was right about that. As we neared the tree line, things definitely began to happen very quickly.

Captain Rich heard the guns first. He said, "We're under fire," slowly and clearly, sort of like, "There's an ant on the table." It was all the warning we needed.

"Everyone, duck!" That was Fritz. He didn't have to say it twice. I saw Lonnie and Margo drop as I went into a crouch.

Captain Rich announced, "North of us. Around two miles." I couldn't see, so I wasn't sure, but I was guessing that he had popped his head up above the side of the basket.

Once I realized we were under attack, I was able to identify the sound. The first few noises were single shots. Rifles, I guessed. There was no way to tell if they were coming close or not. Still, I remained ducked.

Fritz popped up and down. He was in a full standing position as he was checking gauges, and it looked like he was dumping gas. But we continued to rise farther above the jungle, losing any remaining camouflage we had.

"Sounds like .50 caliber. We're probably at the far end of their accuracy, though this balloon makes a big target. Still, I doubt they could hit an elephant from that distance."

Almost as if on cue, we heard a thump as a bullet hit the balloon. Lonnie's eyes were as large as mangoes; Margo's were closed. Captain Rich's were panning back and forth as he surveyed the source. And Fritz's were glued to the gauges.

"How much time do we have before the balloon deflates? And which is going to go first, the balloon or this basket? This wicker isn't going to do us any good. We need to bail." Captain Rich seemed ready to take control.

"Small holes in the balloon won't be an issue. Those are small leaks, and I've got plenty of gas to keep us airborne. It will take a lot more than that to cause any impactful damage." Fritz paused to make sure we were listening. "I don't know which troops are doing this, but they all are fairly underprovisioned when it comes to weapons. They'll probably stop wasting bullets soon. Besides, the whole basket is lined with Kevlar."

"How thick?"

"Thick enough to stop standard .50 calibers. The army doesn't supply troops with armor-piercing shells. They use antipersonnel ammo."

"The entire thing is lined with Kevlar?" Captain Rich was not in a trusting mood.

"Sides and bottom. They are overlapped to eliminate gaps. I had to use body armor, so they aren't big sheets of fabric, but I've got them layered like scales. It's not like I had the ability to import giant sheets—I bought mine over time from the rebels, who stole them from the army, which bought them secondhand from the Chinese."

That's when the machine gun started.

"How many bullets can that thing fire?" I asked.

"Lots."

"Can you put a finer point on that?" I'm not sure why this was a helpful thing to understand, but it seemed like it at the time.

"Depending on the configuration, it could be hundreds per minute, but probably not for any sustained period of time. They are doing a fine job of shredding the jungle." Fritz pointed downhill and to the north, where the bullets were tearing apart the tree canopy. "And they're not using incendiary, so they'll have more difficulty getting their aim down."

And then, as quickly as it had started, the firing stopped. We drifted for a few minutes, Fritz popping up and down to continue making adjustments and surveying the landscape.

"I imagine they are either reloading or have given up. Probably given up. I'd give it a fifty-fifty chance."

If I could have slapped him in the head, I would have, but I wasn't about to stand up based on his fifty-fifty odds.

And then it started up again.

"That's closer." Captain Rich was uncanny. I saw the top of his head as he popped up to make a quick assessment of the situation. He winced when we heard a string of thumps that told us the gunner had found the balloon, but it didn't seem to alter our speed or altitude. And the gunner hadn't known he was on target. The bullets resumed tearing up the jungle, though now it was closer to our altitude and to the south. "And I think they found a better gunner."

A string of bullets hit the basket, sending wicker flying, but it seemed like the Kevlar held. I was hunkered down, so I couldn't see anyone else, but I flinched and almost jumped up. It was all I could do to keep from peeing myself.

"I didn't design for sustained .50 caliber. The bullets may not penetrate the plates, but it won't take many continued hits to break the basket apart. In the event of an emergency, I'll give you the instruction to jump. But we're not there yet." That may have been the most transparent Fritz had been during this whole journey.

Crud.

And then the shooting stopped once more. I didn't have much time to think about next steps—Fritz did that for me.

"Everyone out! Now! Jump!"

Fritz stood up and yanked Margo up out of her crouch, grabbing her pilot chute and dropping it on the floor of the basket. Then he pushed his hand in deeper and pulled out a second pilot chute as he heaved Margo over the side. As she fell, screaming, the pilot chute was pulled from his hand. It took him all of fifteen seconds. No one had time to stop him. I saw her chute open below us and realized I'd been holding my breath. I sucked in a lungful of jungle air.

Fritz had spun around and was staring at Captain Rich as he screamed, "Now!"

"Now! Jump!" Captain Rich screamed at me.

I reached for my knapsack.

"Fuck that." Captain Rich grabbed me and hurled me over the side. I instinctively spread-eagled, grabbed my pilot chute, and threw it. The tree canopy below looked way too close.

The pilot chute did its job. My chute yanked open, and I was gliding, but still way too close to the treetops for comfort. I saw Margo hit the trees and her chute snag. With a quick tug on my riser, I made a sharp turn in her direction. Then I hit the trees, and it felt like I was going through a car wash without a car.

At least the jump hadn't killed me.

Then I remembered the deadly tree snakes.

Crud.

I quickly reassessed my attitude when the shooting resumed. The balloon and basket were taking a lot of hits. Venomous snakes were sounding like the better alternative.

I was distracted from that thought by what I assumed was the sound of bodies crashing through branches, one much louder than the other. As best as I could tell, they were in different directions from where I was hanging.

The jungle was thick, and I couldn't imagine that there was anybody else here other than the five of us. If there were, and I was most worried about soldiers, they would have at least heard our landing. I didn't think I had anything to lose.

"Captain Rich! Fritz! Hello?"

"Can we leave out the 'Captain' part? Kind of puts a target on my back. And there's no need to shout. I'm hearing you five by five."

From the sound of it, he was off to my left and not far away. And based on his jargon, his mercenary training, combined with adrenaline, was kicking in.

I tried to keep it to a conversational level. "Fritz?"

"Here." Off to my right but slightly below me. "In a tree. Nothing broken."

Margo, sounding quite shaken, reported in. She was downslope but within yelling distance. "Lonnie?" After all of his shit, she still was watching out for her teammate.

"He's still with the balloon." Fritz sounded cool, calm, and collected. A surprising reaction for someone who had left a passenger behind.

I didn't have a clear view but could see the balloon drifting upward, rising farther above the tree line. I couldn't tell at first from this new perspective whether the bullets or Fritz's adjustments had slowed the rate of climb.

Then it became clear that the balloon was rising. Fast.

Captain Rich chimed in. "I've got my binoculars on him. Wow, he's way up there. It looks like he's hanging from the basket."

"Yeah!" Fritz yelled. "I hooked a tether to the basket and then to a D-ring on his chute. Hip level, in back. Very hard or impossible for him to reach in his current position. He's not separating from that balloon anytime soon."

I couldn't believe he'd risk letting Lonnie go. "So, he just gets away?"

"Unlikely. His options have rapidly diminished. By leaving, we dumped over seven hundred pounds of ballast. The balloon is rising almost a thousand feet a minute, so he'll be increasingly visible from here on out. In less than sixty seconds, he'll be higher than the ridgetop. After that, more people will see him. Among them will be more people with guns, and the balloon will stand out in the morning light. Whoever is shooting at it, I'm sure, has alerted others to start searching the sky."

"He can jump."

"Even if he manages to unhook and throw the pilot chute, his parachute won't open. The pilot chute is a dummy. And if he figures out that there's a second pilot chute, he'll find out soon enough that the parachute isn't connected to the harness. So, the pilot chute will pull the parachute open, but he'll keep dropping. He'll hit the ground at terminal velocity."

"That's brutal." I felt a bit sorry for Lonnie, what with being screwed over like that by his fellow agent.

"Was that really necessary?" Margo finally reacted, although far less emphatically than the situation deserved.

"He was a loose cannon. The gun bullshit was over the top."

I'd finally sighted Fritz nestled in among the leaves of a tree below me and to the south. He was focused on the balloon.

"They're not having much success targeting the balloon, but they'll likely figure it out. And when they do, they can shred the balloon and make it drop . . ." He paused and listened. "Not yet. They're still just shooting randomly. He has some time, but I'm not sure he can spend it doing anything productive. He's still just flailing away."

It had been at least two minutes since we'd jumped. Or in my case and Margo's, been thrown. I'd climbed higher into the tree so that I could see what was happening. Captain Rich and Fritz had done the same. We were all within two hundred feet of one another. Not bad for an emergency exit.

The stream of bullets periodically stopped but quickly resumed. The balloon had drifted, according to Fritz, to something like three thousand feet above the treetops and well above the ridgeline.

The damage from the bullets was finally becoming evident. The balloon's ascent slowed and stopped as the balloon visibly began to deflate, and then it started to drop. Slowly, the basket gently swaying. Lonnie frantically twisting around, trying to unhook.

"Remember what I said about a sitting duck?"

Someone with more skill, it seemed, had taken over the machine gun. A new stream of bullets hit the giant orb, tearing into it like a knife into a piñata. You could see them slowly working down from balloon to basket. It took a number of hits that sent wicker flying, but then, finally, the basket shuddered and broke into a hundred pieces. Dropping below the mess was Lonnie, his unattached parachute shredded and fluttering far above him.

"Like I said, I didn't design it for sustained fire." Fritz looked ready to cry as his creation broke apart and drifted earthward.

"Any chance he'll make it?" My question was totally about curiosity and nothing about concern.

"I'd say that's about a three-thousand-foot drop. People have survived that before. Under different circumstances." He had a pair of binoculars trained on the balloon, so he was in a better position than I was to assess the situation. "But the pink mist trail he's leaving makes me think he is or will be dead before he hits the ground. Those were .50-caliber shells. It would only take one to ruin his day."

"Then what the hell"—Margo was shouting now, well over the level needed for inter-tree communications—"are we waiting for? You've already signed his death certificate. Let's get out of here before this becomes a hot zone. Captain Rich, Ricky, are you good to go?"

I felt something touch or glide over my head and instinctively reached up to brush it away. Bad move if it had been a snake, but it was just a spider. A big spider, but not a snake, so I was OK with it. But I also noticed a warm, wet feeling on my neck. A gentle check disclosed a gash on my head, but it didn't feel like I had much bleeding.

"I'm not broken, but I think I need stitches."

"Of course you do. You wouldn't be Ricky if it was an uneventful landing."

"Thanks, Cap . . . Rich."

I looked back at the tree where Captain Rich had landed, seeing just his head poking out, and then at Fritz. "So," I shouted, "what do we do now? Just roost here in the trees?" We looked rather comical, all having landed within a couple of hundred feet of one another and each poised in the crown of a different tree.

"Are you OK enough to get yourself down?" It didn't sound like Fritz had a plan B if I wasn't.

"I can climb, but the chute is stuck."

"Just make sure you're stable in the tree, two feet and a hand if you can, or hanging free of branches, and then pull your chute release." Fritz made it sound like it was no more challenging than unbuckling my seat belt in the garage.

"OK. Looking for the release. Got it!"

"Wait!"

That was fast.

"Everyone, listen. You each need to gather up your chute. Wad it up in a ball and drop it. They're camouflaged, but there's nothing to be gained by leaving a potential clue up in the canopy. Especially if all the shooting has attracted copters."

Not the most timely request, but it made sense.

"Margo?"

"I'm good. Just give me a minute."

"Rich?"

"Way ahead of you, mate. Halfway down my tree."

It took a couple of minutes, but I was able to collect most of the chute, shredding it as I separated it from the branches, and dropped it down where I had a clear shot all the way to the ground.

"Ok. Chute dropped. Stable. Pulling my release."

"Oh, and remember to look where you put your hands and feet. Tree snakes."

Freaking snakes. Forget the hands and feet—I'm going for the drop.

I landed on the wadded-up chute, which provided zero padding, with a thud and a grunt. The others all climbed down their trees, some more elegantly than others. No reports of tree snake encounters.

Just a few paces uphill from where I'd landed was a small grouping of rocks. Captain Rich had already plopped down on one, and the rest of us followed suit.

Nobody spoke. I assumed they were all in the same headspace that I was—amazed at what had just gone down.

I leaned in toward Fritz. "I thought you said it was only a fifty percent chance that we'd run into troops."

"See, I was right!"

"OK, sitrep." Captain Rich was in full mercenary mode. Pumped and ready for action. "Ricky, remove your hand from Fritz's throat!"

"In English, please?" I asked.

"Stop choking him!"

I eased up and scooted back. "No, I mean the sitrep part."

"Situation report. What are our known threats? What are our capabilities? What are our liabilities? How are we set for basic needs?"

We took stock of our situation and supplies. Fritz and Captain Rich had both landed with their knapsacks intact. Margo and I, given the way we exited, did not have our bags. I did have some hard-as-rock energy bars in my flight suit cargo pocket. We had about a gallon of water among us. Not enough for even half a day. Fritz had a water decontamination thingamajig. Of course he did.

He also had a medical kit, complete with suturing materials, but no local anesthetic. He and Captain Rich argued over who should have the honor of stitching up my head. In the end, it was agreed that they would take turns. Margo asked to join in, so I granted her the task of shaving around the cut. I knew Captain Rich would go overboard in defining the area to be shaved and didn't trust Fritz's sense of aesthetics. Once I was prepped, the trio happily went about trading off the needle and thread. I contributed a running string of obscenities. After a quick washing and bandaging, I was good to go.

Fritz said, "I'm guessing we have about three miles uphill to get to the ridgeline. Probably about two thousand feet of altitude if we go straight up. About half of it will be slow jungle navigation, but the other half will be quite exposed and even steeper. But at least it's a straight line, fewer snags, and no tree snakes."

Criminy.

"Is there a route that takes us across a lower part of the ridge?" I didn't look forward to a two-thousand-foot grind.

"Yeah, but we'd have a much longer diagonal transit, and we'd be exposed longer. Plus, we'd probably have to stay overnight and then hide all day until dusk. You up for that?" Fritz raised his eyebrows and waited for my reply.

"Like I said, let's go straight up." I wasn't beyond agreeing with logic.

"It's your call, but I'd suggest keeping the flight suits. It's unlikely they'll be scanning for heat signatures . . . but the camouflage will be helpful on the exposed sections. You'll get really hot really fast once the sun hits us, but you can keep it unzipped and the sleeve vents open. Anyone need a bio break before we start hoofing it?"

"Nope," I volunteered. "I peed myself the moment Captain Rich threw me out of the basket."

"Ditto," chimed in Margo, though her cheeks turned crimson as she said it.

"That would be one reason in favor of dumping the suits." Fritz was all business.

"OK, then. Too much information," said Captain Rich, who had already ditched his suit. "Now we walk." He had a noticeable limp as he led the way.

We all kept talk to a minimum. No need to expend energy, and we needed to be quiet to listen for streams. Until we had a replacement opportunity, we were rationing our sparse water supply. Captain Rich mentioned that we could drink our urine in a pinch and that it was a shame that I'd let mine loose while in the air. He and I had agreed to share his water bottle, and I had my worries about how he might be planning on refilling it.

"I'm pretty sure some of it is still pooled up around my elastic ankle bands. These suits are waterproof, and that goes both ways—nothing in but nothing out as well. You can probably . . ."

"I'll get back to you on that offer."

"First come, first serve. You don't want to be at the back of the line."

44

I DID THE MATH

WE'D BEEN ON the ground for more than an hour. We couldn't see the sun yet from our side of the mountain, but it was getting lighter, the air warmer, and the jungle sounds louder. Fritz called for us to take a break. He'd found a shallow pool of water and was going to work his magic with his thingamajig. We passed around and drank our fill from the water bottles. He refilled them and then set to stirring them with the magic purifier wand. I squatted beside him for a little privacy.

"So, you trusted Captain Rich with all of this? The unannounced exit and the Lonnie thing?" I wasn't sure if I should be pleased or worried.

"I wouldn't say 'trusted.' I had to clue one of the two of you in. I did the math, and it said he was the one."

"What math would that be?"

"Essentially, he was bigger and stronger." Fritz looked over at Captain Rich, who was doing stretches against a tree. "If I had picked you, and I was right and he was corrupt, we were screwed. He could have kept you from jumping. At that point, we'd have a hostage situation. If I had picked him and I was right—you were corrupt—you would be unable to stop him from jumping. So, trusting him was the only logical choice."

Logical seemed like the wrong word, but he was being quite free with the information, so I wasn't going to quibble with him.

"I couldn't figure out why anyone would want to rig the nav system." Fritz was as in the dark as the rest of us. Somehow, that made him more reliable. "The only thing that made sense was that someone on the cruise must have wanted to get captured. It was a short jog from that to the fact that only Lonnie and Margo had an agenda and the resources to execute that agenda. That then opened the possibility that they weren't captured but were just masking the fact that they had a prearranged hookup. That explained a whole bunch of things."

He gave me a sad, puppy-dog look.

"And then there was your mom. I'm sorry to say, but a lot of us were amazed you never figured it out. She has always been a fairly obvious spook. I mean, really, you thought she made a living with all those silly jobs? Did you notice that the people she hung out with ended up getting busted, but she never did? And that she traveled the world on, what—discount airfare and youth hostels? By my way of thinking, given that she was, as you so elegantly put it, a spook, it wasn't a coincidence that you were on this trip. For what it's worth, I figured you were too good of a person to be aligned with Lonnie and Margo. I just figured you were a plant to keep an eye on them."

Did everyone else know that Mom was CIA? Please don't tell me you slept with her, too.

"But when it came to getting safely to the ground, you dismissed me and trusted the mercenary?"

"Security consultant." Captain Rich actually seemed offended. I guess our conversation hadn't been as private as I'd hoped.

"Sorry."

"Again"—Fritz was walking a fine line here—"it was the only scenario that could play out with all the good guys on the ground and the bad guys in the sky."

"My mom's a spook. Huh." I'd finally said it. There had always been a weird vibe that had made me wonder. It had even been a joke with some of my friends: "Oh yeah, my mom's not really the school crossing guard. That's just a cover story. Really she's a spy, but I'd have to kill you if I told you that."

"So." I looked at Fritz. "The whole venomous snake thing is just part of the cover story, right?"

"Wrong." He winced. "Worse than I let on. Really, don't grab any branches. If you slip, just go to the ground. Most of them are up in the trees."

45

THE JURY IS STILL OUT

I WANTED TO get as much value out of our break time as possible. Once we reached a populated area, Fritz might shut up tight. Margo, as well, seemed to be trying to figure out where she stood.

"Lonnie. The tether. Was that really necessary?" She made it sound casual.

"You have no idea. Or maybe you do." Fritz had changed. He was now oozing CIA. He seemed taller, more focused, and a lot more unforgiving.

"That's intriguing. Try me." Margo seemed to be shifting into her CIA persona as well.

"Wai had been Thandar's eyes and ears going back to the beginning. Believe it or not, quiet little Wai was really Warrant Officer Wai. Or so he said. I'm inclined to believe him. He latched on to me as I was setting up the gear and you were all napping. Lonnie was playing multiple games. You knew about the uranium skimming." He looked at Margo. "Maybe not, but probably, from the very beginning. But it seemed like, up there, you weren't totally aligned with Lonnie's agenda."

"And what, pray tell, do you think that agenda was?"

I wasn't sure if Margo really wanted to know. Something in her voice.

"From what Wai told me, the back-pocket agreements were to include teak and opium, mostly processed into heroin, in the operation. Makes sense. The Myanmar government would be providing uninterrupted passage for the uranium shipments but wouldn't know that teak and opium were part of the deal. They'd be greasing the skids to get logs, and the custom minishipping containers they covered up, to a harbor near Rangoon. Nobody was going to inspect the cargo. They would have been told to look the other way, so there was no risk of it being intercepted. Lonnie was setting up the receiving end so that he could get his cargo out before it hit the first US inspection. My guess, if he cut good deals, was that he was going to make a killing with the skimmed uranium. There are a hundred bad actors who would be lined up to buy it, and Lonnie probably had that list. But that sort of deal could take a while, so the teak and opium provided immediate profit."

"That's quite a tale." Margo didn't sound very defensive. Hard to tell if Lonnie had been shutting her out or if this was just another deception.

"Prove me wrong."

Margo went quiet. She drummed her fingers to some unheard beat, and her lips were slightly active. She sighed.

"The uranium part is true. We didn't have a GPS

issue. In fact, we were safely outside of territorial waters. We couldn't risk getting in close and being grabbed by a legit government ship. We'd been working a back channel with Thandar for almost a year. He knew where we'd be and when. He was skimming uranium from the mining project and had been looking for bidders. Like Lonnie said, we wanted to keep it out of the wrong hands, so the US was prepared to buy as much of the legitimate product as the government was trying to sell and maybe get a foothold with the current leadership. If we could get that foothold, maybe we could buy whatever the government was shipping out of the country with a guarantee that we'd pay the highest market price. Take the shit out of circulation. And the skimmed product was Thandar's gravy. By buying the skim, we reduced his risk of engaging with people more evil and more conniving than him. But it needed to be off the books. No records. No trail back to the US."

She paused, and they both looked skyward, even though our view was completely blocked by the canopy, as a helicopter slowly flew by. We'd been listening for them ever since the balloon had gone down. Hopefully, there would only be one, and it would focus on the crash site.

Captain Rich seemed amused. "When you say 'evil' and 'conniving,' you mean other than the evil and conniving CIA."

"Sure. Vilify us." Margo shifted among passive, catatonic, and aggressive. Captain Rich had triggered her aggressive state. "We were controlling a threat. You wouldn't be so cocky if you saw Thandar's list of potential buyers. Black market exists for buyers who can't buy through the traditional market. They pay a premium and stay under the radar. Terrorists. Terrorist nations. Basically, the last people on earth who you want acquiring uranium."

"What about the teak and opium?"

Margo's body language was 100 percent defensive. She paused before answering.

"First I've heard of it was just now, when you heard about it. Honest. But I wouldn't put it past Lonnie. The complication was that he had cover and deniability for the skimmed-uranium sale, but teak and opium were out of our remit. Way outside. He'd have major exposure risk. We worked as a team. I'd be involved with the receipt and transfer of the uranium. I can't imagine he could have successfully hidden the opium from me. The teak could be explained away as the means for hiding the containers full of uranium. I'd have known about it, and Lonnie would have expected me to blow the whistle."

"Which is why he's not on the ground with us right now." Fritz scowled at Margo. CIA versus CIA. This was interesting.

"Come again?"

"Educated guess on my part. I figured he'd have stashed the second gun on your side of the basket if you were in on it. Instead, he took the risk of discovery by putting it on his side. I saw him slide it in behind the ballast bag that I'd put in as a counterweight for Captain Rich."

Captain Rich gave a weak smile; he was probably

getting tired of the weight references. "Lot of good that did him." His smile returned.

"Yeah, but at some point during the hike out, I'm guessing once he knew he could make it on his own, he would have tried to take us out. Small man, big gun. Tying up loose ends. Bad news for us. You know, he'd warned Thandar that Tao could be trouble and it would be best if he never made it to camp. Thandar had Wai kill Tao."

Son of a bitch!

That brought the conversation to a screeching halt. We had more pressing matters to deal with, and Lonnie had gotten his karmic payback, but that was a topic that might need revisiting with Margo. My head was spinning, but I pressed on.

"And knowing what you knew about him, you let him keep the second gun?" There were times when Fritz's logic escaped me.

"I pocketed the bullets before we even left the ground. I left the gun so he wouldn't know he'd been exposed. I finally extracted the gun while he slept. That's why he took so long to jump. He was searching for the gun."

Fritz unzipped his jumpsuit, pulled out a gleaming Sig Sauer, and handed it to Captain Rich. He followed it with a handful of bullets.

"The other gun, the one he used to threaten Wai, was a surprise. Luckily, Lonnie wasn't the speediest worm in the compost. You, on the other hand"—he nodded at me—"moved well. Like a gymnast."

"Thanks. It was a wrestling move. Rikidozan. Famous Japanese wrestler. I was named after him."

Fritz nodded as if that was the most natural response in the world.

"So that leaves Margo." It seemed like a good opportunity to find out more about her. She'd wandered off in a huff after the exchange about Lonnie and was sitting on a rock a good distance away. Too far to hear. I had been watching her more closely and kept an eye on her as we talked.

"Yeah, the jury is still out on her." Fritz glanced her way. "But she seems like a straight shooter—we'd been in contact at the beginning of this mission about the possible need for an extraction. I'm one of many she would have contacted."

That was a revelation. I'd never thought the government, our government, would have people embedded in a country like Myanmar. Russia, sure, but Myanmar?

"There are more of you?"

"I'd guess a dozen or more. We don't have contact with one another, but I know there are many exit opportunities within the country. I just happened to be the one best aligned to your escape route."

"I hate to break up this love fest, but we need to keep moving. I'd like to be in the exposed area early so we can plan our route from the shadows. Highly unlikely that the copters will spot us, but I want to maximize the chances of us all making it across the border alive." With that, Captain Rich poured a cupped handful of tepid groundwater over his head, heaved on his knapsack, and headed uphill.

We all scrambled to our feet, some more elegantly than others, and followed.

Fritz's guesstimates seemed spot on. The altimeter on his fancy watch—"nonreflective, shock-resistant, waterproof to three hundred and thirty feet"—told us that we'd gained eleven hundred feet of altitude by the time we'd reached the edge of the jungle. Ahead of us was a mix of timber, scrub, and open ground. Less opportunity for stealth travel.

Those first eleven hundred feet had taken us three hours. We'd had a couple of hours of rest in the shade before venturing upward. The sun would soon be disappearing again behind the ridge, so we'd be able to move out from the scrub and timber. We worked our way progressively up the bone-dry streambeds while mostly staying in the shade from the scrub. Unfortunately, the rocky streambeds retained the day's heat long after they were out of direct sunlight. We were back to rationing water.

Captain Rich's best guess was that we'd take at least two hours to do the last section. Lots of variables. Fritz disagreed. Plus, he had a new plan. "We split up. Captain Rich, you and Ricky continue straight up the way we were coming. We can cut back on the variables by going our separate ways. Less waiting. No standing about below someone when the three people ahead of you have a tricky section. Besides, two people moving through the shadows are less likely to be noticed than four together. But if things get hairy, each two-person team splits up. Every man—person—for themselves. We meet up after clearing the ridge and making it partway down the other side, say two hundred meters down the road."

"How do you think that impacts the odds?" I was pretty sure I already knew the answer.

"I think, working this way, they're about fifty-fifty."

"Fifty-fifty what?"

"Fifty percent chance two of us make it."

"And the other two?"

"Also fifty percent." Fritz seemed to always have an answer.

"And"—I poked my finger in his face—"do you ever give odds other than fifty-fifty?"

"No. I found that if I stick with that as my default answer, I can always say I predicted the outcome, no matter how the dice roll. Don't worry, we'll wait for you."

"Is that what you think? That we'll be the ones lagging?"

"I've been staying in peak condition for five years, ready for this. I've worked out on a climbing wall inside my barn."

Captain Rich didn't even try to hide his eye roll.

"Two teams. You and Ricky, me and Margo. Whoever is the fastest on a team assists the other. Margo and I are going to swing way to the right. We can't take a chance of going through town as CIA operatives. The Shan will be sympathetic to you, but not to us. And frankly, we'd rather keep our faces and presence unknown."

Captain Rich was aggravated. "Well, so be it. Ricky is in tip-top shape and was actually a climber. On real rocks, not a barn wall. I've carried hundred-pound packs up three-hundred-foot sand dunes. We'll be flying up that hill, but we won't leave you behind. We'll be the ones waiting for you on the other side."

He and Fritz did a bro hug. Margo and I just shrugged our shoulders. She feigned a yawn while I shook my head in disbelief. Testosterone can be deadly.

We took a few minutes to hydrate and distribute the water between the two teams. Fritz headed off up and to the right in a deep streambed that was completely in shadow. He was thirty feet up before turning to Margo. "Coming?"

Captain Rich tapped me on the shoulder and gave me a thumbs-up. "Men," he said with a big grin. "So easily manipulated if you challenge our capabilities. I hope you brought reading material for our wait on the other side."

"I'm fine. Keep going."

I then made the mistake of racing up a long, steep, rocky section that would have been a series of small waterfalls had there been any water, without stopping or checking on Captain Rich. In the time it had taken me to clamor up a hundred feet, he'd managed about sixty. His lag time had been slowly increasing as the long-shadow hours fell upon us.

Stopping to scan the horizon, again, he gasped out, "Two hundred more feet, and then we're there."

"Work your way a bit to the right. You're going to end up with an eight-foot climb if you stay in the stream-bed. I know—it was sort of technical. Just use the shade of the scrub."

He managed a gasped "Thanks" as he stopped and paused before dashing to the shade on his right. As soon as he was in covering shade, he dropped to his knees, sucking air.

"You're holding your breath when you're pushing off. Don't. Breath in a natural tempo." It was the third time I'd given that advice. Each time, he'd done it right for a while, but he kept falling back into bad habits.

He shook his head in response.

The scrub became a bit sparser as the ridge turned steeper. The next fifty feet took him fifteen minutes. At that rate, it would be dusk before we hit the ridge. I didn't mind climbing in moonlight, but I was becoming concerned about Captain Rich. The rocks were loose, and he'd already dislodged one, sending it tumbling and sliding twenty feet down the slope. On the plus side, his breathing was more regular, and he seemed to be picking up the pace.

The helicopters had been working along the hillside and ridgetop ever since the balloon had been shot down. The first two had been joined by one more, but that seemed to be the sum total of the effort to find us. With our dark-camo outfits and reduced heat signature, plus working in the shade, there was no way they'd see us. They'd passed over us twice without slowing.

It didn't seem like we were in danger of being sighted, but we'd agreed that no matter what time we got to the ridgetop, we'd wait for darkness and then sprint. Trips and tumbles were far more attractive than gunfire. We'd seen what it had done to the balloon's basket.

And Lonnie.

46

WELCOME TO THAILAND— ALMOST

Do you know that sinking feeling in your stomach when you realize you're out of options?

Fritz and Margo had moved out of sight. They were sweaty and dirty, scraped up and bruised, thirsty and tired, just like us, but both moved gracefully and quietly. We, on the other hand, had already caused two minor rockslides.

Captain Rich pulled me close and whispered in my ear, "We have a complication. Follow my lead."

I wasn't expecting what he did next.

"*Row yum peh! Row yum peh!*" He then said it again, louder. And then, slowly raising his hands, he stood up.

Crud!

"Hands in the air, Ricky. Stand up slowly."

"OK. What does *row* whatever mean?"

"We surrender. I think."

Double crud!

Three soldiers stood up slowly to our right, rifles

pointed directly at us. Up the hill, farther to the right, another two rose. Rifles again.

The soldiers began barking orders and gesturing with the barrels of their rifles, a mix of old bolt-actions and what looked to be AR-15s.

Luckily, I'd peed during our break.

"Lay down, Ricky. Spread eagle. Fingers spread apart. It may not look like it, but this is good news."

Captain Rich remained standing, yelling out something that sounded like Thai. He got a response from the soldier closest to us. Also in Thai.

Thai? Myanmar military? Rebels?

Slowly, with one finger through the trigger guard, Captain Rich removed the Sig Sauer and put it on the ground. He backed down a few feet and dropped into a spread-eagle position.

The soldiers were talking excitedly back and forth. I couldn't make out who the leader was, and they seemed to be lacking in coordination. One was on the radio, relaying information to the others.

I'm no stranger to being arrested, so the sequence that followed was not totally unfamiliar, though these guys used the toes of their boots more aggressively than I was used to. They searched Captain Rich first. Then me. After a few prods and kicks, and a thorough pat-down of my backside, they rolled me over and continued the invasive search. Finding nothing, they backed off.

More radio discussion. Some discussion, still in Thai, with Captain Rich.

At least one helicopter, based on the sound, was working its way up the ridge. Radio guy, who I guessed was nominally in charge, motioned to us with his gun and quietly spoke. We both moved under some nearby scrub brush.

Several minutes later, the copter came by, low and slow. Seeing five soldiers taking a cigarette and water break, guns resting against a large rock, they even more slowly backed off. The soldiers waved. One gave the copter crew the bird until the man next to him elbowed him in the ribs.

There was more chatter among the soldiers and the men.

"We stay here," Captain Rich said, pointing to our position under the scrub, "for a while. There's a delivery coming our way." I had no idea that he was so fluent in Thai. The man was full of surprises.

"How did you know they were there?"

"I heard a safety click. That's always a real pucker moment. In poor visibility, close-action situations, I figured he already had a round chambered."

I was going to have to get some stories out of Captain Rich before I worked with him again. Scary stuff.

It seemed like he was expected to be the liaison. Given my lack of language skills, I was fine with that, even though it did seem a bit presumptuous. And sexist.

I prodded Captain Rich. "Where are we? Already in Thailand?"

"All good. We're in Loi Tai Leng, still Myanmar, sitting right on the Thai border. Fritz mentioned this as a possible crossing site. These guys don't play nice with the Myanmar government. It's sort of a hands-off situation nowadays. They'll get us across the border, no worries."

As reassuring as that sounded, I was going to keep worrying until we got back to Phuket.

About thirty minutes later, the delivery came. Military uniforms. Captain Rich had spent the time checking out our captors—or saviors—and had figured out that they were, indeed, Shan State Army–South. SSAS. That was excellent news. Or so he said. It seemed like we might be home free. They also had rifles for us. Old bolt-action rifles, but rifles nonetheless. I guess trust only went so far.

After we'd changed, and I'd hidden my hair, the two of us fell in with the SSAS soldiers and continued up the hill. To an observer, there was no formation, but neither of us was on the outside, and we were each covered by at least one SSAS guy.

Marching out in the open, I could get a better sense of what had been ahead of us. We had almost made it to the top, which was cleared of trees and brush and completely exposed. I wouldn't have given us good odds if we'd tried to cover that ground in the sight of helicopters.

There were signs of a village as we crested the ridge. The helicopter, or one of the others, made another pass over us as we hoofed it along the ridgetop, but it moved on without slowing. The fact that the group had grown from five soldiers to seven apparently hadn't set off any alarms.

"Welcome to Thailand. Almost."

Captain Rich's confidence never seemed to wane, regardless of the circumstances.

We were escorted—*paraded* would be a better term— through town, past what looked to be a medical clinic, a general store, and a jail, to a couple of noodle stalls.

Next door was a boarding school. Every window we could see was filled with the faces of curious students, giggling and pointing as we awkwardly bent down to get under the overhang of one of the stalls.

Several of the vendors abandoned their stalls to follow behind, curious about these ragtag foreigners dressed in uniforms of the local military.

I still couldn't relax. We weren't in Thailand. We didn't even know if the choppers were told to stand down if we made it across the border. My guess was no. And I wasn't even sure the Shan would put up a fight if the Myanmar Army chose to try to retrieve us before we got to the border. My brain said to move on and over the border, but my stomach said to stop and eat. My stomach won out, and we stopped at one of the Shan shops. The noodles had spindly chicken wings but great spices. I ate two servings and could have eaten a third, but darkness had settled, and it appeared our military host was weary of our presence. He kept checking his watch.

The helicopters had stopped not long after sunset. If they had dropped troops, we weren't aware of it. Thailand beckoned from just the other side of the road, through the nearest town was several hours away. With luck, we might get a ride. Late at night, looking like we did, it would take a lot of luck.

We stripped out of our SSAS uniforms and put our camouflage flight suits back on. Best to play it safe. Mine was beginning to gain a little funk, but the feeling of safety it inspired made it tolerable.

The SSAS troops replenished our knapsacks with flashlights, canned meats, bug spray, bags of sweets, and some extra bottles of water. Captain Rich managed to charm one of them into trading a knife for his precious iPod, which had been cracked in the parachute landing but seemed to still be in working order. Captain Rich also got Lonnie's pistol back, which he'd surrendered when we had run into the SSAS, though he was warned that it might increase his risk of trouble in Thailand rather than diminish it. He took the pistol under advisement.

We were also advised to exit the town quickly and move deep into Thailand, as the Myanmar helicopters and their troops were often known to stray across the border.

The road leading to Thailand lay to the west at a slope far less extreme than the one we had scrambled up. We were assured that the road was safe but told to duck under cover if we heard helicopters.

Not reassuring.

Within minutes of walking on the road, we were covered with dust, and Captain Rich had converted a portion of his T-shirt into a face covering. I borrowed his knife and followed suit, though the aroma from a shirt trapped inside of a nonporous flight suit for more than two days was enough to make my eyes water.

No luck. No ride. We didn't even see a car, motorcycle, or skateboard as we walked the dusty road. But we did hook back up with Fritz and Margo, who were waiting in some roadside bushes, no worse for wear.

We also didn't see a Myanmar helicopter, soldier, or attack dog, either, so—all things considered—it was a good walk.

We found a spur road leading to an area that

appeared to have been harvested of its hardwood trees and was within a short walk of a stream. Fritz's fancy watch told us it was 21:00, so we decided to call it a day. Captain Rich said he had a plan.

While Margo rested, Fritz, Captain Rich, and I set about gathering branches and palm fronds. Using a downed tree near the road, we built a lean-to.

"No fire. I'm still not sure about helicopters, and only use flashlights when absolutely necessary." Captain Rich was in full security-consultant mode. We ate our canned meat cold.

He set about gathering pine needles in large armfuls to make bedding, with which we each gratefully filled depressions under the tree and then fell asleep, still zipped into our bug-proof flight suits.

I awoke a few times during the night, discovering bare spots where I hadn't applied enough bug spray—and once Captain Rich's arm draped over my belly—but I made it through the night without any major bites of any kind.

We all woke up with the sun. Our wake-up meal was dry, day-old sweet rolls that some kind soul had tucked into my pack and may have been the best breakfast I'd ever had. Fritz sterilized more water for us before we set out.

Our luck changed within thirty minutes as a truck, followed by clouds of dust, slowed and picked us up. Behind the wheel was one of the street vendors we'd seen the day before, apparently unfettered by the hypothetical line between his home country and Thailand. His flatbed was filled with wooden boxes containing a variety of glass bottles filled with a brownish liquid, quickly identified by Fritz as moonshine. The only place to sit was on the very back edge of the flatbed, holding on to the ropes that strapped down the cargo. As we settled down, the choking dust cloud caught up with us. It would remain our travel partner for the next ten kilometers.

We then stopped at a Thai border crossing, where our truck was met by a collection of Thais with trucks, cars, and tuk-tuks, who quickly loaded the moonshine into their vehicles, paid up, and began to leave. Our host was in conversation with Fritz and apparently made it clear that this was his turnaround point, but he pointed out one of the Thais as a potential taxi service. Once again, we rode in back, accompanied by the dust cloud.

Forty kilometers later, my butt numb from the ride, we were dropped off on the outskirts of a tiny village, where Fritz arranged for homestays for the four of us— Margo and me at one and he and Captain Rich at the other. The beds were narrow and hard but clean, the food plentiful and spicy, and the air-temperature shower from a garden watering can hanging from a rope was almost decadent. Compared with our past few nights, it was heaven. Our host was anxious to introduce us to the many natural beauties of the village, most of which involved walking uphill, which we politely declined through Captain Rich.

47

BUDDY, CAN YOU
LOAN ME A DIME?

"How THE HELL are we going to get back to Phuket? This hitching is not going to make it," I said.

"I've got cash. A lot."

We all looked at Fritz, who was grinning ear to ear.

"Lonnie's. I saw him slide the envelope into his pack back at the farm. He wasn't very good at spy craft—not at all subtle. I got it out while he was distracted by the shooting. He was curled up in the fetal position on the floor. Oblivious." Captain Rich and I looked at Margo, who was frowning. "Plus," he quickly added, "a wad of my own. And I've got a credit card. Amex. Never leave home without it."

"About how much is a lot?" I had a feeling that there were differing definitions within this group.

"Quick guess? Lonnie's envelope has forty or fifty thousand. There are some big bills, so it might be as much as a hundred."

I sidled up to Fritz, gave him my best flirtatious

smile, batted my eyes, and in what I think was a Marilyn Monroe voice, asked, "Buddy, can you loan me a dime?"

He grinned but made no offer of cash. So much for my Marilyn appeal.

Still staring at the envelope of cash that Fritz held up, Margo almost shouted, "Son of a bitch was holding out! He must have gotten it from Thandar." She went silent and just stared into space. I guess Lonnie's treason was a lot to process.

"That and the gun. I doubt that Lonnie found it. My guess is he was told it would be in the glove compartment. The pathway from the mine to my farm was paved with Thandar's assistance. You could have worn US dress uniforms and waltzed out of the camp in broad daylight. No one would have stopped you. Wai said the Suburban was left right where Thandar said it would be. Shame he didn't include a phone. But I'll take care of that."

And off he went. Five minutes later, Fritz was back with a battered and taped flip phone.

"I can only call domestic, but that's good enough. I gave the Thailand office a heads-up that we might be calling."

The phone, despite all outward appearances, worked. Fritz walked away from us and carried on a hushed conversation. He returned quickly with a big smile. "They hadn't sent anybody to get us yet . . . no way of knowing where we were going to come out. They didn't want to have someone lingering about. Too much attention. They'll call back in a minute."

And they did. After a brief discussion, he handed

the phone to Margo. She didn't say much except to sign off at the end with a curt, "OK, yes, I'll be with them."

"Yep, two cars will be on their way shortly." Fritz was pleased with himself. "First one"—he pointed at Captain Rich and me—"will take you to Phuket. The other will take me to a field office. Margo is going with you. Twenty-hour ride. You'll probably switch cars and drivers in Bangkok. You'll get food on the way. I'm guessing they'll find a place for you to crash in Bangkok.

"Oh." He pointed at me. "It shouldn't have to be said, but this is a covert operation. Don't talk to the driver about what's happened in the last ninety-six hours. Don't ask questions that don't have to do with food or sleep. Don't try to be his friend. Rich, you OK with that?"

"'Nuff said. I'll keep her in line."

"Where, exactly, are we going?" I was thinking of catching a fast plane out of Bangkok.

"You have some serious debriefing. Serious." Fritz added extra emphasis the second time he said "serious" just in case there was any doubt. "You're going back to the harbor where we started. Make the *Valkyrian* your home base. You can call home, but don't talk about the mission or the outcome."

"I think we'll be safe there." I didn't try to hide my disappointment in not being able to put this all behind me. I'd already started making a mental note of people I knew who'd worked in Mozambique.

Despite its broken-down-wreck appearance, the *Valkyrian* seemed to be in a defensible position. "We can defend it, but we won't be able to use it for escape. It's certainly not going anywhere. The thing is ensludged."

"Ensludged?" Fritz and Captain Rich were in almost perfect unison.

"Ensludged. The state of being encased in sufficient sludge beneath the surface so as to hold the boat in place."

"That's not a word." Captain Rich knew his nautical terms.

"It's in Rickypedia. I made it up myself."

"Actually"—Margo popped in from wherever her brain had taken her—"that's a good word. I instantly knew what it meant."

"That's true for all the words in Rickypedia. I've got dozens of them. Back in Egypt, I saw a lady get her hand shredded by a shotgun blast and came up with another entry."

I paused. And waited.

"Are you going to make us ask?" Margo seemed intrigued.

"Please don't encourage her." Captain Rich's face was contorted in pain.

"Handburger."

I crack myself up.

"Can we get back on track?" Fritz was getting antsy. I'd thought of adding *retracked* to Rickypedia but was told it would just cause confusion with *retract*. Besides, it wasn't clever enough.

He got another nod of agreement from Captain Rich, who then gave me an eye roll.

"And here's half of Lonnie's money. You earned it."

Good timing. Win back the attention of the audience.

"You probably earned more, but that's a discussion you can have with Margo and her boss after your debrief. I must say, this was an unexpected change of pace. I was beginning to think I'd never be activated, and I certainly never expected an adventure like yours. And you, sir," Fritz proclaimed, slapping Captain Rich on the shoulder, "are one badass security consultant. Great moves on the basket exit." He merely pointed at me. "And you aren't half-bad yourself, Miss Ricky. You more than held your own. Margo, you got anything else?"

Margo shook herself out of her stupor. "Yeah." The pause was so long that I thought she was going to check out again. But as soon as she got going, she was as sharp as a tack.

"One or two things. So, here's how it's going to play out. You're not going to talk to the press. Nothing good can come of that. Lonnie was rogue. Period. We're going to debrief with my boss, but he's already made this much clear. The story to the press will go something like this. It starts with our cover story, which our agency spent a lot of time putting together. Lottery—they even got that into the news—environmentalists, pollution testing, water testing. Completely benign citizen activity. Reliable boat captain. Meek divemaster."

She stopped to take in a gulp of water.

"Lonnie got distracted while guiding the boat, and we illegally entered Myanmar territory." She gave herself a theatrical head slap. "Maybe there was a failure in the navigation equipment. We'll never know. We were arrested and our yacht confiscated, but it was damaged and sunk. Stupid Lonnie ran back in to get his passport and went down with the ship."

"I did not see that coming!" I was getting to like this storytelling spy craft.

"Yes." She looked deeply into my eyes, selling the story as if her life depended on it—which, perhaps, it did. "The sinking was unforeseen and tragic. Unforeseen and tragic. Lonnie gave his life to get the paperwork. And more. You, Captain Rich, and I were already aboard the navy boat. Apparently, brave but misguided Lonnie grabbed the grenade gun, which was primed and fired, blowing a hole in the hull. He never had a chance and went down with the *Powerballer* in very, very deep and uncharted waters."

Looking at me, and then glancing at Captain Rich, she continued, "Are we clear on that? If there's any point that you aren't clear on, say nothing when asked. We were properly detained, treated well, and then driven to the Thailand border, where the Shan helped us on our way. No mention of uranium. No balloon escapes. Just a kind transport by military vehicle all the way to the border."

I was thinking that the best next step was to completely ignore that set of instructions and contact the media immediately.

She continued. "Now, why will you do this? Because you will get a very friendly cash settlement in addition to the money that Fritz just gave you, which—by the way—doesn't exist. It's not on the books, and you are not to mention it during the debrief. And if you even mention uranium or teak or heroin, we will ruin you.

Passports revoked. Reputations in tatters. Past employers hassled. Probably a Thai prison, if you're lucky, or a special US facility if you're not. We are very good at this, so don't test us."

"OK, play it back for me." Margo was all business. Her stupor seemed to be a thing of the past.

Captain Rich went first.

"Lonnie was an idiot. Couldn't navigate to save his ass and took us right into Myanmar waters. We were captured. The idiot blew a hole in the hull trying to be a superhero, and our beloved *Powerballer* sunk with Lonnie on board because he was stupid enough to go back in for our passports, and then his ego wrote a check his skill set couldn't cash. The Myanmar Army treated us well, interviewed us gently, fed us heartily, believed our story, and gave us a ride in a nice SUV to the border. The Shan helped us from there."

I repeated the tale, with a few choicer words about Lonnie.

"Are we all on the same page?" She looked at Fritz, who responded with a nod. "Yeah, I think that's all."

It was a five-hour wait for the cars, during which time we grudgingly walked up hills to see the views. I still worried about helicopters, but none showed. Our car, a not-too-old BMW, arrived first, as predicted, and Fritz's arrived almost immediately after. We tossed our few possessions, including our foul-smelling flight suits, into the car. We all looked odd with our crop-top shirts, having sacrificed fashion for face coverings, but where we were going, there weren't going to be any pageant judges.

Fritz was way ahead of us and already prepared to

head off. His engine was running and his foul clothes locked in the trunk. I got a big hug before he darted off.

I sort of nonchalantly followed and leaned up against his open window. "Hey, before you run off, I wanted to tell you how much it meant when you decided to trust me. I mean, I was kind of in the way."

"I'm not sure I ever fully trusted you, but abandoning you was an unacceptable option. I figured I could kill you once we hit the trees if I needed to."

"OK. Well, that sort of takes the bloom off the rose."

"Not at all. As you can tell, in my business, trust is a risky proposition. Those were my teammates up there, and I had to assume either of them was prepared to take me out at the first opportunity once I'd gotten their boots on the ground. The moment you four arrived, I had to start planning for any eventuality."

"So, what's next?"

"You know the old saying: 'I could tell you, but then I'd have to kill you.' It's something like that."

"If you ever want to take a break and get in some diving, just let me know. I promise that I won't have any plans to kill you underwater." I was probably coming on too strong.

"What are the odds you can keep that promise?"

"I'd say sixty-forty."

"Sixty yes, or sixty no?"

"I can't tell. It's sort of a toss-up." That got the grin I was hoping for.

Through his open window, Fritz fired off one more salvo. "Adios, motherfuckers." He was getting downright giddy. "It's been real. Maybe we'll run into each other down the road. Once I finish with all of the agency's bureaucracy, I am due a long vacation. I might just buy myself a boat. At this point, the farthest I want to be above sea level is on top of a flybridge. And once I get a boat, maybe I'll get a pony."

Captain Rich grinned. "Lyle Lovett. Good call."

48

NOT A JUNK

A<small>LMOST</small> <small>THIRTY</small> <small>HOURS</small> later, with a good but too-short six-hour sleep at a questionable hotel outside of Bangkok and a quick trip to a tourist-trap store to buy running shorts, tops, and sweat suits, we made it back to the harbor.

The trunk of the BMW was quite ripe by the time we arrived, what with us having added our days' old clothing to the flight suits, but we dragged all our gear out and left it in the parking lot, hoping for a heavy rain. Fritz had told us the flight suits were *uber* expensive and they'd be picked up when we had our debrief, but I couldn't see anyone wanting to wear those now that we'd shed bodily fluids into them for the better part of three days.

"At least the *Valkyrian* is better than our prison-camp accommodations. It's not a junk." Captain Rich's mood had remained sour, even with our return to freedom. Grabbing the railing of the boarding ramp, he pulled himself up, almost immediately falling back with a section of the broken railing in his hand. "Well, so far, so good." He shifted his position and stepped up to the ramp, which squeaked but held as he warily boarded the boat. Margo and I both waited to see if it would hold him.

"Shway!" Captain Rich was looking around and in a worse mood. "He was supposed to take care of that, and a whole list of other things, while we were gone. Five weeks. What's the man done? Shway!"

Once aboard, he moved along the starboard side until he reached the door to the pilot house. "Coming?"

Margo led the way. "No, not the pilot house. Not yet. Let's head down to the cabins. I've got cell phones for you. International plan. You can call your parents from here."

"Ha." I couldn't help myself. "My mom is part of the reason I was almost killed, and I don't even know who my dad is. I can call Pascal, but he's probably not up yet. There's no one else I care to call."

Margo raised her perfectly plucked eyebrow at the mention of my unknown-dad status but didn't tug on that thread.

Captain Rich was always thinking a few steps ahead. "Same. No one even knows I signed up for or went on this shit show of a voyage, and I hope to keep it that way. This sort of screwup can stink up my reputation for years. I just need a passport and a credit card, and I'm out of here."

"Oh, yeah." It hadn't even dawned on me: the paperwork. "Crap! Until then, we're stuck."

"As you might suspect," Margo jumped in, "I actually have connections at the embassy. I think we can get you those replacement passports fairly easily. You've got Lonnie's cash, so that should get you home with lots to spare. Fly coach. First class is a gouge. But pay for one of the VIP lounges. Free drinks and nice chairs before you get on the plane. Makes coach more acceptable. If you really think you need them, we can get credit cards in forty-eight hours. Anybody need a medical kit?"

This was a different Margo than we'd been with. She was actually helpful. We all had scratches and bruises, but no one had mentioned anything serious. She opened the door to the equipment room. The gear we'd ruled out or deemed overkill was piled up on the shelves, along with stacks of packages—batteries, tools, and cleaning supplies that hadn't made the final inventory. It looked more like a dive shop than a storeroom. There were, among all the spares, two full sets of dive gear, plus an extra-large wetsuit they'd bought for Captain Rich before discovering that he had never, ever worn neoprene. He dove in shorts and a T-shirt, and he never came up early. The waters where we'd been were warm enough that I'd even thought of foregoing the suit, except I was down so long that even mideighties water would leave me shivering.

There was a shelf of medical supplies, quite full despite the fact that we'd loaded a lot onto the *Powerballer* for our trip.

"At one time, we'd planned on a larger crew," Margo said. "But the lab grew, and a stateroom got consumed. Captain Rich's qualifications meant one less head count, and we quickly realized Tao—God rest his soul—was able to play many roles, which saved us another."

Margo grew silent. We'd all been so busy and intense, none of us had had time to really process what had happened. Whatever her level of feelings for Lonnie, at the least, they'd had many years together, some amount posing as husband and wife. You don't leave something like that behind without some intense emotions.

Margo was a mess. She sort of bounced around from one place to another, talking to herself, but finding a way to take care of us with some sort of mental checklist. I took the opportunity to go to the cabin I'd used and grab some clean shorts and a tank top. Captain Rich followed suit, coming back in board shorts and a Ramones T-shirt.

Margo continued to putter around, though in a daze. She'd pick up some random item—a book, a screwdriver—inspect it, and put it down again. This went on for the better part of fifteen minutes while we followed her around before she wandered up to the pilot house. For lack of any other direction, we followed. The phone chargers, which she finally found, were empty.

"Um, you're looking for passports?" I was normally the one accused of being spacy, but it seemed like I was going to have to babysit Margo until she got her act back together.

"Passports!" She slapped her forehead. "I was going to get our xerox copies of your passports. Those should help with the embassy. I'll go with you to facilitate. Lonnie had them. Passports. Phones." She looked blankly around the pilot house, still sort of out of it and probably still processing. "One sec. No, they're in the safe." She left us there to ponder whether we should leave her alone. She was definitely not quite all together.

It didn't register right away, but there was a change in the normal jungle sounds, followed by a quiet, but approaching, outboard motor. Captain Rich and I went onto the aft deck and leaned over the railing to get a better view.

It was a nice but small boat. Twenty-five feet or so. It looked familiar. I looked around the harbor and realized it was the same boat we'd left tied up when we had headed out for Myanmar.

49

HE REALLY DID IT

"I GOT ME a boat! I'm Captain Fritz now!"

"You got yourself a fine boat, Captain Fritz," called back Captain Rich. The boat was basically unchanged, except it was now rigged for fishing, sort of. I suspected fresh fish was in our future. Hopefully, nothing on my do-not-eat list.

Fritz pulled up, tied up, lifted a cooler onto the dock, and jumped off, looking every inch the veteran seaman. "You have to see this!"

Margo was back, paperwork in hand. "Who are you yelling at?"

"Captain Fritz. He really did it. He beat us back and already got himself a boat." I was still somewhat fried from our Myanmar escape, and somehow, I found myself giddy over something going right. I might have let out a little cheer.

"He didn't get a boat. That's ridiculous. That's our boat. I told him that he could have it if he was going to stay in Thailand." Margo squinted at Fritz, either confused or concerned.

Fritz was up the gangplank and up to the pilot house with the cooler in a flash.

Damn, he's good.

Before I could process that, he'd popped open the cooler and stood up, holding a pistol. Down on the boat, another person popped up from the tiny cabin—Wai, holding a second pistol.

Margo, it seems, seemed to have only just then figured it out. And by all appearances, she wasn't on the winning team. "Crap!"

Fuck. Double fuck.

Here we were again.

Captives. I couldn't believe exactly how messed up this trip was. With Margo in front, guarded by Wai; me following; then Captain Rich, guarded by Fritz and forced to walk backward, we worked our way down to the aft deck. It was quiet, but I noticed Captain Rich had begun humming. I couldn't figure out the tune at first, but then I recognized it as Sloop John B by the Beach Boys. I didn't know all the words, but I certainly remembered the refrain.

Damn straight. Even my screwed-up home would be better than this.

He barely moved his head, but I could tell, even from behind him, that he was looking for anything that he could turn into a weapon. Unfortunately, I was between him and Wai's gun. Fritz, his other option, had him in an awkward position, and there was too much space between them. No way Captain Rich got to him without being shot. I was prepared to duck if he made a move.

With two pistols pointed at us, there wasn't much choice about what to do. It wasn't entirely clear what our fate was going to be, but charging a CIA agent and a very rogue member of the Myanmar Army didn't seem like the best path to safety.

Once we got to the aft-dive area, Fritz dropped three sets of handcuffs on the deck and kicked two of them toward Margo.

"You know how these work. Cuff them around the base of the crane."

Wai signaled me, motioning with his pistol to take a seat on the deck, backing up to one of our heavy-duty davit cranes. Margo cuffed one of my wrists, pulled the chain around the crane's pedestal base, and cuffed the other.

When she repeated this with Captain Rich, he didn't exactly fight, but he clearly made her work to get his arms behind him. He winced as she closed them, his muscular forearms probably too large for standard cuffs. Fritz checked both sets of cuffs, squeezing mine tighter than Margo had left them. He glanced at Margo. "Nice try."

Wai cuffed Margo to the same crane I was now anchored to. Our arms were pulled back and interlocked, not only making it very uncomfortable but eliminating any leverage we had.

Captain Rich was scanning what part of the marina he could see from his position.

"If you're hoping that Tao's brother . . ." Fritz's tone was almost mocking.

"Shway."

"Yeah, Shway. Anyway, if you're looking for him to come in with the cavalry, you can give up hope. He's with Tao now."

Asshole!

"We're fucked." Captain Rich had a strong grasp of the situation.

I said, "No kidding. Did you have any idea?" It wasn't like him to be so fatalistic.

"Fritz and Wai?" He shook his head. "Looking at them now, working as a team, it should have been obvious that they had more history than we'd known. Did you suspect?"

"Not until Wai popped up. I was, though, kind of surprised that Fritz would come back to the harbor. It's the one place that authorities might be."

"Yeah. Not the move I would have made. Separate yourself and keep adding to the distance."

There was an aspect to Captain Rich's mercenary background that didn't allow for sentimentality. It was more prominent than I had thought.

Margo didn't offer up any commentary.

"Yeah, and I was wondering how he got the channel chain unlocked." The questions were stacking up faster than the answers were coming. I wasn't sure about anyone, captor or captive, at this point.

"That's simple," Margo replied as she slowly returned from whatever place her brain kept going. "I knew he'd be coming for the boat, and I gave him the code. I thought that was a good thing."

Captain Rich was sinking deeper into his funk. "I

should have armed up as soon as we got to the *Valkyrian*. We still had a significant stash of guns on board. Was too slow to react. And it looks like Margo wasn't expecting a double cross." Rich had that bulging-vein thing going on his forehead again. "Margo," he asked snidely, "I'm wondering if you would care to contribute to the conversation?"

Apparently, she didn't.

"We are just full of wonder." I figured I might as well join him in his snidery. I only wished we were as full of answers as we were of commentary.

Wai and Fritz took turns guarding us. I seldom saw what they were doing, but there was a lot of back-and-forth movement between the aft deck and the dock. Of the two, Wai seemed less diligent, often glancing about instead of keeping his eyes on us. This went on for more than an hour. Both of them worked up a sweat.

Margo probably had a better view, but she wasn't talking. I began to wonder if she was part of the plan and had been put there to spy on us.

Finally, both men stopped and settled down on a dive-deck bench. After a great deal of discussion and, apparently, a trip back to his new-to-him boat, Fritz tossed a rash guard and shorty wet suit at my feet and instructed me to put them on.

"I'm a little tied up right now."

Wai had left his gun with Fritz, who stepped a few feet back and behind the rack of tanks. Wai eased behind me, uncuffing one wrist. My shoulders had gone numb from the odd position we'd been left in, and it hurt to move my arms forward. But it felt better once I had. Wai kicked the rash guard toward my feet.

"Turn around, guys. You don't get to watch." I certainly wasn't going to reward their abuse with a peep show.

"No, I won't, and yes, I do." Fritz's smile was more tense than joyful. But his eyes were locked on me.

Dick.

I turned around for at least some measure of modesty, but Wai, who had returned to Fritz's side and gotten his gun back, yelled at me, "Face us! No tricks!"

Modesty was the least of my concerns at that point, so I turned, pulled off my clothes, and put on the rash guard and shorty. Wai pushed me down against the base of the crane and cuffed me again.

"You're not getting a free show from me," muttered Captain Rich. "I work for tips."

"You're fine as is. No neoprene for you. I already heard you brag that you've never dove in it. We want to make this realistic." I had no idea what Fritz had in mind—actually, I had several ideas, and they were all unacceptable.

Fritz had disappeared below but reappeared several times, toting tanks, masks, buoyancy vests, fins, regulators, and even dive computers—all the excess dive gear we'd left behind as overkill.

It appeared we were going for a dive.

"This is going to be tragically simple." Wai was focused and sharp—I only then realized that his English was better than before and his confidence level higher.

Wai kicked Captain Rich with a sweeping roundhouse right in the stomach, knocking the wind out of him. Then he delivered another to Captain Rich's head. He wasn't down and out, but he wasn't in any condition to fight.

Fritz grabbed him by his hair and lifted his head, pouring some expensive wine into his mouth and holding his nose to make him swallow. He repeated that twice before quickly slipping on the full-face mask and securing its regulator. Then he turned on the flow of gas from one of the tanks.

Captain Rich managed to gasp, "Big man, Wai, kicking a cuffed prisoner." He wheezed a bit, and drops of the wine dripped into his full-face mask, making a small, pink pool. "Want to take the cuffs off and try that again?"

Wai kicked him again.

"The two of you are going to take a swim." Fritz still held both guns, aimed generally in our direction. "Sadly, whoever fixed the old compressor on the *Valkyrian* did a poor job. Carbon monoxide seeped into the tanks. Horrors! And shamefully, it appears that Captain Rich had been drinking. Lonnie's finest wine, too." Horrors, indeed. Carbon monoxide was a silent, tasteless killer. Actually, pretty smart on Fritz and Wai's part.

"You'll never know, even at the end. Suddenly you'll just be unconscious, and then you'll be dead."

"Was this the plan all along?" I had a policy with people who were about to kill me—this made five—I wanted to understand why. And stall. Any hope that Margo could be counted on was quickly slipping away as she passively watched without comment or reaction.

Fritz had other ideas. He repeated the kicks with me, and even though I saw them coming, I was in no condition to stop him. He affixed my full-face mask and regulator, then began the flow of deadly gas.

"No, nothing along these lines. The original plan had you living, getting paid for your time, and being sent out of the country. Sworn to silence in the interest of national security. Nobody was supposed to get hurt."

"They killed Tao." I knew I was beating a dead horse here, but their story wasn't aligning well with reality.

"He was expendable. We knew that going in. There was always a chance he'd revert to his training and try to fight us. Although it sounds like he was more Prince Valiant than King Kong." Fritz was clearly up to date on the happenings before we had gotten to his farm. "Thandar's people let him finish early. He was a mercenary. He knew the risks going in. He was actually part of our team and an important part of the plan. Lonnie told Thandar that he was a liability risk. Shame he had to go, but he was a loose thread. His wife and children will be well taken care of. He should have stayed a monk."

"Is that all mercs are to you—expendable pawns? What does that mean for my future prospects?" Captain Rich clenched his fists. I'd only seen that once before, and it had been followed by a very quick and effective beatdown.

"Yes, true enough, but you are currently alive and remain of value. That's not a coincidence."

Fritz was turning out to be a real hard-ass.

50

TOO BAD, SO SAD

"It was really quite a beautifully orchestrated dance," Fritz said. "The CIA wanted to make contact with Thandar. I'd gotten word that he was looking for a customer for the uranium. He was thinking of hosting an auction. I passed it on to my handler, who ran it up the flagpole. Management put together a compelling offer for him. It was all kosher. Stamp of approval and all the right signatures."

Wai paced around but kept his eyes on both of us and kept the gun pointed at Captain Rich.

"But they thought the highest bidder might not be enough, so they decided they'd pressure him by collecting evidence of the uranium mining first. The new regime would have shut him down and arrested him if we gave them the evidence. But that just opened the door for Lonnie. He realized that we could skim the skim and make millions. And we could engage in some side business.

"Then, I guess, Lonnie went behind my back on the

opium and teak, and he became an unexpected complication. I was worried about the scope creep of the
deal. Lonnie was becoming a wild card. Then he became
a liability. And then"—he pointed his gun at Captain
Rich—"rat-a-tat-tat, he wasn't."

Wai sighed, but he never let his gun waver.

"You're missing something," Captain Rich pointed
out. "Why not make me a partner? You no longer have
Lonnie. I've got the training and experience that can
help you deal with these fuckers. I'm the only one who
can handle a boat for you."

I'm not sure how much they heard. The mask muffled his words a bit. Even sitting right beside him, it was
hard to hear. But apparently, they had heard enough.

"The need for a boat is done. Thandar has it. From
now on, they can manage to transport to a discreet
harbor by barge, under the protection of Thandar's
organization and the Myanmar Army. From there, we
transfer goods by a bulk carrier—protected by the CIA.
Everything is hidden in stacks of teak logs that no one is
going to search. Too heavy, too cumbersome, too protected by official documents. It was just going to be a
simple feigned escape, facilitated and executed by Wai.
He was our passport all the way to the border." Fritz was
talking a mile a minute. I grew convinced he was tapping
into the meth. "No one chasing us. Lonnie caught on to
Wai, listening in on his negotiations. Decided he wasn't
to be trusted."

"He must have figured out that I was clued in to his
game, and that's why he went all cowboy on me." Wai's
mastery of the English language continued to impress.

"Lonnie wasn't very strategic," Fritz continued. "He was a 'Ready, fire, aim' kind of guy. He reacted to Wai instead of figuring out how to control him. He wasn't much of a think-on-your-feet field guy. His strength was in the lab. Bad choice for the job. He should have been crew and had a real field agent doing the transactions." Fritz sort of spat out those last two words. I guess he liked his missions locked down nice and tight. "So, Lonnie had to go. Loose cannon."

Fritz looked a bit antsy. He was back up and hopping side to side as Wai tried to calm him down. "Just like your buddy, Tao. Wai saw the tattoo and the scars and realized Lonnie was right—he'd be a handful. Lots of trouble, no negotiating value. So, he took him out. Bang."

I'm going to kill him.

Wai shushed him, then said, "None of us counted on running into a bunch of trigger-happy rebels. Those troops were a big surprise. We'd planned on staying with the balloon, barely skirting the ridgetop, and dropping down safely in Thailand."

Fritz jumped in. "I think that catches you up with the whole story. It's the least we can do. But as far as the official story goes, Lonnie died in the boat, I don't exist, and the three of you made it safely back to Phuket. The CIA will deny any knowledge of you. And Ricky and Captain Rich are the only ones the Shan saw at the border. So as far as the US government knows, all the pieces fall into place. As long as you aren't available for the debrief."

I noticed a little spittle collecting on the corner of his mouth, and his pupils were the size of pinpricks.

"Now it's going to look like the two of you took a pleasure dive with bad gas in your tanks. You'll be found floating on the surface, having dumped your weights in a final desperate, but failed, act of salvation. Too bad, so sad."

I was developing a real dislike for Fritz.

Wai was watching him closely. And frowning. "Fritz has it all figured out. Fritz, are you OK?"

"Yeah, Wai, baby. Just took a little pick-me-up. I'm good. I had to travel through the night to get here and get things ready. Just a little taste. I'm good." He looked far from good. He worked his fingers rapidly, as if playing the piano, but without the keys or any apparent talent. "As far as anyone knows, the two of you have been here all along, working on the *Valkyrian*."

I wasn't sure how Fritz was going to arrange this, but I was intrigued by the way his mind was working.

"Illegally, without work visas, I might add. Tsk-tsk-tsk. It will merit a minor investigation. Nothing suspicious will show up. Your computers will show that you quickly dropped to ninety feet today and then floated to the surface."

He was tying two wrist computers off on the line attached to one of his fishing rods. Pretty clever. He was having trouble, though, with the knots due to his highly energized state, and trying to tie while talking made it even more difficult. It would have been comical under other circumstances.

"Captain Rich here has been buying the diving gear

and food, so nothing points anywhere but back here. Once you arrived, he pretty much stopped going into town. The big South African hasn't been seen for weeks, probably holed up with his American honey. It's a clean, simple story.

"You two, plus Margo, Lonnie, and me, as far as Thandar knows, are dead, but the deal with Thandar will live on. Wai already spoke with him this morning—the reports of the failed balloon escape had already reached camp—no reports of parachutes, but I'll send word that I survived and will work with Thandar to get approval for the next steps. I'll retire to a little place we've picked out here along the coast, and no one will be the wiser."

Things started to click in my head. "But wait—Margo's first pilot chute was a dummy."

"Yeah, that was an insurance policy. I had the option of letting her go over the side with the dummy, but I decided it was smarter to keep her around, so I jettisoned it and pulled her real one. I got a little nervous when you repacked your chute. If you'd worked on Lonnie's or Margo's, things would have gotten ugly quickly. But she lived and served her purpose. She was in the car with you and Captain Rich, so that's been documented. Makes for a better story to have her disappear after the fact."

"Fritz!" barked Wai. "Chill out a bit and bring your boat around. It's time to get the show on the road."

As soon as Fritz left, Captain Rich started thrashing about, jerking back and forth.

"You can keep that up as long as you want, honey." It seemed like Wai and Fritz were in a competition to see who could be more obnoxious in victory. "That crane is rated to hold eight hundred pounds. You're never going to tear it loose. But please, go right ahead. I could use the comic relief."

51

PITY PARTY

I'D BEEN STRUGGLING as well, but without much moving of my body, and had made as much headway as possible for the time being. I was beginning to feel nausea, which could have been brought on by the thought of imminent death or could have been the beginning of my reaction to the carbon monoxide. I figured we didn't have much more time. Captain Rich, though very animated, seemed glassy-eyed. I worried if the thrashing might be seizures.

I turned my head to face Wai, slowly let my eyes droop, and began to mumble. Emphatically, with passion, but without any clear words.

"Trying to get in one last wise-ass comment? Start a little pity party? Maybe throw out one of those French proverbs?" He leaned in, though he kept his eyes on the increasingly frantic thrashings of Captain Rich.

And that was when I punched him in the throat.

I may not be Japanese, but whatever my heritage, I swear my hands really are freakishly small. I wore off a lot of skin and dislocated my baby finger at the knuckle, which hurt like a son of a bitch, but I'd been able to work a hand free of the handcuffs. With my legs tied, though, I had to make sure he was close enough.

After the punch, I grasped a handful of hair and pulled Wai in. I grabbed his throat and began squeezing, keeping his head back with the other hand, despite my injured pinkie. His kicking continued for several minutes, but he finally settled down. I continued to squeeze his throat. I didn't want to discover that he'd been acting.

"Ricky!" Captain Rich had stopped thrashing and was watching the drama play out. "He's unconscious! You can let go."

"I'm not sure! It can take three or four minutes!" I yelled back to make sure he could hear me through the full-face mask.

"He's out. I can tell. You're killing him."

"I don't care. If we're wrong and he's conscious, we lose."

"You're not a killer. Let go. We need to get moving. I don't know how long it will take to get me out of the cuffs and how quickly Fritz will be back."

I still held on.

"Stop and listen. He dropped the gun. I can kick it over to you. Once you've got the gun, you have control over him, and you'll have the element of surprise when Fritz comes around. As long as you wait and surprise him, you can control him as well. Better yet, you can break me out of the cuffs, and I can handle Fritz."

He slid the gun over with his left foot. I let go. Wai dropped like a rock.

"Is he . . .?"

"I don't know, and I don't have time to find out." I quickly untied the rope around my ankles.

"Slide Wai over this way." Captain Rich twisted his body. "I'll squeeze him between my legs. I can keep him in a leg lock for as long as you need."

"Do you want me to shoot the chain on your handcuffs?"

"I'd rather not find out if you have that particular skill. Just pick the lock."

"I have to go find the right wire. And what if Fritz comes back?"

"I haven't heard his engine yet. And I've got a wire for you. My earring."

He was right. The wire hook of his earring was long enough to work. With him holding Wai in an anaconda squeeze, I removed the earring.

"Now bend it into a slanted L and . . ."

"This isn't my first rodeo. I've been in enough handcuffs that I took the time long ago to learn how to pick them, though I may be a bit out of practice."

"OK, I can talk you through it. You first have to disengage the double—"

"I've got this. You're making it harder."

"Remember to have a nub at the end of the pick. Keep it short."

"I'm way ahead of you. It already clicked."

"OK, now—"

"I can leave these on you if you don't shut up. I need to concentrate."

"When this is all over, can we discuss your collaboration skills?"

"OK, one cuff is free; shake your hands. I'll do the other one later. And shut the hell up! If you had kept talking, we wouldn't have heard Fritz's motor start."

I was right. It had. We had almost no time to deal. Captain Rich released the leg lock he had on Wai, who was slowly coming back from the dead, and took the gun.

"Sit on him."

I kicked Wai in the head instead. Then I sat on him. There was a certain satisfaction from the kicking; plus, it disabled him for a longer period. But mainly, I did it for the pleasure.

We heard Fritz's boat bump up against the dock. If he hadn't already noticed the shift in control, he'd see it shortly.

Captain Rich spun and, just as Fritz stepped onto the dock, shot him in the knee. Fritz fell to the ground, screaming. His gun bounced on the edge of dock, teetered for a moment, then dropped over the side.

"Quiet! Shut up, Fritz. I need to think!"

"Don't you think that was a bit extreme?" For someone who had objected to my choking of Wai, Captain Rich seemed a tad hypocritical.

"We were at a disadvantage as long as he remained a threat. I took a nonlethal action that removed the threat. Besides, he kicked me in the head earlier. And no one was going to hear the shot."

He had a point. I hopped onto the dock, walked over to where he lay, and kicked Fritz's wounded knee. The scream was very satisfying.

52

IT'S COMPLICATED, BUT LEGAL

"So, what do you need to think about?"

I nodded over at Wai and Fritz, who were hand-cuffed and trussed up like a pair of Thanksgiving turkeys. "We've got them. They committed crimes on Thai soil. We turn them in to the Thai police and let the politicians and secret agencies battle it out."

"People. A little help over here. I think I need to be part of this discussion." Margo was still handcuffed, despite the fact that we were in firm control and I had demonstrated my picking ability.

"We'll get to you when we're damn well ready." I had six weeks of snarkiness saved up from our voyage and was going to make sure I got it all out while we had control over her. Besides, there had been so many twists and turns in their roles, I had no idea if we could trust her. I saw no upside to treating her as a victim.

"The problem is . . . rather, the problems are, that I"—Captain Rich actually held up the Boy Scout salute—"broke a ton of laws gathering the weapons.

Plus, our story—if accurately told—has us as accessories to Lonnie's death, illegally crossing the Thai border, fraudulently submitting for tourist visas, and overstaying our visas. And then there's the matter of you choking an officer in the Myanmar military and me shooting a CIA agent. I'd add in the recent offense of you kicking the hog-tied agent in his shattered knee."

"OK. I can see how that might look bad."

"I can see more than that. Probably a long sentence in a small Thai jail cell, followed by deportation to the United States for further trials. I can see all of my savings eaten up by attorney fees and my wives in the poorhouse. Thankfully, I can also see some alternate solutions."

"Wives? I knew about one. You have an ex-wife, too?"

"Wives. As in two current wives. It's complicated, but legal."

Yikes. I really don't know him very well.

"I have a headache." It was a splitting headache, to be precise. Likely from the carbon monoxide. Both of us were sucking oxygen from an emergency tank we'd found in the storage room. When I was an EMT back in Hawaii, I'd run into some surfers whose van had filled with the toxic gas while they were using a propane stove to cook Kalua pork, and I'd seen the same signs of poisoning. "Tell me what your alternate solutions might be."

"First," Captain Rich said quite slowly while looking at Wai and Fritz, "we can kill them both. Take them out in the boat like they were going to do for us, weigh them down with anchors, punch a bunch of holes in

TRACY GROGAN

them to let gasses escape so they don't float to the surface, and then send them to Davy Jones's locker."

"Do we punch the holes in them while they're alive or dead?"

"That's really a matter of personal preference. I've seen it done both ways. Either way works just fine, though while they're alive is messier."

My brain instantly tortured me by flashing memories of poor Tao floating away from the aft deck of the *Powerballer*.

"OK, that's one. Do you have a second option?"

"We patch old Fritz here up, rent a van, and take him and Wai back up to the Myanmar border. Hand them over to the troops in Loi Tai Leng with notes on what they were doing with Thandar." Captain Rich leaned back and took a long pull off his second bottle of beer. "There is no love lost between the Shan people and the Myanmar military." He nodded as he spoke. "I'm sure they would love to hand Aung San Suu Kyi's newly installed government a gift—a CIA agent who conspired with a rogue general to illegally mine uranium, harvest precious teak trees, and expand the opium trade. And a coconspirator traitor. Then we make some popcorn and watch the show."

He shot a look at Fritz and Wai. Fritz's eyes were as large as dinner plates, and he was vigorously trying to communicate through the gag in his mouth. Wai was, it appeared, catatonic.

"That's tempting. What about Margo?"
"Hand her off to the US Embassy."
"Right. What's option number three?"

348

"It's a variation on that. We take Wai to one of the official border crossings and turn him over with a note to Thandar explaining that the uranium deal is off, the US government is now aware of Thandar's dealings, and they will be getting in touch with Aung San Suu Kyi's emissaries. We let Thandar go all medieval on Wai, if Wai even makes it that far. We drop Margo and Fritz off at the US Embassy with a note explaining how they and Lonnie have been spending the CIA's money."

"Probably the most ethical of the three." I tried to sound even more pissed than I was. "But I'm not all that concerned with ethics when it comes to this group. I say we go with option one and dump them. It saves us a lot of time. We can avoid the mess by floating them out in the water on air mattresses before we punch the holes in them." Fritz went absolutely crazy as I grinned at him. "Shouldn't have kicked me in the head, jerk."

"I'm not ruling option one out." Captain Rich said that line slowly. "But consider keeping our hands clean and going with option three. Thandar will be more brutal than we could ever be, and the diplomatic attaché at the embassy will probably dispose of Fritz and Margo in a way that we know will ensure they never show up, alive or otherwise."

That got no reaction from the totally stoic Wai. Fritz was thrashing. Margo was hanging on every word.

"Very satisfying."

"So, we're going with three?"

Fritz resumed screaming.

"I don't know. I'm conflicted. Part of me wants to see their faces as they die, but I'm feeling a bit giving, too. The new government could use a nice PR story like this. And we could be repaying the folks of Loi Tai Leng for their kind treatment of us. I may regret it, but I'm leaning toward option two, with one slight alteration."

"I'm not ruling out option two, but what's the alteration?"

I got up, walked over to Fritz, and kicked him in the head.

"Yeah, I guess he had that coming. How about, though, we call it quits with the head and knee kicking? But option two just adds one more act that the government might object to. Handing off a CIA agent to a foreign power must be against some law. I do have an option four."

5 3

JUST ANOTHER LIE

OPTION FOUR REQUIRED we locate a sufficient number of rats to complete the work quickly. And we'd have to locate a jar or two of peanut butter. It also assumed that no one would be visiting the harbor for at least a week. From the perspective of revenge on Fritz, Wai, and Margo, it was clearly the best, but it left a lot of players still out there. And I wasn't ready for a major rat-collection expedition.

I chickened out and was persuaded by Captain Rich to go with option three. It was the only one that made for the greatest amount of accountability. Even the CIA took it in the shorts with that plan. And it kept us far away from US authorities. We figured neither Margo nor Fritz would mention us since we would be most excellent witnesses against them, so we were insulated from both retribution and official inquiries.

Turns out that Margo had our passports on the *Valkyrian* the whole time. She retrieved them from a bag, along with more cash that she'd hidden in one of the unused staterooms. Just another lie to keep us at her hip until she could kill us in a fashion that fit her narrative. That had sort of disappeared as an option the moment Fritz had pulled his double-cross on her.

And as long as no one knew we'd been working for Lonnie and Margo, we had no visa issues. In fact, Captain Rich still had a month left on his visa, and I had two.

We spent the next day chillaxing. Unfortunately, as we chilled, Captain Rich's mind kept working.

"So, exactly how bad was your last convo with your dad? On a scale of one to ten, based on your childhood traumas?"

"Eleven."

"Worse than the birthday party?"

"You have no idea." I was getting twitchy just thinking about it. On the other hand, leaving it as an untold story would just encourage Captain Rich to keep pressing. "He said, 'I'm not your biological father.' OK?"

"Ouch. That'll leave a mark."

"I'm glad you find humor in it."

"OK, I'll be serious. Did he have details?"

"They were seriously thinking about marriage and decided that the best way to figure out if it was the right thing to do was for them to break up and sleep around for a while. It was, he explained, the end of the eighties, and that's how things were done."

"Yeah, no, that was never how things were done." Captain Rich was probably ten years old at the time, but I trusted his historical knowledge. "So, who's your father?"

"Big mystery."

"Your mom couldn't keep track and figure it out with a calendar?"

"She might have needed a stopwatch. As she tells it, a beach party turned into an orgy, and she can't really be sure how many possible fathers were added to the equation."

Captain Rich had met my mother. I suspected that, like a lot of the men I knew, he'd fallen under her spell at some point. "I can see how that might happen." I swear he got all starry-eyed.

"Please." I was on the verge of gagging. "I want to unsee all of that."

The chillaxing was therapeutic, and I found Captain Rich to be even kinder and gentler than I had imagined. But he was getting antsy. As he explained it, when the dust hit his shoes, he just got up and moved. I'm sure that was a lyric borrowed from one of the tunes in his library, but it suited him well.

Once he'd made the decision, he was a whirling dervish of activity. Two days to replenish his basic needs—a cell phone; a new iPod with all his tunes downloaded from the cloud; a few tropical shirts and board shorts, socks, and some running shoes; a total cleaning for his newly acquired flight suit—and he was off by taxi. Thirty-three hours, Phuket to Hurghada, Egypt. Then a private plane to somewhere in Yemen.

"Security consultation. Should be done in a couple of months, knock on wood. It was thirty-six degrees there today, and we're just entering the hot period. That's a hundred degrees, for your way of measure. I like it when things get hot," he said before leaving.

He left me a new iPod with his full musical library. Also a new iPhone. He warned me not to let Sumo touch it. He'd noticed that my previous phone had some fancy malware on it that notified Sumo whenever I powered up the phone, which explained how he and Mom were always able to call me when my phone was actually functioning and by my side. And he'd left a very nice note in the beer fridge, apologizing for recruiting me for the "cruise from hell."

That left me to talk to Tao's sister, TK, which was brutal for both of us. I gave her most of the extra money that Margo had in the passport bag—probably a couple of years' salary at Tao's rate of compensation. But nothing can compensate for the loss of a brother.

Crud. Shway. Two brothers.

After she left, I was all alone in the harbor, bouncing around in the *Valkyrian*, wondering what my next step would be. Living without a schedule. Listening to tunes. Street food whenever I wanted. Getting casual.

I guess I was way too casual.

I never heard a thing. Not the car pulling up or the gate opening, but they must have. I didn't hear footsteps on the gravel or coming up the gangplank. I thought I heard a metallic ping, but the mangosteen trees along the fence line were so ripe that the fruit was dropping at a rate of five or more an hour. I didn't even pay attention to the various pings anymore.

"You really shouldn't be so trusting."

54

CRUD!

I DIDN'T HAVE to turn to know who it was. I recognized the voice. The air of entitlement. The smug superiority. Margo.

It had been almost a month since we had dropped her and Fritz off a few blocks from the embassy—hogtied, gagged, and each of them stuffed into a body bag. We had called a number that Margo had supplied from a pay phone and told them where to pick up the package. I'd included a handwritten note in each body bag about their various activities of the past few months. We were betting that the government would decide that leaving us alone was the best PR strategy. It had gone smoothly.

Until today.

"Margo."

"Riccarda."

There was that metallic sound again as she scooted around beside the chaise lounge on the sundeck, where I was doing my best lizard impersonation, soaking up the rays. But it was an odd metallic sound, like—

Margo put the champagne bucket down by my feet, along with a leather carrying case, and plopped down onto the other chaise lounge.

OK, that was not what I had thought was going to follow.

"Nice boat."

"Not a junk. I've fixed up a few things. The sundeck was neglected, so I've been putting in some hours, bringing it up to code."

"I can tell. Nice work if you can find it."

"This is the shakedown cruise. Very serious. You can test that chaise lounge for me."

"First things first."

She twisted and reached down to the leather carrying case, flipping open its clasps and the twin hinged tops. Reaching in, she pulled out two champagne flutes.

"Care for a drink? It's the best bubbly I could find in Phuket."

I had no idea where this was going but figured I should play along.

"It's a bit early for champagne. Do you have any tequila?"

"Captain Rich once told me your preferences ran a bit edgier. Patrón?" She pulled out a squarish bottle filled with a light-colored liquid. "It's their *reposado*. Captain Rich said it was your favorite."

"Hah! It's his favorite. Mine is the *añejo*. What the heck—I'll go with the champagne."

I was thinking it would be harder to add poison to the champagne. Besides, I'd drink what she was drinking. After switching glasses.

She expertly popped the cork and poured two full glasses of champagne. I paused, not knowing which one to choose. She settled it for me, picking up one and taking a deep sip, then repeating with the other.

"Satisfied? No poison."

I noticed that she left a lipstick imprint on each. Perhaps . . .

"Ricky, chill. This is a friendly visit. You did the right thing taking us to the embassy, though the body bags were a bit brutal."

"Rich's idea."

"Rich? Not *Captain* Rich?"

"No boat, no title. I didn't know he'd gotten body bags in preparation for the trip, and I'm glad I didn't know he had until we got back. He said that they were in case there were interlopers."

Margo took another sip and smiled. "He is an audacious man. Impudent and bold. I plan to stay in touch with him."

"He has two wives."

"Quite legal, he told me. We vetted him well."

I quickly decided this was a thread I shouldn't be pulling on. "So, what brings you out to our humble harbor?"

"A debt. I owe you some answers. And I'm sure they weren't disclosed during your debrief."

"Yeah, I did all the talking."

"I understand you stayed with the story line perfectly. The vulgar comments you made and the nicknames were perfect additions. Lonnie would have been highly offended to find out you called him gerbil face."

"Well, then, it's a good thing he's dead." I was thinking we had made a mistake in leaving her alive, but I'm such a pushover when it comes to not killing people. I was trying to remember if I'd said anything in the debrief she might take issue with. I couldn't remember which of her nicknames I had used. Probably "the iron maiden." That was definitely my favorite. Although it could have been "the chrome nun." Either way, not too insulting.

Margo refilled her glass, noticed that mine was still full, and replaced the bottle in the ice bucket, giving it a little spin.

"One does get used to a certain way of living after spending more than four years undercover. And a certain way of acting. Sorry that I was such a bitch."

"Apology conditionally accepted."

"Only conditionally?"

"If you don't kill me before the end of this visit, I'll make it unconditional."

"Fair enough. That being said, a good cover story is not something to be burned. I am now the bereaved widow of the very brave Lundy Campbell, originally of Aberdeen."

"Who is Lundy?"

"That was Lonnie's original phony first name in our cover story, but we found that *Lonnie* worked better with Americans. It's *Lundy* on all the financial paperwork."

Margo topped off my nearly full glass and her nearly empty glass before continuing.

"There was an urgent need with the agency to clean out accounts that might draw attention. We got instructions to do an intensive analysis of our spend. Word was that an audit was coming."

She stopped to study the bubbles rising through the champagne flute. Her sigh was hard to interpret. Sadness? Contentment?

"I'd found the money. Just over twenty million US. It had been siphoned off by my boss, of all people, and parked in an overseas account that hadn't been used in years. Not some rogue agent—a CPA working with the team that funded contractors. People like Tao. We're talking tens of billions in annual budget, and he was siphoning off about a million a year. Mouse nuts. Decimal dust. Nothing more than a rounding error in our world."

Mouse nuts?

"Easy money with minimal compliance rules and almost no accountability. No paper trail at all. Absolute deniability. As the saying goes, 'If you can't trust the CIA, who can you trust?' Almost everybody else."

"So, the twenty million was like a dark budget?"

Margo laughed so hard she started choking. I took her flute from her until she stopped. She took it back and had another healthy sip.

"Black budget? Hell no. This sort of covert operation is standard operating procedure—not an issue with the audit. No, this falls more in the territory of something like the Contra funds. It came out of the intelligence budget but found its way into a space that was off all books but could be accessed. During that time, it was invested in several illegal but highly profitable ventures, almost doubling its worth."

I had no idea accounting could be so dramatic.

"So, we had to spend the money, and we had to spend

it before the audit. Luckily, the audit was going to take at least three years before it hit us. God bless bureaucracy."

She was definitely oversharing. It could have been the champagne and a need to unload, but nothing had been straightforward to this point.

"Lonnie came up with the idea. He really was obsessive about the Burma uranium mining and its impact. He wrote up a great case. It was accepted before he even left the pitch meeting. The original design was what you saw right up to the point where we were engaged by Thandar's people. By the original plan, we'd have had a meeting on the boat, given them the up-front payment, turned around, and brought the data back to the agency for use in bullying Thandar to ensure he kept his part of the deal. There were elements within Myanmar who would be very interested to know about his mining operation."

I was still waiting for the other shoe to drop. "So, what went wrong?"

"You've already heard chunks of the story, truth mixed in with fiction." She took another gulp of champagne and shook her head. "Politics. The Myanmar election came, and the liberal party won. Thandar could read the tea leaves and knew he had to accelerate his timeline. It was garage sale time. Clearance. Everything must go. Lumber. Uranium. Heroin. Meth. He was going to deliver the entire amount of uranium, five times our original buy, and insisted on half the money up front. We didn't really have any room for negotiation."

She stared at the bubbles in her glass and sighed.

"Plus, Lonnie changed. He started thinking he was

an honest-to-goodness James Bond. Started collecting guns. Took Krav Maga lessons—that didn't last very long. Started practicing surveillance detection. A walk from the office to the local pizza joint took thirty minutes instead of five. He even insisted we refer to each other by code names. And no, mine wasn't the chrome nun."

So much for "just between you and me" agreements during the debrief.

"And the skimming, heroin, and meth?"

"Don't forget the teak. As far as I knew, the teak and uranium were still the plan. No word to me about skimming the skim or drugs. I was even in the dark until after our first two interrogations with Thandar. Lonnie insisted he go in first. He was adamant. I didn't think anything of it at the time. He was the owner of record. And a man."

The path was pretty easy to predict. "He wanted to get his pitch in first. For a share of the skim, the logs, and the drugs. Do I come close?"

"Right." She raised her flute in salute. "Exactly. It wasn't supposed to go as badly as it did. It was a simple negotiation. Neither Lonnie nor I were field operators. He was a lab geek—one with undisclosed delusions of grandeur—and I'm a lawyer and accountant. Mainly I worked on reconciling complex corporate organizations. I was there to make sure that we didn't get cheated as we worked out the money flow for the uranium. And to provide a more complete cover story.

"But once we heard about the garage sale, we had to throw away the old playbook. The reworked plan was for Lonnie and I to hook up with Thandar face to face.

The yacht was CIA property, seized in a raid and off the books. So, it was a great piece of free capital for the deal, in addition to the three million in cash that had been built into the fiberglass hull midship. Thandar's team would make it look like a navigation error; Wai would help the group escape to Thailand safely and then clandestinely return to Myanmar."

"Seems like the wrong set of skills. Accounting and spectro whatever." What it actually seemed like was the recipe for a major muck-up.

"We'd already gone through extensive field training as part of being agents, and it was decided it was easier to teach us about field skills than to teach a field agent to operate the lab and analyze the data. We really were tracking the flow of the uranium. Besides, we'd spent years on our cover story."

"Yeah, about the uranium." I scooted closer to give her my full attention.

"Really small traces. You aren't in any danger, but the agency will pay for all the testing you may wish to get."

"Anyway, easier to train up a geek and easier to train up an accountant-slash-lawyer than to teach a field agent twenty years of accounting analytics. Got it."

Except I had been able to kick Lonnie's ass when he had pulled the gun. I probably would have failed with a real agent. Lonnie was low-hanging fruit.

I'd emptied my glass at the mention of uranium. Margo, without prodding, tipped the bottle my way and—with a little spilling—refilled my flute.

Where is this going?

Margo was visibly more relaxed than I'd ever seen her. It might have been the three glasses of champagne—soon to be four as she emptied the bottle—or the unburdening of telling me the story, but whatever the cause, she was a very different person.

"By the way, we were never in Myanmar waters. There was nothing wrong with the GPS or the charts. We couldn't run the risk of bumping into a real Myanmar Navy boat. Thandar had access to the boat that he used, retired Myanmar Navy boat—off the books—for the uranium trade. We had agreed they'd confront us in Thai waters and claim we were in Myanmar. We got stuck waiting for a few days because Thandar's team was aware of a Royal Thai Navy ship in the area. They had to wait for them to leave."

Things were falling into place. "That's why we shifted to more samples in a smaller area?"

"Yep. We'd sort of painted ourselves into a corner getting that close. We had no idea why the rendezvous didn't take place on the planned date, so we had to muddle around until it did."

I excused myself for a quick bathroom break. The champagne was kicking in in more ways than one. When I came back, Margo was opening the tequila. I went back to the refrigerator, which was acting up and barely cooled anything, and retrieved a bottle of cola. No way I was going to keep up with Margo.

She held up the bottle of *reposado*, but I responded by holding up my bottle of cola. The disappointment on her face was clear, and I had a passing thought that there was a decent possibility that it was a poisoned bottle.

"I swear, it's not poisoned."

"The thought never crossed my mind."

"Liar . . . Fritz had arranged for the *Powerballer* to be boarded and taken to Thandar's operation so we could have the meet and make the deal. The original agreement was just money, and we then got approved for the *Powerballer* and money, but Lonnie apparently tossed in some valuable documents to sweeten the pot. His added incentive to get the side deal."

"We saw. That was the chip he swallowed, right?" I couldn't tell if she had been disgusted or in awe of the move, but it did appear that Margo understood the reference.

"Yep. I don't know what he gave them to grease the skids."

I'm not sure if it was inadvertent or intentional, but Margo's turn of a phrase seemed perfectly aligned with Lonnie's delivery method for the chip.

"Probably some low-level intel. Who knows? Something on possible insurrectionists in Myanmar? Guerilla activity? Known criminals who had done the prior government's dirty work? If I were Thandar, I'd be looking for things that put me in a good light with the new government."

I was still piecing things together. So far, she'd provided explanations for the trip and the capture. But I couldn't extrapolate the river trip. "Why go so far upriver to Thandar's fortress of solitude?"

She smiled a wry, perhaps embarrassed smile.

"That was my idea. If we'd done it in a populated area, a stay of more than a few hours would begin to attract attention. We had a lot of steps to go through, not the least being the details of payments and quality control. We had to have Thandar convince you and Captain Rich that this was all very real. You were our alibi. Nonagency, unaware participants; unimpeachable testimony. But the other reason was that the camp was the closest point to Fritz's farm of any possible locations on our list of options. Besides, I knew Fritz, worked with him on a case once before he went undercover, and I figured he'd go along with the plan. For a healthy under-the-table fee."

"Fritz. He had me totally played."

"Me, too. I began to suspect Lonnie even before we got boarded. He was getting twitchy when we would discuss how to handle the negotiations. After the first interrogation, he kept insisting I shouldn't always be in the room because I was a roadblock to easy discussions. But Fritz? He'd been the voice of reason throughout all the planning. The Rock of Gibraltar. And Wai! Academy Award for him. By the way, Fritz asked me to say hello."

"Really? Fritz? Maybe the kick in the head knocked a few screws loose."

"Well, it wasn't exactly in those terms. But a lady doesn't use the words he used."

"So, you're not going to kill me . . . Wait. You said twenty million. I'm doing the math, and it seems like you spent around eight, including Thandar's money."

"No, I'm not going to kill you. I'm going to thank you again. And you're right: some of our unaccounted-for money is unaccounted for." She gave her turn of phrase a wry smile. "We spent about four million building up our cover story. We had to live like millionaires and leave a proper footprint. The immediate-wealth story of the lottery helped. We didn't have to go far back with that part of the backstory. And four on the boat, the harbor, and incidentals like weapons. That leaves about twelve. Three built into the hull that is now Thandar's. As I said, you don't burn a good cover story, so I'm going to keep up a slightly more conservative lifestyle and wait.

"After you dropped me off, I was locked up for several days while they checked my story. Then I was locked out. They're still not sure if I should be let back in. But in the event I am, they're letting me keep the money. After all, it can't be given back. That reminds me, I have a massage scheduled in less than an hour, and the limo should be coming to pick me up soon."

And here I was thinking about offering her a ride in the super tuk-tuk.

"I'd like to stay in touch. I have your email. What about phone?"

"Yeah, no, I'm not very good with phones. Charging. Listening. Responding. And I think Thandar has my current one. Email is best."

She looked a bit disappointed, but she organized her bags, left me the empties to recycle, dropped an envelope on the chaise lounge, and gave me an air-kiss. She hoisted her bags and headed for the gangplank.

"You seem confident that I'm not going to tell the authorities or the press about this. What if I use it as a bargaining chip in case I ever get in trouble?"

Her smile was so subtle, but smug, that I immediately knew I was in trouble.

"We opened a few accounts in your name. We've been paying you substantial off-the-books bonus payments in addition to the salary we've been putting in your real account. And as of yesterday, you have a healthy, on-the-books bonus waiting for you to spend."

"What if I don't spend it and tell the authorities anyway?"

"Oh, but you have been spending it. Even before you left on this voyage, you and Captain Rich entered a ten-year lease on the marina. Then you two bought that boat sitting at the end of the dock. We have photos of you using the boat before we headed out on the *Powerballer*. You also invested—with me, of all people—in a spa in Bali. It's doing amazingly well, and you've been getting regular income statements. You really should have an accountant handle the taxes. Most of it is tax-free in offshore accounts, but the income isn't."

Crud!

"Oh, don't look like that. Smile. You're a millionaire, and most of it is tax-free. And I'm still going to get my fellow bean counters at the agency to give you the hazard-duty pay that Lonnie promised."

Double crud and triple crud. I never thought I'd be so bummed to be getting a cash infusion.

"Oh, one last thing." She almost fell as she walked down the gangplank. Then she called out from the parking lot, "I was asked to give you a message."

The ensuing pause was uncomfortably long. She

walked farther away, toward the limo that had pulled up at the gate at some point during our conversation.

"Your mom would appreciate a call."

Crap!

As best as I could tell, I was hooked. I even called a legitimate contact in law enforcement to figure out my options. "Hypothetically, if someone . . ."

He listened carefully and then did his aggravating tut-tutting while considering his answer. It was, essentially, the same logic Captain Rich had used.

"Given that this is purely hypothetical, I'll give a hypothetical answer. If this person had turned in the CIA agents correctly, this would easily have gone their way, but doing it anonymously would have removed their best proof of innocence. Shooting one in the knee while handcuffed, even hypothetically, would be a definite problem. Taking the soldier to the border and sending him to a rogue general, for what we can expect to be cruel and unusual punishment, would not help the person's case. Then there's the money."

"Yeah, all the documentation was left behind in an envelope. My hypothetical friend hypothetically checked the accounts. And it's as bad as the hypothetical spy said it was."

"Thank goodness it's hypothetical because otherwise . . ."

"So, your advice?"

"Four things. One, the hypothetical person would do best to never touch or check those accounts again. Two, they should donate all income from the spa to a legitimate charity like the Red Cross. Three, they should get an accountant. And four, if they are ever to call a senior officer in a national police force again, they should limit the conversation to legal scuba activity."

"Roger that. Thanks."

"And Ricky."

"Yeah?"

"You may want to rethink the way you live your life."

55

LITTER

WHILE I WORKED on figuring out my next life step, I'd decided I might as well get some use out of my new boat and my marina, so I did a lot of day trips and some overnight island camping. I slept in the *Valkyrian*, which wasn't bad at all, and worked on my braai skills.

One afternoon, a multiday trip was shortened by a couple of intense squalls, forcing me to rush back in between storms. But I didn't let that harsh my mellow. I'd found a few amazing dive sites that weren't on any maps and one that was, but it was so remote as to be seldom visited. It was a pinnacle that rose to within forty feet of the surface. I hooked up to a buoy that was secured to the reef and back-rolled in. I'd read some good reports on the site but wasn't prepared for what I found.

The current was strong but not unmanageable. I quickly kicked over to the lee side and eased my way down to just under a hundred feet. The fish life was intense. On the lee side, sheltered from the current, were massive schools of angelfish, jackfish, and trevallies.

Tucked into the reef were dozens of moray eels, a bunch of large cuttlefish, and some colorful scorpion fish. Even deeper, a good number of sharks patrolled the water, including some elegant leopard sharks.

I felt tension shedding off me with every kick as I worked my way around the pinnacle. In the current, though, was the best part of the show—a humongous school of barracuda forming a giant cyclone pattern as they swam around and around, keeping an eye out for food.

It was so good I did a second dive there while the squalls battered Fritz's boat. When I surfaced, I noticed a few seat cushions had disappeared in the wind. I was the only person using the boat, so those were more ornamental than utilitarian. And it's not as if Fritz would ever know. Besides, it wasn't really his boat. It was mine.

Fritz. I had probably gone a week without thinking of him. That was a good sign of recovery. The big sign would be when I finally decided what I was going to do next. Up to that point, I'd resisted any urge to return to my old path of divemastering. It seemed like that was a path littered with misery. Or it was just bad luck that followed me around.

I headed back to the marina feeling a little lighter than when I had begun the dive. Unless another squall hit, I'd easily make it back before dusk.

56

BUT WAIT, THERE'S MORE

I TIED UP at the aft deck of the *Valkyrian* and swung aboard, grabbing the davit crane that I'd once been so unceremoniously handcuffed to. I'd raided various rooms on the boat and had bought a few things at the weekend market, nice secondhand pieces of local art, to gussy up my stateroom. It was a pleasant interim home. I'd found a fun thatched hat floating on the surface during my trip back to the boat, so I had hung it to dry in a covered portion of the deck.

I stopped short, though, as I approached the salon. Among the small puddles from the storm, I saw what looked like washed-out footprints—little traces of sand and gravel. I grabbed Captain Rich's replacement cricket bat—he had figured he wouldn't be needing it in Yemen and had left it just inside a utility closet—and eased forward toward the salon. I could hear drawers being opened and closed, not unlike the searches we'd been subjected to by the Thai and the Myanmar patrols. Several possible explanations ran through my head. Sadly, the most optimistic one was burglars.

There was only one way to find out. I knelt to stay below the window line and moved to the open doorway. I was able to keep my head low and check out the reflections in the boat's tinted window. There was someone else on board. They turned.

Crap! Mom!

There she was, holding a wine bottle that I recognized as one that Margo had left as a parting gift, along with two glasses. Kneeling down, going through the drawers, was a muscled but diminutive man.

Triple crap! Sumo.

"Found it!" he cried as he stood up, holding a corkscrew. I could at least thank him for that since I'd never been able to find one and had resorted to driving the cork into the bottle with a pen. That's probably the only thing I was prepared to thank him for.

They both just smiled when I entered the salon. I was still holding the cricket bat, but neither seemed to notice or mind.

It took more than one bottle for us to begin to work through some of our issues. I kept the cricket bat nearby.

Mom was the first to loosen up. "We've been spending a lot of time together, trying to figure out how to fix things with you. There's no justifying the way we handled things, but we're trying to find a way to get back to what we had before."

"You mean like when you dragged me away from Hawaii and my friends, or maybe when you handed me over to a serial killer? That 'before' period? When I literally had to lead you and the authorities to the truth, and you still didn't trust me? When three out of five members of my girl band got killed? That 'before'?"

Sumo smiled a sad smile. He was the band's biggest fan. And roadie.

"Probably before then." Mom was uncharacteristically compliant.

"Sure, yeah, maybe, like, my eighth birthday party? When you chased Sumo through the living room, both of you naked and you swinging a Ping-Pong paddle?"

"Maybe before then."

"Maybe we go back to before I started school, when we'd spend days on the beach and playing in tide pools."

"Those were good times!" That was Sumo's first real contribution.

Actually, I did have fond memories and no traumas that I could recall from that period. Except they had given me permission to wade out into the surf without supervision but had told me stories about the "under-toad" that was known to grab little children and drag them away so that it could eat them. But no harm, no foul. I did go in up to my knees, and maybe that was the start of my path to becoming a divemaster.

"Sumo even took time off last month from the observatory and his research so that we could focus. First vacation he's taken in years." She was holding his hand, which felt very odd. I hadn't seen much physical affection between them in a couple of decades. Sex, yes—and that was an afternoon *not* delight I'd never recover from—but not affection.

"Turns out that I like vacations." Sumo was beaming.

"And we came up with some ideas about how we can help heal our family."

I was not looking forward to hearing this, but the second bottle of wine had mellowed some of my resistance.

"I think we need a third bottle." That came from Sumo. "And I almost forgot. I made musubi."

It turned out we did have another bottle, and it went great with the SPAM musubi. The third bottle was to toast their "good news."

"I am here," Sumo said in a very formal tone, a glass of wine in one hand and musubi in the other, "to ask for your permission to take your mother's hand in marriage. Again."

Luckily, we were drinking white wine, so nothing got stained when I spit out a mouthful on Mom's very cheery Thai Rattanakosin dress. There were several reasons why I then broke out laughing, but the primary one was seeing Sumo, for the first time ever, with the flop sweats.

Mom dabbed some of the wine off her chest but continued without missing a beat. "We're serious, honey. We want you to be part of this and be OK with our decision."

I had tears running down my face. They both restrained from further dialogue until I'd climbed back up into my chair and was able to hold it together for at least thirty seconds. The giggling lasted a lot longer. Of all the conversations I could have expected to have with the two of them, and there were many that I'd imagined over the past months, this was not even on the list.

But I have to admit, it seemed to have changed them both.

It was as if the news had taken years off Mom. She was nervous and coquettish. OK, the coquettish thing wasn't new, but there was a joy and an innocence to it that replaced her more predatory sexual expressions of the past.

Sumo, too, was different. More talkative. Less distracted. Affectionate, but in a way that was probably acceptable, even in public.

"We realized that for all these years, we'd written our issues off as just another of your Ricky-isms." She knew I hated that term. But baby steps. "But we've come to realize that you were always responding to us and our Sumo-isms."

"Or an Ingi-ism," added Sumo with a flinch. But the moment passed, and he gently took her hand.

"What we're trying to say is that we poisoned the relationship, and we want to start over."

I pondered exactly how dense the two of them were not to have realized this decades ago. But this was a time for reconciliation and healing. For forgiveness. For listening and sharing.

Right after I got a few things off my chest.

"Do you even know what I've just gone through? Which, by the way, was in some great part due to you recommending me for a CIA mission without thinking to mention that aspect to me. Is that what we're calling an Ingi-ism?"

"Guilty as charged." Mom held her hands up in surrender. "I was not thinking clearly, but Mary Sue—you know her as Margo—Mary Sue and Marty—Lonnie—made the proposal sound very innocuous. Sort of like a six-week pampered holiday. You weren't the only one they lied to. I got suckered in by them as well."

She was far from done. "What's really going to keep me up at night is that I recommended Tao. I thought he'd do the best job of watching your six. I figured he and Richie"—*Richie? Gag!*—"would be a great team. It was just supposed to be a quick handoff, with the biggest concern being the pirates."

"Which would be really cool." And there went Sumo again. "Being able to say you fought pirates. They love that up at the observatory. Things get kind of slow up there sometimes. A good story can go a long way toward keeping people sharp."

"So, I recommended Tao and Richie and suggested to them that he partner with you, which may have been out of line. I just thought it would be a good break for you after the messiness in Dahab and Palau. You needed a break from stress."

Captain Rich? I am so going to punch him.

"It's such a tragedy about Tao. He was such a sweetie."

"Mom, he was a monk!"

"Not when I met him. I called him the monk hunk. What a body! But I don't like what you're implying. I never laid my hands on him. Just my eyes. I am sorry." It seemed like she actually thought this was working. "It sounds, though, like you had quite an adventure and got some very juicy revenge."

"And you got to ride in a balloon! Cool!" Sumo

really needed to work on his timing. It was like being with a teenager.

"And how exactly do you know that?" My blood pressure was rising.

"People talk."

"People? People like CIA agents? You're a spook, aren't you, Mom? I knew it! All these years of you taking weird jobs, and it was just a cover."

"I was never a spy. Technically. My role was what they called 'an asset.' I was sort of eyes and ears in places they found of interest. I liked the crossing-guard job. It got me outdoors, and I got to meet a lot of people."

"Monica Schlegel's dad got arrested in Germany that year. She was my best friend. The only one who didn't call me the giraffe."

"Yes, well, that's sort of the whole idea. Not the giraffe part, but the arrest. He was very talkative after a few cups of coffee in the morning. They did, in their defense, wait until after her birthday party. And he was a very bad man."

"You two have lied to me from the moment I was born. In fact, I was a lie from the moment I was conceived. And you think that getting remarried is the fix?"

"There's more." Mom was atwitter.

Criminy. Don't tell me I have brothers and sisters.

"I want you to be my maid of honor, and Sumo wants you to be his best man. Double duty. You can plan my bachelorette party and Sumo's bachelor party."

"No strippers! I'm quite adamant about that." Sumo really had a talent for saying the absolute wrong thing.

Actually, that's unfair. It would have been worse if he'd said, "Lots of strippers."

"You two are clueless."

The waterfall of laughter resumed. In between fits of belly laughs, which had my parents nervously reconsidering this conversation, I was able to spit out a few more words. "This is totally bizarre. You two are quite possibly the worst parents I could ever have had."

Sumo beamed and nudged Mom.

"Did you hear that? She called me her parent."

EPILOGUE

It took a few months, and a long, nonworking trip to Indonesia paid for with the last of Lonnie's cash—it didn't appear that the much-promised end-of-trip payout would be happening anytime soon, Margo's last words as I saw her off—but I began to come around.

While I was gone and out of touch, Mom took a lot of time and enlisted the help of friends in planning the wedding. Their first one had been sort of rushed, what with the bun in the oven, so she wanted this to be everything the first one wasn't.

I distanced myself from that process. We were, though, able to figure out the logistics of me being Sumo's best man and then switching to Mom's maid of honor.

The wedding was held on a full-moon night in August. The next day was Statehood Day, so businesses would be closed, and families, by tradition, spent the day relaxing and bonding. Sumo pulled some major strings, and the ceremony took place at the top of Mauna Kea on a peak just beyond the observatories. The nightly stargazing tour was canceled to provide privacy for the ceremony, with multiple signs to that effect posted at the base and along the road to the summit. The few people who missed or ignored the signs were welcomed to the ceremony anyway.

Two of my old surfing buddies, Waxer and Falstaff, made it, though just barely. Waxer still had sand on his sandaled feet when he arrived. Apparently, it was a good day for surfing.

Pascal had worked out enough issues with the French authorities that he was allowed to leave the country. He hadn't been expected to give a toast, but by the end of the evening, other guests were calling out for him to do so—he has that sort of effect on people. His speech, delivered from the seated position since he was in no condition to stand, was probably hilarious but delivered in slurred French, so no one was quite sure.

Captain Rich showed up. He and Mom had huddled up at one point during the reception, a discussion I immediately broke up. The last time they had talked, I had ended up on the *Powerballer*, and I had no intention of falling into that trap again.

I finally got to meet the Riccardo who was one of my two namesakes. He very happily spent thirty minutes explaining cosmic X-ray sources to me, and I obligingly nodded my head. Later on, talking with Sumo, it turned out that I understood quite a bit of the theory. I decided that the next time Sumo started in on one of his dissertations about work, I would actually listen.

Some of Sumo's family, whom I'd met during a short visit to Japan a couple of years back, came for the event. I hung with them quite a bit at the edge of the mountain, watching the stars like Sumo used to do back on the sand dunes at his home in Tottori City, Japan. Sumo and Mom tracked us down shortly after midnight and stayed almost until the sunrise.

No one mentioned the details of my conception.

Shortly after their honeymoon, spent in the Thai city of Chiang Rai, just across the border from Myanmar—and with my consent—Sumo completed the paperwork to officially adopt me. He texted me a photo of him holding the adoption decree.

It was a positive baby step in rebuilding our relationship. I decided this was best handled with an actual phone call. He answered on the first ring.

"Hi, Dad."

CURIOUS? WANT TO KNOW MORE?

Please note: I've provided these links for educational purposes only. I do not endorse any advertisements attached to these videos. As well, this is not intended as an endorsement of the entities that produced the videos or their activities.

A Spanish dancer, dancing:

https://www.youtube.com/watch?v=V6H01cUSpfQ

Diving the Mergui Archipelago:

https://www.youtube.com/watch?v=AQ_dYCLyDpo

Diving through caves:

https://www.youtube.com/watch?v=xWrYREDiYME

The Irrawaddy Delta:

https://www.youtube.com/watch?v=tlCkktFn2Kc

The balloons of Myanmar:

https://www.youtube.com/watch?v=8epwUR6BBos]

AFTERWORD
FEBRUARY, 2023

Myanmar is a nation in constant change. I relied on first-hand accounts, research papers, and reports by oversight agencies to paint a picture, although one influenced by the biases of the agencies and authors, of Myanmar in 2016. If I misrepresented that state of the nation, the responsibility for those errors falls on me.

Myanmar is a beautiful nation inflicting and enduring much pain. With change comes hope.

On a different political note, I feel compelled to point out that my hydrogen balloon shoot-down scene was written in mid-2022, long before any of us knew of Chinese balloons and before the US used a missile to shoot one down. Score one point for fiction.

YOUR FEEDBACK IS A GIFT

A minute of your time, please.

I hope that you enjoyed *JETSAM*. I would appreciate if you could take a moment to visit the *Divemaster Ricky series home page* on Amazon.com and select *JETSAM* to leave a numerical rating, as well as a short review. These ratings and reviews help other readers find books that meet their expectations, and they help me encourage future readers and secure outside reviews.

Your feedback will also help me understand how I can better create a great reading experience for my audience.

If you prefer, you can contact me directly at *divemasterrickymysteries@gmail.com*. I frequently travel, searching out new locations for Ricky's adventures, so I am sometimes away from the internet for weeks at a time. But I will always reply as soon as possible.

Please let me know if you would like a short write-up on one of my survey trips for the Divemaster Ricky series. For that and other backstories on Ricky, please sign up for my newsletter on the *series' home page*. Your email address will not be shared, and I won't spam you.

ACKNOWLEDGMENTS

I owe thanks to a veritable village of friends and professional associates who devoted their time to helping me improve this novel, step by step. Despite their best efforts, some residual errors may remain—these are completely my responsibility.

This release required special expertise not previously relevant to my previous books, *FLOTSAM* and *DERELICT*.

Special thanks to Pat Pruchnickyj, a balloon pilot who has represented the United Kingdom in international competition, for being a sounding board as I worked through the options of a balloon escape from Myanmar.

My limited understanding of BASE jumping and jumping from balloons (not technically a BASE jump, but using BASE gear) was provided by the very helpful Sean Chuma, the first person to reach five thousand BASE jumps and an internationally recognized trainer and coach. Without him, no one would have survived past chapter 43.

To Dave Marchese, Chard Nelson, and Dana Muir: you were my first readers, and you heavily influenced each draft as I revisited your comments as a litmus test for my progress.

There were many others who took the time to provide me with additional guidance. I appreciate your assistance and value your friendship.

And a special thanks to the team at Kirkus Editorial. From Tom Hyman's collaborative edit, through Christa Titus's copyedit, and finally to Kirsten Balayti's final polish, they provided critical insights and feedback to help propel me to production. Any residual erros are mine and mine alone. (Like the word *erros* in the preceding sentence.)

Finally, to Dana, who had faith in me even when I was lacking and who provided enough kicks in the rear to propel me over the finish line. This novel was written in large part during her academic sabbatical as she traveled the globe conducting research and I trailed along, shirking my domestic duties at every stop. I did manage to squeeze in 136 dives during and after those travels. Thank you. I love you.

Please tell your friends to buy the book (and leave reviews.) Let's go diving and search for Ricky's next destination.

Made in the USA
Middletown, DE
02 April 2023

28135405R00236